SO
VERY
HUSH
HUSH

No-one is what they seem…

TONY McLAREN

SO VERY HUSH HUSH
Tony McLaren

ISBN 978-1-917109-18-5

A CIP catalogue record for this book is available from the British Library.

Published 2024
Tricorn Books, Treadgolds
Bishop Street
Portsmouth PO1 3HN
www.tricornbooks.co.uk

SO
VERY
HUSH
HUSH

ABOUT THE AUTHOR

Tony McLaren was born in Scotland and raised in New Zealand, where he did a BA degree, was a newspaper journalist, then worked his way to London as a merchant seaman, acting on the West End stage and on screen. After many years creating and producing drama and entertainment for ITV he went solo, selling his formats around the world for twenty years.

He now writes and dog walks in the New Forest. His previous Duffy thrillers were THE CHOSEN MAN and BONEYARD.

Contents

CHAPTER ONE

The only sound as the cortège entered Auckland's Purewa Cemetery on that soft sunny afternoon was the lone tui singing sweetly from a flowering pohutukawa tree.

The two gleaming black horses, in leather harnesses and traditional livery, their white ostrich plumes fluttering in the spring breeze, trotted elegantly past the whispering mourners, drawing the hearse behind them.

As was the custom nowadays it was a colourful occasion as the widower, Mungo Swift, had requested no flowers or black ties. Instead the ladies in their exotic fascinators and men in their loud Hawaiian shirts gave the impression more of a day at the races than a funeral, but that's how Grace would have liked it. She'd said she didn't want gloom and doom and tears; she wanted a celebration.

Mungo himself looked like an eccentric movie star, dressed in his Royal Navy jacket with its three gold epaulettes, nicely finished off with a blue, green, and yellow tartan kilt flown in from the Highlands. He knew his late wife's New Zealand rellies would appreciate this subtle nod to her forebears.

Four strapping young men who looked like All Blacks, but were more likely Grace's star drama pupils from nearby Selwyn College, gently lowered the coffin from the carriage and carried it into the crematorium.

Mungo waited for all the guests to file in then followed inside.

He was a cheeky sort of chap who everyone, especially the ladies, was happy to call their friend. Nearing fifty, this larger-than-life Londoner had balding ginger hair, a bit of a tum, an infectious laugh like a braying donkey, and a wall to wall smile. Nothing was ever too difficult for him, he never raised his voice in anger, his glass permanently half full.

He stood at the back of the crematorium and looked around the room.

They were all here today.

Grace's son, Noah, from her first marriage, her parents Jim and Annie, who'd migrated Down Under from Aberdeen, Scotland, in the seventies, their cousins Mac and Jenny, the teaching staff from the college, about two dozen pupils from her thespian course, plus all their local mates who lived near them in Kohimarama.

Trouble was, dear Mungo was hardly ever at home. As Commander of a British nuclear submarine based in Scotland he was often away on duty for five months at a time. Could never say where he was going, what he was doing, when he'd next be back with Grace. But she understood. She knew her husband inside out.

Trusted him implicitly and realised the burden he carried, day in, day out, as he ferried this lethal vessel and its deadly cargo around the world deep beneath the seas.

The female celebrant had begun to speak.

She had a tidy blonde bun, a beige smock, and was nervously fidgeting with several pages of her welcome speech. She had never met Grace, and had known Mungo for only a few days. Such was her job.

"Friends. Haere Mai. Welcome to Purewa. This is a sad occasion but also a time to remember our departed loved one and the many joyful memories we shared with her… I know how Mango must feel today," she sighed.

"Mungo!" shouted out one of the mourners. How dare

8

she get his name wrong.

"Sorry... Mungo... All of us today, we feel for you."

The room murmured agreement. Some nodded back at the stoic widower standing behind them.

"Looking over Grace's life you could say she lived every day to the full...

Her devotion to the college, getting her pupils through Shakespeare, teaching them to sing and dance, and end up in one of our fine television dramas or movies... who knows, even Hollywood... Then she had her charity work with Auckland's city homeless, truly an angel... Amazingly she did Ironman last year and got in the top twenty... that takes some guts... And still found time to sit on the board of the family kiwi fruit business... I'd say Grace's led a stunning life and so tragic it was taken from her at such a young age."

She paused.

"Let's take a moment to look at Grace's journey in pictures."

She played video clips of Grace on a large screen beside her.

Her as a toddler... that first swim in a pool... on a surfboard in the sea... the school running race... her in a wig in a school play... dancing at a disco... embracing Mungo on a ship... their wedding photo.

All to "Somewhere over the Rainbow" by Israel "IZ" Kamakawiwo'ole.

At the end a pause, then the celebrant invited Mungo to speak.

"Let's hear a few words from Grace's loving husband... Mungo."

Mungo rolled down the aisle from the back and took the mike at the lectern.

"Thanks so much Leslie, you done a great job..."

"Lily…" corrected the celebrant.

"Sorry love, Lily… So." He sighed.

"How do you follow that?" He wiped his eyes. "Think I'm welling up here…

But she wouldn't have liked that, not our Gracie. In those final weeks I had to promise her that when it happened, when she went, it'd be one helluva party… She said, get all our mates around, get in the booze, and anyone who can walk home at the end, she'd never forgive!"

The room laughed as one.

"You've heard it all before, but Gracie *was* my rock, kept me in my place, and together we were a team. Now you all know that we both had been married before… she lost her Arnie, and I divorced Bella. Then fate took over. We both went on a singles' cruise in the Mediterranean… it was murder on the dance floor… and bingo… that was it… married in two months… We bought a lovely house down the road here in Kohi… and had the very best of four years together, before the illness took my dear girl from us… bless her. Course, driving a hunk of metal under the sea for months probably was the best way of keeping us together… She never recognised me when I got home, and, after all that time away, I had this insatiable, truly insatiable, lust… for… you know… chocolate fish and pineapple chunks!"

The room laughed again.

"Now. There's one special person here who I'd like to thank for his support over the years… Grace's son Noah."

Noah nodded to him from the front row.

"He's just done a great degree from Auckland Uni and'll be joining the family firm in a few week's time."

Mungo led the room in applauding Noah, who stood and bowed his thanks. He was a shyish lad, about twenty-two, short back and sides, slight scar on his cheek from a bike accident as a kid, with a diffident smile.

"It's time now to farewell dear Gracie... and I expect to see you all down the Thai restaurant in Saint Heliers to celebrate, as she wished... God bless you all."

The coffin started moving towards the furnace as the celebrant played Hayley Westenra singing "Pokarekare Ana"...

*

Duffy woke to a pleasing smell. An expensive perfume that he could never afford, mingling strangely with a musky male deodorant. He lay there a moment trying to work it out. His mind was still fuzzy from all that French plonk watching the English rugby team get severely hammered in Paris, then buckets of cheap fizz on the plane back home. His mouth felt drier than the Atacama Desert. Or an alpaca's armpit.

Whatever.

Then he opened his eyes.

At first all he could see was the stylish ochre ceiling. He liked it. It said class.

Then he saw the hair tumbling on the pillow beside him. Long and dark and luscious. The naked toned back. No stranger to the gym. That tattooed bird in the nape of the neck. It said style.

His head cleared a little.

No idea where he was.

Or who she was.

But did it matter?

He leant across and gently stroked his sleeping beauty's locks.

Who then groaned wistfully and slowly turned to face him.

It was the beard that put him off.

Duffy leapt in the air as if he'd touched a high voltage electric fence.

And shouted.

"No!"

The guy sat up quickly. Saw Duffy. And shouted.

"No!"

Then suddenly from behind Duffy a third body threw back the Emperor duvet and shrieked.

"No!"

All three sat up and looked at each other.

"What the fuck!?"

Duffy was the first out of bed.

"Who the hell are you?" shouted the third body. She had short dark hair with a cute fringe, clear blue eyes, and a very pert nose.

Duffy was quietly impressed.

"Have we met?" he asked politely.

"You're in my bed! My flat!" she seethed.

"Who's this?" asked the long-haired bearded male, looking at Duffy.

"Shut up Max!" cried the fringe. And turned again to the singing detective.

"So? Explain yourself…"

"It's all a blur… but I think we might have met last night flying back from Paris?" said Duffy vaguely.

The blonde quietened.

"From Paris..?"

Duffy nodded.

"I think we drank champagne together. Lots of it…"

"And shared a cab into town…" sighed the fringe.

"I wasn't expecting you back so soon Sis... Sorry." interrupted Max.

Duffy understood in a flash.

"Jeez. You're brother and sister... I thought we just did a threesome."

"Over my dead body mate," said Max.

"And mine"... added the fringe.

"That's a whole lot of corpses," smiled Duffy.

The fringe leapt out of bed starkers and draped herself in a towel.

"I think you'd better go... whoever you are..." She started quickly dressing.

"I'm going to be late for work."

Duffy pulled on a hoodie and jeans.

"Did... did anything happen... last night?" He asked the girl.

"Bloody hope not," she snapped.

Then he saw what the fringe was wearing.

A uniform.

"You're a cop!"

"Inspector to you sunshine!"

Duffy moved to the door.

"What's your name Inspector?"

She hesitated then. "Kate."

"Duffy. Here's my card."

He dropped it on a table and exited pretty damn quick.

Had great respect for the Met but didn't want to get that close.

*

Mungo had booked the top floor of the Chim Chim Thai Kitchen in St. Heliers for Grace's wake, though by seven o'clock it seemed more like a boozy hooley. They were playing all her fave Barry Manilow hits full volume, serving Crying Tiger, Deep Fried Snapper, and Drunken Spicy Duck, washed down with buckets of the best New Zealand sauvignon blanc. But Grace was not just there in spirit, for, sat beside Mungo at his window seat, was a small oak casket containing her ashes, so she'd made it to the party after all. Bless.

There must have been sixty well-wishers squeezed into the place, though Mungo wondered how many were along for the free meal. Well, the free wine.

Two of his neighbours pushed through the throng and nodded to their host.

"Gonna miss her Mungo," said Sal. "We did pilates then went for lunch. Best bit of the week. That lunch… Boy could she drink."

"And we don't see enough of you Mungo," added Ross. "All those months away – must drive you crazy mate."

"It's a weird job Rosso… 140 sweaty bodies squeezed into that sardine can … and no contact."

"Can you get emails?" asked Sal.

"Na… we're allowed two familygrams a week – that's a 60-word message sent from home… but… we can't reply."

"Can't reply? Shit - why not mate?" asked Ross.

"Security… have to stay hidden… the silent service… not give away our position."

"Trident. You should be bloody proud mate… Putting your life at risk for us lot," added Ross.

Sal tapped her nose. "So very hush hush…"

"Right on Sal. Right on."

"Has anyone asked you yet?" she asked with a twinkle.

"Eh?"

"What you're wearing under your kilt?"

Mungo collapsed in laughter, as Grace's son Noah came and joined him.

"What a view... picture postcard."

They both looked out over Auckland harbour's mirrored waters at Rangitoto, an iconic dormant volcano on the horizon, shimmering in the sunset.

"I'll never forget this place Noah, Godzone..." mused Mungo.

"What – you're not coming back?" joked Noah.

"And miss all this? But I will miss Gracie..." patting the casket. He turned all serious and faced Noah. "By the way, I haven't forgotten Noah... that transfer. Once I get to the airport tonight, I'll send you over Grace's million, as promised."

"Thanks Mungo. Much appreciate it."

"A whole new life beckons for you old son... wish you all the very best."

"How long away this time? Can you say?"

"Deployment should be four months... then I'm taking a holiday... here on the beach!"

"That'd be great... Just great."

Mungo stood and looked around the crowded room.

"Forgive me Noah. Been a tough day. I'm going to quietly fade away... I'll do that transfer later... and see you in... a few months... Take care my boy."

He punched Noah playfully, picked up the oak casket, and quietly exited the restaurant.

*

Duffy parked his Harley then pushed his way through the posh shoppers into Fortnum and Mason, the luxury store on Piccadilly, best known for its picnic hampers and inventing the Scotch egg.

Looking younger than his thirty-something years, with his broken nose, messy quiff, stubble, and red string wristband, he had that "je ne sais quoi" with the ladies.

They could never put their finger on it, but Sherlock the rock star, had the kind of charisma they would risk their marriage for, and some did.

Professionally he had a unique selling point.

A singing detective with no office and no home.

His office was the winery in Fortnum's basement and his home was wherever he could find a bed for the night. Some called him a "free spirit," which was the way he liked it.

Toto, his black barman buddy, welcomed him as he entered the wine bar.

"Morning squire... How was Paris?"

"Crap match... but the after party was fun, I think..."

Toto poured him a large chardonnay.

"How so?"

"Ended up in bed with a girl I met on the plane... and her brother."

"A threesome?" laughed Toto.

"I hope not. It was all a mistake – the brother didn't know we were in bed with him."

"Just saw another flying pig..."

"You what?"

"Listen man, you never know what you're doing after a few drinks... and after a rugby match, then getting pissed on the plane..."

"You saying I did have a threesome?" whispered

Duffy, looking across at the two middle-aged ladies in the corner sipping martinis who were obviously enjoying the conversation.

Toto shrugged and smiled. "Ain't saying nothing man… Just sometimes when we drink, we do some very stupid stuff."

"I didn't tell you… Kate. She's a cop!"

Toto winced as Duffy's phone pinged. A new email.

"Shit. She just called. And we only just met."

"Must like you…"

He read out the message.

"Duffy… run off my feet today but wonder if I can ask you a small favour?"

"What she want – her back rubbed?" smiled Toto.

"Doesn't say…" He emailed back offering to help.

Almost immediately he got a reply.

"It's my brother's birthday tomorrow and I wonder if you could help me out by getting an Apple gift voucher from a supermarket… around £100. Shouldn't ask but you seem a nice guy. And I'm in wall to wall meetings. Will repay when next see you. Promise. Kate."

"Well?" said Toto thoughtfully.

"So? It's not a problem… I get the token, she pays me, and I date Kate!"

"For a hundred quid!" laughed Toto. "You think it's genuine mate?"

Duffy sighed. "Sometimes, sometimes Toto, I wonder if we're living on the same planet."

He gulped down his wine.

"Now. Where's the nearest supermarket?"

Toto quietly shook his head as Duffy stalked off with a smile.

*

Mungo paid the Uber driver and entered Auckland's International Airport, carrying a small case and that precious oak casket containing Grace's ashes.

The place was heaving with other passengers off to travel the world. Young bright-eyed Kiwi students in their gap year visiting New York or London or Beijing... shrieking mini skirted girlie groups popping over to Queensland for a bachelorette weekend party... dour pensioners in safari jackets and walking boots off for hunting treks in Kenya... and those smiley single mums with three tiny kids out to sabotage the peace and quiet of everyone else sitting around them on those never-ending overnight flights.

Still wearing his naval jacket and kilt, Mungo made for the nearest mens' loo.

Inside a locked cubicle he quickly changed into a t-shirt, jeans, and a leather jacket, leaving the funeral clothes on a hanger behind the door. Then exited to the nearest café where he ordered a coffee and croissant, sitting at a far corner table.

He took out his Apple iPad and punched in some numbers.

Peered at the screen.

It was a joint bank account belonging to himself and his deceased wife.

In front of him he had a big choice to make.

Before Grace's death he'd promised her that he'd transfer her million dollar profits from the family kiwi fruit business across to her son Noah.

Only an hour earlier he'd repeated that same promise to the boy.

But now, in the cold light of reality, he hesitated.

Back to that big choice.

He could do as he promised.

Or.

He took a sip of the cold coffee.

Nibbled at the stale croissant.

Then did the transfer.

Gave the son Noah two thousand New Zealand dollars.

And gave himself the remainder of Grace's one million.

He hesitated.

Had he done the wrong thing?

Then made a change.

Giving Noah just one thousand, instead of two. After all, this lad's got the whole of life ahead of him. Can't spoil them at that age.

So in two taps Mungo was nearly a million dollars better off.

And why not.

He snapped shut his iPad and unzipped his case.

There strapped to the lid were five burner phones.

Each one had a number. 1 to 5.

He carefully extracted phone No.2, kissed it with a broad smile, and threw it in a nearby bin.

Patted the precious oak casket.

Grabbed his case and quickly exited the café, a renewed bounce in his step as he headed for the Departures gate.

The café waitress saw the smart oak casket containing Grace's ashes sitting alone at the table and looked around for the absent-minded customer.

But Mungo was already taking off his belt and shoes and happily going through the security body scanner, en route for London without a care in the world.

*

Duffy stood on a small stage at the Victory Services Club near

Marble Arch, wearing a camouflage jacket and pounding out Status Quo. It was a members' club for military vets and tonight, lining the long bar and sprawling at tables, were dozens of square- jawed soldiers, young and old, attending this Special Forces reunion.

There was not an SAS hard man in the room who was not swaying and singing badly along to the chorus : "You're in the Army now!"

Duffy got thunderous applause at the end and joined the two old muckers who'd helped organise the party.

"Bloody amazing mate – the SAS salutes you!" smiled Bonzo, a beaming unshaven six-footer in khaki t-shirt and jeans… doing a mock salute.

At his side a smaller tattooed ball of bulging muscle, Spud, shook the singer's hand.

"Should tour the bases Duffy - Special Forces sweetheart!" laughed Spud.

"Not often I sing to trained killers!"

"We're all teddy bears, you know that," laughed Bonzo.

"Who just got back from 'somewhere' in the Middle East…"

"Shush Duff "… hissed Spud. "We was never there."

Duffy looked across the room at a massive guy sitting alone downing three pints and three chasers. Black chiselled beard, flinty eyes, flat top haircut, mean lips.

"Who's the big ugly in the corner?" asked the singer.

"'Psycho'. Don't do eye contact - he'll come butt you!" urged Bonzo.

"Psycho"?

"Loves the smell of blood," added Spud.

"Desert last month took out six jihadis bare-handed…"

"Then scalped them."

Psycho glared across at the singing detective.

"Jeez. No eye contact, promise!" said Duffy and promptly looked away.

"You dropped something mate" said Bonzo, handing him a card.

"Ah. My gift voucher…" said Duffy. "This little beauty has just bought me a date with a lovely lady."

"Eh?" asked Spud.

Duffy told them about Kate's email, asking if he could help out and get a £100 voucher for her brother's birthday.

Just then his phone pinged. A new email.

From Kate again.

Duffy read it.

"Ah. She wants the numbers off the card…"

"Who?" asked Bonzo.

"I told you. Kate."

The two SAS guys looked at each other then sniggered.

"Do not reply mate."

"What?" said Duffy.

"You, my dear old plonker, have just been scammed!" smiled Bonzo.

"Never…"

Suddenly Barry White interrupted singing "The First, the Last, my Everything." Duffy answered his phone.

"Kate? Just been talking about you… What? Shit. OK OK. No problem…

Catch up later, I hope."

He ends the call.

Spud looks at him. "She was hacked?"

Duffy quietly nodded.

And handed the boys the gift voucher.

"I *was* a plonker…

Bonzo took the voucher. "Thanks mate. We'll put it in a raffle. Oh, and…"

"What now?" sighed Duffy.

"You gotta change that fucking ringtone."

*

Mungo walked through the Arrivals entrance at Heathrow airport after his long gruelling stinking flight from New Zealand. He scanned the crowds waiting for family and friends, ignored the endless taxi driver signs looking for their pickups, and there they were, waiting to greet him.

Monica, just turned forty, arms wide open, with a new coloured hair style, pearl necklace, and tweed suit… Donna, nearing her twenty-first, but looking much more mature, ready for that Vogue cover shoot… Riley, at fifteen a foot taller than when Mungo last saw him… and young Sam, at eight, beaming the cleanest teeth and brightest eyes in the terminal.

Mungo hugged them all at once.

Back home at last with the wife and kids.

CHAPTER TWO

Mungo raised his glass of Montepulciano and looked around the table at his family.

He had to raise his voice to be heard over the din in his favourite Harrow pizza parlour.

"First, it's great to be back home with those I love most in the world."

Monica and the three kids smiled, pleased to have him back safe and sound.

"Second, let's raise our glasses to our lovely Donna on her twenty-first birthday!"

On cue two waiters in red bow ties and aprons appeared from nowhere carrying a large cake with twenty-one sparkling candles, and the whole place erupted, singing "Happy Birthday!"

Donna, her auburn hair tumbling down her shoulders, wearing an over-sized All Blacks rugby jersey, leant over and gave Mungo a long hug.

"Thanks Dad... and ta for the shirt!"

"Sorry it's so big babe... bit of a rush at the airport."

"It's perfect Dad... perfect!"

Monica put her hand on Mungo's.

"And how was Down Under?"

Mungo took a long swig of his red and sighed.

"As usual love, I can't say much."

Monica nodded. "I understand. So very hush hush..."

"But... This time it was a Russian whistleblower. He'd come to us with all this hot intel... and needed protection...

so we put him in a safe house in New Zealand. Somewhere deep in the bush where no-one'd think of looking, not even the possum hunters."

"Ah... Clever, love." whispered Monica.

"Trouble was, their agents did come looking for him."

"KGB?" asked Riley with sudden interest.

"FBS now son," said Mungo. "So... got a bit tricksy... know what I mean."

"Were you ever in trouble Dad?" asked Riley.

"Let's just say we sorted the problem Riley... we sorted it. Now. Anyone want tiramisu for pudding?"

"You got a gun Dad?" piped up young Sam.

"Really can't say Sam."

"You must have... fighting all those baddies round the world."

"I think Daddy just wants a rest tonight Sam..." said Donna.

"I want to see it," persisted the eight-year-old.

"One day when you're a bit older Sam..." hinted Mungo, slowly nodding his head, as if he did own a gun.

"You can make them yourself these days, from a 3D printer..." said Riley. "I often thought..."

"Don't go there son."

"When you next off Dad?" asked Donna.

Mungo sighed.

"End of the week."

His wife and kids groaned.

"Where this time Mungo?" asked the long-suffering Monica.

"The States. Going part of a team. Some 'wrong un' from here causing trouble - need us to track him down, sort him out..."

"Sounds like my Dad's a bounty hunter," laughed Riley.

"Sometimes I am son."

"And sometimes you're undercover," added Monica proudly.

"Depends on the job love."

"If you don't have a gun, you can't catch the baddies," added Sam. "I think you're making all this up… you're probably just away on holiday all the time!"

"Sam! Don't be rude to Daddy…" laughed Monica. "He's very tired, and he works very hard."

Mungo patted Sam on the head.

"No, Sam's right. One day soon I will show you that gun…." He points to the menu. "Now. Did we decide on pudding?"

*

Duffy was sitting with Kate at a bar in Covent Garden. She was wearing a bright summer dress and looking more attractive than when she was in police uniform.

"I am so sorry Duffy…" she said.

Duffy shrugged. "Thought I'd never hear from you again."

"That was the intention. Then I saw your card and for some mad reason popped your email address into my phone. Few hours later some arsehole got onto my contact list and sent out that same message to dozens of my friends!"

"Can you help? Go buy a £100 gift card for my brother's birthday…" laughed Duffy. "Certainly caught me love."

"So simple, so clever. If they'd said £200, people would have sussed it was a scam… but this way…"

"The one good thing Kate, it brought us together again."

She shrugged with a smile. "Let me give you that £100."

"No way… Anyway it's gone to an Army charity, a good cause."

"So… You're an investigator?"

Duffy nodded. "I try. Go looking for missing cats or help a dotty old dear who can't find her car in the station car park."

"I'm sure it's more than that."

"And you? What crimes are you solving right now? Or can't you say?"

"Trying to keep the streets clear – everyone wants to protest these days and bugger up ordinary people living their lives."

"Was that really your brother in bed? Max? Or some saddo ex-boyfriend?"

"My dear brother. He was flat-sitting, sleeping in my bed, but got the dates wrong… hence the fuck-up."

"Or not the fuck-up… I hope."

"Duffy. Again, thanks for your patience and sorry you were scammed."

"Life's rich pattern." He goes to pay the bar bill. "Shit." He pats his jacket pockets.

"Don't tell me…"

"Lost my bloody wallet… probably at Fortnum's." He shrugs.

"No matter, I'll pick this up. You can do it next time."

Duffy perks up.

"Next time?"

*

Mungo drove his grey Skoda into the sprawling industrial estate in Pinner and parked outside the Solar Global factory.

He entered the office, nodded to Sheila the receptionist,

and walked on through to the executive suite.

Charlie was watching a horse race at Wincanton, shouting at the screen. Then went quiet and collapsed into his leather sofa as Mungo entered, carrying a bottle of sparkling wine.

"Get some glasses Charlie... Cloudy Bay fizz all the way from Down Under!"

Charlie, around sixty, dyed black hair and beard, glasses, four stone overweight, leapt to his feet.

"The conquering hero returns! Mungo Mungo !" And gave him a bear hug.

"Good trip old bean?"

"More than paid for itself Charlie. Those Kiwis are gagging for anything that helps save the planet, so our solar panels..."

Charlie put two glasses on a table as Mungo popped the cork, and poured.

"Quite a killing, in more ways than one... reckon we should go back there in a few months to build on our contacts... possibly double the profits."

They clinked glasses.

"Well done that man."

"Only one problemo mate."

"What's that – you'll get that bonus in your pay packet, promise!"

"Na Charlie – it's such a boring bloody job – solar panels!"

"Listen old son, don't complain... we are raking it in... Most buggers don't get off their arses and sell globally. Most talk the talk. We walk the walk!"

"Off to the States this weekend," said Mungo.

"Targeting California?"

"Silicone Valley to San Diego. I'll need two or three weeks. To meet and bed in with some fruity deals, know what

I mean."

"Trust you with my life Mungo, I truly do. And I'm thinking, perhaps perhaps we should ratchet up our prices, just a mite?

"You're the money man Charlie. I'm just the gopher."

"Then let's 'gopher' gold!"

And clinked glasses again.

Mungo looked at Charlie. "Know anything about 3D printers mate?"

*

Duffy in a cool DJ was at a wedding gig in an old Georgian pile somewhere south of Guildford. The guests had mostly coptered in and a few nouveaus arrived in limos.

The gels were all Fuschia or Saffron and the chaps Jazz and Buck. How times had changed.

The singing detective had them all on the dance floor and was just winding down with the final Elvis lyrics : " For I can't help falling in love with you…"

There were cries for an encore but the lad was parched and headed for the bar.

No sooner had the Provencal rose wet his lips than she was at his side.

"My… everybody's pin-up date…" she oozed. She was a dazzling blonde, very tall and smiley, glam and shapely like that Hannah something on the telly.

Looked like the red satin had been sprayed on.

Duffy froze. Already his neck was hurting from looking up at her. But he enjoyed the pain.

"Drink?" he asked tentatively.

"Got to be a dirty martini…" she said, the corner of her

lips creasing in a bent smile.

The singing detective ordered. "I'm Duffy."

"Of course you are... everybody's pin-up date."

"What?" he asked.

"Right now you're trending on DateFunk. All over it. Like, come and get me girls... Here I am."

"What the hell's DateFunk?"

"You're kidding me... The sexiest thing on screen and you pretend you don't know."

Duffy shook his head. Liked the attention but no idea what this classy Amazon was talking about.

She took out her cell and showed him the DateFunk site.

Clicked in and there he was talking to camera.

Our Duffy astride his Harley, looking cool as ice, and asking any girl that liked to have fun, to get in touch with him, on the DateFunk number.

"That's not me!"

"It so is!" She insisted.

Duffy stared at the screen.

"That's my picture and me talking... But I never did that, never said that. It's a fake!"

"So you don't want to meet lovely ladies?"

"Course I do, but on my terms – I'd never put my name to that... someone's taking the piss!"

The girl shook her head and was about to go.

"Wait. What's your name?"

"Tiger."

"You're joking."

"Blame my parents."

"They here today?"

She nodded.

"They own this hovel." She gleamed. Then looked long

at him, her eyes narrowing like sizing up a gold sequinned Balmain maxi dress in Harrods. "You want another drink big boy?"

Duffy nodded almost imperceptibly, gazing up at her.

He realised he had a challenge on his hands and tonight perhaps, perhaps he was on a winning streak.

*

Mungo had done his homework. If he really wanted to get himself a gun he could either buy a 3D printer and try make one himself, or, visit the most notorious gangster drinking den in town, the Blind Beggar on Whitechapel Road. It was here the legendary Kray brothers hung out; where in 1966 Ronnie had shot George Cornell, a member of a rival gang, the Richardsons, as he was sitting in the saloon bar.

Surely somewhere like that there'd be a bent guy who knew someone who knew someone who could quietly get him a gun.

First problem was what to wear.

Something naff. Like a shiny suit and a chunky necklace.

Or more down and dirty.

Torn leather jacket and ripped jeans.

He made a third choice.

Polo shirt and chinos.

That way he could be a dodgy geezer off the golf course or a flash harry trying to hide his working class roots.

Second problem was what to say.

Waltz up to the barman and... "Hi mate, anyone you know can sell me a second-hand Glock or an Uzi?"

Or...

With more of a streetwise drawl and quiet menace...

"Here sunshine, I'm looking on the quiet for a shooter… a piece… so I can get tooled up… get my drift?"

Mungo stood outside the pub, took a deep breath, and entered.

In the nearest corner was a raucous hen party, about a dozen near naked girls in their early twenties… in the other were two very old pensioners, sipping pints and sucking on their gums. Apart from them and a few spotty teens necking, it was empty.

Mungo went straight to the saloon bar. Where Ronnie had done the deed way back when. And ordered a scotch.

The ugly barman who'd just got out of Parkhurst on a grievous bodily harm charge was in fact a pretty brunette with too much makeup, painted eye brows and those swollen lips that were all the rage these days.

The solar panel salesman sat a moment then turned to the barmaid.

"Quiet tonight?"

"Always like this now. Every weekend we get coach loads of bloody tourists coming to see where the Krays drank, and that's that. Most punters go up west these days."

"So now it's squeaky clean?" asked Mungo.

"Than a baby's bum," she smiled.

But Mungo realised that a baby's bum was never clean. Perhaps she was telling him something. In code. Perhaps he looked like a gun for hire. A hitman.

He cleared his throat.

"I… I…" he hesitated.

"Yes love?"

"I know a friend who's looking for something…"

"Oh? What a cat… dog… somewhere to live?" she asked helpfully.

He shrugged.

"More like something this friend could carry around to protect them… make them feel safe."

"Mmm. Like some kind of alarm… self-defence spray… perhaps a baseball bat?"

"Something more lethal than that love."

"How much would they pay?"

"About five hundred quid…"

"A monkey?" she asked.

"Five hundred quid," repeated Mungo on the verge of giving up.

"Why don't you leave name and number and I'll see what I can do."

Mungo wrote his contact details, emptied his glass, and left, wishing he'd never got into this. Made him feel like a total plonker… acting like he was in some old black and white Cagney gangster movie. One thing he realised for sure. There was no way that pretty young barmaid was going to find him a bloody gun. Monkey or no monkey.

*

With his wrists and ankles tied by rope to each corner of the four-poster, Duffy wondered when the torture would begin. Bloody freezing without his clothes on. Then he heard the squeaking from above. It sounded like a pulley that needed a dose of WD-40. His eyes strained in the early dawn light filtering through the wine velvet curtains and didn't know whether to laugh or cry. For she – Tiger – if that was her real name, was slowly lowering her fulsome body down towards his, from the top of the bed.

The blonde Amazon's eyes dazzled as she got closer and

closer and closer.

The pulley squeaked louder and louder.

Then stopped.

Her gleaming body swaying above him.

Five inches away.

She was teasing him, her legs wide apart.

They were very nearly touching.

Both of them quivering.

He could smell her desire.

Then he felt it.

A wet feeling on his face.

And woke with a start.

He was lying fully clothed on an old sofa with two large Great Danes licking his cheeks.

"My alarm call - at last you're awake!" cried Tiger from the doorway.

Duffy peered through the gloom. She really did look like that Hannah thingy on the telly.

"Come join us for kedgeree..." and she was gone.

Five minutes and a face wash later the singing detective joined the Amazon and her parents in the breakfast room.

They were all sat at a very long wine-stained table, while on a side cabinet were laid out vast plates of kedgeree, porridge, muesli, fruit, and two coffee urns.

Blanche, Tiger's very aristocratic mother, beamed when he entered.

She had long greyish hair, sculpted cheekbones, and her daughter's sunshine smile.

"My... you look younger than your picture on DateFunk! That was so so wow," she drooled.

Duffy sighed. "I told Tiger... that wasn't me... Well, it was, but someone put those words into my mouth."

"Who the hell's Tiger?" asked the suave daddy with a frown. He was greying in a sophisticated way, dressed in a silk robe, and looked like he should have worn a cravat. His voice richly theatrical, mellowed by years of fine wine and Havana cigars.

Duffy nodded at the Amazon.

"Izzy – you been playing games again?" laughed the Amazon's father. "Next she'll tie you to the four-poster!"

Duffy looked around this wacko family and wondered if in fact he was still dreaming.

"Poor boy – you're looking like a rabbit in the headlights!" said Izzy.

Just for once Duffy wished the earth would open up and swallow him. There were comfort zones and comfort zones.

"Eat up dear boy – you look famished, and we all loved your singing at the wedding," said Blanche.

"Sorry," said her father, extending his hand to Duffy. "I'm Patrick… and Blanche."

After copious servings of breakfast fodder, Duffy relaxed and felt at home, especially after the two brandies.

"You a fulltime singer?" asked Patrick.

Duffy shook his head. "Work as a private investigator… keeps me busy."

"Ha!" replied the father. "Never know when we might need your help."

"And you?" asked Duffy. "Retired?"

"Not yet. I was Army most of my life. Northern Ireland for my sins… Still limping from those little scrotes skimming paving stones at our knees."

"Shit…" said Duffy.

"But now, keeping my hand in doing a bit of charity work here and there, giving back what we took out."

"Very noble sir."

"Keeps the wolf from the door… speaking of which…" Patrick stood. "Must get on Duffy… good to meet." And left the room.

Duffy stood.

"I'd better get going… back to the office. Nice to meet you all. And you…

Tiger… Izzy."

Izzy slipped him her card.

"Ever want a free lunch in South Ken… do call."

They pecked each other and the singing detective left on his Harley for the hour ride back to the smoke.

He really fancied the girl, whatever her name. She was a one-off. And now he had Kate, his police inspector, also on his to-do list.

Then he remembered DateFunk. It all looked like some weird scam. But why would anyone target him. A P.I. with no office or home. Not as if he could pay a blackmail bung or anything.

He was just approaching the London ring road when this zooty little red MG swerved past him, too close for comfort.

A mile further on he spotted it in a layby.

Minutes later it had crept up behind him again and this time was right on his tail.

It drew closer and closer, then rammed the back wheel of the Harley.

The bike spun full circle, sending Duffy into the air, landing on the grass verge. His Harley was still in one piece. Scratched but would live to ride another day.

And no MG in sight.

Duffy wondered why some arse ran him off the road? Which angry husband, which unhappy client, which ex-lover… No idea.

Hands bruised, neck aching, and still shaking all over, our singing detective rode soberly on his way into London, keeping an eye open for any further surprises.

*

Mungo held his family in one huge hug. It seemed only yesterday that they'd met him at Heathrow as he flew back from Auckland, and now he was off away again.

They were all huddled outside their home at Trafalgar Terrace, Harrow-on-the Hill. Been there now for over twenty years… and ever so happy.

"Thanks for that birthday party Dad," sobbed Donna.

"Been good to catch up, hear your stories," added Riley.

"Still wanna see your gun Dad," chirped Sam.

"And so do I love," laughed Monica. "As soon as you get back."

"And you will – I promise!" smiled Mungo, as he turned and leapt into the waiting Uber. "Stay safe – back soon!"

And off they drove.

"Mayfair mon brave," he told the driver. "Luxe Barbershop…"

He was dropped at the upmarket hairdresser where he went with his balding ginger hair and had a blonde rinse. Took years off him.

Popped into Harvey Nicks for a cool dusty blue cotton linen blazer and fresh new white t-shirt, and came out a new man.

Then headed to Heathrow, International Departures.

Checked in for his flight to Los Angeles.

And went through security.

In the duty free section he bought a massive pink teddy bear and a bottle of Jack Daniel's Tennessee whiskey.

His cell phone rang.

"Is that Mister Swift?"

"Speaking…" answered Mungo.

"I think we can help each other."

"Who is this ?"

"You could call me 'the blind beggar'…" answered the stranger.

"Ah," replied Mungo, nervously fiddling with his teddy bear.

"You was looking for some merchandise?"

"Ah… maybe… maybe not."

"I got it right here mate, but first I'd like you to do me a wee favour…"

*

At around midnight that same day a car quietly pulled up outside Great Ormond Street Hospital – London's most prestigious children's healthcare centre.

Someone in a hoodie ran to the front entrance, lay down a bundle on its front steps, then drove off.

Moments later an off-duty nurse came down those same steps, saw the bundle, examined it, then quickly turned and carried it into the hospital.

CHAPTER THREE

Duffy sat thoughtfully at his Fortnum's wine bar office sipping a flat white, while Toto wiped clean the lipstick off a champagne glass.

"Must be in a state of shock if you're not drinking..." said the barman.

"It was so out of the blue Toto – never saw it coming. Could have wrecked the bloody Harley."

"And you man."

"Just don't know why they did it... who it was."

"Some dick getting a kick."

"Perhaps, wrong time wrong place."

"As for you on DateFunk..." Toto laughed. "You must've been right pissed when you did that."

"That was not me!"

The barman shrugged in disbelief.

"If it looks like a duck, quacks like a duck, walks..."

"Swear to God, I never set that up."

"So who the fuck did man?"

Duffy shook his head slowly.

"I wonder... you haven't seen my wallet have you?"

"Not another tab behind the bar?"

"Seriously, must have left it somewhere."

"Not here man. You see this?" Toto threw him a copy of the Evening

Standard. "Talking of dicks, who'd dump a baby out in the cold like that."

Duffy looked at the story.

"Jeez. It was already dead. Only a few weeks old."

Suddenly Madness broke through with "It must be Love, Love, Love…"

"New ringtone," explained Duffy and answered his cell. "Duffy… private investigator at your service."

A male around forty, dark, balding, droopy moustache, haunted expression, filled the screen.

"Rocco Mars. I need come to your office Mister Duffy."

"How can I help?"

"It's life and death."

"Always is… Fortnum's wine bar in the basement. Five o'clock."

"Got it. Thanks."

"What's the story?" asked Duffy.

"That dead baby dumped at Great Ormond Street."

"Which some bastard…"

Rocco was silent a moment. "That bastard was me." Then hung up.

*

Flying into California always gave Mungo a thrill. It was those final minutes before landing as the plane circled and you could see the "Hollywood" sign on those distant hills. Then when you came through Customs at LAX out into the air and that bright bright sunshine blinded you, then the tropical heat bowled you over, that and the sight of those tall swaying palm trees. You realised you were suddenly in another world… paradise. Well, sort of.

He'd had a lot to think about on the twelve hour flight from London.

That surprise call from the guy at the Blind Beggar pub

had thrown him.

They'd come back so quickly with not only the offer of a gun, a real gun… but they wanted him to do some favour in return. This worried him a tad. Didn't want to do something he'd regret in his world where everything was micro-managed to the final minute, carefully day by day, location by location.

But right now there were more pressing matters to consider.

On landing he'd gone to the bathroom and spruced himself up. Taken a shower, slapped on an expensive deodorant, and emerged feeling ready for anything.

He'd opened his case, viewed the four remaining burner phones, grabbed No.3 and made a call.

She answered.

"Hi honey. I'm home!" cried Mungo with a new American lilt in his voice.

He heard her whooping with delight, then killed the call.

Coming out of the building he saw a large grinning Hispanic with his name on a sign waiting for him.

Mungo threw his case, giant pink teddy bear, and bottle of whiskey into the limo and sat back as they hared across to a fenced compound where the private helicopters were housed.

He looked at his watch and changed it to L.A. time.

One hour before noon.

All going smoothly.

Within minutes he was in the air in a private copter, flying up the beach line, avoiding Los Angeles city, heading for Malibu, home of just about every movie star you've seen on screen.

The sun was high and the sky clear blue.

Below on the beaches – Manhattan, Playa del Rey, Santa Monica – he could see the surfers, the swimmers, the family picnics… what a different world from doomy gloomy grey old London.

"Landing in five, sir," cried the female pilot over the engine noise.

"Thanks ma'am." answered Mungo.

He stroked his blonde hairs, patted down his smart new blazer, now sporting a red carnation he'd imported from Heathrow, took a deep breath, and allowed himself the briefest of grins.

"Going in to land now sir," shouted the pilot. "One minute."

"You can land on the beach?" shouted Mungo.

"Said it was an emergency…" laughed the girl.

"It could… it just could be," laughed the passenger.

And they landed on the sand in a large privately roped off area.

Zuma Beach in Malibu.

A guy in a suit met him at the copter door and took all the luggage.

Then Mungo saw her.

And the bridal arch made of driftwood, adorned with sparkling lights.

And the mariachi band of Mexicans with their trumpets, guitars, and violins.

And the angel choir of thirty wide-eyed school girls in white, hired from a Santa Monica theatre school.

It was West Coast noon precisely when he embraced her.

"My darling", whispered Mungo, his breath scented with peppermint to hide the stench of cheap wine from the flight over.

"My sweetest," she replied, looking up at him with tears in her eyes.

Janie Schwartz was ten years older than Mungo and a multi-millionairess.

Also about a foot shorter in height, with short-cropped grey-blue hair, bright blue eyes and the most youthful face seen outside college. She'd had work done but then everybody in California had. It was a rite of passage for every female over forty.

Even some of the men.

She didn't suffer fools and always got what she wanted. Which first was money and then husbands. Money she made from her property empire in Beverly Hills, Pasadena, and Burbank. Husbands she bought and discarded like her condos.

Behind her back she was known as the rich bitch princess of Bel Air... the powerhouse killer queen who sacked her pool cleaners on a daily basis.

In a few minutes time Mungo would be Janie's fifth husband. And he was determined he'd be her last. She was quite a find. He was shopping in a Valley superstore, and nearly crashed his car into hers. They got talking. She liked his English accent, divorced Eddie, and the rest was soon to be history.

Janie was dressed in a body-clinging white silk wedding gown, showing off her generous bosoms, and which looked like it cost a million bucks. The dress, that is.

The breasts looked way more expensive.

Mungo gently took her hand.

The Mexican band played "Here comes the Bride".

And the priest in a bright red blouson and black leather skirt crisply read the vows.

Mungo placed the sparkling diamond ring on Janie's finger.

They kissed, like for the very first time in their lives.

The band played a tacky version of "Pretty Woman".

The married couple danced badly in the sand.

Kissed again.

Then walked towards the waiting limo.

"I am very very happy Mungo," cooed the bride. "I'm in love…"

"So am I, my darling girl, so am I," echoed the adoring husband.

*

"Tell me about this baby you dumped," said Duffy.

Rocco took a long swig of beer at the bar. He was dressed in a tatty old duffel jacket, soup stains down one sleeve, looking like he'd not slept for a month.

Duffy wasn't sure about this case. Not sure about anything involving a dead baby. And anyway, this guy had serious halitosis.

"OK. Jade and I been trying for a babe for years but got nowhere. We was getting desperate. Adoption people were hopeless - I had a criminal record, so no way."

"You been inside?" asked Duffy.

Rocco nodded. "Two years. Then we saw this advert. If you wanting a new baby, get in touch…"

"Which you did."

Rocco nodded. "Met this very smart bint in a Kensington hotel. She could find us a 'bespoke' baby."

"Bespoke"?

"Name the colour, eyes, hair… and bingo, we'd be Mum and Dad!"

"The catch?"

"We had to buy it."

"Buy a baby?"

Rocco grunted. "We argued like crazy. Should we just pay up and shut up... Or…"

"Tough call Rocco."

"Tell me."

Rocco sat in silence a moment, took another sip of beer.

"You bought it." said Duffy quietly.

"Handed over twenty grand cash."

"Twenty grand! Shit! That's a bloody fortune man!"

Rocco nodded painfully. "Put everything on the line. And I mean everything. Borrowed from mates, parents, and whatever we could squeeze out of the bloody bank."

"And the baby?"

"It was beautiful. Sorry 'she'... Dark hair, laughing eyes... Sheba. An old Hebrew name meaning 'promise'."

Rocco bent forward, bit his lips, as if to stop from crying.

"And?" asked Duffy softly.

"She… Suddenly died. TB. Then next few days Jade got it too... got infected…and right now… right now, she's on life support."

"So sorry mate. That is awful. But where'd it come from, this TB?"

"Dunno. Guess the baby had it early on, then Jade caught it from her sneezing, coughing."

"Shit."

"I didn't know what to do with her. Sheba. Our guilty secret. I tried contact the woman we bought her from, but no reply. So I left her outside the hospital."

"That is so tragic. But why me Rocco... not go to the cops?"

"For the moment, low key. I dunno what we did was illegal

or not…"

"What you want me to do?"

"Stop those bastards selling babies! And… I want that money back!"

Duffy paused.

"Better get me the advert. I'll have to find myself a wife, then go shopping!"

He leant forward and clasped Rocco's shaking hand.

This was not just a tragedy, it was a crime. And he was determined to get justice for this guy and his wife. And for that poor little girl Sheba.

*

The wedding reception was at Geoffrey's, a Mediterranean-style restaurant and favourite celebrity haunt in Malibu.

Janie had hired the patio overlooking the Pacific Ocean so they could see the sun go down as they feasted on their grilled swordfish, surf' n' turf, and rib-eye steaks, washed down by Bread and Butter chardonnay from Napa Valley.

Mungo quietly thought to himself it was only two weeks since looking out over that very same sea when he dined at the Chim Chim Thai for Grace's wake in New Zealand. Funny thing, fate.

Janie stood and clapped her hands.

The large pink teddy bear in the chair beside her nearly fell over but the guests immediately quietened.

"Thank you all for coming on this very special day."

Some of the younger guests hooted.

"Sometimes as we make our journey through life you meet someone and you know, you just know, that this is the person you want to grow old with. Not that I have to say, I will ever grow old!"

Her guests laughed politely.

"But. That person is my adorable husband Mungo. And I look forward to sharing my life with this man, my husband."

The patio cheered.

And Mungo stood to reply.

"Friends, new and old… I am flattered to be here today to begin a new life with my wonderful wife Janie. I know it won't all be easy – they say she's a tough cookie."

The patio laughed again.

"But I'm sure if she does everything I say, we'll get on just fine."

More laughter.

Janie shook her head in mock anger.

"As a movie producer I travel the world, but I'm hoping to spend more time working on new projects here in Hollywood, spending more time at home!"

He raised his glass.

"Ladies and gentlemen. A toast to the lovely bride… my Janie!"

All raised their glasses and toasted the happy bride.

And Mungo sealed the wedding with another wet drooling kiss.

*

"How'd you like to be my wife?" asked Duffy as he and Kate wandered slowly beside the Serpentine in Hyde Park.

Kate stopped abruptly.

"This some kind of joke Duffy? I know we've slept together but that doesn't mean I want to marry you."

They sat on a bench beside the lake.

"Perhaps I should explain."

"Please do. And hurry up – I've a briefing in half an hour."

Duffy told her how he'd met the guy who left that dead baby on the steps of Great Ormond Street Hospital. How the couple had trouble having a child, plus as he'd been in prison they couldn't adopt, so they'd answered an advert, met a woman who promised them a "bespoke" baby, and, for twenty grand, bought a brand new baby. Trouble was, it had already caught TB... it soon died, but not before the wife got infected, and was now struggling to stay alive.

"That's a shit awful story," cried Kate. "Why didn't he come to us?"

"For the moment, for the moment Kate, he wants to keep this under the radar... hence talking to me."

"So why involve a police woman?"

"Being honest, you're the only one I can think of right now who could play 'mummies and daddies'!"

"Guess I should be flattered. But I'm not."

"All I need is someone to come with me when I track down this mystery woman who's selling babies."

"So how will you find her?"

"Rocco – the guy – showed me the advert he answered, but now the phone goes dead. So I'm going to drop by the hotel where they met and see if I can get a name or something."

Kate stood, looking at her watch.

"Course I'll help you Duffy. This sounds real seedy... My cup of tea."

"Appreciate it Kate." Duffy pecked her on the cheek. "I'll let you know when I find this bitch."

"And remember, if you want uniform involved, do call. We've got thousands of people doing this stuff every day, all those resources."

"Understood. But for the moment I'll do the legwork myself, like the guy asked."

"Good luck Duffy."

And she walked off briskly to her meeting, leaving the singing detective to take a photo of baby Sheba from his pocket.

It took some repugnant behaviour like this to make you realise there were some really heartless people out there, breathing the same air as him.

*

The newlyweds, Mungo and Janie, both in the buff, lounged in their steaming hot tub under the Californian stars, sipping margaritas.

Bel Air was the most expensive Los Angeles neighbourhood, a ritzy enclave in the Santa Monica foothills.

Two stately entrance gates off Sunset Boulevard led to winding streets lined with lavish mansions and their pools and tennis courts. Popular with celebrities and media executives, it was also home to the legendary Hotel Bel-Air where caviar cost over £300 a pop and the exclusive Bel-Air Country Club with its annual membership fees upwards of £130,000.

And so it was into this brittle world of excess riches and faux refinement that Mungo had tentatively stepped, wide-eyed and bushy-tailed, pinching himself regularly to check that his carefully planned fiendish dreams had indeed come true.

"What shall we call your company darling?" purred Janie. "Mungo Productions?"

"Janie and Mungo Productions..? JM Entertainment?"

"No no dear," insisted Janie. "You are now the mover and

shaker! I'll fund to start off, then when you get some big deals and movie franchises going, we'll take another look at the finances."

"You are so caring my love," oozed Mungo.

"Call it… call it 'Mungo's Movies'. That's catchy. People'll remember that. And makes you the star of the show!"

"'Mungo's Movies'?"

"Why not dearest?"

"I like it. Simple. To the point. Does what it says on the tin, and all that shit."

"Now." Janie emptied her glass. "I'll put in ten mill for the first year…"

"Ten million?" Choked her husband quietly.

She nodded. "That'll show the world you're a real player, babe!"

"That would be great my love."

"So… what's your schedule tomorrow?"

"Tomorrow? Oh… lunch at The Ivy… meeting some guys about a script."

"Perfect. I'd come along, but doing some hot deals in Burbank… Another drink?"

She rubbed his thighs…

"Or… shall we go to bed my darling?"

Mungo smiled and held out his glass. "Please."

He wanted to put off bed as long as possible. This woman under the sheets was insatiable. Better to get pissed and have a good night's sleep… though he did like her breasts.

Next morn Mungo showered, put on a lightweight cotton summer suit, had a standing breakfast – peach pancakes and a caramel latte - with his new lady in her outsize kitchen with an island the size of Majorca - waved as she was chauffeur-driven away in her white Rolls, then exited in his soft-top powder blue Jaguar F-Type for his first meeting of the day.

Half an hour later, sweating like a pig on heat, he parked in the Commerce Center at Glendale, a bland business park of large square boxes, about ten miles drive from Los Angeles. Driving across town he'd noticed the number of homeless living on the streets in tents had increased, more druggies around. Shit happened.

He grabbed his briefcase, wiped his brow, and headed for the building marked "Global Energy."

His last visit had been six months earlier when he did an unbelievable deal on the solar panels. This time he hoped for more. Much more.

Dakota in reception remembered him and kissed his cheek. He wondered why, then recalled he'd taken her for a beer and burger and all had become a blur when she'd made him smoke weed. Right now she was standing there in front of him, wanting another invitation. Long blue hair, bright red eye makeup, stud through her chin, tattooed dragon on her neck, pink chiffon dress pulled down one side to expose a beach-bronzed naked shoulder.

"Hi Dakota. I think Brett's expecting me ?"

"You in town long babe?" she smiled, showing the fake diamond in her teeth.

"Leaving today my dear," answered Mungo, wanting to get in and out mighty quick. His personal life had got busy enough without this temptation.

Dakota sighed.

"Go straight through. He's waiting."

Mungo walked into Brett's office to find him not alone.

He was behind his long desk as usual, adorned with models of solar panels and wind turbines. Anything that could make L.A.'s foul air that much cleaner.

The walls were lined with team photos of the Los Angeles Lakers over the past twenty years, and a basketball hoop hung from the far corner, so the main man could try get a goal into the basket from his office chair.

An obvious sports fanatic, Brett had an old-fashioned crewcut, a square jawline, and a cheesy grin. He always had his hands on a ball… a baseball, basketball, a football. Usually Mungo had to be on his guard that his buddy would not throw one at him as he walked through the door, then yell 'catch!' but today was different.

On either side of him sat two smiling Asian gentlemen in identical elegant white suits with silk kerchiefs.

Brett stood. "Mungo, you're looking great my man, looking great."

Mungo shook his hand firmly. He liked this guy. He'd been a good business partner for some years and now he hoped to not only increase his sales output, but also the prices.

"Always good to see you Brett…" Mungo nodded at the two Asians.

"Ah," said Brett, almost apologetically. "Meet Mr Sun and Mr Yi from Shanghai. My new business partners."

Mungo was a little taken back by this but beamed his best.

"Howdy," he said in a fake American accent.

"He's British," explained Brett to the Asians who smiled back.

"Mungo. My new friends here have taken over the company. I'm working for them and they want to change our working model."

"Change?"

"They want to order *twice* the number of solar panels from your company."

"Shit! That's fantastic Brett! Thank you, thank you," he

said nodding to Messrs Sun and Yi, who both bowed and broadly grinned back.

"But, in return for this increase in your export profits…"

"Yes?" asked Mungo hesitantly, wondering where this was going.

"They want you to do some importing."

"Like what?" asked Mungo.

"Blades. Wind turbine blades. That you find on those offshore wind farms."

"Wind turbine blades?"

Brett nodded. "So this is in keeping with your ecologically friendly business. Solar panels, and now… wind turbine blades."

"But why us?"

"You're a well established global exporter, keeping the planet clean. So you bringing these into the U.K. makes sense. All that climate change stuff."

"What would it cost us?" asked Mungo.

"Absolutely nothing."

"What?"

"That's the deal. We double the order for your solar panels, and you import our blades for nothing. For us. Plus… we're happy to pay a tad more on top."

"What's the catch Brett?" asked Mungo warily. This was too good to be true.

"No catch old buddy. These guys here want a toehold in Britain's eco biz and you're the way in. Brit politicians are madly racing to get to net zero before anyone else… more fool them. So, our guys want part of the action."

"OK so what's their strategy?"

"Trojan horse, buddy. Our Chinese friends want to get in on the ground floor of the wind farm bonanza, then, eventually start their own business in the U.K., build their own blades, and get a monopoly going... They see this as the next gold rush!"

Mungo thought a long moment. It was a canny deal, and least they'd double their profits if he accepted.

"I'll have to run this past Charlie back home." He stood and nodded, smiling again at the two Asians.

"Totally understand kemosabe. Let me know soonest. These guys want to get cracking... get a share of that gold!"

Mungo made for the door.

He wondered what Mr Sun and Mr Yi were up to. Perhaps as Brett said, they wanted to be part of the crazy race towards net zero in the U.K., perhaps they wanted to make the planet a cleaner place, or perhaps something much more sinister.

*

The two swarthy owners of the Ambassador Casino in London's Leicester Square looked through the smoked glass window at the tables below and didn't like what they saw. All the gamblers, all the croupiers, all the games were closely covered by the in-house security cameras. Any guest they thought might be dodgy they'd do a close-up and watch them very carefully. This was one of those times as the same guy had come in each night, three days running, and was taking home a fortune. Over one hundred grand. He just had to be cheating them.

Olaf, one of the Romanian owners, spoke into a mike on his desk.

"Jerry – go get his ID. I wanna know who this asshole is..."

They watched six-foot pock-marked Jerry move nimbly to

the centre table and speak to the high roller.

"Excuse me sir," said Jerry politely. "Could we have some ID please."

The guy turned, looking puzzled.

He wore a wide-brimmed fedora, shades, velvet DJ and a yellow bow-tie.

"Not a problem." His accent sounded pukka public school. He took out a credit card.

Jerry peered at the name. Then up to Olaf in his office behind the glass.

"According to his credit card his name's... Duffy."

CHAPTER FOUR

Duffy bounded up the steps of the Kensington Grand Hotel. He was feeling pleased with himself as he'd just got onto the DateFunk people and insisted they took down the fake photos of himself and some geezer using his voice. So least he had that behind him.

In his pocket, a photo that Rocco had taken of the woman who sold them the baby under this very same roof. She had a dark bouffant hairstyle, brown eyes, and a deep tan from weeks lying on some private beach in the Caribbean. Expensively dressed in a well-cut suit and pearls. The picture showed her passing the tiny baby Sheba across to Rocco's wife. It looked like a happy family scene, not like a cold- hearted financial transaction.

At reception Duffy was about to ask for the manager when an old acquaintance passed him, on their way out.

The tall bombshell from the country wedding and that four-poster fantasy.

"Well eat my knickers!" she laughed.

"Izzy!?"

"Mmm… you here for some tryst Duffy? Meeting some lady under the covers… or doing a bit of crooning in the bar?

"Ha – playing Sherlock this time… sniffing around a bit. You?"

"Live down the road… pop in and use their pool."

"Keeping the body beautiful…"

"I try."

"Listen. I know nothing about you… What do you do?"

asked Duffy.

She sighed. "Long story. Been a trolley dolly for Virgin... ran a Chelsea catering company... did a bit of modelling... now just helping out a bit with Dad's charity stuff."

"Impressive." Duffy felt this girl was way out of his league, but you never knew.

"I looked for you on DateFunk – but you'd disappeared..." she said.

"Closed it down just in time, before I got into trouble."

"Pity... Hey, when you want that drink, give me a call – you know where I am."

And she'd gone, playfully flicking her swimming towel at him on the way out.

Duffy made a mental note to follow up the invite. She really did look like that shapely Hannah thingy off the telly. Awesome.

He sighed and turned back to the receptionist and asked for the manager.

Several minutes later an important little man in an important little suit asked him to follow him into an important little office. Mister Bruce. Duffy wasn't sure if this was his first name or last. But it sounded important.

Handing over Rocco's photo Duffy explained he was a private detective, trying to find this woman.

"Ah. I do recognise this lady. She often comes into our lounge for tea in the afternoon," said Mister Bruce. "Very often with friends... she leaves a generous tip."

"Does she ever bring babies with her?"

"Sometimes. Sometimes I have seen babies."

"How often does she visit?"

Mister Bruce shrugged. "Nothing regular. Perhaps once a month. Is she in some sort of trouble? Should I be concerned with this lady?"

"Not at all sir. But. Next time you see her in here, I'd be much obliged if you could call me." And handed over his card. "A very good friend is trying to track her down..."

Mister Bruce agreed and Duffy went on his way, realising that this woman could be using many other hotels in London to do her dirty business.

Hopefully very soon the important little man would make an important little call to our singing detective.

*

Mungo came out of Brett's office and headed for the loo. He needed time on his own to think, and talk to Charlie. He went into a cubicle, locked the door, and took out his phone.

This offer was one helluva deal for Solar Global of Pinner. They could make bloody millions.

They were going to double their solar panel exports into the U.S.A. plus get paid more on top, in return for his company bringing these wind turbine blades into Britain for Messrs Sun and Yi, at no extra expense.

It could simply be as obvious as it sounded. China was by far the world's biggest producer of greenhouse gases, accounting for 27 per cent of global emissions, compared to 1 per cent for the U.K. Which meant the guys from Shanghai had the biggest guilt trip on the planet. Or, more likely, as Brett said, they wanted to get in on Britain's burgeoning net zero industry and cream off the dosh from those ugly onshore wind farms, more than 3000 new turbines soon to spread across the South and Home Counties.

Either way the boys from Pinner were the winners.

He woke Charlie at his Wembley home and explained the offer.

His business partner as usual was totally pragmatic. Saw both sides of the issue and suggested they give it a green light.

Mungo agreed. What could possibly go wrong?

He flushed the bog and walked out through Brett's reception. Was tempted to tell his buddy their decision there and then but thought would look too keen. He'd call him later.

Dakota was at his side.

"Flying home today then sir?"

Her eyelashes fluttered for California.

Mungo stalled and had a thought.

"Maybe, maybe not. Hey, you fancy a bite?"

"Like when Dracula?" asked Dakota, all a quiver.

"Right now my dear..."

She reached for a mirror, checked her face, flicked back her blue hair. "Ready to go capitano!"

Half an hour later Mungo pulled his Jag into the valet parking area at The Ivy in West Hollywood and entered with Dakota trailing behind, smoking a vape.

He was sat outside in the shade beside a small palm tree and asked for the menu.

"What you celebrating Mister Swift?"

"Life"… replied Mungo, feeling rather mellow.

He looked around at the other diners. No celebrities here today, just himself, he thought.

"Shute! Here's here," hissed Dakota.

"Who?"

"My bad boy."

Mungo twisted his neck and in a far corner spotted Brad Pitt in shades.

"Target at five o'clock… going in…" said Dakota, and raced across through the other diners towards the star's table.

"Holy shit!" sighed Mungo, who stood and peered after her.

By the time he'd reached Brad's table Dakota had pulled up a chair and was sharing a glass of fizz with him and his female guest.

"Mister Pitt... Mister Swift. A very famous business guy from England."

She pronounced it "Eng-er-land" as she introduced them. "Brad – used to be my big bad boss."

"What?" asked Mungo, nonplussed.

"Daks here was my nanny, man... and real good she was too," smiled the movie star. "Pity she moved on."

Dakota sighed. "Sorry Brad... but kids..." She shook her blue head. "I went off and did dog-walking for a year... much easier."

Mungo saw a moment of opportunity. And handed her his cell.

"Dakota – 'Daks' – could you possibly..?" Meaning take a photo of me and Brad.

"Sure. You want me in it too?"

Mungo shook his head and smiled sweetly. "Just me and Mister Pitt please."

She took the photo, then endless selfies of Brad and herself.

Mungo grabbed his phone back and motioned to Dakota to join him back at their table.

"Privileged to meet you sir – love your work," crept Mungo, bowed as he backed off and pulled Dakota back to his table.

Brad waved after them.

"We could've joined him if you'd asked," sighed the girl.

"Another time perhaps... now we've met."

Mungo realised the import of that chance meeting, in his new role as a Hollywood movie producer. He parked that connection and the shared photo very firmly in his memory bank for use at a later date.

"Now 'Daks'... tell me all about working as Brad Pitt's nanny."

*

Duffy was nibbling a stir fry at Fortnum's bar when they entered.

She was cute like a pixie and he was big like a bodybuilder.

Neither of them was smiling, but both made straight for the singing detective.

"Duffy!" the guy cried aggressively.

The P.I. spun on his barstool and raised his eyebrows as the guy raised his massive hairy fist.

"Who'd you think you are mate!?"

"What's the problem?" asked Duffy, trying to quieten him down.

"You on CutieBoy!"

"What's CutieBoy?"

"You bloody well know – you were begging me for money…" cried the girl.

"Start. Start at the beginning," begged Duffy.

"Sheila here – my sister – went on CutieBoy last night and started talking to you."

"Yeah, you Duffy! And within minutes you was wanting me to give to charity – your charity – two grand you was asking!"

"Show me", said Duffy quietly.

The hairy fist pulled out his phone. Tapped away and up

popped the singing detective, like DateFunk sitting on his Harley, and talking to screen. Once again it looked like him and sounded like him... Asking punters to call a number and have a romantic chat... On CutieBoy.

"I phoned you up on that number - you said we must have dinner by candlelight - so cheesy... then you tried to make me send you cash, to an online account!" said the girl.

Duffy put both hands in the air.

"Stop stop. I am so sorry guys – but this is all fake. They just did it on DateFunk, which I've closed down. It's a con... Let me buy you both a drink... That is not me!'"

"We don't believe you mate – but you'd better stop or I'm coming for you!" said the guy, who pulled his sister off and out the door.

"You at it again Duffy?" smiled his barman friend.

"Someone's targeting me Toto – just dunno who."

"Close down that account mate, before you get more visitors."

Duffy pulled out his phone and went to dial CutieBoy when it rang.

It was his Mister Bruce from the Kensington hotel.

The woman was there in the lounge right now, talking to a young couple.

Duffy killed the call and exited fast.

*

Mungo and Dakota were just washing down their grilled giant prawns with Napa Valley's finest Duckhorn chardonnay when he saw her enter.

West Hollywood's most celebrated restaurant, The Ivy, was at maximum buzz with Brad Pitt laughing in that far corner, beautiful blondes with flawless faces nibbling zucchini, and chubby rich guys quaffing champagne with their pretty grand-daughters.

"Fuck," muttered Mungo.

"What honey?" asked Dakota.

"Someone I know just came in… she's… she's a fantasist… thinks I'm her husband… that I'm a movie producer."

"Wow – that is so dope."

"I need you play along… just be careful what you say," urged Mungo.

Janie suddenly saw her new husband and came over to their table.

"Well, what a surprise!" cried Mungo.

"Hi babe – I got away early… thought I'd join you," smiled Janie, looking expectantly at the strange girl with blue hair.

"Oh… this is Dakota… a screenwriter… we're just discussing her next project."

"Well, that is wonderful. I'm Janie… Mungo's wife."

She sat at their table and summoned a waiter.

"Ah… so nice to meet you… Janie," grinned Dakota from ear to ear.

Janie ordered what they were having, then turned to the writer.

"So what's your big idea my dear?"

Dakota looked at Mungo a long moment. Then.

"A flying pig," she said suddenly.

"Really?" asked Janie wide-eyed.

"Yup. Everyone's always talking about flying pigs… so. That's the big idea."

"And?" urged Janie.

"I think it's still in development babe," covered Mungo.

"Well…" continued Dakota, grasping for words. Then sees Brad Pitt at his far corner table. "There's this real handsome guy… who decides to keep a… a pot-bellied pig."

Janie nodded. "I remember a few years back, that was all the rage… Instead of dogs, you walked down the street with your little piggy."

"So this guy, he decides he wants to try make his pig fly… way up in the sky."

"What's it called?" asked Mungo, getting interesting, although he knew she was making this up as she went along… It wasn't a bad idea… In fact he might steal it.

"Greta."

"Greta. And?" asked Janie again.

"And…. This guy and his nanny go hang-gliding together every weekend, so decide to take Greta along… In the end they tie the pig into her own glider and the three go way up into the heavens together and never return… End of."

"That is magical my dear," sighed Janie. She turns to her husband. "You got to option this for Mungo's Movies!"

"Mungo's Movies!?" laughed Dakota.

Mungo nodded and winked again.

"Told you I was a movie producer, girl." And winked again.

"And who's your big star? You need someone who'll bring in the crowds, bring in the cash."

Mungo got out his cell.

"Shall we show her?" he said to Dakota.

She nodded. "Why not?"

Mungo tapped his phone and showed Janie the picture. "There's your big star…"

The photo of Brad and Mungo.

Janie was dumbstruck.

"That's not all... I worked for Brad as his nanny."

Dakota stood and waved across to the movie star in the far corner, who waved back.

Janie looked from Dakota to Brad Pitt to Mungo.

"That's what I call networking darling."

"It's called : 'Pigs Can Fly...'" chirped Dakota, not knowing if this was all a crazy game or for real. Though right now she was enjoying every minute of it.

"You got a script?" asked Janie.

"Not yet."

"Show us a script and we'll show you a check." Janie stood, pecked Mungo on the cheek, and shook the girl's hand. "Gotta fly – like the pig – great doing biz with you..." And shot off.

"So," asked Dakota. "Who's living in the real world? You... or her?"

*

On getting Mister Bruce's call that the baby woman was at the hotel, Duffy leapt on his Harley and raced around Hyde Park to Kensington.

Dashed up the steps, past reception, and into the lounge.

It was quiet as a university library. Mostly old folks sipping tea and chewing scones, speaking sotto voce, not wishing to disturb the others.

Duffy scanned the room.

Then saw her sitting alone on a sofa. Dark long hair, scarf round her face, pulling on a woolly overcoat. She was just leaving. Couple long gone.

He could confront her face to face now. Or he could let her go and follow.

Decided the latter.

She was nearly six foot tall and walked in a rolling long gait. Probably been a runner in her younger years.

She exited via reception and the main entrance.

Duffy left a healthy distance between them. Didn't want to scare her off.

She walked through the hotel car park, and crossed the main road on foot.

Duffy was about fifty yards behind her, walking casually along without a care in the world, in case she suddenly turned and spotted him on her tail.

As he followed, he wondered what on earth would make a woman get into such a seedy trade... selling other people's babies. The big question was where did they come from in the first place, and who was masterminding the whole racket.

Could be a gang abroad somewhere like Albania, similar to them sending the asylum seekers across the Channel on boats. But that was for another time. Right now his first stop was this woman who'd cheated Rocco out of twenty grand, put his wife in hospital, and caused the death of little baby Sheba.

Up ahead she turned into an alley.

Duffy paused.

Counted to twenty before he too turned down that alley.

No-one in sight.

Given him the slip or gone into a house or garden along the way.

He jogged along the alley, looking left and right into the back gardens of the grimy terraced houses. Rusting mowers, torn trampolines, kids' broken toys. Decay.

Got to the end of the alley, looked both directions.

She was off one hundred yards to the left.

Looking behind her every few seconds.

Duffy knew he'd been sussed.

He walked faster behind her, trying to narrow those hundred yards.

She walked faster ahead.

He broke into a run.

She took off her high heels and sprinted.

He spurted after her, gagging for breath.

As she turned right into another alley.

Duffy raced after her, his lungs burning.

Got to the alley and it hit him slap bang across his face.

Her handbag. Weighty and hard, like a sledgehammer.

Duffy fell to the ground, his nose gushing blood. He could smell it.

She stood over him, a self defence spray in one hand, phone in the other.

"I'm calling the cops, you little shit…" she spat.

"I am the cops," snuffled a bleeding Duffy.

Now he could see her clearly.

The scarf had slipped from her face.

She was dark and tall and smart but not her in the photo.

He'd been chasing the wrong woman.

*

After the inspiring lunch at The Ivy, Mungo packed Dakota back to work, then wandered alone into the five-acre vineyard behind Janie's mansion. He wanted a clear head, some time and space on his own.

First up he called Brett to confirm he and Charlie would love to progress the new deal – double the solar panel exports, increase the costs, plus happy to bring in the wind turbine blades for the Chinese guys.

Next he took out his No. 1 burner and phoned Monica at home in Harrow with the kids.

"Just checking in love... Can't talk long," he whispered.

"All very hush hush Mungo..." she replied.

"Of course. But all safe this end. Home in a few weeks. Kids OK?"

"Everyone is just fine dear, looking forward to your return."

"Lovely lovely Monica. Looks like I have to go... an emergency!"

"Bye love, bye..."

Mungo put burner No. 1 away and got out burner No. 4.

Dialled and waited.

A female answered. French accent.

"Margot! C'est moi! J'arrive... demain ma cheri... tomorrow."

And ended the call just in time.

Janie was calling for him from the house.

He put away the phone and wandered back into his wife's mansion.

"Where you been honey?" asked Janie, a gin martini in her hand.

"Plucking a few grapes..."

"They ripe yet?"

"Not quite. Few more weeks."

She moseyed up close to Mungo.

He could smell her Parisian perfume. Only the best. Her eyes glowed.

"I think today I discovered a star..." she whispered.

"The writer girl with the blue hair?"

"You stupid! That was one amazing session. You meet the

girl. She's got the idea. And you get Brad Pitt thrown in... That is way something."

"Right time right place."

"Oh no – that was pizzazz! Your pizzazz."

"Thanks babe... you know how to flatter."

"You are going to go far sunshine..."

"Ah! Talking of going far... There's this media market in Cannes this week... Loads of TV and movie deals... I thought I should fly over, take a look, meet a few investors, you know the stuff."

"We could both go... make it a long vacation... our honeymoon?"

"Oh no. That's gonna be a surprise – I'm still fixing that one... don't want you knowing anything about it."

"So no Cannes for me?"

Mungo shook his head slowly.

"This time better babe, probably better if I focus on the deal, you know?"

Janie hugged him hard.

"Sure I understand. I can't wait to hear about the honeymoon..."

"It'll be fun, promise." He kissed her brow. "So, tomorrow at noon, I fly out to Nice for this market... and be away a few days... week or so."

"You're the boss darling," swooned Janie. "You're the boss."

*

Duffy, his face bruised from chasing the wrong woman down the wrong alley, sat at a quiet table in a corner of Fortnum's bar. He was sipping a scotch and soda with Rocco, both were peering at a stained page torn from a local newspaper.

"It was just pure chance that I saw it… eating my fish and chips wrapped in our local paper. It was the same advert we called about our Sheba."

Duffy peered closely.

"So." He reads: "If you have fertility problems but cannot adopt, we can help you find your very own special baby… Highly reputable firm with many satisfied customers. Please call this number…" He looked at Rocco. "Brilliant. I'm going to meet your woman with 'my wife' and ask all about getting us a brand new baby!"

Just then there was a slight rumpus at the bar.

Toto was trying to quieten down two customers, both male, loud, aggressive, and very threatening.

"Where is this Duffy!?" shouted one.

"I thought he worked from here?" cried the other.

Toto shook his head. "Not been here for a while gents."

"He's been cheating in our casino and our boss wants his money back!" shouted one.

"That's a hundred grand to you mate!" cried the other.

"Jeez", sighed Toto, genuinely amazed at this accusation.

But not as worried as Duffy who sat in the corner quietly listening to these threats. At first he'd thought this was another CutieBoy allegation, but couldn't be as he'd already closed down that site earlier in the day. No, this was something else that he couldn't account for.

One of the thugs picked up half a lemon from the bar and squeezed it all over Toto's head.

"Tell this Duffy, we never let go…" he spat.

"Tell this Duffy, we're coming for him," spat the other.

And they were gone. Leaving a waft of cheap aftershave

in the air.

Toto wiped his hair, looked across at the singing detective and shrugged his shoulders.

Duffy came over, shaking his head.

"What the fuck? I haven't been in a casino for years… and as for owing a hundred grand."

"Listen mate, face the facts. You lost your wallet… your credit card…all that dating shit online… someone out there's pretending to be you!"

"What?" said the singing detective.

"There's another Duffy out there."

"Please no…"

Toto nodded solemnly.

Duffy sighed. "ID theft… there's bloody two of us!"

CHAPTER FIVE

That night Duffy slept out under the stars in Hyde Park. Made him feel safer. Not that he got much sleep. Too much to think about. First up, who in hell was behind the ID scam? Nicking his persona, pretending to be him, and deliberately getting him in trouble. Big trouble. Those dodgy geezers meant business if they thought he owed a hundred grand. As if. But someone. Someone had looked deep into his lifestyle, where he worked and hung out, and was wanting to hurt him bad. But for all those wide awake hours that night he simply had no idea who wished him such harm.

Serious harm. Gouging his eyes out harm.

He got up at dawn, had a cool dip in the Serpentine, then headed for Fortnum's to wash and shave in their loo. Despite no sleep he felt razor sharp.

Probably knowing there were two guys in town trying to track him down for a small fortune someone else had nicked in his name.

He decided to put that at the back of his mind for the moment and ordered a large expresso from Toto to get the adrenalin pumping.

Least he now had a lead on the baby racket and around eleven made the call to the mystery woman who could magic you up a baby from nowhere.

She answered almost immediately. Her voice was educated, confident, and calm. She was totally in control. And wanted to know where the caller had seen the advert.

Duffy said his wife had spotted it in the local paper. They'd been trying for a baby for years, couldn't adopt for various reasons, and would do anything to have a child before it was too late. He arranged to meet her for tea in the Kensington hotel the next day at three.

Then he called Kate.

She was a bit brisk as was in the middle of a team briefing but promised to come with him to the meeting as his "wife."

Duffy went walking through Soho, trying to work out his strategy.

He and Kate had to appear totally naïve and desperate to do anything to get themselves a baby. Play it by ear... see what this woman recommended... then follow her to her home or next contact to expose how this baby selling racket worked.

He stopped in a doorway near Ronnie Scott's jazz club in Frith Street and called Rocco. Told him about the meeting and suggested he turn up out of sight so he could confirm it was the same woman who sold them Sheba. His wife was still in a coma, struggling to survive the TB she'd caught from the twenty grand baby.

As he turned back towards Piccadilly a large black shiny SUV stopped beside him and two hairy thugs jumped out.

Everything went dark as a hood was pulled over his head and he was pushed into the vehicle.

He heard growling voices, the engine revving, and felt the fist ramming the back of his neck. Hard. Then nothing.

Some time later, his heart thumping, he opened his eyes and faced the glaring light in his face.

He was handcuffed to an iron bedstead.

"He's woken up," said a voice sweetly.

"'Bout bloody time."

Duffy felt his shoulder being shaken.

"Now, you clever dick, my boss wants to know where you put that hundred grand?" asked another voice. Not so sweet.

"He wants it back sunshine. Like now…" said the first voice.

Duffy went to speak but his throat wouldn't talk.

"Louder! I can't hear nothing!"

Duffy croaked. "You got the wrong guy. I was never in your casino… don't gamble… was someone else."

"Your name Duffy?" asked the sweet guy.

Duffy nodded.

The second slammed his fist across his face.

"Then you're our man!"

"Again. Where you put that dosh?" asked the sweet guy, ever so sweetly.

Duffy tried to sigh but his neck hurt. "ID theft. You understand? I lost my wallet, my credit card… some arsehole's pretending to be me!"

The two looked at each other and laughed.

"You think we're bloody fools mate!?"

"Not! Me!" shouted Duffy in despair.

"We'll come back with the boss… he'll make you talk," and exited the room, leaving the singing detective very much in the dark.

Once alone he reached down with his free arm and took a shoe off.

Pulled out a tiny phone and dialled.

"Bonzo. I need your help mate. Bring a bloody hacksaw!"

Within thirty minutes Bonzo and his SAS buddy Spud had tracked the phone, broken down the door, and released Duffy from the handcuffs.

It was a basement under an empty office in Battersea.

The hairy bruisers were nowhere in sight.

The singing detective took the boys for a drink in a nearby pub and explained how now there were two Duffy's on the loose in London.

One making a shitload of trouble for the other.

It must have been fifteen minutes before Bonzo and Spud stopped laughing.

For some reason Duffy didn't see the joke.

*

Mungo had flown into Nice wearing an unbuttoned linen shirt, skin-tight chinos, and an "I Love L.A." baseball cap. He thought he looked cool. But at his age.

Margot was there to meet him, crazy as ever, holding his name on a card upside down as a prank. She was in her late twenties, wore a red hibiscus in her tousled golden hair which reached her waist, a low-cut floral dress, and bare feet.

He'd found her one bright sunny morning in a Cannes flea market selling her paintings. Immediately he was taken by her mischievous eyes, her teasing sultriness.

He'd found his street urchin, his gamine. Not much older than his daughter Donna back in London, but they had an unspoken affinity. They belonged.

As she threw her arms around him at the Arrivals terminal he noted the bronze curtain ring he'd given her on the last visit. It was their "engagement ring". Still there.

"Papa..!" she cried. Ever the joker, she took his hand and skipped alongside him like a petulant child. "I have booked your favourite."

"Chez Xavier?"

She nodded.

They grabbed a cab and headed into Cannes.

Half an hour and a hundred quid later they were drooling over pizza du pecheur in his favourite café off the Rue D'Antibes.

"How's the painting going, cheri?"

"Not good when you are not here... You are my muse... so when you come home, I am inspired!" she giggled. "Tonight I will paint till dawn... well, not all painting," she laughed cheekily.

"How's the flat?"

A year earlier Mungo had invested some of his savings in a small attic in an old farmhouse in the hills overlooking the Mediterranean. It was bohemian, chic, full of light... everything Margot had ever wanted. It was their home on the Cote D'Azur.

"Parfait!" sighed Margot. "Now I have everything, thanks to you Mungo. Except... except..." She tapped the curtain ring on her finger.

"Ah," smiled her benefactor. "I have to go away again next week."

"But you promised... Where you go this time?"

"We're touring London then perhaps America for a few weeks."

"Tell me exactly what you doing."

"Like I said before. We're called 'The Invisible Orchestra'. We pop up in places where you never expect it. Like those restaurants used to do. One day it's a piece of empty ground. The next we have twenty musicians there playing the best tunes in the world. The next day we're gone!"

"I must see this."

"We will come to France soon."

"And you are playing?"

"The kettle drum."

"Ah… You make much money like this darling?

Mungo shrugged. "We make enough. And there are charities who help us."

"Then you are my star! Very special… and, like me, very crazy!"

"Merci Margot."

"But…" She tapped the curtain ring on her finger again.

"OK my sweet. You've been very patient. We'll make a date. Six weeks from Saturday."

"What?" Margot's mouth fell open.

"We get married in six weeks…" whispered Mungo.

Margot sat still a moment. Then whooped for joy, called the waiter over, ordered a bottle of champagne, and went from table to table telling the other diners she was about to get married and they must all come to the wedding.

Leaving Mungo with a mellow smile, carefully poking his teeth with a tooth pick, looking quietly philosophical.

*

Back at Fortnum's, Duffy called Kate to tell her how he'd been duffed up by strangers who thought he'd broke the bank in some casino – which he hadn't – and wanted to go over their strategy as 'husband' and 'wife' before meeting the baby seller woman the next day.

"I'm really really sorry Duffy… but I can't make it,' said Kate.

"You don't want to be my wife?"

"It's Max. My brother. He gets these turns…"

"Shit. Can I help?" asked Duffy.

"Thanks, but it's personal. Sometimes he gets very needy… almost possessive, and I have to take time off to calm him down."

"I can easily pop over, a second pair of hands?"

"Most kind. But it's a one on one thing. I'll deal. And so sorry to let you down."

"Understood Kate. As if you haven't got enough on your plate."

"Good luck with that woman. Let me know what happens… And be careful… these people could be dangerous." And she was gone.

Duffy stared at his phone.

"Damn."

"We could be a gay couple?" offered Toto the barman with a wry twinkle.

"Fuck off mate!"

Toto passed him a glass of chardonnay.

"I have an idea," said Duffy. And dialled a number. "Izzy?"

*

Mungo was rolled into a cab from the pizza joint late that night and headed with Margot back to their arty attic in the hills above Cannes.

The young fiancée guided him up the stairs and he collapsed on their double bed, out like a light.

She looked at him a moment then went to his jacket and searched through the pockets. Found his purse. Took out a hundred Euro's and stuffed them down her skirt.

She then tiptoed out of the flat and made her way back into Cannes.

Waiting for her in a tiny quayside bar was a young unshaven boy, wearing a dirty hoodie, in his early twenties. He had a dark sallow look, was possibly from Algeria.

Margot kissed him on the cheek and took the beer he'd ordered for her.

"He's asleep Sami. Pissed. The old fart," she hissed.

"So?"

She passed him the cash she'd stolen from Mungo, which he pocketed.

"We have a wedding date."

Sami high fived her.

"When?"

"Six weeks," replied Margot, grinning from ear to ear.

"Parfait…"

"He keeps giving me this shit about some pop-up orchestra, says he travels the world… and I know, cos I saw it in his case, I know he's just a bloody salesman, of solar panels!" cried Margot.

"But he's rich?" asked Sami.

Margot shrugged. "He bought the flat. That's worth something."

"Sure. That's worth something… Once you are his wife then we make sure he leaves you everything if he dies," whispered Sami, ordering more beers.

"Then he dies and we get the flat, and anything else he has."

"We gotta plan it careful Margot. It's gotta look good."

"We can poison him slowly," she suggested.

"Or some kind of crazy accident."

Both clink their glasses and dream of the small fortune they'd make in the coming months.

Meanwhile back in the attic flat Mungo had been wakened by his bladder, and realised he was on his own.

He took a long swig of tap water and slumped back on the bed.

Where was Margot?

He noticed his jacket had fallen on the floor and looked through his pockets.

He was a hundred Euros short.

He sat back down again, thinking hard.

Just for once. Just for once it looked like our global swindler had met his match.

*

At three the next day Duffy left his Harley in the Kensington hotel car park and made for reception where'd arranged to meet Izzy. He'd explained the whole deal. That he was on a job for a client who'd paid twenty grand to buy a baby. Today the two of them were posing as husband and wife and wanted to get more info from the woman involved in this wretched scam.

Duffy was in his usual jeans and leather jacket, Izzy looking very 'mumsy' in a long pink coat and beret. They were Jack and Lucy Baker. Desperate to get themselves a new baby, whatever.

"But I hate kids Duffy," spat Izzy. "Gimme a dog any day."

"Bite your lip and smile. And remember you're my wife."

"Mmm... you're quite butch at times."

Also in reception was Rocco, discreetly waiting behind a newspaper, who nodded to Duffy, confirming the baby seller woman was sitting next door.

They entered the lounge and saw her immediately.

Dark bouffant hairstyle, cool, stylish grey suit, like an international business executive.

She stood with a pert grin to meet them.

"Rachel Storm."

"Jack... and my wife Lucy... Baker."

They all shook hands and sat.

"So... You'd like a baby?"

"We would love a baby," oozed Izzy.

"We been trying a couple of years now, ain't that right darling," said Duffy.

"Zilch. We think Duffy might have a wee problem."

"Well, it was never proven love."

"I think you'll find it was darling... all those tests... remember your embarrassment."

"This can happen..." said Rachel sympathetically.

"We thought of adopting," offered Duffy.

"But they're so very fussy," added Izzy.

"Said we were too old."

"It got just complicated – easier to get a puppy," joked Izzy.

"Which we did think of," added Duffy.

"But we argued about the breed."

"I wanted an Irish wolfhound," said the detective.

"I wanted a Hungarian Vizsla."

"Boy or bitch?" sighed Duffy.

"And the name."

"I thought 'Clancy' was perfect."

"I preferred 'Zsa Zsa'."

Rachel Storm cleared her throat.

"A baby?"

"Sorry," smiled Duffy sweetly. "We both... really do want a baby."

"Do anything," added Izzy.

"Do you have a nice garden for children to play... a special bedroom for your little newcomer?"

Izzy laughed. "We've already painted the baby room and bought the cot."

"I suggested blue," added Duffy.

"But I preferred pink."

"Got a trampoline for him on the lawn."

The business woman suddenly became professional and sat erect.

"We offer a bespoke service," she clipped.

"Bespoke?" sighed Izzy.

She heaved a thick catalogue onto the coffee table between them and opened. Page after page of babies. Different skin tones, different eye colours, different hair colour, different sexes, different religions.

Duffy and Izzy were speechless.

"It's like choosing a new home or car or holiday... You tell me the baby you're dreaming of and we'll match it."

The pretend husband and wife silently poured over the photos with near genuine amazement..

"Wow wow wow," said Duffy.

"This is going to be really difficult..."

"There's no hurry – you have all the time in the world. The babies won't go away."

Duffy looked at Izzy.

"This is going to be tough..."

"Let me show you our contract."

She handed Duffy a form which he quickly read.

"So we can't return once we've bought the baby."

"Most parents would never dream of returning their new babe. The moment you hold it, the moment it cries, moment you change that first nappy."

"The moment it's sick down your front," laughed Izzy.

"What if it gets ill and dies?" asked Duffy.

Rachel Storm went silent then looked serious.

"That... would never happen."

Oh yes, it would, thought the detective, thinking of Rocco's Sheba.

Duffy looked at the woman. His turn to be serious.

"Where do the babies come from Rachel?"

She hesitated a nano second. "As you can guess... many girls have accidental pregnancies, which is where we help out... we step in and lend a hand."

"So you're a lifeline - stopping abortions?"

"That's how we see it. Like a charity, looking after young girls who are not ready to be mothers... we compensate and take the babies off their hands."

"Very admirable. Dare I ask how much... what it would cost to take a new baby off your hands ?" asked Duffy.

Rachel Storm paused a long moment.

"Twenty grand Mr Baker."

"Twenty grand!? That is massive."

"Remember it's for life."

"Like a puppy," added Izzy sweetly.

"We might need a week or two to try get that money together."

"Of course," smiled Rachel. She felt that the deal was almost done.

"And yes, we'd be happy to take any little babe, long as it's smiling and well and got all its cute little fingers and toes... Yes darling?"

"Sure thing. Let's do it."

"Excellent."

Rachel snapped closed her catalogue.

"Why not borrow this baby file, have a think, then call me when you've made a decision."

She stood and shook hands with Mr and Mrs Baker.

"Immense pleasure doing business with you both," and left.

"Bloody hell!" seethed Duffy.

"Where you getting twenty grand Duffy?"

He shrugged. "I'll find a way."

"What now then?" asked Izzy.

"I'm shooting off to find out where our Rachel lives… catch up later."

He rushed to the hotel entrance and into the car park, just in time to see the baby seller drive off in a sleek black Audi and noted its plates.

Walking away from Duffy's Harley was a tall guy wearing shades, a wide-brimmed Fedora, velvet jacket, and a yellow bowtie.

The singing detective hardly noticed him and roared off on his bike, chasing Rachel Storm.

As they reached a T-junction Duffy slowed to follow left.

But the brakes failed.

Been cut.

And crashed smack bang into the iron railings ahead of him.

The Harley lay there, wheels spinning in the air.

Duffy in a crumpled heap, motionless.

CHAPTER SIX

Abigail Clements-Brown was nearing eighty, whip smart, and didn't suffer fools.

She sat with her walking stick, peering at a massive screen in the large luxurious living room of her Thameside penthouse apartment.

Looking younger than her years, she had light greyish short-cropped hair, an aristocratic hooked nose, slender but whimsical lips, and radiant green eyes.

She was not only intelligent, it had been her profession.

Following her Oxford degree she had joined GCHQ and worked in the analysis unit before moving into cyber crime. But, after many years in "The Doughnut" at Cheltenham, she grew restless and joined MI6 as a foreign agent, which meant she travelled the world and lived on her nerves. Rubbing shoulders with piano wire technicians in Tehran, Moscow, and Istanbul.

But those days were now behind her. Sort of.

Her husband Jeremy had died several years earlier, leaving her a small fortune from his furniture design empire.

But she was desperately bored and spent most days watching dreadful television or even worse movies on her 12-foot TV screen, "The Wall".

Which is why she'd had called in an old work friend Hanny to help organise some fun before her time ran out.

Today was the first of her experiment.

She was not even sure where it was going.

Hanny had arrived at noon and poured them both a stiff

gin and tonic.

She, like her colleague, was Oxbridge, bright, and had lived her life on the edge. Mid-seventies, shoulder-length darkish hair, and deep brown eyes. Never married, but had many affairs in the field over the years. Very self-sufficient and a dependable rock to her tight-knit group of wizened spooks put out to grass.

On the huge wall screen was a live picture of Piccadilly Circus.

So large, so real, you felt you could walk right into it and feed the pigeons.

In the centre that statue of Eros, the winged archer poised with his bow.

All those flashing neon signs on the buildings around the circus… the Criterion Theatre… the roads connecting Piccadilly, Regent Street, Shaftesbury Avenue, the Haymarket, and Coventry Street, along with the London cabbies, double-decker buses, the white van men, and mad cyclists braving the traffic.

"How many assets on the ground Hanny?" queried Abigail.

"As you asked Abigail, three," answered Hanny.

"Perfect my dear, just perfect."

Abigail closely watched the crowds moving around Piccadilly Circus on the giant screen.

She giggled a moment. "I feel like I'm back in the field again."

"Can't believe we're watching this live, as it happens, like a hugh window," added Hanny, mesmerised. "Anyway, what's the plan old girl?"

"Fishing. We're going fishing. But first. Let me play a game. Spot the assets… Three faces in that crowd. Trying to blend in and not be spotted. Looking as if they're window shopping, tying their shoelaces, reading the paper, asleep on a bench..."

"You've got about three hundred faces on that screen, all moving about...tricky challenge," mused Hanny.

"Let's see... we've got punters coming up from, and going down into, the underground... tourists taking selfies around the statue... some rushing to meetings or dates or lunch... others just selling dope or crossing the street."

"Tricky, like I said," replied Hanny.

"Asset 1. Nine o'clock... leaning again that pillar, lighting a cigarette and showing he's never smoked in his life..." Abigail paused. "Asset 2. Three o'clock. Young girl asking directions. She's been doing that over and over."

"Very good."

"And Asset 3. Sitting right under Eros and pretending to be asleep, with one eye open."

"Too bloody right that girl – you should've been a spy!"

"Random."

"What?" asked Hanny.

"I want to choose three strangers, totally at random."

"Go on then."

"Here we go," said Abigail. She spoke into the mike she was holding.

"Asset 1. I want you to target the young guy on crutches, hobbling towards Piccadilly."

Asset 1 replied: "Broken nose, stubble, leather jacket?"

"Affirmative," replied the handler. She went on... "Asset 2. The girl crossing into Regent Street... pretty brunette in a pink plastic mac."

Asset 2 replied: "Too much makeup, painted eye brows and those swollen lips that are all the rage these days."

"Affirmative," replied Abigail once more. "And Asset 3. The young lad, early twenties, very short hair, looking a bit lost, exiting the tube."

Asset 3 replied: "Looks like a tourist, bright-eyed and bushy-tailed... bit of a tan, possibly from Oz."

"Affirmative," answered the ex-MI6 agent.

"Now. All assets... I want you to follow and find out the life story of these three random strangers... Get back to me in 24 hours... Good luck. Over and out."

She froze the screen picture and turned to Hanny.

"The game is on," smiled Abigail.

"You've caught three little fishies..."

Abigail nodded with secret excitement. Back on the job.

"You own them," added Hanny.

"And they don't even know it," chuckled Abigail.

"What next old thing?"

"Well, we went fishing. Now let's see what we've caught..!" twinkled Abigail.

*

Cannes that week was abuzz with 10,000 bodies from all over the world. It was the annual **MIPCOM** market where the producers and buyers and sellers of screen shows – dramas, comedies, quizzes - from Albania to Zanzibar came to shop in the Rue d'Antibes, dine on the Carlton Beach, and do a little television business on the side.

While the flamboyant and the beautiful flowed into the Palais des Festivals for their endless meetings, Mungo stood on the steps grabbing anyone who'd stop for a selfie to send back to Janie in L.A., as he needed proof he was shooting the breeze with the cool creatives on the French Riviera.

Right now he was grinning ear to ear with two young pretties from Milan who flinched and disappeared into the throng when he suggested lunch.

He'd been taking photos for twenty minutes and was about to give up when a chubby garlic-breathed guy in a bright yellow shirt accidentally bumped into him.

"Scusi!" he smiled.

"No problema," smiled Mungo back.

The guy held out his hand.

"Wim De Groot…You Italian? I saw you with those girls?"

"British mate. British."

"Producer?"

Mungo nodded.

"Pitching some movie stuff."

"Ah."

"And you from Holland?" asked Mungo.

Wim nodded.

"Investment. Always looking for the right project to put our money into…"

Mungo thought a moment.

"Got time for a drink?"

Minutes later they'd crossed La Croisette, avoiding the elegant grandes dames with their pampered poodles and henpecked husbands, and found a backstreet bar.

Wim stared at Mungo's business card.

"Shit – you based in L.A. 'Mungo's Movies'. What you selling?"

Mungo told him about the Brad Pitt project with the flying pig.

"That is awesome man… We might be interested in the world rights."

Mungo ordered a bottle of expensive wine.

"Tell me how much you invest…"

Two hours later Mungo had agreed to stop over in Amsterdam on his way to London. Wim promised him the world and Mungo was beginning to enjoy his new role as a movie magnate, when a tap on his shoulder shattered his dream.

"You been hiding from me!"

She pulled up a chair and sat beside him.

Margot, in a long flowing sundress and floppy straw hat.

Mungo turned, slightly tipsy and slightly irritated.

"Baby!"

She looked at Wim.

"You part of his orchestra?"

Wim looked puzzled.

Mungo quickly explained. "I play with a travelling band… like to keep my hand in, you know."

Wim nodded and felt he should move on.

"You have my card Mungo. We will meet…" And vanished.

Margot looked at Mungo.

"You're drunk."

He shook his head.

"I been looking at wedding dresses. I think we need a big bad yacht for the party… What you think my darling?"

She grabbed his hand.

Mungo sobered up and looked her beadily in the eye.

"Where'd you go in the middle of the night cheri… you were out for hours?"

"I could not sleep – I am so much in love."

"You took a hundred Euro's from my wallet."

Margot paused as the waiter came over and asked Mungo.

"Another bottle monsieur?" with a sickly grin.

It was Margot's Algerian friend… Sami.

*

89

A bruised Duffy sat in his corner of Fortnum's bar with a pair of crutches at his side.

He was sipping a flat white and looking forlorn when she entered.

"You have to be kidding Duffy! What you done now?"

She was around thirty-five, attractive, expensively dressed. His ex-wife.

"Zandra... who you paying to beat me up!?"

She nodded to Toto for another coffee and sat down.

"OK. What happened?"

"Rammed off the road. Two times this week. Seems there's someone out there pretending to be me, and I'm getting the blame for his shit!" sighed Duffy.

"Oh dear oh dear. ID theft. Lots of it around. Scammers everywhere... dodgy phone calls to old dears trying to get their life savings... others calling to say your bank account's been emptied... Not good."

"I been hoping it would go away, but..." He shook his head.

Zandra sighed deeply.

"Apart from this disaster how you doing? Still no office... still no home?"

The singing detective shook his head.

"Still crooning?"

"When I can. And you? Dating? Engaged? Wedding on the horizon?"

Zandra shook her head.

"The odd spotty toyboy. Nothing serious." She looked at him, almost with pity. They'd had some fun times together. But she knew he'd never settle down. Too much of a free spirit. "So?" she asked. "You must be wanting something Duff?"

As one of London's top barristers she knew that he knew when he was in a hole he'd come calling, and she was right.

"I'm on this case…"

Zandra nodded. "You always are love."

"They're selling babies."

"Babies!?"

"And they want a massive fee."

Zandra looked at her feet.

"Yes?"

"Twenty grand."

She stood quickly. "Tell me you are joking!"

Duffy did his best puppy look back.

"That… that is way…" And just shook her expensively-shorn hair.

"It's got to be stopped. And the only way… is go along with it… expose them… and get your money back!"

Zandra sat again slowly.

"Twenty bloody grand Duffy… Never asked that much before."

This time he stared at the floor in silence.

"OK OK. I have an idea. See this watch." She took it off. "Hermes. It's worth twenty grand, give or take." And passed it across the table to her ex-husband.

"Shit Zandra," sighed Duffy. He realised this really was crossing a red line.

"I can't. That must have memories."

"It does. He was a very rich Arab. Who was very pleased when I got him off."

"Damn."

Zandra stood suddenly.

"I'm in court in an hour. Take the watch. But when you catch them I want it back. Comprendo?"

"Comprendo," whispered Duffy guiltily.

And watched as Zandra waltzed out of his life once more.

He picked up the timepiece with great hesitation and hoped to high heaven he'd be able to return it in the coming days.

*

It only took Mungo a couple of hours to fly from Nice to Amsterdam. He was glad to leave Cannes for two reasons. First, the place was simply overrun by the media circus attending the television market; second, Margot was beginning to get on his tits and he was wondering if the marriage was a good idea. He adored her fancy free nature, walking the streets barefoot and looking like a street waif. He adored her wide-eyed innocence but alarm bells were starting to ring. Was the conman being out-conned by this youngster? Did she feel anything for him... was he in some kind of danger from her... or was he still suffering from that third bottle of red in that seedy backstreet café?

As he walked through Arrivals at Schiphol, Wim was waiting there to meet him as promised.

He drove his guest into the city in an old white Mercedes and stopped by a modern block of flats.

Mungo had never been to Amsterdam and was surprised by all the cyclists, the river meandering through its centre, the cobbled bridges, and the tall medieval houses bordering the canals. Everywhere the smell of pot, coming mostly from the waterside cafés.

They drove to the Prinsengracht district and found a quiet Indonesian eaterie.

Wim ushered him to a corner table where an exotic

woman was waiting for them.

"This is him my darling," said Wim, as they sat.

She stood politely to greet them, did a little bow, and smiled. "I am Putri."

"Mungo Swift." He squeezed her hand gently and gazed into her eyes. This must be the most gorgeous girl he had ever met.

She was probably thirty, long dark shoulder-length hair, with wide Asian eyes, and a bewitching smile.

"This is my wife," said Wim with quiet pride. "We met in Bali three years ago… got married after six weeks. Made in heaven."

"I am privileged," whispered Mungo.

Wim beckoned a waiter and ordered Bintang beer and Nasi Goreng for three.

"Now. Down to business… I wanted to discuss your movie projects and our investment."

Mungo nodded, still looking at Wim's enchanting wife.

"I am all ears my friend…"

"Of course, it's always a two-way thing… funding for TV or the movies. Ideally we try do cross-over productions, so we can invest with your shows and you can invest in ours."

"What exactly are you doing right now Wim?" asked Mungo.

"We have about five shows up and running. A game show, a quiz show, a travel show, a documentary about a famous Dutch footballer, and a live soap opera."

"That's fantastic," said Mungo, impressed. "Then why do you want me?"

Wim shrugged. "You do movies. I want to do movies… so we become partners and make magic together."

"Sounds like a plan."

"So. I could invest say a million Euros in your next Hollywood film… and, you could invest a million U.S. dollars in our next drama?"

"Very interesting."

Mungo, the solar panel salesman, was still feeling his way around this media bullshit but thought he could just about stay ahead of his new best Dutch friend.

"Let's think about deals my man… Deals… But first, got to go pee."

He left the table and went to the bog, leaving Mungo alone with Putri.

"I love your name – what's it mean?" he asked.

"'Putri' mean 'princess' in Malay," she said sweetly.

"Wim's a very lucky guy."

"He is kind. But be careful…"

"What? Why Putri… this is your husband."

"Like I say he can be kind… but in business, always be careful."

"I think he's a guy I can trust…"

"Be. Careful."

And Wim was back at the table.

"What you been talking about? You got her phone number yet?" joked Wim.

"Not yet…" laughed Mungo. "Not yet."

"Now. We were talking deals… If you were to invest in my shows… like I said, a million dollars, then you'd find the profits pretty damn good."

"What about my movie?"

"That will happen. Sure. But as you're here in Amsterdam, we could start with you helping on some of our homegrown stuff, becoming a partner in a new business venture, right here and now!?" He leant across and tightly grabbed Mungo's wrist.

"What do you say old buddy?"

Mungo sipped his beer and realised Putri's warning was right.

There he was all alone in a city he'd never been before, with this new best friend suggesting he gave him a million to put into his own shows.

Alarm bells were ringing.

He felt like he'd just walked into a massive bear trap.

Only one thing was certain about this meeting of minds. By the end of the evening he vowed to have Putri's number on burner phone No.5.

*

"So let's get this right. We've chosen Baby No. 22 in the catalogue. Little guy with blonde hair and blue eyes?" asked Izzy.

Duffy limped along on crutches beside her as they entered the lounge at the Kensington hotel.

"I got 'heads' when we flipped the bloody coin. So it's a boy, sorry."

"And I decided to call him 'Byron.'"

"We sure about that?" laughed Duffy.

"I see a storm on the horizon," whispered Izzy.

"What?"

"A Rachel Storm. Baby seller of this parish."

There she was on that same sofa. Still in that prim grey suit. Still looking very businesslike. She stood as she saw them coming.

"Greetings," she oozed with great fake charm.

"Hi there," cried Duffy as he slumped into a chair, and

Izzy plonked the baby catalogue onto the coffee table.

"You had an accident?" asked Rachel, looking at his crutches.

"Fell off my bike," replied Duffy.

"I'm sorry…. So… Decisions?" she asked politely.

The other two nodded silently.

"No. 22." said Izzy. "We've chosen that cute little blonde boy."

"Mister blue. Great choice."

Duffy cleared his throat.

"The payment."

Rachel Storm looked a trifle anxious.

"Yes?"

"We have a proposal. We do have the amount. Twenty grand."

"But?"

Duffy took out the Hermes watch and put it on the table.

"This watch is worth twenty grand. Perhaps more."

"Oh. We do prefer cash Mr Baker…"

Duffy sighed. "I can go sell it if you wish. Might take a bit of time… or, if you want a quick sale."

Rachel Storm was inwardly irritated and said nothing. Then.

"Let me check this out." She took the watch then googled it on her phone.

The others looked at each other in silence.

"OK. As you say… worth just over twenty grand. I'll take it."

The others sighed relief.

"Wouldn't normally do this. Against procedure, but."

"That's a relief," said Izzy. "We thought we might lose our baby boy."

The seller pocketed the Hermes watch and stood.

"Same time same place next week?" she said.

Duffy shook his head.

"No. No watch until we have our baby. With respect."

Rachel Storm coolly gave him back the watch.

"Of course. Next week you have your baby…" And left looking far from happy.

"She nearly nicked your watch…"

"Nearly," added Duffy.

"Shall we follow?"

"Next week… If she brings a baby we might see her collect it from someone else."

"What now then?"

"Let's go celebrate being a Mummy."

"Why not… Daddy?"

Duffy limped off on his crutches towards the nearby bar and turned.

"A dirty martini, if I remember correctly?

*

Monica was hoovering the front room of their tiny terraced cottage at Harrow-on-the Hill when the doorbell rang.

With Mungo returning from his mystery job in the States in the next few hours, she could hardly contain himself. He'd sent the odd text from Los Angeles and hinted that they – probably him and the CIA – had tracked down the fugitives and were bringing them to justice. She always prayed when he was away that he'd come to no harm. She knew her man could be very determined once he had a challenge but was not sure whether he could defend himself in a fight. But then he must have had military training which he didn't want to talk about. He was like that.

Kept certain things very close to his chest.

So. That morn she'd been to the hairdressers first thing. Bit of colour and a blow dry. Then the butcher and bought him six venison sausages. She knew he loved cooking them whole in a vegetable stew with plenty of red wine. And his favourite bottle of Rioja. Not that she spoiled him. Just liked to make him happy. He was one in a million.

They'd met just over twenty years ago at the Hammersmith Palais, just before they pulled it down. She was still in her teens and he was about ten years older. A great mover and shaker on the dance floor. Had a worldly way about him. Had no parents – was an orphan – and the poor thing had been brought up in kids' homes across the country. But oodles of cheeky charm and a way with the ladies. In those early days he was with the SAS… going away on missions behind enemy lines, into Libya… Iraq… who knows where, who knows why. He could never say. But she was ever so proud of him.

Monica turned off the hoover and looked at her watch.

If it was him he wouldn't ring the bell, unless he was playing games, which he did, sometimes.

She opened the door with a flourish.

On the step stood a young man with a shortish haircut and a clipboard.

"Good morning madam."

"Hello?" said Monica wondering what this was about.

"I'm from the council and doing a quick door to door census. Can I ask a few questions?" he asked.

"Of course love. But I've not much time…" cautioned Monica.

"Just getting a few names and numbers of local residents. All ready for the next election," said the young man.

"Not a problem. But…" paused Monica. "You've got an accent. Australia?"

The young man nodded with a broad smile.

"Never can lose it."

"Thought so."

"Now. Am I right that the householder is a Mungo Swift?"

"Correct."

"And…" Looking at the hoover behind her. "You are his… housekeeper?"

Monica shook her head.

"His… sister?"

Monica shook her head again.

"His wife."

The young man quietly noted this on his clipboard.

"His wife?" he confirmed curiously.

Monica nodded. "Nearly twenty years now."

The young man looked at her a long moment.

"Any… family?" |

"Three children."

"Three children?" he repeated. "And can I take the profession of Mr Swift please?"

"Sorry. I can't say… It's sort of…"

"Hush hush?" offered the young man.

Monica smiled.

"So very hush hush," she added.

Noah, the New Zealand stepson that Mungo has diddled out of nearly one million N.Z. dollars, smiled back at this woman with the hoover in the doorway.

"How very interesting… Mrs Swift. How very interesting."

CHAPTER SEVEN

Mungo sat with his business partner Charlie in their Solar Global offices in Pinner sipping a very large scotch.

He'd had a very frantic couple of days.

Juggling his crazy gamine fiancée Margot in Cannes who was planning their big wedding in six week's time, with a party on a luxury yacht in the marina… could she be trusted.

With his new Dutch showbiz buddy Wim and gorgeous wife Putri as they bullshat each other in Amsterdam on fantasy media deals where each was trying to rip off the other.

Leaving behind his new super rich wife Janie in L.A. who was convinced he was developing a Brad Pitt movie about a flying pig, inspired by the wondrous scribe, young Dakota… the solar energy receptionist with the blue hair and chin stud.

On top of which was dear Monica and the kids. She'd greeted him home with his dream meal of venison sausage stew and a fine bottle of red. She really was to die for. The only credible being in his entire life. He wondered why he played these games with his ladies, with his wives. It was something in his genes… in his persona… he simply couldn't help himself… he saw a lovely lady and he wanted to marry her. Wasn't perverted or criminal or bad, just that, that was the way his romantic juices flowed.

And of course dear old Charlie knew nothing of this. Merely thought Mungo was the best salesman of their solar panels on the planet and always returned with mind-blowing contracts that made them both ever so much richer.

"They're flying in tomorrow," he burped.

"Who?" asked Mungo.

"Your Chinese mates."

"Ha – Messrs Sun and Yi… they seem keen to get their stuff going."

"Probably got endless funding… I've had to empty out the big hangar for their turbine blades – they're anything between 30 and 100 metres long!"

"What?" gulped Mungo.

"Yup… mega… But if these guys want to get in on the start of the onshore winds farm bonanza, this is very very clever."

"Agree," nodded Mungo. "They start bringing them in through our company.

Then buy an industrial space and build their own… Get a monopoly going, up the prices… and hey bingo!"

"Perhaps we should go partners?"

Mungo shook his head. "Too much hassle when we're doing just fine with the solar panels."

"Where next maestro? Where next will you sprinkle your sales magic?"

"I was thinking of selling to the Eskimos… No, just kidding… Charlie, I guess after a break here in London I'll wing off again to do California, France, possibly Amsterdam and the Low Countries."

"You got the gift Mungo. Always knew you had."

"Yeah, but like anything, you can overdo the good luck stuff… One day, one day my dear friend, that magic might turn to dust."

*

Duffy sat with Izzy waiting for Rachel Storm to arrive with their baby.

"Here she comes," whispered Izzy.

From the far end of the lounge she cruised towards them with a fake smile, in that same prim grey suit, clutching a baby's carry cot.

Duffy stood and nodded as she approached them.

The baby seller delicately placed the cot on the coffee table.

And there he was.

A tiny blue-eyed blonde baby boy.

Crying.

"Here's the little chap you've been waiting for."

"Oh my God…" whispered Izzy. She picked up the babe and rocked it in her arms. "There there…" The little boy looked at her and went quiet. "Shit… he likes me."

"From this moment on," smiled Rachel Storm, "you're his Mummy."

"What about me?" asked Duffy.

Izzy handed him over. "Here you are Daddy… say 'hi' to Byron."

Duffy took the baby awkwardly and blew gently in his face.

The baby started crying again.

Rachel Storm sat on the sofa and got down to business.

"Right. You have your baby… Now. About that payment?"

Duffy fumbled in his pocket. "Of course. The watch…" He reluctantly handed her Zandra, his ex-wife's, Hermes watch. "That's twenty grand for you."

"Thank you Mr Baker. Mrs Baker… You've signed our contract so all is in order. I wish you both many many happy years with your lovely little boy."

She stood, bowed slightly, ready to leave.

"Wait," said Duffy. "What if I need to contact you for

anything... even get another baby?"

"That number stays valid for a month. After that, you'll have to keep an eye out for new adverts... But nothing can possibly go wrong."

Izzy, holding the little boy. "He is so sweet."

"We do try," smiled Rachel Storm. "Good luck!", turned and walked out of the lounge.

Duffy leapt to his feet.

"Cold bitch. Right," he said. "This time we follow her."

As they exited the hotel entrance they saw Rachel Storm talking with a tall guy on the far side of the car park. He was leaning against a large white van.

She was obviously in charge as he stood there nodding away, then got into the van and slowly drove off.

"So who do we follow?" asked Izzy. "The bitch or white van man?"

"The van," replied Duffy. "Might give us a clue where the babies come from... or not."

Izzy handed the baby to Duffy.

"OK Daddy. I'll drive, you change nappies."

The singing detective tucked the cot under his arm and hobbled on his crutches to her car.

An hour later they were steaming down the M3 south of London, past Basingstoke and Winchester, taking the M27 and heading for the New Forest.

"I hope he's not going to Bournemouth for a dirty weekend," sighed Izzy.

"Shit knows where he's heading..."

But thirty minutes on they had the answer.

Lymington.

A quick Google search told Duffy this was a harbour town and major sailing centre on the Solent, with cobbled streets, a history of smuggling, and two private yacht marinas with deep water berths for vessels 30 metres long. Plus a frequent ferry service across to Yarmouth on the Isle of Wight.

"Mmm…" murmured Duffy. "This is getting interesting."

"Why so cowboy?"

"We're wondering about the babies. Where they come from."

"She said they helped out young girls who were pregnant."

Just then their newly bought son started howling again.

"Shit. Probably needs feeding," said Izzy.

Duffy had the cot on his lap.

"So what do I do?"

"We'll have to buy food at the nearest shops."

"What about white van man?"

"He'll have to wait."

"No way Izzy. We've driven all this way."

"Correction. I've driven all this way."

The white van was still one hundred yards ahead and driving down Lymington High Street.

"Gimme ten more minutes Izzy. I'm sure we're nearly there," he shouted over the crying baby.

The van turned into the Lymington Yacht Haven and parked.

The large guy they'd seen with Rachel Storm got out and walked along a wooden pontoon between dozens of moored yachts.

He looked around carefully then jumped aboard a 30-metre luxury cruiser – a veritable gin palace – named "Delphi" – and disappeared below.

Duffy handed Izzy their shrieking blue-eyed little boy.

"Wait one minute."

He limped down to the boat and peered more closely.

It was registered to Piraeus, Greece.

Probably a hire job.

There was no sign of life apart from the big guy below deck.

Duffy could hear the baby howling so returned to the car.

"Izzy, I'm going to stick around here for a few days."

"You what!?"

"That guy on the boat – I've seen him before… don't know where."

"You're leaving me with the baby?"

"Just a few days love…"

"Duffy – this is your bloody baby!"

"Ours darling – ours… Just a few days… promise… you'll be fine."

And hobbled off towards the gin palace for a further peek.

If looks could kill, Duffy was a dead man walking.

*

Mungo sat in his car outside The Blind Beggar pub and made three calls.

Burner 3 to California. Breakfast time in La La Land… Janie was in the hot tub sipping carrot juice. She was sorely missing her new husband and couldn't wait to get him home. Mungo explained that he could be getting some co-production cash from a Dutch producer he met in Cannes, so all going well. He'd flown on to London to visit studios there and be back in Bel Air very soon.

Next Burner 4 to Cannes. Margot took ages to answer and told Mungo she was looking at other properties. She thought that after the wedding they should move from their tiny attic flat to something bigger near the sea, Antibes or St Tropez.

Already she'd found several homes that she knew he'd love. One just yards from the beach.

Mungo told her that was amazing though privately knew there was no way he was going to buy a bigger place for him and his bare-footed street urchin. She was one adventure he would make the most of, while it lasted.

And finally, Burner 5 to Amsterdam. He caught Putri at a good moment. Wim was out at a business meeting so she could talk. Mungo told her he'd love to see her again but, as she was married, realised it was not easy. Putri was interested. She would like to see him again. When would he visit Amsterdam? Mungo looked at his diary. He'd try see her in a few weeks, depending on his busy schedule. And hung up.

This girl was a diamond, really special. But with Wim around, it was complicated.

Mungo sighed deeply at being such a lucky guy and entered The Blind Beggar.

That same pretty brunette with too much eye makeup and those swollen lips was at the saloon bar.

He ordered a double scotch and reminded her who he was.

"Came in a few weeks back love. Told you a friend of a friend was looking for a shooter... You said would cost five hundred."

Cheryl the barmaid called behind her. "Dad... that geezer's back!"

A large guy about seven foot tall, just as wide, nose broken a dozen times, came to the bar and looked Mungo up and down.

"Swift?" he growled.

Mungo nodded. "I came in a few weeks ago."

"I know who you are. Checked you out. Just don't look

like a gun for hire."

Mungo shrugged. "Your girl said… a monkey."

"Yeah. I got one for you."

"OK…" said Mungo tentatively, not knowing where this was going.

"Thing is. If I hand over the shooter there's a job I want you to do."

"Job?"

"Let me explain. From time to time some of my contacts get in touch with a little job they want done. Quick and easy. Which is where you come in."

"Why me?" asked Mungo.

"Clean skin. You're new around here. Never get traced."

"You want me to shoot someone?"

"Teach them a lesson. Bullet in the leg. The arm. The knee. Not fatal. Know what I mean? Oh… and there's ten grand cash in it."

"Ten grand cash!?" repeated Mungo. This was not what he wanted to do.

Enough on his plate. But. Ten grand cash… He sighed… "Who is this guy?"

The burly giant turned to his barmaid daughter.

"Cheryl?"

Cheryl bent down and retrieved a brown envelope from under the bar.

Her dad opened it and pulled out a photo taken at The Ambassador Casino in Leicester Square a few weeks earlier.

The target was wearing a wide-brimmed fedora, shades, velvet DJ and a yellow bow-tie.

"This is our man. I know where you can find him. Name's Duffy."

*

107

Noah was still inwardly reeling from the shock of finding out that his stepfather Mungo Swift had been married for years, while at the same time playing husband and wife with his recently deceased darling Mum, Grace.

It seemed only days ago that they had both attended the funeral in Auckland.

He'd been much moved by the service and, especially, by Mungo's charming speech. But that was the problem. That guy had oodles of charm, which was how he'd trapped Grace in the first place, persuading her to marry him. And now he was exposed as a bastard bigamist. Which would put him behind bars for seven years.

Though, knowing this slippery shit, he'd probably get off with a fine.

And then there was the company cash. Grace had expected that million to be transferred across to him on her death, but instead Mungo had creamed off most of it for himself. Noah wondered if this guy had been after the money from the very start. No feelings for his Mum, just her bank balance.

As for his job. Was he really running nuclear subs around the world, which gave the perfect excuse to be away for months at a time so he could see his other wife in London? The woman Monica that he'd met on the doorstep had hinted he was doing something "hush hush", which could have been the same job, or something else.

Whatever, Noah was determined to confront this jackass and get the cash back. Knowing what he now knew, he could even blackmail him for more?

He looked across again at the café waitress.

She looked about twenty, had long gingery hair, and was wearing a baggy All Blacks rugby jersey.

He waved to her and she came over.

"Another bacon sandwich?"

"Why not." He nodded at the jersey. " Don't mind me asking, but you a Kiwi?" asked Noah.

"No no. Local girl… this was a birthday pressie. But you… you got an accent… You from there?"

"Too right. Just over meeting family," smiled Noah.

"I hear it's a beautiful place."

"Godzone, they call it."

"Just so far away."

"What was the birthday – something special?" asked Noah, genuinely interested in this pretty girl.

"Twenty-one. I'm a grown up now," laughed the girl.

"It's my first trip to London… If you ever have some spare time… be great to have a drink perhaps?" asked Noah.

The girl was taken by surprise but looked thoughtfully at this cheeky visitor from Down Under. "Why not? I could show you round town…"

"I'm Noah, by the way."

"Pleased to meet… and I'm Donna."

*

Abigail was sipping yet another gin and tonic in her Thameside penthouse with Hanny when the door buzzer went.

"That'll be them," said Abigail. "I'll let them up."

She pushed a switch on the wall and turned back to Hanny.

"This should be fun my dear."

"I do hope so."

Two minutes later the three "assets" entered.

"Thank you all for coming and I look forward to hearing what you've got." said the retired spy. "Do sit down please."

There were two young men and a girl, all casually dressed,

all looking fit and razor sharp.

"Right. Let's get going."

She turned on her massive wall screen which displayed the frozen picture of Piccadilly Circus which they'd viewed the previous day.

"Yesterday you three were stationed as instructed in Piccadilly Circus. I chose three random strangers from the crowd. Two men and a girl. And asked you to find out all you could about them."

She turned to one of the men.

"Asset 1. You had the man on crutches… broken nose… stubble… leather jacket."

Abigail clicked her screen control which zoomed in on that target.

Asset 1, replied: "Name, Duffy. 35. He's a private detective who works out of Fortnum's wine bar in the basement and sleeps where he can find a bed. No partner.

No home. Also does singing gigs in clubs and bars. Came off his bike, hence the crutches."

"Well well well, interesting bod, eh Hanny?"

"Very," agreed her old friend.

"Asset 2. The girl crossing into Regent Street… pretty brunette in a pink plastic mac… Too much makeup, painted eye brows and those dreadful swollen lips that are all the rage these days."

Abigail clicked her screen control again which zoomed in on the female target.

The young girl, Asset 2, replied: "Cheryl Lloyd. 23. Barmaid. Works at the Kray's favourite pub, The Blind Beggar. Her father Eddie's been in and out of jail for minor offences. Nice East End girl, still single."

"Mmm…" mused Abigail.

"And finally… Asset 3. The young lad, early twenties, very short hair, looking a bit lost, exiting the tube, possibly from Oz."

Abigail clicked her screen control one last time which zoomed in on the third target.

Asset 3 replied: "Noah Barton, 22, a tourist from New Zealand, in London looking up family. Just lost his mother Grace in Auckland. Plans to go into the family kiwi fruit business. Nice lad. No downsides."

Abigail and Hanny both applauded the three assets.

"Job well done, all three of you. Thank you so much." She nodded to Hanny who plied them with gin and tonics.

"So. We've identified the three random strangers. A singing detective. A barmaid from a dodgy pub. And a Kiwi tourist."

"What now Abigail?" asked Hanny.

"Now Hanny? Now we talk about our old friend. Iran…"

*

The sun sparkled like diamonds on the Solent waters as Duffy sipped his beer, not taking his eyes off the big guy in the shadowed corner. He was sitting on the wooden deck of The Haven Bar that overlooked the yachting marina in Lymington.

And white van man from the gin palace was just about to leave. Duffy still could not pin him down. Face hidden under a baseball cap. He knew he'd seen him somewhere before. Just couldn't place him.

But the big guy was on the move.

Out of the bar and across the marina pontoon. At pace. Purpose in his step. A man on a mission.

Duffy, still on crutches, struggled to keep up.

The guy, his back still turned to the singing detective, leapt aboard "Delphi" and went below.

Duffy spotted a young crew member cleaning the anchor chain up at the bow.

No-one else in sight.

He stood a moment, scanning the other boats on the pontoon, then limped quietly across the roped gangway onto the polished cedar deck.

Froze a long moment.

Listened.

No noise, just the distant sound of Sinatra crooning somewhere.

There was a large cabin just feet away.

Duffy crawled in.

A chart table with piles of maps and documents.

Duffy listened again. Still Sinatra. And looked around. Coast still clear.

He sat at the table and found the boat hire agreement.

From Lesbos, Greece.

Then a navigation map showing the route from Lymington across the Mediterranean to the Greek isles.

And a photographic drone's eye view of... the Lesbos refugee camp.

Shit, he thought. This was it. The baby supply. They're taking babies from these homeless refugees. Probably for a few quid, then selling them for twenty grand.

There were pictures of the camp. Syrians, Iraqis, men, women, babies.

Duffy took out his phone and took photos.

He stood quietly and peered down the steps going below.

Crates of canned food lining the corridor.

From the labels, looked like baby food.

Suddenly Duffy's ringtone broke the silence.

He'd changed it to "Mr Blue Sky"…

"Sun is shinin' in the sky

There ain't a cloud in sight…"

He answered quickly.

Izzy.

"I'm covered in poo!" she shouted.

"They're bringing the babies from Greece," whispered Duffy, and killed the call.

He raced towards the gangway, dragging his crutches, but standing blocking his way was white van man.

Black chiselled beard, flinty eyes, flat top haircut, mean lips.

Now Duffy remembered where he'd seen him.

The SAS reunion at The Victory Club.

The big ugly Special Forces crazy who scalped guys.

It was Psycho.

CHAPTER EIGHT

Toto was explaining to the two wide-eyed girls from Milwaukee how to get to see the dinosaurs at the Natural History Museum when he heard the noise.

It sounded like a baby crying.

It was.

A flummoxed Izzy flounced into the bar carrying the cot and wee Byron.

"Have you heard from Duffy?"

"Not a peep…" replied the barman.

"He's not answering my calls."

"Probably singing on stage."

"No – I left him on the south coast… Lymington… stooging round a yacht marina."

"Sure he's found a pub by now."

"He left me with this…" Izzy nodded at the cot.

"That is so cute," counted one of the American girls.

"Such beautiful eyes," added the other.

"Boy or girl?" asked Toto.

"Boy…"

"You must be very proud," said the first girl.

"Is he your first?" added the other.

Izzy sighed. "He's not mine. Well, he is. Mine and Duffy's."

"Shit, man, he never said. Never told me he was going to be a Daddy!" chirped Toto.

"No – it's not really his, or mine… We're… He's on a job!" snapped Izzy.

"Look - can I have a double gin and tonic!"

As Toto went to pour the drink, Mungo entered the bar carrying a briefcase.

He'd never handled a gun in his life. No need to. But for some crazy reason he'd gone and got this bloody pistol from that East End pub. And now he'd agreed to shoot some stranger's leg or arm for ten grand cash. He couldn't believe what he was doing. Enough juggling all those bloody women in his life without getting mixed up in some sodding gangland feud. And what if he missed? What if there was a punch-up and this Duffy pulled the gun off him? What then? He could die for absolutely nothing! And yet. And yet there was always that walking blindfold into the dark, taking ginormous risks, that fantasy adventure into the unknown, that waited our unflinching hero Mungo Swift around every corner of his never boring life.

He took a deep breath, knuckles white around the briefcase handle, and headed straight for the barman.

"I'm looking for a Mister Duffy," he said with a nervous smile.

"Aren't we all love," smiled Izzy.

"Oh?" said Mungo. "I was told he used your place as his office?" he asked Toto.

The barman nodded.

"Right now he's down in the deep south, so it seems," he answered, looking at Izzy. "And this little beauty is his baby." He rocked the baby cot that sat on the bar.

Mungo turned to Izzy.

"Then you must be Mrs Duffy?"

"Just good friends." Izzy gulped down her gin. "Does he know you?"

Mungo shook his head.

"I've been put in touch. Like to meet him."

Izzy drained her glass and grabbed the baby cot.

"If it's urgent, you can come with me. But it's a two hour drive."

Mungo thought it over. "OK. If I'm not getting in the way."

"Warn you, I don't know what's going on…" said Izzy. "He may be in a wee spot of trouble."

Mungo patted his briefcase knowingly.

"No problem. I can look after myself."

Izzy just hoped he didn't mean what she was thinking, as she yanked Byron from the bar and exited, with the chubby stranger hot on her heels.

*

Kate sat with her brother Max in her local health club cafe, sipping carrot juice.

"You've lost the beard…" said Kate.

"Knew you hated it."

"I did… How'd the interview go?"

Max shook his head. "Think I was too young or too old. Usual shit."

"I can fund you another month or two but you really must start earning, Max."

He shook her head. "No need sis, got plenty of dosh thanks."

"You're not still gambling?" she asked with concern.

He shook his head again, more slowly.

"Then what's the matter. What's going on? I can't help you if I don't know."

"You and that Duffy… really getting on my tits."

"What?"

"You bring him back to your flat that night."

"Eh? I was pissed Max – so was he!" said Kate, puzzled at his venom.

"And you're still seeing him."

"We meet sometimes… I feel sorry for him… He was scammed over a bloody gift voucher he thought came from me… then he lost his wallet and now someone's running around pretending they're him… ID theft!"

"Serves him right, bloke like that," whispered Max.

"Like what?"

"That guy is prize one bullshit. Wouldn't spend a minute of my time with him… and you do Kate, you do."

"Hang on here Max. You're beginning to sound a bit obsessive love. You don't own me… I'm your bloody big sister… and a cop. I can look after myself."

"He's gotta be taught a lesson."

"What for?"

"To remind him, to keep his space… out of your life."

Kate stood suddenly. "You Max are getting controlling… I don't like it. This is not my brother talking… You on drugs again?"

Max stared bank blankly.

"Anti-depressants."

"Jeez love. You should have said."

She sat back down again and put her hand on his.

"Sorry if I snapped at you. You're going through a tough time."

Max stared into the bottom of his empty glass.

"Even since Mary walked out, I just feel angry. Doing stupid stuff. Wonder who I am sometimes… I get fixed on things… can't sleep."

"Hey. Come back and stay with me a while if that helps."

"Just you and me?"

His sister nodded.

"No boyfriends?"

"I'm married to the job, silly. You know that," said Kate.

Max leant over. Gave his sister a long kiss on her cheek.

"Yeah, I might just do that Kate. Thanks for the invite…
Bye love."

He pulled on his coat, grabbed his wide-brimmed fedora,
flicked on his shades, and headed for the door, leaving Kate
looking somewhat bewildered and just a little anxious.

*

Izzy was halfway down the M23, just passing Winchester
on her way to Lymington and Duffy, when her passenger's
phone rang.

Mungo opened his briefcase and took out burner No.1.

Izzy glanced across and saw the phones in his case.

She also saw the pistol. A Sig Sauer P320.

She swerved and pulled into a layback on the motorway.

Mungo had answered the phone.

"Monica?"

He listened a moment then. "So? Don't worry – Donna's
turned twenty-one – she's a big girl now. Can take care of
herself… Who's the date – let's hope he's rich?" He listened
again. "So, sounds like he's a nice young holidaymaker…
let her have fun love… Yeah, back in a few hours… ciao
bambino." And killed the call.

The car engine was turned off and Izzy was glaring at
Mungo.

"What the fuck!?"

"Eh?"

"You got a gun in that case!"

Mungo was placing the burner back with the other three.

The pistol was lying there, gleaming, happy as Larry.

"Don't worry love. My job. I do undercover. This and that. Hush hush. Know what I mean?"

Izzy breathed a sigh of relief.

"You should have said earlier... You might come in handy with Duffy."

"How so?"

Izzy sighed. "He's looking into something. Buying babies. Already cost us twenty grand."

"Shit. Double shit," swore Mungo.

"And... it might get a bit rough, when we get there... But. If you're a man of action... no problem."

Mungo gulped inwardly, and was closing his briefcase when he remembered.

Took out the brown envelope with Duffy's photo.

"Got this snap of your lovely hubbie."

The guy in the wide-brimmed fedora and shades.

"That's not Duffy."

"Eh?"

"That's not my singing detective."

"He's a detective!?" asked a surprised Mungo.

"Course he is. And that guy is not him. Look... look... in the background.

Croupiers, punters. This was taken in a casino. Duffy drinks, but doesn't smoke and doesn't gamble."

"Then, then who the hell is this wanker?" spluttered Mungo.

*

119

Donna was shown to a candlelit table for two in The Golden Dragon eaterie in London's Chinatown.

It was her first date outside the Harrow area and her heart was thumping.

First, because she didn't know what to expect. This guy had been a customer in the café where she waitressed. He could be a scary weirdo or a dream catch.

Second, her Mum had really moaned about her going out with someone she and Dad had never met. So she just hoped that her fears would not come true.

And thirdly, her heart was thumping because it was so bloody hot in the place!

Noah sat there quietly waiting for her in a pink hoodie and a wide smile.

As a well brought up boy from Down Under he stood on her appearance and timidly shook her hand.

Donna's confidence surged. Seems her date was as shy as she was.

"Gidday Donna – glad you made it. Thought you might've brought your Mum along as a chaperone!" he laughed.

"Don't joke – that nearly happened!"

Noah pushed the chair in under Donna then sat back down himself.

"Like some wine or a beer?"

Donna nodded. She hardly ever drank, though sipped beer sometimes in the summer with the barbecue.

"Beer would be great."

Noah ordered drinks and an assortment of Dim Sums.

"So Donna. Tell me your life story."

"You got all night? Or… really, just a few minutes – I've not done much really… still deciding what I want to do… perhaps be a nurse or join a charity."

"Ah… a do-gooder. Very admirable."

"You… Noah. It is 'Noah'..?"

He nodded. "Sure. Like you, early days. Done a bit of studying… probably waste of time, and might end up working in the family firm."

"What's that?" asked Donna.

"Food export. Bloody boring, but good salary."

"Mum and Dad still around ?"

"Na. Sadly both gone. Just me and a dodgy step-father."

"Why dodgy?"

"Think he lives in a dream world. Never sure what's true or not. Claims he's commander on a nuclear sub, away underwater for months at a time."

"Perhaps he is?"

"I've tried to check him out – no luck so far."

"But isn't that job classified – official secrets I think they say?" said Donna sweetly.

"Yeah sure. Anyway, enough about me. What about your family?"

"Got two little brothers. Lovely Mum and Dad. Though, like your step-father, he works around the world and can't say too much. We think it's MI6… always undercover… always in danger, but he can't tell us… bless him."

"So very hush hush," joked Noah, tapping his nose.

Donna put her hands to her mouth and laughed.

"That's exactly what Dad says… 'hush hush'!"

"Perhaps they're the same person!?" said Noah with a wry grin.

"I reckon they could be," giggled Donna.

"When we met, you said you were twenty-one."

"Just twenty-one," answered Donna. "This month."

"And I'm twenty-two. Not far apart… Another beer?"

She nodded. Both smiled silently at each other. When you're 11,000 miles from home on your own, this lovely girl with the deep brown eyes could just be the comfort that Noah was looking for.

*

Abigail and Hanny sat on two wobbly plastic chairs at the London Aquarium watching the sharks being fed, as they jostled and bared their vicious white choppers.

"Reminds me of GCHQ, only tamer…" mused Hanny. "I do miss those wonderful days… never knew what was round the next corner."

"Which is why I contacted you my dear," smiled Abigail. "We've work to do."

"But we're retired old fogies," laughed Hanny. "Put out to grass."

"Not any more." She paused. "I received a call from Sir Geoffrey."

"He's still alive?"

"Still working my dear," said Abigail.

"Oh my God."

"Wait for it," teased Abi.

"Go on."

"He's resurrecting Shadow Unit. Wants you and I aboard."

"Shadow ? I don't believe it… Is this why we used those three assets… found your random strangers?"

Abigail nodded.

"And you said something about Iran?"

"Precisely. Sir Geoffrey wants us to clean up some of their agents, right here on British soil."

Hanny sat to attention. "All ears Abi."

"Well… Since that Hamas attack on Israel, our friends in Tehran – who probably masterminded the whole ruddy thing – have inspired at least seventeen plots against UK targets."

"Seventeen! Right here? Dear God."

"Intel says they plan to use proxies to do their dirty work."

"Proxies?"

Abigail nodded firmly.

"According to the CIA, the more space you create between yourself and pulling the trigger, the more comfortable it is… provides them with 'reasonable deniability'."

Hanny nodded thoughtfully. "So how exactly are they using these proxies?"

"Well… U.S. agents recently uncovered a spy network who'd used detectives and gangsters to unwittingly carry out reconnaissance for Tehran."

"Useful idiots?"

"Absolutely. So now you see my fishing experiment at Piccadilly Circus has hooked us in our very own… proxies."

"How so?" asked Hanny.

Abi sighed. "Quite by chance, two of the three random strangers I chose have turned up trumps… We have this Duffy, a private detective… and the girl Cheryl, barmaid at The Blind Beggar, whose family are probably linked to organised crime."

"Detectives and gangsters. I'm impressed," said Hanny. "But how do we use them?"

"Entrapment. Sir Geoffrey wants us to catch a particularly nasty pair of spies."

"Go on."

"Soraya and Darius Akhtar. They pose as a married couple but are both deadly assassins."

"Soraya and Darius," repeated Hanny. "Delightful. And?"

"And, like that poor bleating tethered goat in 'Jurassic Park' that lured in the monster flesh-eating dinosaur…"

"Oh don't…. I nearly cried."

"… we'll use Duffy and Cheryl as bait… to catch these two very bad actors!"

*

Izzy and Mungo drove into the Lymington yacht marina and quietly parked. Byron the blue-eyed blonde woke immediately and started crying.

"Shit shit shit!" seethed Izzy.

"Want me to sing to him – usually does the trick?" suggested Mungo.

"What? My covert action man kills babies too?" snapped Izzy impatiently.

Mungo turned in his seat, picked up the baby and quietly sang :

> "Ol' man river
> That ol' man river
> He must know something
> But he don't say nothing…"

At which Byron suddenly went quiet. Either because the singing was shit or he was dead tired.

Mungo shrugged and looked at Izzy.

"OK smart arse, let's go find the real Duffy!" she spat.

They locked the car, leaving Byron fast asleep in his cot, and headed down the pontoon where Izzy had last seen the singing detective.

There it was at the end.

A luxury cruiser called "Delphi".

Izzy remembered Duffy spotting the white van guy boarding this very same vessel.

But for a dim light below, there was no sign of life on board.

"What we looking for?" asked Mungo.

"Shush!" whispered Izzy.

She bent low and crept across the gangplank onto the polished cedar deck.

Mungo followed close behind.

"Got your gun?" hissed Izzy.

Mungo shook his head. "In the car..." Safest place for it, he thought.

Izzy went and sat at the chart table.

Then spotted them in the corner.

Duffy's crutches.

"Looking for something darlin'?" asked a deep voice behind her.

She turned and was confronted by this massive man with a dark beard and mean lips. White van man who they'd followed from London.

"You must be Duffy's girl?" he smirked. "Lucky boy!"

"Where is he?"

"Safe and sound love. Come down and see..."

"No thanks."

Izzy spotted the boat hook in the corner, grabbed it and swung it at the leering giant.

He caught it in one fist, snapped it in two, then grinned again.

"Fancy a Greek cruise love?"

She could feel the boat swaying.

Heard a rumbling engine and the anchor chain.

A sudden jolt nearly knocked her over.

They were moving.

The bloody boat was leaving port.

Turned around to Mungo, but he was nowhere in sight.

Back to the deadly moron who was slowly coming for her.

She realised she had little choice.

The baby was still locked in the car.

So took a deep breath and did a lightning back flip high in the air.

Over the stern and sank deep in the freezing salt water.

She swam to the surface, gulping for air.

"You'll never see Duffy again!" shouted the Special Forces killer.

As "Delphi" quietly pulled away from the pontoon, heading off on its long journey to Lesbos.

Izzy slumped puffing on the quay.

Wondering what this crazy had done with the singing detective.

And where the hell was Mungo?

CHAPTER NINE

There were two things that really upset Mungo and right now he'd managed to combine both at once. Boats and closed spaces.

The moment he stepped aboard a boat he'd feel seasick. Even if it was moored in harbour, he'd get that sicky feeling in his gut and rush to the nearest railing. He remembered that singles' cruise where he'd met his late Kiwi wife Grace.

Despite getting pissed and having an outrageous time on the dance floor and in the bunk, his lingering memory was that never-ending heaving motion as the ship carved its way through the Mediterranean swell. Not even rough, but enough to make him puke.

As for closed spaces, he was seriously claustrophobic. Even getting in a lift meant sometimes having to get out a floor or two early before he collapsed. An experience he was relieved none of his ladies had ever witnessed.

So right now, hiding in the small dark locker along with the life jackets and ropes and boat fenders, our Mungo was a very unhappy boy.

Feeling seasick in a tiny cramped space… both his nightmares at once.

But what was even worse, he now realised they were up and moving and heading for the high seas, with him still on board!

And what on earth was he doing there?

All because some dodgy geezer in an East End pub had offered him ten grand cash to duff up some stranger called… Duffy.

Then he'd met that attractive tall blonde – Izzy – who was the spitting image of that glam Hannah something on the telly. She'd said that the guy in the photo was not Duffy, and that she was going to meet the genuine article. Poor old Mungo had stupidly tagged along, because he'd fancied the blonde, driven all the bloody way down to Lymington, and right now was trapped on some boat with a giant crazy. He'd heard Izzy speaking but now all was quiet. He wondered if both she and this Duffy had been snuffed by the white van man, as she'd called him. In which case his own life was not looking too healthy.

He opened the door a touch.

And heard distant voices.

Opened the locker wider and quietly crawled out.

Two large fenders crashed out onto the polished cedar deck.

Mungo froze and listened.

No response from anywhere.

He crawled on his knees towards the saloon lounge.

Beyond, on the bridge, a young guy was at the wheel, peering ahead, wearing earphones. No wonder he heard nothing.

Mungo heard those voices again. Below deck. Probably some cabin.

He spotted stairs near him and climbed down as quietly as he could.

It was the giant crazy, aka white van man, laughing.

"Your singing mate, it was crap! But must admit, thought I'd never see you again…"

Another voice. More a dry whisper. "Why you doing this – you're SAS… this is a real shit job… selling babies?"

Mungo suspected this must have been the Duffy he wasn't looking for.

The private detective, who sang.

"Money, arsehole. Why you think? Better than the army where they treat you like scum. This is real dosh and very soon I'll be chucking it in and buying my own boat. Then fuck off and sail the world... That will be something."

"Why don't we do this together– tell me how it works and we catch the arseholes running it... you can disappear, not be involved?" croaked Duffy.

"But I am involved man. I want to be. Like I said, this is my lifetime pension.

Dream come true. I play delivery man. Bring home the babies. And make a lot of desperate young couples bloody happy. Almost feel proud. And, just for once I'm not sodding killing anyone!"

Duffy went quiet a moment.

"So you're taking babies from the refugee camp on Lesbos? Paying them a month's food or less, then making a fortune selling them off in the UK?"

Psycho grunted. "So easy mate. We hire this gin palace in Greece for two weeks. Motor from Piraeus across to Lesbos. Our guy there has about thirty little buggers screaming in cots, which we load aboard. Turn round and race back to Lymington. Up the M3 in our van and sell them to rich pricks who know no better!"

"It's a dirty bloody scam!" spat Duffy.

"I don't give a toss what you think, wanker. And you shouldn't worry your pretty little head no more."

"You'll be banged up for years."

Psycho laughed loud.

"Correction. First, I've some very important friends, so that's never gonna happen. Second, this is your last trip at sea."

"What?" asked Duffy.

"You're quite the man about town. I guess you like French seafood?"

"Eh?"

"Well, in a few hours we'll be off the coast of France. Which is when we're going to feed you to the French fishies… dump you overboard my son… and all that stuff I just told you will drown with you!"

Psycho laughed loud once more.

Duffy said nothing.

And Mungo, crouching near the cabin door, felt his whole body shaking.

Now he wished he'd brought along that bloody gun.

*

An exhausted Izzy flounced into the Fortnum's bar and plonked the baby cot on the counter. Again.

"Selling him already?" joked Toto.

"Don't go there…" she sighed. "I've been up all night feeding this little brat!"

"Where's his Daddy?" smiled the barman.

"If you mean Duffy, he's in deep doo-doo."

"What?"

"Remember I went back to Lymington looking for him with that guy Mungo?"

"Yer … the yacht marina…" replied Toto. "Chasing the gang selling babies."

"We got there. And went straight to this gin palace, 'Delphi,' where I'd left him."

"And?"

"I found the guy – white van man – on the boat but no Duffy. There was a little difference of opinions… he said I'd

never see Duffy again – and I left... Something like that."
She bit back a tear.

"You say Duffy?" said a female voice from behind.

Izzy stared at her. It was Kate, in civvies.

"Don't tell me, you're after him too?" sighed Izzy.

"Only for a catch-up – he's a mate. I let him down recently..." She saw baby Byron on the bar. "This little boy is just so cute." She played with his fingers. "So... cute."

"On borrowed time," smiled Izzy.

"Oh God." said Kate. "He asked me too... Did you play 'Mummy'?"

Izzy nodded through gritted teeth.

"That's me."

"I let him down at the last moment – brother trouble. Mental health issues, and all that bullshit."

"So I got you to blame."

"Did he get what he wanted – solve the case – catch the woman selling the babies?" asked Kate.

Izzy shook her head.

"Our Duffy's in big trouble – was hoping he might have called here."

"Oh shit," said Kate, sitting in the stool next to Izzy. "What's happened?"

Izzy brought her up to speed. Him going aboard "Delphi" to find white van man. Disappearing. She going after him. The fight. And now the boat was heading for Greece with the singing detective on board.

"Jeez," breathed Kate. "I better try track them down... contact the coastguard... get a copter up."

"Who you kidding love?"

"I'm with the Met."

"A copper?"

"We'll get in touch with the JMSC and they…"

"Who?" chipped in Toto.

"Sorry, Joint Maritime Security Centre – their lads'll track down your boat in no time… When did it leave the marina?"

"Three hours ago."

"Fine. Probably piddling down the French coast by now."

Kate held out her hand to Izzy.

"Kate. Kate Sanders."

"Izzy Green. How you know our fella?"

"We met on a plane from Paris…"

"And he sang at our family wedding bash."

"Anyone ever say you look like that Hannah thingy off the telly?"

"Yeah yeah."

"If he goes…" mused Kate. "If he goes."

"He'd be sorely missed!" added Izzy. "Come on then. Let's track the bugger down. And hope we're not too late!"

"What about the other guy?" asked Toto.

"What other guy?" asked Kate.

"Oh. Mungo. We met in here, this bar. He was looking for Duffy too. Some case, I think. Anyway, he tagged along with me to Lymington. Got to the boat and he bloody disappeared!"

"He could be in trouble too then?"

Izzy shrugged.

"Hope there's room for two on that copter!"

Kate pulled a face, took out her phone, and quickly called a number.

"'Delphi' you said, Izzy?"

"Yeah – 30-metre gin palace… they can't miss it!"

*

132

Abigail and Hanny sat in the saloon bar of The Blind Beggar sipping stout and nibbling crisps.

"These are probably the most foul chips I have ever devoured," wheezed Abi.

"What flavour dear?"

"Cajun Squirrel. Though I don't believe any were killed in the making."

"I've got Builders' Breakfast. Faint taste of smelly socks. And the little black bits between your toes," sighed Hanny.

"Oh don't! Otherwise we'll need a bucket!"

"Haven't done this for a while. Quite exciting."

"The crisps?"

"The job," whispered Hanny.

Abigail cleared her throat and carefully looked around at the other drinkers.

"Reconnaissance. An exploratory military survey of enemy territory."

"I feel shivers going down my spine, dear."

"Good. Means you're paying attention."

"And I can see the target."

"She's the ruddy barmaid."

"Cheryl. The girl you chose from Piccadilly Circus."

"Exactly. Way too much makeup. Silly painted eyebrows and those ghastly trout lips. But underneath, I suspect she's a very sweet girl, just needing a bit of tender loving care."

"And you think there might be criminal activity going on here Abigail?"

The old spy sighed. "Well... bit unlikely. Here we are in the Kray's old boozer in Whitechapel. Busloads of tourists piling in to take photos."

"But. That's it Abigail," said Hanny. "It is so obvious that... something could be going on here... 'in plain sight.'"

Abi shrugged and picked up a potted history of the pub, lying on their table.

She read aloud : "In 1904, 'Bulldog' Wallace, a member of The Blind Beggar Gang of pickpockets who frequented the pub, stabbed another man in the eye with an umbrella."

"A brolly? Bet that hurt."

Abi continued : "It gets worse : On 9 March 1966, Georgie Cornell and his friend Albie Woods entered the pub, ordered some light ales and then sat upon stools next to the bar. At around 8:30pm, both men were approached by Ronnie Kray and a Kray associate, Ian Barrie; upon seeing him, Cornell smiled and said sardonically, 'Well, just look who's here'. As a warning to the barmaid and the few others in the pub, Barrie fired two shots into the ceiling, while Kray walked towards Cornell, took out a 9 mm Luger, and calmly shot him once in the forehead, just above his right eye.

The men turned and departed to a waiting car on the street. Kray was sentenced to life imprisonment for the murder three years later and remained in Broadmoor Hospital until his death in 1995."

Hanny sighed deeply. "Talk about living history. We're in the very same room that the murder happened all those years ago."

"And look around you now Hanny. Couple of odd blokes over by the fireplace. Probably planning a local bank robbery, perhaps a mugging."

"Or simply moaning about their wives or their prostate."

"And that group of girls in the corner… could be a gang of shoplifters dividing their spoils."

"Or simply a hen party celebrating a last night of freedom before the wedding."

"You're not helping me breathe in the dodgy atmosphere

dear. I want to imagine this place could be a den of thieves and our Cheryl part of it."

Just then a voice interrupted them from behind.

"Another drink ladies?" asked Cheryl the barmaid.

"Why not? smiled Abigail. "We're loving this place, so much colourful history."

"This is where it happens love, mark my words."

"Oh… we're writing a book on the London underworld and thought we should visit here," said Abi.

"Must meet my Dad sometime – he could tell you a tale or two."

"Is he here tonight?"

"Na – off with the lads, if you know what I mean ladies," she twinkled.

"Is he the owner?" asked Hanny.

Cheryl nodded.

"Yeah, there's a sort of consortium…"

"How fascinating," said Abi. "We'd love to have a chat with him about the pub, and the underworld, and gangs… if you know what I mean."

"Next time, next time I'm sure I can put you together…" nodded Cheryl, who walked off to get more drinks.

"Methinks we might have come up trumps old dear," mused Abi.

"Methinks you might be ruddy right!"

And clicked their empty glasses together.

*

Noah had returned to the café where he'd first met Donna and was eating a bacon sandwich. Seems her shift hadn't started yet.

He was still mulling over what to do about Mungo, the shitty step-father who had waltzed off with nearly a million of his inheritance cash.

He could do the obvious physical confrontation. Now he knew where he lived and had met the other wife, Monica. So, nothing to stop him banging on his front door and threatening to hand him over to the cops, now he knew he was a bigamist. That way he might write him a cheque there and then. Or he might not.

Or he could try something more subtle. Like get someone to follow him 24/7. Find out what he was really doing for a living. If he was conning other women around the place, going after their money. This chubby bastard could be making mischief all over the world.

He took another bite of his sarnie, and googled "detectives" on his phone.

One guy stood out from the others.

Duffy. Very cool, sitting on a Harley. Even worked as a singer on the side.

No office, worked out of a wine bar at Fortnum's in Piccadilly. No home either.

Noah liked him instantly and made the call.

Went through to voicemail.

Tried again.

No luck.

This guy must be really busy.

"You're very persistent," she said.

Noah looked up from his phone and saw Donna standing over him.

He sighed deeply. Life was looking up again.

"Hi again," he said simply.

"I just loved that Chinese meal, thanks Noah."

"My pleasure, promise."

Donna was looking depressed.

"Oh shit – your Mum's told you not to see me again?" he asked with a grin.

She shook her head.

"It's Dad. He's gone missing."

"What? That's terrible – what happened?"

"Went out on some job and never came home last night," she said.

"Isn't that what he does – covert stuff... man of mystery?"

"Sure but he'd promised to take us to the movies. And never turned up.

He's not answering his phone. Something's wrong Noah... Something's very wrong."

Noah squeezed her hand.

"We'll find him babe, don't worry. We'll find your Dad."

*

Charlie was sat in his giant leather chair at Solar Global when they arrived by helicopter. Must have cost a bomb.

He'd arranged for Sheila in reception to bring in the best Chinese takeaways in Pinner at precisely one o'clock along with the crate of lagers. Chicken balls and chips was his personal favourite.

It was starting to drizzle as he ran out with two brollies to meet his esteemed guests, just flown in from California. His new business partners, Mr Sun and Mr Yi.

They embraced on the tarmac outside the offices.

Charlie noted they were both shorter than himself, with immense grins that never seemed to go away. And style. White suits and silk kerchiefs.

The trio ran back into the offices and, after much mutual bowing and scraping, sat at the long table in his boardroom.

Sheila served English tea and ginger nuts.

Charlie thought it seemed appropriate to show his visitors maximum respect and introduce them to the local customs. He quietly dipped his biscuits in the tea, savoured the taste, and the two Chinese guests copied his example. They too appeared to savour the taste.

"I am looking forward to doing business with you both, Mr Sun, Mr Yi…and we've put aside a very big hangar here for your products, the wind turbine blades."

"Thank you, thank you," said Mr Sun.

"We can see?" asked Mr Yi.

"Of course. Follow me," replied Charlie.

He grabbed the brollies and led them out through reception and across a yard to the very long hangar that would house the giant blades.

His two guests seemed delighted with the size of the building.

"Very long, very good," said Mr Yi.

"And security…We bring our own security," added Mr Sun.

"Oh no," said Charlie. "If you want that we can get some local lads in to help out, no problem."

Mr Yi's smile vanished and said emphatically. "We will provide the security please Mr Charlie."

As Mr Sun also stepped forward. "There is no argument here Mr Charlie.

We insist. Our security."

Charlie was a little taken back by their tone. Couldn't see him getting pissed with these two.

The Chinese sensed this and patted him on the back.

"We like very much, thank you," grinned Mr Yi.

"And look forward many years doing business," added Mr Sun.

Charlie steered them back to the boardroom where, as ordered, Sheila had delivered the cartons of chicken balls and chips.

"I've ordered Chinese takeaway for you," said Charlie, rather humbly.

The Asians bowed with great politesse.

"Most kind but never eat takeaway," smiled Mr Yi.

"Must go now to more meetings," added Mr Sun.

They bowed farewell to Charlie, turned on their heels and trotted out to the waiting helicopter.

"That went well then," Charlie muttered to himself. "Bloody well."

*

Mungo had spent two hours hiding in the saloon lounge, covered in a tarpaulin. He no longer could hear the big guy shouting at Duffy below and wondered if he'd topped the detective already.

He was just dozing off when something suddenly woke him.

His stomach. The boat was lurching left to right and back again. The sea out there had just got seriously rougher and his tum was not liking it one sodding bit.

From under his sheet he heard footsteps running towards the bridge.

He peered out.

The young guy, carrying a half empty bottle of beer, and totally starkers, had run up from below and was pulling frantically on the wheel. Must have left the boat on autopilot and gone off for a kip, thought Mungo. Silly bugger.

Then he heard a pitter patter.

Mungo took another look.

A girl. Very dark. Wearing a see-through black sarong had joined the lad at the wheel. She put his arm around him.

Now it was making sense.

She must be the cook. Or a nurse to help with the babies.

There were three of them on board.

And he'd been below having nookie when the going got rough.

The lad set the boat on autopilot again and led the girl past Mungo back down the steps.

Mungo thought carefully. Now it was him against the big guy plus these two.

Very soon, as promised, big guy was going to dump Duffy overboard.

Our chubby fantasist made a decision.

He'd try isolate the opposition.

He crawled out from under the tarpaulin and looked around the deck.

There were two boathooks in a corner.

And a large fire extinguisher on the wall.

Thought a long moment.

Then grabbed the boathooks and quietly crept down the steps to the lower deck.

Listened.

Sinatra was still gently singing from a cabin. Mungo suspected this was where the big guy was sleeping.

Further along, from a smaller cabin, he could hear groaning, louder and louder.

The young couple enjoying themselves.

Mungo went to their door and carefully wedged the boathooks across the handle. Rock tight. There was no way the two lovers were getting out of there.

He then retraced his steps and went back up to the saloon lounge.

Took the fire extinguisher off the wall and read the instructions.

Point at the fire and foam would extinguish the flames.

Then he heard voices coming his way.

Coming up the steps.

Duffy was shouting: "I got mates who know where I am – you know that – you'll get caught man!"

From his tarpaulin Mungo observed the big guy dragging Duffy up the stairway into the saloon lounge.

"Don't give a damn – I'll say you swam ashore… must've drowned along the way… I'll even cry a tear for you…" laughed Psycho. "Now. Stand up, you little prick!"

Mungo saw Duffy had his hands tied behind his back, and had difficulty getting to his feet.

The big guy pulled open the door to the stern deck and the cold night air stormed in, reminding the chubby fantasist that the moment of truth was nigh.

Within a minute or two the singing detective would indeed be feeding the French fishes, as promised, and he himself would be a very unwilling stowaway.

The big guy had now pushed Duffy out the door onto the stern deck.

No railings, just the open ocean beyond.

It was now or never.

Mungo leapt into life.

Aimed the fire extinguisher at the big guy's head and shouted : "Hey!"

Psycho turned quickly, surprised there was anyone there.

Mungo spirted the foam into his eyes, covering him in white snow.

Blinded but not out, the big guy lunged at Mungo.

Who, with all his chubby strength, threw the heavy extinguisher at his head.

Pyscho rocked back and forth, slowly swayed, then fell off the stern deck into the dark murky sea.

Mungo searched the waves.

The big guy had vanished.

Nothing.

"Shit shit shit – didn't mean to kill him…"

He turned back to Duffy and ripped the ropes off his wrists.

The singing detective hugged the stranger tight.

"Jeez – that was close man – you saved my life!"

Above in the sky a sudden searchlight beamed down on them.

They heard the thrumming engine.

A copter was circling the boat.

"Seems like the cavalry's arrived… a bit late," sighed Duffy.

He and Mungo slumped panting on the deck.

"I didn't mean to kill the big guy," repeated Mungo.

"Not your fault mate… accident. He was one tough nut." A thought. "But listen…" Duffy looked him in the eye. "Are you Special Forces too?"

Mungo quietly shrugged his shoulders and smiled back.

CHAPTER TEN

"My heroes!" shouted Izzy as a disheveled Duffy and a weary Mungo entered the Fortnum's bar. Kate the cop was also sitting there, alongside Byron the sleeping babe.

Duffy sighed deeply. "What I would give for a large chardonnay!"

"Me too," gulped Mungo.

"Coming up gents!" smiled Toto the barman.

The two guys pulled up stools and joined the girls.

"So what happened – the rescue copter get there in time?" asked Kate.

"Almost, thanks…" smiled Duffy. "I was about to meet a watery death, when Mungo here came from nowhere and dumped the big guy in the sea… saved my life."

"Him or me mate," added Mungo diffidently.

Duffy shrugged with admiration. "I owe you man."

"I hear there were two youngsters on board… but they're not talking," said Kate.

"Yeah," nodded Mungo. "The lad was steering… and the girl, who knows."

"What were you doing there?" asked Kate.

"Looking for Duffy, but seems I got the wrong bloke."

"Oh?"

Mungo took out the photo with the guy in the fedora.

"Someone asked me to find this guy… who gave his name as Duffy."

Duffy peered. "Nothing like me, though does seem rather familiar."

Kate took one look then winced. She recognized her

brother Max, but said nothing.

"Find him why?" she asked carefully.

"Think he's rubbing up some people the wrong way… at a casino," replied Mungo.

"Ah," replied Kate. This meant that Max was back gambling again. And getting into trouble.

Then Duffy twigged. "Hang on – I got grabbed by two thugs saying I owed their boss a hundred grand – the Ambassador Casino… which I didn't."

"They came in here after you man," added Toto. "I remember."

"This fedora guy must have my credit card… remember I lost my wallet Kate… this is the bugger pretending to be me!" He stabbed his finger at the photo.

"ID theft," nodded Mungo. "Now it makes sense."

"Find him, get your life back," added Izzy.

"Let me deal with this Duffy," said Kate crisply. "This is ID fraud… stealing your personality. Give me a day or two!"

"I wouldn't mind saying hello… if you ever catch him love," smiled Mungo.

A muffled phone started ringing.

Mungo opened his briefcase, and took out burner No.3 : "Hi babe! Still in London… all looking good… see you in a few days… ciao ciao!"

He explained to the others : "My new wife… California…" He shrugged with a smile.

"Lucky old you…" laughed Izzy. "Quite the beach boy, huh!"

The baby started crying.

"Oh shit – he's missing you already…" said Izzy. She picked up Byron and put him in the detective's arms. "Go to Daddy."

"So. Back to the baby scam," said Kate. "You got rid of the guy running the boat to Greece to pick up the kiddies. Now we need to get this woman who's doing the selling... and find out where they're keeping the babies... who's running the show."

"Yeah," nodded Duffy. "There's got to be a home, a cosy building somewhere that's housing them all."

"There's got to be nurses or carers looking after them – you can't just dump a load of them in a basement like putting them in the freezer – they've got to be fed, watered, looked after, have their nappies changed," added Kate.

"I'll go back to meet the woman at the hotel... say little Byron's sick or something."

"Or we could buy another little one, dearest?" teased Izzy.

"Oh shit..." said Duffy softly. "He's been sick down my trousers."

"That's my cue!" piped Mungo... "See you round Duffy – hope you catch the fake guy." He made for the door.

"You know where to find me matey," cried Duffy.

And Mungo left.

"Dunno what makes him tick..." said Izzy softly. "He's got a load of burner phones and a bloody gun!"

"Wish you'd told me minutes ago – I'd have nicked him!"

"Bollocks Kate – whoever he is, that man saved my life..." mused the singing detective. "My hero."

*

Abigail and Hanny sat primly sipping afternoon tea at The Ritz, looking like a couple of eccentric country dowagers in their tweeds and brogues, rather than the razor-sharp undercover agents they really were.

"Sources tell me that Soraya and Darius – Mr and Mrs Akhtar – have just landed in Manchester, having flown across from Dublin," said Abi. "Probably gone from Tehran to Istanbul to Rome... the usual route. Then pop up here posing as tourists."

She placed a photo of an attractive couple in their late thirties, both dark- haired, sallow features, sophisticated, standing in front of the Colisseum, on the table.

Hanny sniffed and took a closer look.

"Mmm. Rather snazzy. Both of them. Wouldn't look out of place at a royal garden party."

"That's their USP. They can be special or ordinary. Blend into the background or foreground. Be visible or invisible. These are possibly the best two spies coming out of Iran. They're aristocracy. They've had years of training. Spent time in Washington, Paris, Moscow... even Canberra. They know how to dress, how to talk, how to walk. And most of all, when it comes to realms of the imagination, they know how to kill. Simply and cleanly. Using methods never seen before. Always very hard to pin it down as murder, least of all find any evidence. Always emphatically deadly."

"Sounds like a challenge."

"Oh, they will be Hanny. And they'll also be chasing the very top targets in the country."

"Not the P.M.?"

"Not far off."

"Oh dear."

"They'll arrive here with a list of names. Around ten, I'd guess. There'll be journalists from television and newspapers who've been rubbishing the Tehran regime; there'll be young female students and models who refuse to wear the compulsory hijab headscarves as in Iran; there'll be male students urging the overthrow of the autocratic ayatollahs; and of course activists in the gay community… so no shortage of targets."

"You said you'd use Duffy the detective and Cheryl the barmaid to trap them?" asked Hanny. "How so?" Abi nodded.

"They very cleverly – Soraya and Darius – try and keep at a distance from the people they kill. So if they can get others unwittingly to track down these people, on their behalf…. then it's an additional protective layer of cover, smoke and mirrors, they can hide behind, if you get my meaning Hanny."

"He who sups with the devil should have a long spoon."

"Exactly. It means the useful idiots do all the dirty work, leading the killers right to their target's door, for them to give the coup de grace and disappear into the ether!"

"Do I detect the Islamic Revolutionary Guards Corps pulling their strings?" Asked Hanny.

"I.R.G.C.? Bloody right girl… their ghastly little Unit 840 tasked with eliminating dissidents on British soil."

"It sounds like you know these two intimately Abigail?"

The older agent looked long at Hanny with a wry smile.

"We have met. Once. In an Istanbul nightclub. Standing in a terrace bar, sipping vodka martinis, overlooking the Bosphorus. I was very taken by Darius.

Young enough to be my son. He had no idea who I was or what I did. But I knew exactly what he was up to. Why he was in Turkey. But I got the timing wrong. I thought I had 48 hours. He took my number and promised to call the next day for a drink."

"And did he?"

"No. Instead I read that very morning an American diplomat was shot in a back alley near his embassy. That man had been attacking the Iran regime for months.

Darius did the job a day early then vanished. I think he knew who I was after all. I think he knew we were onto them. I never saw him again."

"My God."

"But… he was very dishy," whispered Abi.

"So… you might meet again."

"We might. And then there was her…"

"Soraya?"

Abi nodded, poured more tea, took a scone and carefully buttered it, before spreading on the apricot jam very thickly.

"She's the most evil of the two."

"Have you met her?" asked Hanny, her mouth agog.

"Tel Aviv."

"My God, Israel?"

"Yup. A females only sauna. We all sat there in the nuddy, sweating like pigs to the slaughter."

"Abigail – what on earth were you doing in a place like that… were you having a 'Sappho' moment!?"

"Our hands did brush in the steamy gloom Hanny, but no… I was simply tailing her and getting a bit too close for my own good!"

"What happened?"

"We both sat there for half an hour… no eye contact… nearly fainting with the heat… then she suddenly got up, kissed me on the cheek and vanished."

"Gosh."

"I waited a few minutes and followed, but she'd gone."

"Then what?"

"Well… as an Iranian assassin in Israel you knew there'd be trouble.

And there was. The next morn. The whole breakfast floor of the Paradise Hotel was bombed, killing five Israeli generals. But not before Soraya was seen eating scrambled eggs there… fifteen minutes earlier."

"She had cheek."

"She had something," added Abi.

"And why did she kiss you my dear?"

"To this day I'll never know. Did she fancy me? Or was she saying, I know who you are?"

"Well, very soon you may find out," smiled Hanny.

Abigail sat up straight and breathed deep.

"Now Hanny. Twenty minutes ago I told you that Soraya and Darius had just landed at Manchester airport from Dublin."

"Yes."

She placed her phone on the table.

"Any minute now this little phone will ring."

"And?" asked Hanny.

"My man on the ground will tell me he's lost them."

"How do you know?"

"Because they're good. And they know their tradecraft. I suspect."

Her phone interrupted her.

She answered.

"OK Brutus. Thank you."

She put down the phone, slowly shaking her head.

"He's lost them."

"Oh dear."

"Which means, without our eyes on them, they could split and turn up in different locations… instead of a couple, we could be chasing two lone assassins!"

*

Duffy had a load on his mind. He'd had a narrow miss with

Psycho on the boat, in fact if the mysterious Mungo had not leapt from nowhere when he did, there was no doubt the singing detective would be swimming with the fishes. The whole baby smuggling racket was still needling him... least now he knew where the kiddies were coming from, but had yet to track down this posh saleswoman, where the babies were kept, and who was backing them. This was his first day without crutches, so that was something positive, then he remembered the twenty grand he owed his ex-wife. Getting that watch back to her was a no-brainer or his head would be on the block. And what about cute little Byron... giggling and gurgling away in that carrycot without a care in the world. Guess some couple would end up adopting him.

But his most immediate irritation was the guy in the fedora who'd been impersonating him and using his credit card. Was it just luck that he'd found Duffy's wallet or had he been deliberately targeted by this weirdo... was it him who ran him off the road on his bike... was there some more personal reason... had he screwed this guy's wife in the dim and distant..? And what was the Mungo connection? His gut instinct was not good when he heard his hero was carrying a gun, and wanted to meet the fedora guy. What in hell was that about? Lots of questions.

Right now, he aimed to find out some of the answers.

As he walked into the Ambassador Casino and looked around.

It was packed with the usual crowd of gamblers. Earnest, seedy, sad. Old, overweight, rich guys, there to pick up the crumpet and make or lose a few bob.

Anything to get away from the wife. Then there were the younger players, taking the tables very seriously, watching the others' moves, planning their strategy, not giving an inch.

They all had poker faces but you knew they really hurt inside every time they lost. And the girls. Always there like pop band groupies in the old days.

Sniffing around the men and their money. Didn't matter how old, just how much they might make.

The croupiers all had that pained veneer of perpetual boredom. Thinking about what they'd be eating that night, where they'd be drinking, who they'd be sleeping with. And how in the hell they could get a job somewhere else… doing anything but this ghastly robotic mindless tedium.

Duffy spotted a six-foot something pock-marked thug wearing a tux and a wire, moving quietly around the tables. Realised he must be the main man, talking directly to the bosses upstairs behind the smoked glass offices.

He went over and introduced himself.

"Hi there… my name's Duffy – I'd like to speak to the management."

Jerry did a double take. "You say 'Duffy'?"

The singing detective nodded. "At your service."

Jerry grabbed Duffy firmly by the elbow and ushered him to a nearby lift.

Moments later they were in Olaf's office that overlooked the casino floor.

"Got something special for you boss."

Jerry pushed Duffy towards the Romanian.

"A mister Duffy… the guy who walked with a hundred grand."

"That was not me," said the detective firmly.

Olaf pointed at a chair where Duffy sat.

"You owe me," whispered the casino boss, cracking his fingers.

Duffy whipped out the photo of the guy in the fedora.

"Take a look. That is not me. He stole my credit card. Took my name.

I'm a private detective. I don't gamble."

Olaf looked carefully at the picture then back at Duffy.

"Detective?"

He waved it at Jerry.

Jerry peered at Duffy and the fedora guy.

Shook his head.

"Not him boss."

"You sent two guys after me… handcuffed me… made threats."

Olaf poured a scotch and offered the glass to Duffy.

"Mistake. It happens. He took a lot of money that I want back. He was a cheat."

"Glad you admit it mate." Duffy sipped the scotch. "Clears the air."

"Mister Duffy… if you are a detective… perhaps you can find this little shit?" smiled Olaf with a toothy grin that showed off his gold fillings.

Duffy shrugged.

"Tell you one thing. I'm wanting to find this cretin as much as you!"

*

Mungo had spent lunchtime with Charlie at their Pinner office and heard all about the arrival on their premises of Messrs Yi and Sun. They seemed to live in a parallel universe with their fancy helicopter and insistence on providing their own security for the wind turbine blades. No matter, the contract was all signed and the first payments were incoming. That meeting with them had been both a surprise and a bonus.

Thinking of California, he'd made a second call to Janie saying he'd be back home with her in L.A. the next day and just couldn't wait to hold his new bride once more.

He'd also got a message from Margot in Cannes who'd found a diaphanous silk wedding dress for five grand which he agreed to buy for her. It was the twenty grand expenses for the wedding party that worried him.

And that very brief chat with Putri in Amsterdam, who was now well and truly hooked. Wanted to see him as soon as he could get back in town. Trouble was, the husband. For once Mungo was not sure how he'd react if or when he found out he was carrying on with the lovely wife. There was something in Wim that Mungo recognised in himself, something wild, something dangerous.

Finally he dropped by The Blind Beggar to give the guy a heads-up on tracking down the fake Duffy. Told him all, and promised he was still on the case, that there were others also after this tosser, and very soon, very soon he hoped to fulfil that ten grand cash deal and put a bullet in the guy's knees, or worse.

Monica leant across the dinner table, asking if he wanted more potatoes, smashing Mungo's train of thought. She'd been desperate with him away all night but relieved he'd been trouncing some villain in a gin palace on the high seas… always a hero.

"No more thanks love," he said. "Trouble getting into my trousers as it is."

"So off again tomorrow then?" she asked. "My action man."

He nodded. "Los Angeles. Signing off on that bounty hunter case… then back home darling." He squeezed her hand. Monica was the one trusting constant in his whole life.

153

Her and the three kids.

"You got that gun yet Dad?" squeaked little Sam. He'd not forgotten.

"Working on it son, promise."

"Oh yeah," the boy scoffed.

"So Donna... I hear you've a boyfriend," said Mungo with a twinkle.

"Sort of Dad... Just a guy for a date. Nothing special," said Donna.

"What's he do? Doctor, lawyer, or something hush hush like me?"

Donna sighed. "All these questions... I think there's a family business.

He's been studying and soon joining the firm."

"Ha," said Mungo. "Methinks I smell money?"

"No Dad, nothing like that. He's... he's just a nice guy."

"We should meet him love," suggested Monica.

"P'raps," sighed Donna.

"That'd be nice," said Mungo. "I'll treat him to a nice meal in town."

Donna shrugged, wishing her parents would get off her back.

"P'raps."

"That's a date then... in the diary when I get back home!"

Donna left the table without saying a word.

Monica and Mungo looked at each other and shrugged.

"Kids..." whispered Mungo.

*

"What the fuck is going on Max?" spat Kate at her brother.

They were sitting in a cosy snug at their local pub.

"What you mean Sis?"

"You pretending to be Duffy."

"Don't be stupid! I'm nothing like that prat, who'd want to be."

"He lost his wallet... probably left behind at my place that day when we were all pissed... You found it. Next thing you're in a casino using his credit card and saying you're him. You are in deep doo doo... Duffy's after you and sounds like the casino mafia got you in their sights too! They have your photo in that same bloody fedora!"

She nodded to the fedora on the hat-stand beside Max.

"No way."

Kate simply glared at him in silence.

"OK. OK. I... I found his wallet. And I hated him on sight. That morning, us three in bed together. Total prick. And... and I hated you Kate for liking him.

For going out with him. Hated you for fucking screwing him. You're my sister.

You're... special." His voice trailed away and he began to look pathetic.

"What are you saying Max? You jealous of me? That is so weird."

"I just don't want anyone coming between us."

"You are jealous. Jeez Max... are you on medication still?"

Her brother sighed.

"Just for depression."

"And still gambling when you know you get addicted, get into debt... like before."

"Only that once."

"Did you cheat at that casino... they want their money back."

"I'll mail it back... today, promise." He took her hand. " Kate, I am so sorry...

I just have these funny days and do stuff I regret later."

"Was it you who ran Duffy off the road, put him in crutches?"

Max said nothing.

"Shit!"

Kate could not believe it.

"OK. You seem to forget I'm a cop. I could turn you in now and you'd get a sentence, no problem. But... just this once... you're family... understand?"

Max meekly nodded.

"Give me Duffy's wallet and his cards."

Her brother stood and took a wallet from his overcoat. Handed it to Kate.

"We will never speak of this again."

She stood.

Stared long at her brother.

And walked briskly from the pub.

*

Duffy sat on a small stage in a drinking club off Notting Hill High Street, a single spot shining on his face, as he sang the final chorus of Peter Sarstedt's classic :

"I know where you go to, my lovely
When you're alone in your bed
I know the thoughts that surround you
'Cause I can look inside your head
Na-na-na-na, na-na-na-na-na-na-na
Na-na-na-na, na-na-na-na-na-na-na..."

The room rocked with applause as he grabbed a bottle of lager and stepped across to sit at a corner table.

A male fan came and joined him.

"Mister Duffy?" asked the stranger.

"That's me."

"The singing detective who rides a Harley?"

"Unless I'm getting knocked off," joked the singer.

"I've got a job for you… if you have time."

"Slay me."

"I have a step-father who's just ripped me off."

"A wicked step-father?"

"My name's Noah. He was married to my Mum who died recently. There was a family inheritance of nearly one million New Zealand dollars he promised to transfer to me, but kept most of it for himself."

"A very wicked step-father."

"I also just discovered he already has a wife and family here in London."

"Mmm… bigamy can get seven years and a fine."

"I don't care too much about that but I think he's a crook and I want my money back."

"Who is this guy?"

"He claims he's doing some hush hush job… but I think it's bullshit."

Noah showed a recent photo to Duffy.

"Mungo Swift."

Duffy's face fell.

"My Mungo? This guy can't be a crook – he's the Special Forces hero who just saved my life!"

CHAPTER ELEVEN

Duffy had spent a long evening in that Notting Hill dive with the young Kiwi, Noah.

They'd cracked a couple of bottles of sauvignon blanc and put the world to rights, especially when it came to Mungo.

Our singing detective was cautious in blaming the guy. He would not have been on that gig that night if he hadn't been rescued from certain death from Psycho the crazy scalper. But. He also recognized this was an honest lad with a problem. If Mungo had half inched that legacy cash then Duffy would try sort it, mate or no mate.

As for the bigamy stuff, that was personal. It was also criminal, but not exactly chopping anyone's head off. Duffy also remembered Mungo taking that call from California in the bar, claiming it was his "new bride"... Good luck to you buddy, thought Duffy, if you can get away with it, why not. Though looking at the guy, he was not exactly drop dead gorgeous... More like someone serving in a chippie. But these days you never knew. As for being Special Forces, Duffy gave him the benefit of the doubt... he just wasn't sure. But promised Noah he'd follow through on the money he was owed.

Right now he'd persuaded Kate to contact the baby seller, Rachel Storm, who'd just walked through hotel reception at the Kensington Grand in that same prim grey suit she wore on the last meetings, looking again like a very serious businesswoman.

The story was that Kate, posing as a would-be mother, wanted to know about buying twins, if that was possible, and how soon she could see them.

Duffy meanwhile was hiding behind a yucca plant in a far corner of the lounge, listening to every word through an ear-piece.

"So same time next week, I could see a pair of twins, in the flesh?" asked Kate.

"Absolutely my dear. I'll bring you a selection... three pairs... you take your choice," smiled Ms Storm.

"What... How much?" She seemed to hesitate.

"The outgoings?" helped Rachel with a charming smile.

Kate nodded, looking nervous.

Should have been a bloody actress, thought Duffy.

"Well, normally for one baby we ask twenty grand. Two would be forty. But.

In your case, for twins, same bloodline, we'd ask just thirty-five."

Kate sighed. "My God."

"See it as a lifetime investment. One day you'll be talking with your twins over a glass of champagne and you'll tell this story. You'll realize they are priceless.

Money just doesn't cut it."

Kate stood.

"You're right of course Ms Storm. Thank you so much."

They shook hands.

"Same time next week. With twins."

Rachel Storm left the hotel first with Duffy starting up the Harley in the shadows.

He watched her drive off in her sleek black Audi and followed two hundred yards behind.

Always allowed one or two other cars between them in case she spotted him in the rear mirror.

Twenty minutes later they were driving through the

tree-lined suburbs of Ealing, all very respectable, and not somewhere you'd associate with a baby smuggling racket.

Rachel Storm pulled up at a large Victorian brick mansion.

A brass plate outside said : "God's Work Hospice – Caring for Pilgrims".

Rachel parked outside and, taking several cartons of canned baby food from her car, carried them around to the rear of the building.

Moments later she emerged again, took out more cartons, and carried them round the back out of sight.

Then she got into her Audi and drove off.

Duffy was intrigued and just a little gobsmacked.

A highly respectable hospice, linked to the church, where terminally ill patients normally went to quietly die, was posing as a possible front for a baby selling scam. You couldn't make it up.

*

Mungo felt his heart thumping the moment the plane turned to circle before landing and he spotted that Hollywood sign on those far off hills. Always happened. Every time he flew into Los Angeles that same tingle, that same buzz. About to touch down in "the land of the free" where anything could and would happen.

As usual, the moment he walked through LAX customs on arrival, out into that warm tropical haze that nearly bowled him over, and saw those tall palms swaying high against the crystal clear blue sky, he knew he was back in paradise.

He took out his Burner No. 3 and made the call.

"Hi honey, I'm home…" he joked.

Janie was a tad peeved he'd been away for so long but

then softened. She'd booked lunch at Geoffrey's in Malibu to celebrate their first three weeks of marriage.

An anniversary, she said.

Over champagne Mungo told his new Californian wife what he'd been doing in Europe. Well, a sanitized version. How he'd met loads of producers at the Cannes media market and gone on to visit Wim in Amsterdam who was anxious to develop movies together. How he'd met other new contacts in London. How Mungo's Movies was moving ahead at lightning speed.

Obviously he didn't tell her about Margot, his young fiancée in Cannes, Putri, his married interest in Holland, or Monica, his long suffering wife of twenty years in London. Nor tales of adventure about getting a gun from a dodgy geezer in an East End pub, nor fighting for his life aboard a motor cruiser off the coast of France.

Though surmised this was all ripe fodder for a movie in itself.

"So what next my darling?" chirped Janie.

"Next?" said Mungo, nodding at a stunning starlet at the next table. "Next, I flesh out the flying pig script with that writer."

"Dakota? She was sweet dear – you should ask her over for dinner... she's really going places, I can tell you."

"Why not. We'll do that. And then I want to talk over other ideas with other writers while I'm here."

"You're not going away again so soon – you've just arrived!" sighed Janie.

"Not yet babe. But got to tie up a few loose ends, do some deals abroad but not yet babe."

"And what are these other ideas? Something big you planning to spend my money on?"

Mungo looked thoughtful as he emptied his glass.

"I want to do a movie about this guy. A fantasist. You never know if he's in the real world or living a dream. Everywhere he goes, he finds love. Can't meet a pretty girl without saying 'marry me'."

"That could be very funny."

"Two versions... Comedy... Call it 'The Ballooning Bigamist'. Everywhere the balloon lands he gets married. So he's floating around the world. With a wife in every country."

"Wow – I love it. How does it end?"

Mungo shrugs.

"The balloon gets ripped and won't fly. So he's stuck with his last wife. A terrible choice when he was drunk. For ever and ever... locked in a marital cage with the wrong woman."

"I love it," squeaked Janie. "What's the other version?"

"A thriller. 'The Waster'. He's a crazy who chases rich women, marries, then wastes them."

"Don't like that version. Stick with the balloon guy."

Mungo nodded at the stunning starlet at the next table again and looked at his watch.

"Hang on big boy – that fantasist's not you is it?!" smirked Janie. "A girl in every port?"

Mungo shrugged. "Sure babe, that's me. Listen... got to fly. Development meeting. But I'll be back in time for that hot tub cocktail."

He pecked Janie on the cheek, quietly passed his card to the next table girl, and left.

Half an hour later he'd arrived at Brett's Global Energy office in Glendale.

There in reception was a beaming Dakota.

"My dream's come true! You're back again," she laughed.

"Hi Dakota."

"Now tell me. Is that Janie for real – she your wife or is your wife in London, like I thought?"

"She's a dear old friend. Likes to pretend we're married."

"I can see she's old… But she got cash for making movies?"

"Oh yes she has."

Dakota nodded thoughtfully. "OK."

"Is Brett in?"

"Sure he is Mungo. But first…" She opened a drawer and pulled out a document of some kind. Offered it to him.

"What's this?"

"'Pigs Can Fly'" … the script… first draft."

Mungo flicked through the pages.

"This looks great. But you can't write."

"Just did."

"Let me take a look. And show Janie too."

"When can you pay?"

"When we like it babe."

He kept the script, kissed Dakota on her forehead, and walked on into Brett's office.

"My man!" cried Brett, leaping to his feet. "Back in town."

"Had to thank you again for the Chinese deal… they came visiting Charlie in a bloody copter. Seems they like the big hangar we gave them for the blades… but weirdly want to have their own security."

'No probs Mungo – they do the same here with us. They rent two massive sheds for their wind turbine shit and won't let us near it. We don't mind, long as we get their checks."

"Guess you're right. These Asians like to keep a tight control, I heard that."

His smartphone rang.

It was Willow. The stunning starlet from the next table at Geoffrey's restaurant in Malibu. She was still hungry.

"Chateau Marmont. Thirty minutes. Reception."

He ended the call and looked back at Brett.

"Talking of tight control mate... got a sudden meeting."

"Enjoy..." smiled Brett.

And he was gone.

*

It made the front page of The London Evening Standard. A beautiful girl in her twenties had committed suicide in South Kensington. Afareen Azad. She'd been working as a freelance reporter in the U.K. for just six months. Her brother had been imprisoned in Tehran for three years for his political activism and the story suggested that Afareen was putting together evidence to prove his innocence.

"What it doesn't say," said Abigail to Hanny, "is that she lived just around the corner from the Iranian Embassy... and that to fall to her death from her apartment meant squeezing through a window gap of ten inches."

"Murder not suicide?"

"Just so. I suspect she was snooping on the diplomats – half of them are government agents – following them in and out, hoping she might spot something she could use against them. And the fact she was taken out, probably means she did just that. Found something valuable. Someone she could blackmail to help free her brother. Then they turned on her and liquidated the problem. End of."

Cheryl the barmaid at The Blind Beggar interrupted her.

"Another round ladies?" she asked.

Abi nodded back beamingly.

"You don't think... your friends?" asked Hanny.

"Soraya and Darius? Quite possible. It's their sort of

killing. Made to look like suicide when it was murder. Except. When you look closer you know it's not easy to squeeze out through a narrow window."

"Not easy but possible. I remember a top telly boss doing that years ago.

Everyone thought the windows didn't open. But he managed. And that was…suicide."

"However."

"However?" asked Hanny.

"I've used some of my contacts to get near the medical report."

"Don't tell me."

Abigail nodded.

"There was a whiff of chloroform on her lips, and faint traces of bruising around the neck."

"Ah."

"Her iPad was still beside her bed, but wiped clean. Like brand new. Same with her phone. No contacts, no messages. And of course, no prints in the flat.

"Then that gives the game away – if her stuff was wiped clean we know she had intruders… we know she was killed."

Abi nodded wisely.

"I suspect this was a 'warm up' for our lovely couple. Like before playing the big match… loosening the sinews… deep breathing exercises… fifty press-ups on the turf. Also sets a marker to people in the biz like us Hanny… Tells us they're back in town."

"You said they'd arrive with a kill list. Do you think this Azad girl was on it?"

"Undoubtedly. Cameras outside the block saw an elegant blonde visit about thirty minutes before the death."

"Blonde?" asked Hanny.

"Our Soraya was very proud of her disguises. One minute a spotty shop girl with a pony tail, the next an old crone on a mobility scooter."

"Mmm. So what's the plan dear?"

Abigail gently waved to Cheryl the barmaid.

The girl came across. "Everything alright ladies?" she asked.

"You might remember us from last time..?" asked Abi.

"Of course. You're writing about the underworld... want to meet my Dad."

She turned back to the bar. "Just a mo'..."

Moments later she came back followed by a large guy about seven foot tall, just as wide, nose broken a dozen times.

"Ladies... I'm Cheryl's Dad, Eddie. How can I help?"

He sat beside them, taking up two chairs.

"We're Abigail and Hanny. Writers. Doing a book on the gangland haunts of old London town."

"Ah... Place changed a lot in the last ten years. Wouldn't recognise it now.

Lot of newcomers, shall we say. Too many. Far too many."

"Times have changed," agreed Abi. "But round here, are there many gangs operating... drugs, guns, or worse?"

Eddie looked her over very carefully.

"I realise, at your age, you're probably retired... but. The questions you're asking – you're not cops are you... undercover or something? What you're asking, not something I'd discuss with strangers, get my meaning?"

"We're not cops dear," assured Hanny with a flaky grin.

"But we are asking sticky questions Eddie. We want to get the facts on what goes on now in gangland. Don't need names, just get a feel of what's going down...

To give our book a bit of authenticity, a flavour of the real

East End."

Eddie sighed deeply.

"Go on. Ask away. You got me for five minutes ladies."

"We read in the papers there are different gangs operating in this area…

Albanians, Romanians, Turks… and I assume some home-grown local boys?"

Eddie nodded slowly.

"Wherever you go, you'll find some dodgy geezers love. If there's money to be made by smuggling in something – drugs, guns, people – someone'll do it for the right price. If there's stolen goods on the market, there'll be a fence happy to sell the stuff on. If someone wants to warn someone off, teach them a lesson, there's always a kid with a baseball bat or chisel who'll do the deed. None of this is secret – we all know it happens. Always has, always will. Where you get poverty and greed, shit happens."

"What about guns for hire?" asked Abi with a knowing twinkle.

"I wouldn't know meself… but guess they're around. Is that why you're really here – you want to teach someone a lesson?"

"Don't think so Eddie…" smiled Abi. "But, final question. Do you ever get foreigners asking you, or your mates, to find people for them? Give you a name and see if you can get an address where they're living… nothing more. Track down a lost relative or old mate, that kind of thing?"

The pub landlord went quiet and thought long.

"Mmm. That happened once. Couple of years back. They paid well too. Can't remember where they from. Middle East for sure. Yeah… we found a young student for them. Really happy. Big reunion they said."

Abi looked at Hanny and nodded slowly.

"Eddie. That's just the sort of story we want for our book. Local colour.

Strangers looking for old mates. You helping track them down… Emotional catnip.

That bloody sells books!"

"OK…" replied Eddie, a trifle bewildered. "OK."

"So, promise me. Next time you do that – a foreigner asks you to find someone, could you give me a call… and we'll make it worthwhile."

She handed him a card.

Eddie shrugged. "Sure. If that's all you want. Not a problem ladies." He stood. "Give them a drink on the house Cheryl… nice to meet." And vanished behind the bar.

"That went well," whispered Hanny.

Abigail nodded with a serene smile. "Taken the bait."

*

When you're nearly twelve thousand miles away from home, it can get lonely. Very lonely. And right now Noah was feeling it. Wondering if making that long plane trip from Auckland to Heathrow - over 24 hours in the air – where your brain went numb, the food was disgusting, and the bog like something in a horror movie – was really worth it. The motivation was getting that money back from Mungo. A legacy that was truly his, promised by his dear deceased mother. But, shit, some things in life were more important than money. Or were they? He'd found Duffy, the private detective, who'd promised to confront his step-dad over the cash, so now he was playing the waiting game. Though the water was muddied by Mungo saving Duffy's life. Plus he still felt very alone in this huge bloody dirty city where he knew not a single soul.

Well, he knew Donna. They'd only met a few days earlier in that café where she worked, then they'd had that Chinese meal... She was a lovely girl but Noah didn't want to get too serious, too quickly. Not sure he even wanted to sleep with her.

Yet. That way he could get her pregnant, then there'd be a wedding. Then the big emotional choice – does he stay in London for the rest of his life, or drag her crying and screaming to his island home on the far side of the planet? She'd surely love it there, the most beautiful place on earth, but she'd have no family, no friends... What if he died early, she'd be stuck, probably with a few kids... alone. Like he was now.

Eileen had been his first Kiwi girlfriend. They'd met at his school, Selwyn College in Kohi. Both in the fifth form, both sixteen. She had long blonde hair, and a massive smile. Was captain of the basketball team, and ran cross-country. Noah at the time was the school mile champion so it seemed a good match. They'd meet a few times a week after studies and went swimming or walking or running together. They had a feel good bond, nothing sexual, but both felt really close to each other. Then suddenly they went in different directions. It might have been interfering parents, or simply they'd changed their courses at school. Eileen was chasing a P.E. course, while Noah had gone all arty, getting into History and languages. Every summer break he'd work for six weeks in a freezing works, stacking boxes of butter, dressed in snow gear, it was so cold. Soon he'd saved enough to get himself his first car, which again opened up his life more. He now started going on surfing breaks up in the Bay of Islands, going to moonlit piss-ups on the beach, and meeting wild girls with dyed hair and tattoos and ear-piercings. His social life was starting to roar… The second serious girl he found at Auckland Uni where he was studying for a B.A. degree. This was Lola, an exotic goddess with a Brazilian mum who was as much a man-eater as the daughter. They both shared French and Philosophy classes… plus the backseat of his Holden car where, every Saturday night, he'd park in a quiet avenue where both would strip to the waist and fumble awkwardly in the dark. It was only after a very boozy Uni hop one steaming night that they went further. All the clothes came off and they had sex. Least that's what Noah thought it was. No condom or pills. Just basic animal lust. Then afterwards, the fear. Both worried shitless that she could be pregnant. Waiting and waiting for those days to pass. But nothing happened. And, several months later, Noah's mum died. That really knocked him.

He'd lost his Dad some years earlier and now to have no mother as well was a severe kick in the gut. His new Dad on the block, Mungo, was a mystery. Away most of the time in his nuclear sub, so he said, he and Noah never truly connected. The lad felt it was all an act. And so it proved to be.

Right now the young lonely Kiwi was heading to Flora's Brasserie in Covent Garden where Donna had booked a table and promised him a 'surprise'. Knowing how liberated these Me Too Brit girls were, he prayed she was not getting down on one knee and giving him an engagement ring. For that he was not ready. Or perhaps she'd gone and booked a holiday for two… in Scotland or the Med or the States. But that was crazy for this girl had no money – she was working in a café for goodness sake. Nevertheless, any surprise did make the back of Noah's neck nervously tingle just a tad… He hated surprises. Liked to know what he was walking into.

And then he saw.

Through the window at Flora's Brasserie.

Donna sat at a table waiting for him, with another female.

An older woman, who must be her mother.

Noah's heart missed a beat as he recognized her.

The woman he'd met on the doorstep at Harrow-on-the-Hill, who said she'd been married to his step-dad for twenty years.

This was one earth-shattering surprise.

Donna, the girl Noah was dating, must be Mungo's daughter.

*

Duffy was sipping his second flat white in a rundown café, mulling over his discovery that the baby smuggling racket was run from the "God's Work Hospice" in Ealing.

It was an outrageously clever ploy. Who on earth would think that this religious charity where people went to die, was behind a seedy business where migrant babies from the Lesbos refugee camp were smuggled into Lymington marina, then sold off to the highest bidder in a posh Kensington hotel.

He called Kate but no answer. Wanted to thank her for playing Mummy with Rachel Storm, and talk over when to raid the hospice.

Then got a text from her.

Which sounded like a romantic invite.

"Come over to mine at seven. Bring a bottle."

Duffy looked at the time. Just after six. Went and washed up in the café loo.

Brushed his hair and popped a mint in his mouth. Ducked into a supermarket and grabbed a bottle of Montepulciano.

Ten minutes later he was tapping on Kate's door.

No answer.

Then noticed it was ajar and pushed it open a jot.

Could see a dining table with two candles already lit.

This had promise, thought Duffy, as he walked inside.

"Kate?' he softly called.

In a split second a rabbit punch sent him thudding to the floor.

Everything went black.

Then he heard a voice.

His head ached and he felt dizzy.

He was roughly tied to a chair.

Opened his eyes and didn't like what he saw.

Kate's brother Max standing in front of him, drinking from a bottle.

That beard he had when they met in bed, had gone.

"Thanks for the wine Duffy – I love Montepulciano."

It got worse.

Max was wearing makeup and wearing a dress, probably Kate's.

This guy was seriously fucking weird, thought Duffy.

Then saw a fedora hat on a sideboard. That photo. Max was the guy posing as him in the casino!

"It was you!" shouted Duffy. "Stole my ID!"

The painted face nodded with glee. "It was such fun… You left your wallet here… so I used the cards… scammed those dating sites… went gambling in the casino… and ran you off the road darling… I became Mister bloody Duffy, ha!"

"But why Max, why?" seethed Duffy.

"Kate and I are very close…" persisted Max. "I told you to keep away."

Duffy noticed his voice was slurred… probably on drugs.

"I did Max. Not seen her for days."

"Liar! You were with her today!" he shouted.

Duffy sighed. Of course he'd seen Kate at the hotel.

"We were on a job together."

"At a bloody hotel! You don't work at a hotel; you fuck!" Max shouted again.

Shit, thought Duffy. This guy's really out of it. He's following me… and Kate.

"I warned her, I warned Kate not to see you!"

"Won't happen again mate, promise" whispered Duffy.

"You're right mister private detective… you're right." His voice had softened in a sinister way. "It won't bloody happen again."

He turned up the volume on the sound system. So loud Duffy's ears hurt.

"Hope you like Wagner!" he yelled over the music.

Then picked up something from a side table.

A mini chainsaw. Not the usual biggie for tree trunks. A smaller more subtle version for branches or fingers or legs.

Max laughed and started the saw.

It whirred and whined as he menacingly waved it in the air, to and fro.

Threw it from hand to hand like a deadly juggler.

"Coming to get you!" he cried, his eyes bulging, dribbling red wine from his lips.

"No!" shouted Duffy as the smiling druggie staggered towards him.

Then, in a mirror on a far wall, Duffy saw a flicker, a sudden brief movement.

He could smell Max's bad breath.

The saw was nearing his throat.

Felt the air from the blade.

When he saw a flash in that same mirror.

The music so loud he heard nothing.

Max threw the whirring chainsaw high in the air and crumpled in a heap.

He didn't move.

Wagner still blared.

But Max, the druggie brother wearing makeup and a dress, breathed no more.

Someone had come in the door behind Duffy and shot him stone cold dead.

CHAPTER TWELVE

It must have been thirty minutes at least before an irritated neighbour who didn't like Wagner had barged into Kate's flat and found the corpse lying beside Duffy. The singing detective was relieved to be alive. This was getting a very bad habit. Not long ago he'd been run off the road on his Harley, and had his brakes cut, apparently by Max, then nearly drowned in the briny by the SAS monster Psycho… and now, seconds away from having his throat slit open by a mini chainsaw, his life had been spared yet again. Question was, who shot Max?

There were several possible suspects.

It could have been sister Kate herself. Returning to her flat and interrupting her brother's ghoulish game with Duffy. If it had indeed been her, then the singing detective would never find out. She would have shot her own sad brother and hated herself for it. A secret she'd take to her grave. The shame, and the fact that she pulled the trigger, could never ever be admitted. Duffy also wondered if he should reveal that Max was the guy in the fedora… behind the ID theft… motivated by some weird jealousy over his sister… But then by now she would have seen the hat and put two and two together. Or not. For the moment Duffy decided to say nothing.

Or the shooter could have been Mungo. Duffy knew that he'd been looking for the guy in the fedora that cheated the casino out of one hundred thousand cash. He knew he carried a gun. So? He might have been offered a payment to eliminate the man in the hat, but it would not have brought back that cash. And, hang on, didn't the chubby charmer say he was off to California to visit a new bride? Or was that just a fake alibi… smoke and mirrors?

Or, staying with the casino, it could have been the two mobsters who'd dragged Duffy off for questioning, thinking he was Mister Fedora.

Any of the above, thought Duffy. Any of the above.

When she suddenly rang him.

Kate.

In a terrible state. Just heard about him and Max and could not believe it.

Duffy, back with Toto in the Fortnum bar, played it cool. She could just be double-bluffing, having shot him herself, or, be genuinely shattered by his death. Or both.

"I'm gutted Duffy," Kate sobbed.

"I nearly was."

"So so so sorry… I didn't know Max was that crazy… he must have been drugged up… and now… now he's gone… my only brother."

"Do you want come over for a drink?" soothed the gumshoe.

"No thanks Duffy. I need… I need to keep working."

"OK. Your call… Why don't we pay that baby place in Ealing a visit… check them out – we could play Mr and Mrs again?"

He arranged to meet Kate outside the joint in an hour, when he heard a familiar but unwelcome sound.

It could have been a Patagonian mountain goat or the lesser spotted peewit.

But no.

It was a baby crying.

"Oh shit," he mumbled, as Izzy stormed into the bar carrying baby Byron in a cot.

"You avoiding me sunshine?" she snarled, dumping the cot on the bar, then turned to Toto. "Double scotch on the rocks."

"Just trying to stay alive Izzy."

"So am I! With this bloody baby round my neck!"

"Not much longer babe... We've found where they're holding them..."

"Lost Property at Waterloo?"

Duffy ignored her sarkiness. "A hospice in Ealing, would you believe... off there in a mo'... then close them down and sort out young Byron here."

"What you mean – 'sort out'?"

"Well. He and all the other babies they're hiding there, waiting to sell off... We've got to... sort it," blustered Duffy.

Izzy nodded slowly and sipped her scotch.

"That I understand Mister bloody private detective, but how?"

Duffy drained his gin martini and thought hard.

"They'll have to be properly adopted, cared for. We'll go to Barnardo's who do that stuff... or any adoption agency... or local councils... Plenty of safe places to find them new homes," said Duffy.

"Without gullible families forking out twenty grand?"

"Exactly love." Then remembered. "Jeez – I got to get that Hermes watch back for Zandra – she'd kill me if I lose it!'"

"I don't like it though... it's like treating them as stray dogs and taking them to Battersea Dogs' Home!"

"Any better idea Izzy?" sighed Duffy. He knew it wasn't perfect. Knew it was all a bit inhuman, but what was the alternative?

Izzy shrugged. Then turned to the cot and tickled Byron

under his chin.

"He is quite cute Duffy."

"Careful Tiger... you're sounding a bit mumsy."

Izzy pulled back from the cot.

"You're a bloody cold fish sometimes Duffy – don't you feel anything in those ice-cold veins?"

"Listen. I nearly lost these veins last night when some nutter came at me with a chainsaw."

"Oh yeah," laughed Izzy. "Anything to change the subject."

Duffy got off his stool.

"Just a few more days baby-sitting Izzy. Promise. Then we'll find our boy Byron a happy home and get back to living our usual boring lives."

He patted the baby's head as he would a puppy, pecked Izzy on the cheek, who flinched, and headed off to meet Kate at the place where sick people went to die.

*

"This is a fucking amazing script babe – for a new writer!" shouted Janie at Mungo who was floating, eyes closed, in their pool, listening to Supertramp on his earbuds.

He saw the old girl waving at him and stopped.

He was in another world.

Still in Room 33 of the Chateau Marmont with the girl from lunch, Willow.

She must have done ballet training as a kid as her legs could open wall to wall wide. Mungo almost took photos. He'd now put her carefully on speed dial so, once the coast was clear, he could relive that ecstatic experience. Not that it was bad with Janie. Just that Willow had more energy, more imagination, when it came to trying out new stuff.

"What?" he cried back to his wife.

Janie waved the script in the air.

"Love it!"

Mungo woke up, pulled out the buds, and climbed out of the pool.

"We should get Dakota over for a meal," suggested Janie.

"Mmm... not sure," mumbled Mungo. He didn't want Janie finding out the girl had never written anything before and was a receptionist for Global Energy in Glendale, of all places. Didn't want her finding out he was really a solar panel salesman with a wife and family in London. Our Dakota knew all this shit, so the chubby charmer had to keep her on a tight rein.

"Could look a bit too keen Janie... bit unprofessional. Better I meet her and discuss before we start doing social stuff?" smiled Mungo.

Janie shrugged. "You're the big bad producer darling. Whatever you say... But it really shows promise."

"I thought so too." A sudden thought. "Hey, why don't I see her today after breakfast... try move the show forward... get a meet with Brad Pitt perhaps... if he likes the script?"

"Adorable. You are so... adorable." As she grabbed Mungo round his flabby waist. They kissed wildly, stepped backwards, and both fell into the pool.

After their juices and over easy eggs, Mungo in a silk hoodie and neatly ironed white shorts, headed to a bistro garden on Sunset Boulevard. It was all palms and orchids and very camp waiters. The beautiful people of La-La-Land were quietly assembling for the late morning imbibings.

Dakota arrived exactly at noon as requested.

Mungo had bunged her a thousand dollars as an advance

option on the script.

If they liked it, she would get more. Much more.

But already that cash showed. She was glowing.

The long blue hair had been cut in a Beverly Hills salon and was now a short greyish blonde… the stud through her chin had gone, replaced by two long diamond earrings… and the dragon tattoo on her neck covered by an expensive silk trouser suit, probably bought on Rodeo Drive.

Mungo just sat and stared in admiration.

If nothing else, he'd given this girl some class and sophistication.

And now, if they could get her script off the ground, a life-changing shot in Hollywood's ruthless fame game.

Trouble was, nobody knew that Mungo was totally out of his depth in the movie world. His filmic pedigree was a cosy cinema in Harrow where you could book a sofa seat and take in a cheap glass of plonk. He was simply a rather slick solar panel salesman. But, even in Hollywood that was all it took. He'd heard of a London hairdresser whose wife wanted to act so they moved to L.A. and now both were bigtime, with the snipper a top producer and her starring in a network comedy. So, as they said in the States, anyone could make a fortune if they had the balls.

"You look great girl," praised Mungo.

"Thank you mister producer," smiled Dakota from under new long lashes.

"Three words."

"What?" asked Dakota.

"We love it."

"What?"

"Your script. We should run it past Brad."

"Hell! Fuck! What!?"

"It's funny and sexy and cool…"

"Wow."

"So. Brad Pitt. Should I send it to his agent or, can you get it to him direct?"

"Hey – I was his nanny. As they say…we know where you live… and I do!"

"You happy to drop it off there…?" asked Mungo, sucking hard on his pina colada.

"Sure… if you think it's that good."

Mungo nodded. "We'll pay you the full option fee now… we are on a roll!"

"Shit. And I wondered about you Mungo. The game you playing… one day you selling solar panels, the next a Hollywood producer making movies… one day a wife and kids in London, the next a fantasist wife in Bel Air… What the fuck!?"

"Dakota. You and I have had some fun. We know each other pretty well.

But now you know my secrets. I have to seriously trust you. Can I?"

She stared at him through the new long lashes and beamed.

"You're my buddy Mungo. Making me a movie writer. That is something."

"Promise me not a word to Brett about Janie… or the script you wrote. He mustn't know I'm doing this movie shit. It'd spoil everything."

"I promise. Coz one day I hope to leave Global Energy as receptionist and become a fulltime screenwriter!"

"We'll do it together girl. To 'Pigs Can Fly'!"

They clicked glasses.

Then Dakota looked coyly at Mungo.

"I want some personal advice," she said.

"Try me."

"You know the Chinese guys we're doing business with – Sun and Yi?"

"Yeah," replied Mungo, getting very interested indeed and not a little nervous.

"Well, Chang Yi… that's his name… has asked me out to dinner."

"What?"

"Should I go, or politely say fuck off?"

"Well… tough choice. Brett – and I – are working with them… they're bringing us in good money."

"So it's a 'yes'?"

"No pressure. You decide. But be careful. I'm not racist, god forbid, but these Asians are known to be inscrutable… never know what they're thinking… so, don't take chances… stay in control babe, polite but firm, know what I mean?"

"I'll take the risk then. He's mega rich – promised a Beverly Hills supper then a West Hollywood nightclub."

"What's not to like babe," smiled Mungo, suddenly feeling paternal towards this wayward free spirit he'd known for quite a few years. Right now she was on a roll – just written a great script for the first time – and didn't want to take a wrong turning in her personal life that could screw everything!

"You enjoy… but take care."

Dakota smiled back.

"Don't worry Mungo…" She tapped her nose. "Hush hush."

*

"What on earth are we doing in the Scottish Highlands?" asked a bemused Hanny as she shovelled down another spoonful of lukewarm porridge.

"It's Alfred Hitchcock's fault dear," mumbled Abigail, through her kedgeree.

"Why?"

"I saw 'The 39 Steps' last week with Robert Donat being chased across the moors and thought that's what we want," said Abigail curtly.

"What dear?"

"Mettle. Something to test our mettle. Put us on edge... push the boundaries, mentally and physically... these coming weeks are not going to be easy, trying to catch our Iranian friends... at our age."

"But why come here – the middle of nowhere?"

"A weekend in Scotland – why not? Here we have this bonnie wee hotel nestling in the braes... haggis and heather... what better location for our challenge?"

"What challenge Abigail? I'm finding all this very... bewildering," sighed Hanny.

Abi leant forward over the toast and malt whisky marmalade. "We're going to shoot a stag."

"Don't be bloody stupid!" she whispered sotto voce.

"What?"

"You need a licence, a gillie, a rifle."

"Normally Hanny. Normally it costs £700 a kill. But we ain't normal, remember. We're Shadow Unit. And gun?" She patted her tweed jacket. "Beretta M9."

Hanny's mouth fell open as she looked around the tiny dining room with its paintings of Mary Queen of Scots and Sir Walter Scott, hoping no-one had heard her.

The other two couples looked rather prim and proper as

they peered at their newspapers and said not a word. Talk about God's waiting room.

"You can't shoot a stag with a pistol!" she whispered. "You can't wander onto private land and chase deer!"

"You can do anything you want if you bloody put your mind to it," snapped Abi. She pulled a map from her pocket. "Now. It's a three hour walk from here up into the crags. If we get stopped, we're lost. If not, we're hunting deer."

Abigail stood.

"Come on girl. Let's see what we're made of... let's get stalking."

And led her astonished friend from the small austere hotel out onto the moors.

They were both wearing sensible brogues and carrying ram's horn walking sticks.

Hanny was still shaking her head in disbelief as they climbed the first hillock, covered in bluebells, heather, and thistles... a shining waterfall tinkering down from the heavens in a distant valley on the horizon.

"Isn't this just something?" sighed Abi, pausing to take in the view.

"What's in your bag?" Hanny asked, dreading the answer.

"All we need. Map, compass, camera, binoculars, a hip flask of scotch, and a chunky venison sandwich from the hotel kitchen, my dear."

Hanny shrugged resignedly and followed her old friend.

After several hours tramping over the heather moors, they climbed a gentle hill and peered around.

Abi perched on a large boulder and scanned the horizon with her binoculars.

"We're not lost are we, old thing?" panted Hanny.

"I think I can smell deer."

"Probably that venison sandwich."

"No really... Breathe it in Hanny... the heather... bluebells... and now... there's a new scent out there."

Hanny inhaled deep then shook her head.

"There you are! I have it. See... on that crag... twelve o'clock... against the sun... a stag!" whispered Abi, handing her the binoculars.

Hanny squinted and saw the silhouette.

About a hundred yards away stood this noble creature. Looked about eight feet tall, with antlers a metre or so long.

"Majestic Abigail... that is stunning!" she trembled.

"Shush!" snapped Abi. "Get down. Slowly... Don't let it see us."

Both elderly ladies sank to their knees and lay flat on the ground.

"We're going to crawl forward... until I get close enough."

"To do what?" asked Hanny nervously.

"Shoot it," answered Abi quietly, as she started moving forwards across the heather.

The stag stood on the hillock, not moving. Possibly sensing humans, possibly just posing in case a pretty young doe came by.

Within minutes the two spies were twenty yards from this handsome beast.

Abigail turned to Hanny.

"Do - not - move!"

"You're not?"

"Shush. Going to shoot this beauty." And quickly pulled an expensive Kodak camera from her bag... aimed carefully... and took the shot.

Abigail sighed relief.

"That is something I've wanted to do all my life," she grinned at Hanny.

"I don't understand…"

"Shoot a stag. Visit the highlands and get a close-up photo I can frame for the fireplace."

"You said you had a gun!"

"Just winding you up dear."

"That was not funny Abigail." muttered Hanny.

"Listen. We've both got out of London and breathed the country air. We've both stalked a bloody stag and shot it… figuratively speaking… A total refresh for both of us old dear!"

"Right now, I could do with a swig of your bloody scotch."

As Abigail handed her the hip flask with a wide grin.

All was well with the world once more.

*

Noah stood frozen for several minutes as he stared through the window into Flora's Brasserie. This had to be Donna's surprise for him. She'd brought along her Mum to meet him and that Mum was married to Mungo, his dastardly step-dad.

His immediate response was to flee and wipe Donna from his mind.

Then his gut instincts kicked in. He'd learnt it on the rugby field at Selwyn College… never run from danger, face it head on. Like if the cops pull you over for drink driving or whatever, get out of the car quicker than them and walk towards them. Take the high ground and keep it.

He gritted his teeth and walked in.

Donna beamed and her lady guest looked quizzical.

"You came Noah," said the young girl.

"I came…" added the Kiwi with a sweet smile.

Donna turned to the woman.

"This is my surprise… my Mum."

"I'm Monica," said the woman..." and I think, I think we've met?"

Noah went all thoughtful.

"You're right. Never forget a face."

"Remind me," said Monica.

"That door-to-door survey... I came knocking... did a few days work for the council."

"Of course you did. Now I remember."

"I didn't know this," said Donna a bit nonplussed. "You working for the council Noah?"

He nodded.

"Just a few days... get some extra cash."

"You were from Down Under if I remember?" asked Monica.

"Can't hide the accent."

Noah sat at their table.

"Donna, this is a wonderful surprise, and so glad to meet this lovely's girl's Mum!"

Monica laughed. "You're a flatterer... How long you here Noah?" she asked.

He shrugged. "Not sure right now. I thought I'd stay a few months tying up some family business, but, now I've met Donna, who knows?"

"He's got a degree Mum," added Donna with pride.

"Mmm. You know who this young man should meet Donna?

"Who?"

"When he gets home from California, your Noah should meet my Mungo!"

"I should love that Monica," grinned Noah. "I should just love that."

187

CHAPTER THIRTEEN

Duffy met Kate a few doors down from the hospice. It was just getting dark as he parked his bike and she silently walked towards him in the drizzle. He grabbed her and hugged her tight. Nothing was said for a minute or two. He could feel her pain.

Her body sobbed in his arms.

"So sorry Kate," he whispered gently.

"What a fuck-up... my own brother."

"Guess he had problems... nobody understood."

Kate eased out of Duffy's arms and stared at him through the tears.

"I should have understood Duffy. He'd been through a lot... drugs, drink, gambling... I just didn't realize how crazy he'd got...how jealous... how fucking bonkers!"

"It's tragic love, but it happened."

"And all that time he was the one who was stalking you... who stole your credit card... your identity... posed as you on those dating sites... and got that casino mob chasing you!"

Duffy shrugged.

"I think he was just being protective Kate... his little sister... in the end it was all about you... he must have loved you a lot."

Kate sighed.

"Too much Duffy, too much."

"So... who shot him Kate?" asked the detective softly.

She shook her head slowly and wiped her eyes.

"No bloody idea. But... thank God they did."

Duffy looked away and wondered if she was dodging the truth, or if in fact the shooter had been a total stranger... Perhaps he'd never know.

Kate cleared her throat and grabbed Duffy's arm.

"Come on my friend... let's go play Mr and Mrs."

The singing detective squeezed the cop's hand and together they crunched up the gravel drive to the God's Work Hospice.

Duffy tapped the brass knocker on the large wooden door.

Nothing happened so he tried again.

Still nothing.

Tried again more loudly, and a white-haired woman in her seventies, wearing a floral dress, pink cardigan, and a hearing aid, poked her head out.

"Have you been here long – I didn't hear you?" she said sweetly.

"Not long," answered Kate with an equally saccharine smile.

"My wife and I would like to talk to you about the hospice... I've an aunt who's sadly dying," said Duffy.

"Do come in, please," said the old girl. "My husband can help you."

They followed her into the hallway. Very Victorian with high ceilings and faded wallpaper. An old painting of the Queen, and one of the new King, alongside Jesus on the cross. Muzak softly playing in the background. A musty stale smell.

The woman paused a moment and turned around, still blissful.

"I'm Mary Durant by the way."

"Kate and Godfrey Plumb," added the cop.

"Godfrey?" whispered Duffy. "Plumb?"

189

The pensioner led them into a dimly lit office.

"And this is my husband, Cecil."

He sat at a long desk piled high with files. Must have been well into his eighties, wore a vicar's collar, a lived-in jacket with leather patches, and looked quite exhausted.

"Dearest – Mr and Mrs Plumb – who'd like to talk about a dying aunt, God bless her."

Cecil gestured for the couple to sit, as he cleared his throat.

"Tell me all, dear people…" he said.

"Well… Annie, she's just 84, been suffering lung disease for a few years now, and looks like we're in…" started Duffy.

"… the final few months," added Kate.

"Ah… God bless her," murmured Cecil.

"So we wondered if?" added Duffy.

"Of course, of course. Our hospice cares for the frail and ailing… Is she a Christian?"

Kate nodded. "A regular church goer."

"Excellent," sighed Cecil.

"So we could bring her in for a visit… a look around?"

"We have a spare room. Bring her tomorrow and she can stay if she wishes."

"That's most kind. We'll donate to your charity of course," added Duffy.

"Anything is always welcome my son," gleamed Cecil.

Suddenly the distant sound of a baby crying.

"Oh, how nice. You have babies here?" asked Kate.

Cecil nodded. "Families visiting – we let them bring in the children to see their relatives."

"Keeps us on our toes," smiled Mary.

Kate's phone suddenly rang. She listened a moment then turned to Duffy.

"Little problem at work. Must dash… catch up later."

And she was gone.

"And what does your wife do Godfrey?" asked Cecil.

"Head teacher," answered Duffy. "Trouble at school."

He stood to leave.

"Thank you both for your time – I'll bring our aunt Annie in tomorrow around noon, if that's OK?"

"My pleasure," charmed Cecil. "Nice to meet."

Mary led Duffy to the front door and bade him farewell.

The singing detective trudged across the gravel to his Harley then froze.

The sound he'd heard earlier.

Babies crying. This time more than one.

Mary was still waiting in the doorway, still grinning, waiting for him to leave.

He waved with a nod, started the bike, and rode off around the corner.

He had a plan.

He was going to head back to the rear of the building, where he'd seen Rachel Storm carrying the canned baby food, and find out exactly what was going on.

*

"Back to Europe tomorrow Brett, then we'll confirm all those new exports, plus do final planning for the wind turbine blades," chirped Mungo.

"Our new Chinese partners are over the moon about this deal old buddy, and promise there's a load more shit where this is coming from," replied Brett.

"They certainly got an eye on the main chance – these ugly fucking wind farms are popping up all over the place back home – hate them myself, but can't complain about the dosh."

191

"Know that you mean – the climate change crazies seem to ignore the number of birds they kill... if there's no wind they don't work... if the wind's too strong they bloody blow over! But... we... we're doing OK."

Mungo nodded, bear-hugged his L.A. partner, and made for the door.

"Anything you want me to bring back from Blighty?"

"I'd say Taylor Swift, but she's one of ours."

"Take care my friend," cried the chubby charmer who exited into reception where Dakota was waiting to ambush him.

"You want the good news or the bad?" she whispered.

"In the car park..." muttered Mungo.

Dakota followed him to his soft-top powder blue Jaguar F-Type and leant in close.

"Brad loved the script, but he's tied up for the next two years!"

"Damn!" spat Mungo. "Seemed like we had it on a plate."

"There's plenty more big boys out there Mungo."

Mungo nodded. "Got time for a drink?"

Dakota thought a moment. "I've got to drop off some files... that can be my excuse."

She went back inside and returned with a satchel of documents.

"Got to drop them off to the money men..." she explained. "Brett'll understand." Then climbed in beside Mungo.

As they drove away, her boss peered from his window, hoping that Mungo was not fucking his receptionist. That would be unprofessional, but, knowing his buddy, quite probable.

Half an hour later, the pair were knocking back Feeling Pretty cocktails in the Blvd Lounge of the Beverly Wilshire.

"Guess we could always cast a Brit who can do an American accent," suggested Mungo.

"Na babe… we need the real thing."

"Or, by the time we get it ready for filming, he might be free!?"

"Say that is cool. So you book him now… and we got him in two years."

"Mmm… let me run this past Janie – she's funding the fucker."

Dakota leant back and looked Mungo coyly in the eye.

"You haven't asked me."

"Asked you what – you got the script money OK?"

"Yeah – that's fine. No - about my date."

"Date?"

"With Chang Yi. The wind farm guy?" she reminded him.

"Ah so. How was it ? Fun or scary?"

"Bit of both. We dined in Beverly Hills – at this new joint called 'Clove', then the party started… we went to three clubs… ended up in Santa Monica, dancing on the beach… and watched the sun come up!"

Mungo was flabbergasted.

"We talking about the same guy?"

Dakota nodded with a broad grin. "Oh yes. One of the Chinese suits. And you should see him without it!"

"Well I never…" mumbled Mungo, a little put out that his lovely girl was off with other guys… "Were you OK?"

"Was I OK? I was flying Mungo… After the meal, he started handing out spliffs… and then, on the beach, in the sand, we hit the pills… I was really flying."

"Oh jeez Dakota. Don't go back on drugs… please… you know it messed you up girl… you can't go back to that!" urged Mungo like a kindly uncle.

Dakota squeezed his hand.

"I'm a big girl now Mungo, and don't you worry – I'm not going back to those shit awful days."

"You seeing him again?"

"Sure. He's a riot. He looks about fifty, but he's only thirty. And so so rich… I think you'll do well out of this connection… He said he liked you and I promised you were a big star!"

Mungo nodded quietly with a smile then made his excuses. He had to get back to Janie and pack before he flew to Cannes and Margot the next day. His little French street urchin had been sending him endless texts and wanted to sit down and make final arrangements for their upcoming wedding… It seemed she was spending money like it was going out of fashion. Or she was printing it herself.

When he arrived at the Bel Air mansion his new American bride was waiting for him with a massive grin.

Janie's hair had been freshly dyed and cut, probably by her usual guy she coptered in, sharing him with all the top Hollywood stars. She'd obviously just done a Botox session too as there was not a line on her face. And the pristine makeup made her look twenty years younger.

"Janie!" cried Mungo, sucking in his breath. "What do I do to deserve this darling? You look a-maz-ing!!"

"I wanna look good for Europe."

"You what?"

"I can't have my hunky new husband trail around all those sexy places on his own, can I? Baby, I'm not having you lonely over there any more… while I sit here twiddling my thumbs doing nothing… it just ain't fair."

"What?"

"I know you're doing deals… getting finance… for Mungo's Movies… but we're in this together… we should go out there as a team…. pitching side by side in Cannes, Rome,

Amsterdam, London… wherever… whatever."

"But what about your property business – it can't run itself," blustered Mungo.

"Sure it can honey babe. I don't want you to worry about anything… I'll just be there at your side… giving comfort and support. To my little boy."

"I… I…" stuttered Mungo, avoiding eye contact.

"I've packed my bags. Ready to go at dawn." Then added firmly. "Whatever you say my darling Mungo… I'm coming with you!"

And, just for once, the cheeky charmer was totally lost for words.

*

"Know thine enemy…" muttered Abigail, as she placed the final jigsaw piece - a cartoon picture of a bearded old man - on the table she was sharing with Hanny.

Both sipped a glass of sherry in front of a roaring fire in Abi's apartment.

Both still appreciating the warmth after their icy safari in the Highlands.

"The big bad wolf," added Hanny.

"Eighty-five and still going strong - Ayatollah Ali Hosseini Khamenei – Supreme Leader of the Islamic State of Iran."

Abi picked up a cheese knife and playfully stabbed at the man's bearded face.

"Looks like he could play Santa…. Yet… this sweet old pensioner's causing so much bloody mayhem in the Middle East… the world would be a much safer place without him."

Hanny nodded. "Indeed. His evil tentacles stretch into every country with a yashmak - the Houthis targeting cargo ships in the Red Sea… Hezbollah launching rockets at Tel Aviv."

"And… thanks to him arming Hamas for that ghastly October attack… followed six months later by firing 300 drones and missiles at Israel… the whole ruddy area could blow up into World War Three, " seethed Abi.

They sat in silence a moment sipping their sherry.

"So… It seems saving Western civilisation rests firmly on the shoulders of two tipsy old biddies doing jigsaws," sighed Hanny.

"Joke not my dear – we'll play our part. Small but vital cogs in serving our country and bringing Iran's killers to justice. Fancy something stronger?"

Hanny nodded, surprised that Abi needed fortifying after their usual afternoon dip into cooking sherry.

"Hanny, I hope I didn't throw you too much with that trip to Scotland, but I desperately needed something to blow away the cobwebs… a total refresh if you get my meaning… so we could focus more on the job in hand."

"Soraya and Darius?"

"Precisely."

Abigail handed Hanny a very large tumbler of malt whisky.

"My dear. I think the game of cat and mouse has started a little sooner than I'd planned."

"How so?"

"I didn't say, but when we got back from Inverness, I had a strange tingle on the back of my neck as I unlocked the door."

"Oh dear… Trapped nerve?"

"Silly girl, no. Gut instinct. Alarm bells. You see, whenever I go away I do the usual trick of sticking a piece of hair across the door so that if anyone came trespassing, the hair would be moved, and I'd know I'd had an uninvited guest."

"Oh lord… And?" asked Hanny.

"And this time, as belt and braces, I did two other things… left a champagne cork tucked into the bottom left corner of the door, plus a teensy piece of cellotape across the right top corner."

"You certainly covered everything."

Abi nodded. "So when I opened the front door I checked that the hair was still exactly in the same place… the cork still nestling on the floor…. But …they'd not spotted the ruddy cellophane!"

"Meaning?"

"It had totally gone. No longer sticking across that top corner. In fact…." Abi looked pleased with herself. "I found it on the carpet just four feet inside the flat!"

"Clever old you!" smiled Hanny.

"I thought so. Quite pleased that a simple bit of childish tradecraft can still catch them out!"

"Were you burgled?"

Abi shook her head. "Nothing. Nada. They snooped around, moved my laptop a fraction, but… Well. There was something quite amusing."

"Yes?"

"You know I'm a mingy old cow with my drinks… I always mark the level on a gin or scotch, even wine bottle… to show me how much I'm using, or not."

"I have noticed dear," sighed Hanny. "Strange habit."

"Well, the only thing I spotted they'd stolen, was two fingers of my favourite scotch!" And she held up her own glass of whisky, before emptying it down in one swig.

"So they have good taste, whoever they were!"

"And that's the point Hanny… I have to ask myself, were my visitors Soraya and Darius, the bad actors we're planning to trap… or, were they friends of dear Sir Geoffrey, doing a little checking on me… making sure I'm up to the job?"

"I expect we'll never know… but that's so creepy, knowing there was someone in your home while we were in Scotland… perhaps lying on your bed, peeking in the fridge, using your loo."

"Ah! I did have one further clue."

"Go on."

"I don't know why, but I asked Alexa to play the last song she'd played for me."

"Oh?"

"And up came Gloria Gaynor with 'I Will Survive'! Now Hanny, that's something I'd never ask for… far too unsubtle for me… far too loud."

"That's very much a gay anthem Abi … so it certainly could have been one of our more camp agents sniffing around."

"Or… our very dear Soraya taking the piss!" sighed Abigail, standing up.

"What now?"

"I think it's time we try to find our singing detective, Duffy, in his office."

"The Fortnum's wine bar?"

"Why not. I'm running short of Oolong tea."

*

Noah was feeling stir crazy. Still mentally numb from learning Mungo was Donna's Dad. He'd worked out with lightning logic that they weren't actually related, save from that phony marriage to his dearly departed Mum... But it had seriously shaken him... worse than a kick in the goolies on the rugby field. That girl who he fancied was actually the fruit of the loins of that arsehole who'd stolen his inheritance an shown no signs of giving it back. However. However, now the boot was firmly on his foot with Monica arranging a family meal together when the toady bigamist got back from L.A. and whoever he was shafting in California. Noah had already planned to take an instant photo of the guy's face when he entered the room and was introduced as the new guy in his daughter's life. Probably have a heart attack. Hopefully would.

But right now Noah was stir crazy.

He'd hardly slept a wink after that gobsmackingly awful meal.

So now he was pounding London's streets trying to walk off his anger, his frustrations.

It was mid-morning and he'd had his first flat white at a little bijou café tucked away in Mayfair. He felt such an outsider, peering in at those vast brightly-lit offices where sexy young girls and hip cool guys leant over their computers, looking so much at home with themselves and each other. He wished he was in there, out of the cold, sitting with his mates, feeling part of a team. He missed that. He missed having familiar friends around him. On the terrace at Eden Park watching the All Blacks. The beery bars. The burning sand. The twinkling sea. That bloody sun. Godzone.

He dodged a pile of dog shit on the pavement and trudged on through Piccadilly into Chinatown. This was another world within a world. The sweet smell of pungent herbs and spices, the dumplings, the dim sums, the exotic dazzle. The restaurants with names like Golden Dragon, Plum Valley, The Lotus Garden.

Looking up he saw a young smiling Chinese girl waving to him from a third floor window. She leant out and called : 'Number 7', then went inside again.

Noah stopped in his tracks, causing a family of American tourists behind him to spill their coffees… He apologised and looked up again. He knew who she was and what she wanted. Question was, did he know what he wanted.

His heart was still racing with confusion from the Donna and Monica drama.

Perhaps this was just what he needed. No commitment. Get it out of his system. A quick bang and move on.

He looked around at the other passers-by… visitors like him, local Chinese making deliveries… And went to the door beneath the girl's window.

He pushed the bell for No.7. and the door opened.

He hesitated a moment then ran up the stairs to the third floor.

She stood waiting for him.

Late teens, very pretty Chinese girl, with a little too much makeup, and a big wide smile. Draped in a black chiffon wrap which allowed him to see her naked body underneath. She had petite breasts, he noted.

She beckoned him into her room with her forefinger.

He followed, almost meekly, under her spell.

In the centre of the tiny room was a narrow bed, with a bin, towel, and condoms to one side.

In a corner to his left, almost hidden beside a sink, sat an ageing Asian woman with few teeth, knitting quietly away and whispering to herself.

"One hundred," smiled the girl, standing beside the bed.

"One hundred?" repeated Noah, thrown by the cost, and the old girl knitting.

The girl dropped the wrap and sat back naked on the bed, her legs teasingly opening and closing in front of him.

"You like, big boy?" she purred, licking her lips.

He was tempted. Shit he was tempted.

"Must pay first," wheezed the old crone from the corner.

Then Noah suddenly saw Donna's face as he looked at the girl.

Turned quickly on his heels and ran down the stairs out into the street, all the way across Piccadilly Circus, along the street until he reached Fortnum and Mason, where he rushed in, and went straight to the wine bar on the lower ground floor.

"Duffy around?" he panted.

"Out on a job mate," answered Toto. "What you having?"

"Something strong enough to forget who I am and why I'm here."

"Shit – you're having a bad day man… Leave it with me."

As Noah slumped on a bar stool and put his head in his hands…

*

Duffy crept around to the back door of the old Victorian mansion with its brass plate that said : "God's Work Hospice – Caring for Pilgrims". He could still hear babies crying inside. There were three or four windows, all with curtains closed, all with lights on within.

He leant against the brick wall and listened further. No

voices, just the babes wailing.

Tried the door handle.

Not locked.

And opened it gently.

Listened again.

No sound of anyone moving around.

Poked his head in and there they were.

Rows and rows of tiny cradles with little babies inside. Some sleeping, some crying.

At a glance Duffy thought there must have been six rows of ten... sixty babies... at twenty grand a pop they were worth over a million smackers. So if their turnover meant a monthly trip to Lesbos and back they could be making a small fortune each year, without anyone knowing.

There was another door on his right. Closed.

He checked there was no-one around then sidled over and peered in.

This time another shock.

About a dozen coffins, all lying with their lids open, waiting to be filled with the dead bodies from the hospice upstairs, as the terminally ill passed away and were sent off to the nearest crematorium.

"Here! What you doing here?" snapped a female voice behind Duffy.

He turned to face a rather large woman dressed as a nurse, holding a clip board. If looks could kill.

"Delivery. Got some more baby food to bring in but there was no-one here love," smiled Duffy.

"I thought we had this week's deliveries." She said, staring him down.

Duffy shrugged. "Got some more outside – I'll bring them in."

He moved to the door but the nurse blocked his way.

"You're sniffing around son – you should not be here!" she seethed.

She moved in on the singing detective and went to smash him with the clip board.

He ducked and wrestled with her.

But she was heavier than him and pushed him against the wall, squeezing his wind pipe.

Duffy lashed out with his right fist, hitting her to the ground. Then quickly dragged her through the second door into the coffins parlour, and locked her in.

He leant against the door getting his breath back. A close shave. But now they knew someone had been snooping, he had to call in the cavalry.

Got out his phone to get Kate and her cops over soon as.

When something thudded into the wall beside him.

An axe.

Someone had thrown an axe at him.

Duffy looked about, saw no-one.

Then a second axe pinned his jacket to the door.

Still no sign of anyone.

And then he saw the assailant framed against the naked light bulb in the ceiling.

This guy was massive.

Black chiselled beard, flinty eyes, flat top haircut, mean lips.

"We meet again Mister Duffy", he snarled.

The singing detective's mouth dropped open.

"You thought I was bloody dead?"

The big ugly Special Forces crazy who scalped guys.

It was Psycho.

Very much alive.

CHAPTER FOURTEEN

"What the hell am I drinking Toto?" slurred Noah, sitting in the Fortnum wine bar.

"One of our signature cocktails sir…" replied the barman. "It's a 'Jubilee Beacon'… our own Dry Gin, mixed with Dubonnet, Royal Vermouth, Royal Blend Tea and Honey Bitters."

The Kiwi sighed. "If I'd wanted tea mate, I'd have ordered chocolate fish and pineapple chunks!"

"You what?"

"Old custom back home, no worries… Let's try something new."

"Coming up," said Toto as he turned back to the cocktails.

At that moment two elderly ladies in tweed entered.

Abigail and Hanny.

They were about to take a corner table then spotted Noah, and seemed to recognize him. The young tourist from Down Under they'd targeted in Piccadilly Circus from their 'fishing expedition' weeks earlier. Fallen into their hands like a sun- kissed kiwi fruit.

They decided instead to sit next to him at the bar.

"Is this taken?" Abi asked the youngster.

"All yours Ma'am…" answered Noah with a polite smile.

The pensioners sat on two stools at the bar.

"Can I help you ladies?" said Toto.

"We're looking for a private detective," said Abi.

"Who sings…" added Hanny. "And owns a Harley."

"He works here… or from here?"

"Duffy. This is his daily office ladies, but right now he's out in the field, as they say, getting into trouble one way or another I guess," smiled Toto.

"Oh, well in that case we'll have a couple of single malts... Glenfiddich..." said Abi.

"Think I might join you girls on that, if you don't mind, thanks Toto."

Toto nodded and poured three glasses.

"We'd be only too pleased young man... It's so nice to meet someone with old-fashioned manners these days," said Abi.

"And no tattoos or ear studs," added Hanny.

"Are you Wellington, Auckland, or Christchurch?" asked Abi.

"Is it that obvious ladies?" laughed Noah. "How'd you guess?"

"Oh we know our accents don't we dear," answered Hanny, winking at Abi.

"We both worked in security."

"All our lives..." whispered Hanny.

"Don't tell me – 'so very hush hush'... keep meeting people like you, though never sure if they're the real McCoy," said Noah.

Abigail cleared her throat archly, like a dowager Maggie Smith. "We most certainly are the real McCoy, I promise you dear boy."

"Ah... I'm Noah by the way, from Auckland, as you guessed."

"And we're Abigail... and ..."

"Hanny."

"Are those code names ladies?" asked Noah, slightly taking the mick.

The two agents smiled back serenely and shook their heads.

"Seems we're all looking for the elusive Duffy," said the Kiwi. "You know him?"

"I've met him – watched him sing – bloody good... and he's meant to be doing a small job for me... just chasing him up really."

"Are you visiting Noah, or do you live here now?" asked Abi.

"Passing through... looking up an elusive step-father."

"Perhaps we could help... part of our old job, looking for people," said Abi.

"Kind, but that's what I got Duffy doing... when he's got time."

At that moment Kate, looking flustered, in her Met police uniform, rushed into the bar.

"Don't arrest me occifer," slurred Noah.

"You heard from Duffy, Toto?" asked Kate, ignoring the Kiwi.

The barman shrugged. "Everybody's favourite dick! These guys are looking for him too."

"Gidday," smiled Noah.

"Afternoon," said Abi.

Kate nodded to the others then back to Toto. "Rather urgent – he's not taking my calls... or texts... nothing."

Toto shook his head. "Not a peep... Probably singing in some dive and turned off his phone."

Kate thought then quickly dialed a number on her phone.

"I think we have a problem... I want a Section 17 entry and search – now - get a patrol over to that hospice pronto - I'm on my way!"

And rushed from the wine bar.

*

Mungo felt a weird mix of embarrassment and pride sweep over him as he saw the young barefooted waif waiting to greet him at Nice airport. He almost pinched himself to prove this earthy urchin with the long golden hair was really interested in him. It was either his seductive way with the ladies or his cheque book. He rapidly parked that thought and embraced her tight as he came through Arrivals. Margot smelt fresh and wholesome and sweet as corn in a summer breeze, her warm wide eyes dispelling any doubts he had about her. This was real. The bronze curtain ring was still there on her finger. This was his girl and very soon they would wed.

It was thanks to his imaginative dexterity and creative gymnastics that Mungo was free to visit Cannes without his latest wife Janie clinging on his arm. He'd tried every trick in the book to come up with a wish list of reasons he should travel alone.

The deadly new Covid outbreak sweeping the South of France... the vile cosmetics restrictions the Customs there placed on American ladies of a certain age... and the lethal food poisoning bug that was closing down the classiest joints on the Cote D'Azur.

Eventually Janie resigned herself to staying at home while her producer hubbie did his deals in Europe alone. At least this time he promised to return to California in ten days and to call punctually at her bedtime so they could talk dirty over the phone while she lay naked under the duvet. That latter stipulation was a deal breaker.

"Papa!" Margot cried. Still the same joke thought Mungo as she took his hand and skipped alongside him like a petulant child. "Booked your favourite."

"Chez Xavier?"

She nodded.

Always the same shit, but it was comforting to the chubby charmer. Felt like coming home, felt like family… He noted she was carrying something wrapped in brown paper but he didn't comment in case it was a surprise.

They grabbed a cab and headed into Cannes.

Once they'd ordered the usual seafood pizza and guzzled several glasses of red plonk, Margot got inquisitive.

"So how was L.A. this time… how was the 'invisible orchestra'… and you playing the kettle drum?"

Mungo put on a serious face. "Great success. Next time we're gonna pop up at the Hollywood Bowl."

"Chut… that sounds like a big gig cheri."

"The biggest."

Margot put her hand on his.

"Mungo, my darling fiancé… what do you really do? You think I'm stupid, but all this pop-up stuff is fantasy… You know it and I know it. I'm young, but I'm not a child!"

Mungo sighed long. "OK OK. I do do other stuff around the world, but it's sort of… under the radar… know what I mean?"

"I understand."

"I have to sign the Official Secrets Act… I can't speak about it baby."

She leant across and kissed him on the lips.

"I am very proud of you my little James Bond… For a moment I thought perhaps you did something boring like… sell solar panels or something."

Mungo gulped quietly. Either she knew the truth or had made a lucky guess.

He smiled. "About our wedding."

"Ah! I waited for you to say this, not me… I get too excited."

She suddenly placed something wrapped in brown paper on the table.

"It's a little wedding present for you darling."

"Wedding present?"

Mungo took it… it looked like a board or something.

"Shall I open?"

"Of course… I hope you like."

"Let's see… a new pair of silk underpants… a toupee… a collapsible zimmer frame," joked Mungo.

"Zimmer frame?" asked Margot.

Mungo tore off the brown paper and looked at the surprise present.

It was a head and shoulders portrait of himself in oils.

"Wow wow wow… I just love this Margot! You painted this?"

"Bien sur." she murmured.

Mungo held it above his head and showed it to the other diners who applauded as one.

"Genius! Margot – you are a genius!" And kissed her on the lips.

"Glad you like cheri… So. The wedding… when?"

"Well… Last time I was here we said six weeks time. So, once I get back again, in three weeks, we will do it, I promise!"

"Three weeks! Why not now, today, while you are home… We can do the party in here… go buy a ring… sign everything and I am yours for ever!"

"Wonderful Margot, but I want to do it right. Choose the date, arrange the party, and think about the honeymoon."

"OK you win. Three weeks time. Then we do it… But no honeymoon."

"No?" asked Mungo.

"I have a better idea. Something I've always wanted to do

209

with someone I love."

"Go on... surprise me."

Margot's face lit up in a massive grin.

"I want to skydive over the sea."

"Skydive!? You are joking," said Mungo, "I'd probably have a heart attack!"

Margot smiled blissfully.

"I've been talking to the Parachute Club – they do it every weekend – it's quite cheap and totally safe."

"Why on earth do you want to do this Margot – we could go to Paris for a few days... a luxury hotel."

"Paris we can do anytime. But to free fall... flying up there like birds on the wing... it's magic Mungo... you fall at 200 kilometres."

"Shit! You done this before?"

"In my dreams."

"I really don't think this is a good idea Margot."

"No wedding then!"

"What?"

"You will love it cheri... We can hold hands up there... a diamond ring on my finger... Monsieur and Madame Mungo... in Heaven!"

Just then the waiter interrupted. It was Sami, Margot's Algerian friend and co-conspirator.

"Encore du vin monsieur?"

"Sure – another bottle of red!" said Mungo.

"Celebration?" asked the waiter cheekily.

"We're getting married in three weeks," answered Margot.

"Three weeks," making a mental note, said Sami. "Then the wine is on the house... Felicitations!" And went to get another bottle.

"We seen him before," mused Mungo.

"Sure, that's Sami – he moves around the cafes, nice guy."

"And you really want to skydive?"

Margot nodded slowly.

"Perfect end to a perfect day… we get married… have a party… then go skydiving up in the blue, before going home to bed to make mad passionate love!"

Mungo shook his head slowly…

"I like the last part… I'm going for a leak… when I get back we'll talk more about the wedding… the details." And vanished to the loo downstairs.

As Sami arrived with the free bottle of red.

"I told him about the skydive," whispered Margot.

"He agreed?" asked Sami.

"He's shitting himself… but I'll convince him."

"We gotta plan it just right… make sure he signs the apartment over to you… then fix his parachute on the big day."

"Relax Sami… He's eating out of my hand."

"This'll make us both very rich," smiled Sami.

"Then we find another sucker," added Margot with a twinkle.

As the chubby charmer returned from the loo and flopped in his chair.

Their table sat almost directly above the ramshackle toilet he'd just visited downstairs which meant he could hear much of his fiancée's conversation with the Algerian waiter. The tone had been intimate and the content quite alarming. It sounded like the pair were plotting against him, possibly to bump him off, which suddenly gave that free fall suggestion a whole new meaning.

"I been thinking Margot."

"Oui?"

"That skydive idea sounds just fantastic – now I've had time

211

to mull it over – the perfect end to a perfect day, as you said."

"Merveilleux cheri! I hoped you would love it too."

"I must read up all about it – how it works… don't want to jump off with no chute!" he joked.

"I think we have to do some practice jumps to start off," said Margot. "Then we can go up and try solo, but with an instructor."

"Whatever… Now Margot, the wedding. Let's make it Saturday in three weeks… Do you want to do a church… a beach… a boat?"

"Oh baby there's this superyacht in the harbour – straight out of the movies… we could hire it for the ceremony then do the party there… followed by the crazy skydive."

"I'm going to dress posh for you girl."

"'Posh'?"

"Classy. Top hat and tails. Like the nobs do in England… I'm going to jump out of that plane in my posh clobber, and you got to wear the wedding dress."

"I gotta paint that… great picture."

"And, I guess I should do a will with you, making sure you get the apartment in case anything ever happened to me, what with all my travels around the world."

"No, no cheri – that is too depressing."

"You don't want to inherit the flat?"

"Well… that is kind…" She leant over and kissed him on the cheek.

"Oh, and best man. I need a best man for the wedding… except I don't know anyone in Cannes except you baby."

"We are two little loves alone… Unless…" said Margot, looking around the café.

"Unless?"

"Unless we ask Sami?"

"The waiter!?"

She shrugged.

"Why not. We have no real friends... He could do the job... I have seen him around the place for years so he's no stranger."

"Makes me look like a saddo... choosing a bloody waiter... but... for you... why not darling?"

Margot looked across at the Algerian who was serving cocktails a table away, and beckoned him over.

"It's Sami, isn't it?" asked Margot.

"Bien sur."

"Mungo – my fiancé – would like you to be best man at our wedding."

"Best man!?"

"Stand beside me, give me the ring... all that stuff," mumbled Mungo.

"Pouf – that would give me great pleasure m'sieur... you are sure?"

Mungo nodded hesitantly.

"We are sure Sami – thank you."

"Three weeks – I will be there... for you both... wild horses will not keep me away..." and walked away beaming.

"There you are my darling... The trap is set."

"Trap?"

"When I lock you in my cage for ever..."

Margot grabbed the chubby charmer's hand and squeezed.

"My darling Mungo, you would not believe what this means to me."

"Oh I think I have a very good idea my dearest Margot... a very good idea."

*

213

Duffy had to think lightning fast if he was to survive to live another day. There, just a few feet away, was the monstrously dangerous Pyscho, the ex-SAS warrior, who scalped his victims alive. The singing detective's jacket was pinned to the door by the second axe the madman had thrown at him. This guy was the powerhouse behind the baby factory scam – who sailed from the Lymington yacht haven to the Lesbos refugee camp where he cheaply purchased dozens of babies from their impoverished parents and brought them back to childless couples in the U.K. It was a clever racket that made the gang a small fortune, and right now Duffy was threatening to blow their cosy business sky high. From Psycho's angle there was only one simple answer – this private eye geezer would never see the light of day again. In fact, he would vanish off the face of the earth.

Duffy took a deep breath – felt the energy and adrenalin and fear coursing through his veins – as he ripped his jacket from the axe pinning him to the door… grabbed the chopper and threw it blindly at the hulk looming close behind him.

Psycho ducked instinctively and kept coming.

Duffy fell on all fours - raced through the giant's legs – and was out the door.

He hared down the gravel drive, out the gate, across the road to the row of Victorian semis opposite.

Looked behind him.

A grinning Psycho was twenty feet behind, waving an axe in the air.

Duffy banged on the front door of one of the houses.

No answer.

He burst inside.

Again with the big man not far behind.

Down a carpeted corridor stinking of cats.

In the lounge to his right sat an old couple watching a game show on telly.

Their mouths dropped open as they saw they had intruders.

Duffy ran past the stairs and headed through the kitchen with its stained wallpaper and angry parrot leaping about its cage.

"Fuck off!" shouted the bird. "I hate cats!"

"You fuck off!" roared back Psycho, which silenced the feathered fop.

Out the back door onto a small lawn and dirty fish pond.

Leapt over a little gate and dashed along the muddy track behind the houses.

Pyscho was still not far behind, still grinning, still waving that bloody axe.

Took a sharp right, over a barbed wire fence, into a concreted back yard, avoiding the kid's plastic tractors and the doll's house, ramming into another neighbour's back door.

Small tacky kitchen with a dog bed on the floor.

Up the narrow staircase.

Into the first bedroom.

Two naked bodies writhing on silk sheets, froze then screamed as Duffy entered and exited through their window.

Slid down a drainpipe.

Could hear an angry dog attacking Psycho in the bedroom behind him.

And out into a grassy field.

Duffy had left Psycho behind, and sprinted towards the distant woods.

Another thirty yards and he'd be free.

When the axe hit behind his left knee, bringing him hard

to the ground.

His cheek ached and eyes blurred, then he heard that voice, then nothing…

*

Kate arrived at the hospice at the same time as her two patrol cars. They immediately arrested the old couple who were running the place – Mary and Cecil – who, despite their pleas of innocence, must have known about the baby factory being run from the rear of the property. They also found a nurse locked in a back room with a load of coffins, then called in the Barnado's charity to take care of the dozens of babies being kept like battery hens in the basement.

But of Duffy there was no sign. His Harley was still parked around the corner, so he couldn't be far away.

Kate went back into the hospice and checked out the upper floors where the many terminal patients lay in their beds, waiting for their moment to come. She could hardly believe the ruthlessness of this gang to hide their seedy business behind these sad ailing people waiting to die.

As she peered from a top floor window she saw a hearse drive slowly away down the drive. Another death, even on her watch. Some things waited for no man, or woman.

Then a sudden thought.

She talked on her intercom to one of the team.

"Ask those two – Mary and Cecil – where the hearses go."

They came back. To the nearest crematorium. Couple of miles away.

Kate raced downstairs and leapt into her car.

The hearse had turned right and hopefully she could still catch it up.

Then she saw it. Two traffic lights ahead of her.

She turned on her blue light and siren.

The hearse saw her too.

Took a hard right and picked up speed.

Kate was caught behind a bus and lorry.

Couldn't overtake.

At the next lights she shot through the red but the hearse had vanished.

She pulled over and googled the nearest crematorium.

A mile away.

She crashed two more red lights narrowly missing a woman with a pram and an oldie with a zimmer, then saw the sign for the Hightown Crematorium.

The hearse was parked outside.

And the doors to the crem closing.

Kate leapt from her car and ran inside.

A giant of a man was at one end of a coffin, and two others at the front.

It was being placed onto the loading table outside the red curtains and the furnace beyond.

"Stop!" shouted Kate.

The men ignored her as the giant pushed a button on the wall and the coffin started slowly moving towards the cremator. You could feel the heat and hear the flames roaring in the incinerator.

Any second that wooden coffin would ignite.

Kate took out her pistol and shot Psycho in the leg.

"Stop!" she shouted again.

Psycho fell to the ground holding his knee in agony as the two men vanished through a side door.

The coffin was halfway into the oven.

You could smell burning.

Kate quickly scanned the buttons on the wall.

And randomly pushed one.

Nothing.

Then another.

The loading table suddenly juddered to a halt.

Three officers joined Kate and all four heaved the smoking coffin back into the room.

She prised it open.

And up sat a very pale blinking Duffy, gasping for breath.

"Am I in heaven?"

CHAPTER FIFTEEN

Duffy and Kate sat at the Fortnum's wine bar peering into their glasses.

"There are close shaves and close shaves..." mused the singing detective. "I could smell my hair burning."

"Another few seconds Duffy."

"I owe you big time..."

"Ah, but they say it's not over till the posh lady sings." smiled Kate.

"Our Rachel Storm?"

"Yup. We've got your monster guy from the SAS locked away... we've got the old dears running the hospice, plus the nurse... But. Who's behind the racket ... who thought through the concept... the business plan? None of the above. And our dear Rachel I suspect was in it for the money, no more."

"So you think we're looking for a Mister or Mrs 'Big'?"

Kate nodded.

"Someone out there was creaming off those profits... millions a year... from that very clever baby scam. That's who we've got to close down next."

"But now you've arrested the hospice mob, Rachel will go to ground, we'll never find her..." Then he remembered. "Except. Except I have her number plates – for her sexy little black Audi... and I still have that phone number to call to buy babies."

"Bravo detective. Give me the car stuff and my guys'll try get an address."

Duffy showed her a plate number on his phone.

"And there's the other loose ends."

"Hmm?" said Kate, noting the number and texting her cop colleagues.

"My ex-wife Zandra wants her watch back, worth about twenty grand... which I gave to Rachel... plus I've got to meet Rocco again – the poor Dad who started all this rolling and whose twenty grand baby died... and I've got to do something with the baby poor Izzy's been caring for all this time."

"Byron. She'll be glad to get him off her hands."

"I'm not so sure Kate... methinks there's a Mummy instinct beating in there somewhere."

Kate put her phone away.

"OK. Hopefully we'll track our Rachel down soonest... Right now I want to unwind... blot out the past 24 hours. Any ideas?"

"Well... there's this cute little club in Chelsea where I'm due to sing in about thirty minutes time."

"Sing what?"

"Oh, romantic slush."

"Sounds perfect – let's go!"

And she dragged him not quite screaming from the bar.

*

Mungo spent two days with Margot in Cannes plotting the French wedding. He was also quietly plotting his own survival strategy. It was now plainly obvious that his flirty little minx was after his money and was possibly planning to bump him off during the skydive. It looked like Sami the Algerian waiter was in on the scam, and even her lover, when Mungo was out of town. To think the chubby charmer had agreed to have him as his best man. He'd walked right into that one. So. He had several choices. He could quietly sell off his attic apartment in that old farmhouse overlooking the Med and never step foot on French soil again, hence avoiding the whole melodrama. Or fight back in his own quiet way, which might be more fun. But now he had more pressing business. He'd just landed at Schiphol Airport and was cabbing across to Amsterdam.

It was just one night before heading home to London.

He'd called the gorgeous but very married Putri several times from L.A. on Burner No.5 and made a date with her that very night in his canalside boutique hotel.

He'd been avoiding husband Wim who'd been calling him constantly over recent weeks trying to get him invest in his rather dull Dutch projects. Mungo thought the only investment this very eve was going to be in wooing his sultry partner. The princess from Bali... he couldn't wait to see that sweet Asian smile again.

At precisely eight p.m there was a gently knock on his door.

Mungo had ordered in a platter of seafood and a bottle of champagne.

He had dressed in a casual white linen suit which he hoped he would not be wearing for too long.

He opened the door and there she was.

His angel delight.

Putri's face lit up when she saw him. She was clad in silk, a gentle teasing pink outfit that flowed from her tiny shoulders and pert breasts to her painted toenails.

"My darling", soothed the chubby charmer as he took her in his arms.

They kissed a long moment then gently closed the door.

"Hello Mungo," whispered Putri.

"It's wonderful to see you again."

He broke away from her and poured two glasses of bubbly.

"Do we have long?" asked Mungo.

"I'm at a book club with my girlfriends," replied Putri, a little nervously.

"And what are you reading?"

"That old Dickens classic. 'A Tale Of Two Cities'."

"Ah. 'It was the best of times, it was the worst of times, it was the age of wisdom, it was the age of foolishness…'" quoted Mungo.

"Exactly."

"And how is our Wim?"

"Oh… Still a bully… still wanting to do business with you… and take your money."

"I've been avoiding his calls."

"So he tells me."

They sat on the large double bed and ate mussels and prawns.

"Do you love him?"

She shrugged.

"We've been together for three years but it seems a lifetime. He can be kind.

He can be… cruel."

"Do you want to leave him my darling?"

She sighed. "I don't know… I really don't know…" She suddenly looked Mungo eye to eye. "I never asked… Are you married my sweet?"

The chubby charmer put aside his plate and ran his fingers through Putri's hair.

"Am I married?" he repeated softly.

"Of course he is!" snapped a third voice.

And there in the doorway stood Wim, all smiles, taking endless shots of the two together on the bed.

Putri dropped her glass in shock and Mungo leapt to his feet.

"Wim!"

The Dutchman entered and closed the door behind him.

"My darling Putri, this man has just got married in California to his new wife Janie. We spoke on the phone just an hour ago… She sounds very cute."

"What?" gasped Mungo.

"I told her how we'd met at the Cannes TV market – which we did – and how you were wanting to invest a million dollars in my projects."

"A million!?"

"That's just the start Mungo… I think you and I have a very long business partnership going, which, looking into the future, could go on for years and years."

Mungo slumped back on the bed.

"You're blackmailing me," he sighed.

"Not at all old chap. I can see that you like my wife Putri, and I like your money… I can't wait to call Janie back and tell her that you are part of my darling's book club."

"OK, OK… I'm sorry for flirting with your wife… she's very beautiful… but you know I can't give you a million."

Wim smiled and dialled his phone.

"What are you doing?" yelled Mungo.

"Calling your wife… as your partner she might agree to transfer the cash immediately, once she knows you've been kissing Putri in your hotel bedroom."

"Give me some time Wim. Give me some time…"

Wim put his phone away and grabbed Putri's arm.

"We'll talk again in the morning... A good night's sleep might make you see sense... and give my love to Janie!"

The door slammed and the two were gone, leaving Mungo looking

gobsmacked. In just one phone call this Dutchman could bring his Californian empire, dreams, and marriage, to a very brief and bloody end.

He took out his phone and called The Blind Beggar pub in the East End.

"Is that Cheryl's Dad? Eddie. It's Mungo Swift. I was the clean skin you met a few weeks back. The shooter - yeah... Listen. I'm in Amsterdam and need your help mate."

*

"It's barbaric!" hissed Abigail as she read The Telegraph. "This lovely Iranian girl refused to wear the hijab so they gave her 74 lashes!"

"Sounds like a medieval torture chamber," added Hanny.

Abi read aloud: "'Ever since their 1979 Islamic Revolution, women are required by law to cover their neck and head'... and that's what happens."

"But not the men."

"Oh no, the men in Iran treat women like slaves, and get away with it."

"Did she live?" asked Hanny.

Abi nodded. "Long enough to board a plane for London. She landed this morning and hopes to get a job as a journalist... wants to publicise how badly women are treated back home."

"Ah. So with Soraya and Darius in town that means there'll be a large target on her back."

"Precisely. I'm told she's staying with an aunt in Hackney till she gets a place of her own… Sir Geoffrey gave me the heads up."

"So?"

"So I think we should do some collecting for charity, door to door, if you know what I mean dear… before those two assassins get there first."

"Now?"

"Why not. Let's seize the moment…"

An hour later the two oldies in warm coats and woolly hats were knocking on front doors in a small cul-de-sac in Hackney.

At the first house a male pensioner opened the door, took one look at their collection box, and slammed the door in their faces.

At the second, a young mother cradling a baby came to the door looking exhausted, said she was too busy, and smiled them off.

But at the third, a woman in her fifties answered and asked what they wanted.

Obviously a foreigner. Abi explained they were collecting for Battersea Dogs and

Cats Home. The lady did not quite understand why animals needed money.

"Can I help?" said the young girl who approached from behind her aunt. Her English was perfect. She was attractive, about 25, with olive skin, and dark hair tied back in a red ribbon.

Abi recognised her instantly from the newspaper – the girl who'd been given the 74 lashes in Teheran.

"I think I saw you in the papers," she said. "I feel for you."

"Thank you."

"She no talk," said the aunt, pushing Abi and Hanny away.

"No no... I am happy to talk... come in and have some tea, please."

The two wrinkly spies followed the Persians inside and collapsed on a dusty sofa beside a bad-tempered smelly cat.

"My name is Ava... this my aunt Nasrin.. and the cat is Ayatollah. He is always angry and very spiteful."

"Abi and Hanny. We're old friends... do a bit of charity work to keep us sane."

"Already I like your country. So free and easy. So safe, compared to mine."

"Ah, but be careful my dear," said Abi. "Like everywhere we have bad people too... even some of yours."

Ava nodded. "I've been warned. Next week I start work with a small Farsi podcast where I will tell the world the truth about Iran... what they are doing to our girls and boys... what they will do when they get the big bomb."

"You know about this?"

"I have an engineer friend who has many secrets – how they are making the nuclear device in the desert. He is very brave and would die if he is caught talking."

"Ava. You do not know us. You must be very careful who you talk to...even in London," said Hanny.

"She's right. We have friends in the media... it can be very dangerous if you open your mouth at the wrong time my dear," added Abi.

"Were you allowed to work when you were young?" asked Ava.

"Allowed? Of course – everyone here can work if they want. We were both teachers... we still do some writing for magazines, you know."

"So you are both writers. Then we shall meet again... You must show me the best places to eat and drink and laugh... You are allowed to laugh here?"

Abi nodded with a smile.

"I am joking," said Ava.

Her aunt handed out cups of tea.

"Ah. Cinnamon tea – I've not had this for many years... Not since I was younger and travelled," said Abi. Thinking it was in her spying days in Turkey and Iran that she enjoyed such Eastern delicacies.

A silver framed photo on a bookcase caught Abi's attention.

A handsome dark young man, obviously taken about ten years earlier.

She recognised him and nearly spilt her tea.

It was the Iranian killer they were targeting.

Darius.

"Who's that good-looking man?" she asked innocently.

"Ah – that's my cousin, Darius. I'm hoping to meet him sometime when he pops over from Tehran."

"Well it's good to have family around you my dear." said Abi. "Makes it a home from home."

She gulped down the tea and motioned to Hanny to hurry up.

Abi's mind was racing. Either this girl Ava was a red herring placed by the Iranians to distract and mislead the U.K. security forces... The whole lashes story could have been a fake... If so, then they had been very successful already and the two veteran agents had walked straight into the spider's web. Or. This was simply a very naïve girl with a cousin who was an assassin and didn't know it.

"We must meet again," said Ava, as she saw her guests to

the door.

"That would be nice," smiled Abi.

"Here's my number, and a fiver."

"What for?" asked Hanny.

"The dogs and cats – you were collecting."

"Thank you my dear," said Abi, taking the cash. "We'll phone you and go somewhere exciting for lunch."

"I'd like that," said Ava, waving as she closed the door.

"Well," sighed Abi, as they walked away.

"Well indeed."

"Either we've revealed ourselves to Tehran as two over-eager dotty old spies who overplayed their hand… or have simply connected with a sweet idealistic girl whose cousin is a monster unbeknown to her."

"Time will tell dear, time will tell," muttered Hanny. "Now. Shall we go and get a proper drink?"

"I think we deserve it," sighed Abi deeply.

*

Mungo sat fidgeting at an outside table of The Black Cat coffee shop beside the Keizersgracht canal. The smell of weed drifting from inside was enough to make him float away in a warm fluffy dream. But he had more pressing matters to worry about.

His plane to Heathrow was taking off in three hours, and, more importantly, Wim had called him at midnight to arrange an urgent business meeting there over breakfast. But he was late.

The chubby charmer had already sunk two mugs of strong black coffee to keep him awake. He'd been up all night, not slept a wink. Well, how could he, when this arsehole was threatening to wreck his marriage to Janie unless he got paid a million. Mungo had panicked and called the East End publican who he knew was involved in dodgy dealings. The kind of stuff that could solve problems very easily at not too much cost. He'd told the guy he wanted Wim 'closed down', and got a promise this would happen within 24 hours. For five grand.

Then, sometime around four in the morning, Mungo had second thoughts.

OK, he'd done some very silly things in his life, not least having five ladies on the go at once, each on the end of a burner phone, two or three of them married to him or about to be…but never, never had he deliberately killed… put out a hit on someone. That would seriously cross the red line.

Just before dawn he'd called the geezer at The Blind Beggar back to cancel the contract. He was furious – sure he'd got the cash transfer – but once you agreed a deal like that there was no going back. And he'd hung up. So Mungo was left wondering whether he could stop the killing himself by warning off Wim.

He'd gone walking around the canals, trying to straighten it out in his head.

Trying to avoid the late night drunks coming home from the clubs, or the druggies wanting to mug him but too stoned to stand. Weighing up the pros and cons… pay the guy the million and he'd just come after more… top him and end up in jail for the rest of his life.

The sun had come up over those tall narrow teetering Dutch houses beside the bridges and the waterways… the rush hour had kicked off around seven when young and old had started flooding the streets on their bicycles, like some weird silent slow motion wheelie marathon… girls in big straw hats, guys in yellow or green or red jackets... a kaleidoscope of colour... all smiles and grace and elegant calm.

Except Mungo sitting at that table on the stone cobbles, sipping his third mug of coffee, tapping his feet, and glancing again at his watch. Anything but calm.

Wim was nearly an hour late.

There was still time to call him and warn him. He'd kept putting it off for hours. Still not sure what to do.

When the phone rang.

Putri popped up on Mungo's screen.

In tears with a very black eye.

"Mungo," she sobbed.

"What... what's happened Putri – did he beat you?"

"He's gone."

"What?"

"He left here an hour ago on his bike to meet you... Then I got the call."

"What call?"

"The police. An accident. This van knocked him into the canal..."

"A hit and run?"

She nodded slowly. "When they got him out... he's dead Mungo... my darling Wim is dead... I don't know what to do... help me please."

*

Duffy and Kate sat in an unmarked police car across the street from where Rachel Storm lived. Kate's team had tracked her to a quiet Victorian cottage in Richmond.

Very classy, with period windows and a lush hanging basket outside the bright red door.

"She's done well for herself," muttered Duffy.

"Probably got a big bonus from selling the babes."

"She can't have any morals doing that… stealing little kids from refugees then make a massive profit from saddo couples who can't have their own."

Kate sighed. "Takes all sorts Duffy."

"You OK Kate?" asked the singing detective.

"What?"

"You been through a load of shit this week… your brother Max goes manic with a chainsaw and gets shot… then you rescue me from getting scorched in that bloody crematorium!"

"Can't say it's been fun… but least you're still around."

"I remember that morn when I woke up in your bed after flying in from Paris and you had no idea who I was!" said Duffy.

"Yeah… could have been the milkman, postman, and I landed a bloody private dick!"

"Hang on," said Duffy, peering across at Rachel's front door. "Bit of action."

Rachel, in a black satin dressing gown, had come out to see off a guest.

"Looks like she has a boyfriend," whispered Kate.

The guy looked about sixty, quite classy, in chinos and a cashmere jacket.

Looked like he should have worn a cravat.

"Bingo…" breathed Kate.

"What?"

"This could be the moneybags behind the baby scam… the 'mister big' we're looking for."

"Or just her weekly bonk."

"No Duffy… something tells me this could be the guy… he reeks money, importance, corruption."

Duffy took a photo of the man on his phone.

"I feel like I know him."

"Really? Who?"

"Dunno. Back of my mind I can see him somewhere… probably wrong."

"Let's see where he goes."

And Kate pulled out behind the guy's Mercedes and followed at a subtle distance.

An hour later they were still tailing him.

"Probably lives in France," joked Duffy.

They had just driven south of Guildford when the lover pulled down a long country drive.

"I… I've been here before," gasped Duffy.

"So?"

"I did a singing gig… a wedding… weeks back."

Ahead of them loomed a vast Georgian pile.

"And?" asked Kate.

"Shit!"

"What?"

"I know who it is…"

"Yes Duffy?"

"He was ex-Army… doing charity stuff."

"Who?"

"He's married… To Blanche."

"So?"

"Patrick."

"Patrick?"

"Patrick… It's Izzy's Dad!"

CHAPTER SIXTEEN

When Mungo received that fateful call from Putri saying that Wim had been knocked into the canal and was dead, everything went numb. He had just taken someone's life.

Swotted them aside like an irritating fly. Pulled the trigger and shot him between the eyes. Whatever. If he hadn't phoned the dodgy geezer at The Blind Beggar pub, Wim would still have been breathing, still have been able to blackmail him for a million and wreck his marriage to Janie. On second thoughts he told himself, he did the right thing. If only he'd kept away from the married Putri this would never have happened.

He'd consoled her over the phone, checked he could still catch his flight to London, and promised to see her when he was next in Europe. Well, he'd do a rain check on that when he worked out if he could happily handle that Burner No.5 assignation or not. For once in his life the chubby charmer was thinking perhaps he was juggling too many ladies in his life... tempting too much trouble. At his age perhaps having three loves was more than enough... Monica, his long-suffering mother of three in Harrow, Janie, the newly-wed bride in L.A., and Margot, the soon-to-be-married minx in Cannes...

As his plane circled over the Houses of Parliament and Big Ben and the dirty old Thames, Mungo felt a pang in his gut. Home James... this was the one place he really felt at home in all the world. He'd received a text from Monica saying there was a steak and kidney pie warming in the oven and a nice bottle of red… Manna from Heaven, he thought… manna from Heaven.

Once through Customs he made his way straight to the Solar Global offices in Pinner, gave Sheila the receptionist a bunch of tulips from Holland, and interrupted Charlie watching a horse race from Salisbury.

He leapt to his feet and gave Mungo the usual grizzly bear hug.

"My hero returns! Wonderful to have you back old bean," he roared. He went to the fridge and plucked out a bottle of champagne.

"Wonderful to be home old buddy," cooed Mungo. "We celebrating?" he said, smiling at the fizz.

"We are indeed, the first cheque has been banked from Messrs Sun and Yi… and the first batch of their wind turbine blades arrived yesterday!"

Charlie poured two glasses and they clinked them together.

"That is very good news," said Mungo.

"Certainly is… they're going to bring in more cash than the bloody solar panels."

"Just shows, you never know what's round the corner… If I hadn't popped into Brett's office in L.A. that day."

"We'd both be a way lot poorer!"

"And all going smoothly – with the blades?"

"Absolutely – no problem – but they are so bloody long… come out and see."

And Charlie led his partner outside to the long hangar that was housing the blades.

As they went to open the door, two Asians in khaki security uniforms blocked their way.

"What the?" cried Mungo. "I did warn you – their security – the Chinese insisted - but they know me now

234

- I bring them burgers at lunchtime."

He nodded to the burly duo who nodded and stood aside.

"Cheeky buggers," muttered Mungo.

There, stretching from one end of the hangar to the other, lay about ten blades.

"Jeez," said Mungo. "You said they were long…"

"About 50 yards long… need two or three lorries to carry them."

Mungo was impressed, shaking his head.

"I'm staggered… These Chinese are really onto something… this Charlie, this Charlie, is the future…"

He stroked one of the long shiny white blades. Then tapped it.

"Sounds like they're hollow… made of fibreglass."

"Yeah – they make them light as can be… carbon fibre and balsa wood."

"So what's the turnover?" asked Mungo.

"They plan to move these blades in a few weeks – erecting them somewhere in Suffolk… then get a much bigger load in next month."

"No wonder they're taking over the world, the Chinese…" said Mungo.

"When they want to do something… they do it. For us, like HS2, takes bloody years!"

"Come, let's open another bottle…" said Charlie, heading back to the office.

"Not today my friend… got to get home and sample some real food with Monica… steak and kidney pie… my stomach's going crazy after all that Californian bloody lettuce!"

He high-fived Charlie and headed for Harrow.

She was there waiting for him in the doorway.

Hair neatly done, nice simple makeup, a clean pinny, and

a wide smile.

You are the genuine article my dear, thought Mungo. None of your Beverly Hills vacuity, that all-American schmaltz, that desperate fake wokery…

"Hi honey, I'm home," toned the chubby charmer in a mock L.A. accent.

"Shut up and come here," said Monica, giving him a long wet kiss.

Mungo followed her inside.

"Where is everyone?"

"The boys are at games and Donna's working at the café."

"So, mummy and daddy are alone at last?"

"Now that daddy, the 'so very hush hush' spy, is back from his wanderings."

"I think it's time we both went… undercover," whispered Mungo.

And dragged his English wife slowly upstairs to the main bedroom.

*

"Crying over you
　　Crying over you
　　Yes, now you're gone
　　And from this moment on
　　I'll be crying, crying, crying, crying,
　　Crying, crying, over you…"

Duffy signed off gently to Roy Orbison's classic, midst whoops of applause in that dingy basement club off the King's Road.

"Nearly had me in tears." said Izzy, rocking baby Byron

to and fro in her arms. "As for him, you sent him to sleep."

Duffy smiled at his tall blonde goddess. Still thought she was stunning. She made him laugh. They could almost be a couple with a baby... as several in the club had thought earlier... Careful he thought. Now you're getting broody.

He sighed inwardly. He had a lot to tell Izzy.

Or not to tell Izzy.

He could reveal they had closed down the baby scam network. The hospice oldies where the kids were kept, and the dreaded Psycho who was now safely locked away. The cops were yet to arrest the posho Rachel Storm who could do a flit once she found the game was up.

And he could reveal that Kate and he had followed Rachel's apparent lover from her home to a mansion near Guildford... who might also be the kingpin behind the whole racket and that he was... her father!

Or perhaps they got it wrong.

Perhaps Patrick, her father, was simply Rachel's rich uncle, or an old boss dropping by... or anything.

Either way Duffy had to say something.

Bravery was not always one of his best qualities.

But it was not just that.

To arrest Patrick the Dad, the cops needed proof that he actually was running the scam.

Better to tiptoe around the subject, for the moment.

But then he had had a cunning plan. Or so he thought. A master plan.

"Shouldn't we get going?" he asked Izzy.

She looked at her watch.

"Shit. If we're late for Mum's dins she'll go nuclear!"

"Let's hit the road then," said Duffy and carried Byron to her car.

One hour later they were driving up that same country lane that he and Kate had visited the night before when tailing her Dad Patrick, back from Rachel's place.

Was it a love nest or not? They'd soon find out. As they entered the huge oak door to that Georgian pile somewhere south of Guildford.

Duffy had arranged that dead on midnight Kate and her team would do a very silent raid on the house and take Daddy away for questioning. It was Duffy's job to somehow get him alone from the others so they wouldn't know what was happening until it was over.

He was welcomed with open arms by the charmingly flamboyant mother Blanche and given a firm handshake by the debonaire Patrick.

The parents seemingly had already fallen for young Byron with each taking turns to walk him round their drawing room, singing bawdy rugby songs.

Dinner was pheasant shot on the estate, washed down with an Italian Barolo.

"So how's business Duffy, or are you too busy singing?" asked Patrick.

"Ha. It's juggling that work/lifestyle balance you read about... very tricksy."

"But you're solving the baby racket... that's taking up your time," said Izzy.

"Oh yes... we're still trying to close that down... find the Mister Big behind it."

"Any clues?" asked Blanche with a twinkle.

Duffy nodded, avoiding eye contact with Patrick. "Clues aplenty, but not enough evidence... so far."

Byron started crying.

Izzy went to his cot and carried him to the stairs.

"I'm putting him to bed."

Duffy stood.

"And I must go."

"No no," said Blanche. "You're staying the night – and that's final."

As she took a phone call and disappeared into the kitchen, suddenly looking anxious.

Duffy shrugged. "Most kind."

With Izzy away with the baby and Blanche in the kitchen, he whispered to Patrick. "I need a quick word with you… on your own."

"Of course dear boy. Come into the study and we'll have brandy and a cigar.

Never disturbed in there."

Duffy peeked at his watch. Quarter to twelve. Minutes away from the police raid.

The study was very stylish period, with oil paintings, leather chairs, and a very long oak table.

True to his word, Patrick handed Duffy a cigar and glass of brandy.

"Now?" he asked.

"You asked about work. That baby racket. Got nearly everyone… but think there might be someone still out there… in charge."

"The Mister Big?"

Duffy nodded then looked hard at Izzy's father. He knew he was about to drop a bomb. A big one.

"We followed you last night," he said softly.

"You what!? Followed me?"

"From Rachel Storm's place. It doesn't look good. Any minute now the cops are coming to question you Patrick."

"What!?"

"I wanted you to hear it first... to give you a chance mate... to explain."

"I'm sorry! The police are coming here... to question me?"

"We saw you..."

Patrick sighed deeply, then smiled.

"You saw me... with Rachel?"

Duffy nodded, checking his watch again.

"Damn. OK. What can I say... I was with Rachel Storm for a short visit yesterday. You see, since Izzy met that baby – your little Byron – she's a changed girl. I wanted to meet the woman doing these ghastly deals and make sure Izzy could keep him... for herself."

"Meaning?"

"I paid the woman cash so we could have him. No questions asked. But now... but now, now you've got in the bloody way."

"So she's been paid twice!" snapped Duffy.

"I don't care. I want my Izzy to be happy. This Duffy is the happiest I have even seen her. It's bliss... for me and Blanche. She knew I was visiting Rachel Storm... We did it for our Izzy. I'm sorry if we led you astray... We did it for the family... The family, Duffy. Do you understand?"

Patrick now looked furious.

"Really?"

"Really my boy. For Pete's sake!" he spat.

It was five minutes to midnight.

Duffy thought hard, looked at Patrick's rigid expression, then called Kate.

"Sorry... Abort Kate, abort. We got it all wrong..."

Just then the detective smelled smoke and looked out the study window into their walled back garden.

Blanche was out there in the dark, burning wads of paper on a bonfire.

"What's she doing?" he asked Patrick.

He stared into the dark and shrugged with a smile.

"Blanche? She loves her bonfire – says it's primal."

"Primal? At this time of night?"

"At any time…"

Duffy tried to read Patrick, who again flashed his teeth.

Then looked at those roaring flames outside.

*

A prerequisite to be a successful spy in today's cut-throat world was not just keeping your mind as sharp as a tack but ensuring your physique could deal with every eventuality wherever and whenever. Which is why Abigail and Hanny were listening to the songs from "South Pacific" as well as trying to balance on one leg for their weekly Pilates class in South Kensington.

Abigail, for her years, stood rigidly to attention on her left limb while the right stuck out behind her like a boat's rudder.

Hanny, on the other hand, was very gently swaying in the breeze to "Bali Ha'i", summoning all her fading muscles to keep her erect on the mat and not topple over. And would have triumphed had the phone not rung.

Its sudden chirp sent her sprawling to the ground as Esther, their trainer, cried:

"No phones in class!"

Abi waved her hand in the air as an apology and quietly answered.

"Ello love… thought I'd let you know. Some foreign geezer's asked my lads to track down a TV presenter, find out where they live… take photos. Might make a good story for you writers?"

It was Eddie, the publican from The Blind Beggar.

"Where they from, your geezer?"

"Middle East, reckon."

Half an hour later the two elderly gymnasts were downing pints of cider with dodgy Eddie in his East End boozer.

"This is who they're looking for… said he was a long lost cousin from Turkey… who might be working in telly here… Hassan Bijan."

Eddie showed the ladies a photo on his phone of a young man in his twenties, quite good looking, and certainly Middle Eastern.

"And if you find him?" asked Abi.

"Ten grand and give them the address. Said they wanted to surprise him… for the family back home like."

"I bet they do," smiled Hanny.

"Eddie. This is really interesting. And thanks for calling us. It could make great copy for us."

"What I thought," said Eddie.

"So. Start at the beginning. Who said what to whom?"

"Eh?"

"Tell us about the Middle Eastern geezer your mates met, love," added Hanny.

"Ah. Well, we have this gambling syndicate, about ten of us. Anyone's in trouble, we look after you, watch your back, know what I mean?"

Abi looked at Hanny knowingly and nodded patiently.

"Roddy was approached in his pub down the road by this guy. Real smooth.

Bit of a looker. Bit 'oily', he said. Anyway, went on about a missing relative and if he knew anyone who could help find him. Roddy tells me so we're all in it. Easy money if we can find him."

"How does it work?" asked Abi, gesturing Cheryl for more drinks all round.

"OK. Guess you could call us a gang... Well. Me and the lads got together and have put that photo round every pub we know... We'll split the finder fee if we have to, but right now, if that guy's in town, then we'll get him, always do...

Someone'll see that picture and remember him from the corner shop, down the market, at the movies... then we close in... follow him... and give his home address to the smoothie guy."

"You don't speak to him?"

"Na. That gets complicated and then there's no surprise. Smoothie chops made it clear he wanted the surprise element... for the folks back home, he said."

"I bet," said Hanny.

"And how do you contact Mister Smoothie Chops?" asked Abi.

Eddie patted his jacket pocket.

"Got a number love."

"Name?" asked Hanny.

"Something like Bert, but reckon it wasn't real."

"Could we see that number Eddie?" asked Abi.

The publican hesitated. "Sorry love. This is business. Ours. Just thought you could sort of tag along and get the story. Not be part of it."

"Totally understand Eddie."

"Anyways," he said standing. "Got to race off but will let you know what happens."

"Just one favour?"

"Yer love?"

"Could you let us know when you find him…before you tell the smoothie… we won't queer your pitch… promise."

Eddie looked at the two old dears. They were no threat to anyone.

"Course I will, you're my mates now!"

And he walked off behind the bar.

"I have him," whispered Hanny in Abi's ear.

"What?"

She thrust her phone in her friend's face. A picture of an olive-skinned young man.

"Hassan Bijan. He was a reporter at the Farsi TV station here that's always hitting on Iran."

"Ah…"

"Their embassy's been trying to close them down for months… always banging on about Tehran's human rights or lack of."

"Of course – he had death threats then disappeared."

"Which means he's hiding from the Iran bad guys, who're using useful idiots like this gang to flush him out," said Abi. "Just as we predicted."

"And no guessing who the illustrious smoothie guy must be, behind this surprise man hunt."

Abi nodded. "It just has to be my old friend, Darius."

*

For the first time in months Mungo felt totally relaxed. His whole life had been on fast forward for too long now and he just needed a moment or three on his own, to relax, to wind down, to enjoy his existence.

He'd had a hearty breakfast with Monica and the kids then driven up to Hampstead Heath where he sat on a bench overlooking the London skyline – the best view in town.

In the newspaper he'd read the idiot politicians were planning to fast track covering the country with the wretched ugly bird-massacring wind farms, which meant he and Charlie would be raking it in for years to come, thanks to those bloody Chinese. So financially he was on a roll. Not to mention the riches he'd gained from marrying Janie across the pond. Funny old world. One minute you're a dreary old git slumming around trying to sell solar panels that only hippies and middle-class eco- nutters wanted ; the next you're swimming in money. Bless.

But then you were also a murderer. Though only a few bods on the planet knew that – Eddie from the Blind Beggar who helped solve his problem in Holland, plus the guys who actually ran Wim off the road into the canal. That decision would never ever leave Mungo. But. It was that or have his life with Janie ruined. It had to be the right choice. Even if he still regretted it. He wasn't all bad. In fact in Mungo's head, he wasn't bad at all.

"Mind if I sit down?" asked a gloomy male voice beside him.

He was middle-aged, unshaven, and smelt of booze.

"Sure," said Mungo, hiding himself in his newspaper. His peaceful solitude had gone, wrecked by this plonker.

The stranger sat on the bench beside the chubby charmer.

"Come here every day. For the view."

"Very special," said Mungo, now thinking of moving on, quickly.

"Today'll be the last," said the guy.

"Uh huh," nodded Mungo, not interested and beginning to roll up his paper.

"Going to top myself."

Mungo froze. "You what?"

"Today I'm going to die."

"You sick?"

"No – sick of living."

"You can't do that – kill yourself," said Mungo.

The man shrugged.

"Nothing to live for."

"You got this view for a start," said Mungo.

"All I got."

"There must be someone…"

"Just me. And an ex-wife."

"Some friend?"

"The bottle…" The guy turned to Mungo. "Before I die, got any spare cash… for a final drink?"

Mungo looked closely at him. Was this all a con to get money for the next drink? He decided to ignore the plea.

"How will you kill yourself?"

"Not sure. Spur of the moment. Walk under a bus. Jump off a building. No planning. Just do it. No regrets."

This guy didn't seem like an alkie thought Mungo, despite needing a shave and the stink of cheap wine. Something cerebral about him.

"You got a job?"

The man paused a very long moment. "Dr Death."

"What?"

"Doctor. I was a bloody doctor."

"But that's great, you've spent your life saving others… bringing joy to strangers."

"Yeah… But sometimes they die and it's your fault."

"That's tragic, but guess we all make mistakes."

"That's murder, if you kill someone."

"You can't blame yourself… every day we take risks… we have to, otherwise we'd be wrapped in cotton wool and do nothing."

"I cut the wrong vein and a youngster died on my watch. I saw those parents in tears, wrecked their bloody lives for ever… all my fault."

"You can't carry the blame… they'd understand… shit does happen."

"So I resigned, and now my life's over."

They both sat staring into the middle distance, outwardly calm but both minds racing.

"I killed someone this week," said Mungo quietly.

"You what?"

"Ended someone's life. Got them… terminated."

"Shit. Why?"

Mungo breathed deeply and turned to the guy.

"I was seeing his wife and he threatened to blackmail me."

"So you topped him?"

Mungo nodded silently.

"What did the wife say?"

"She thinks it was a road accident… and now misses him. It was all a bloody mistake."

"Why tell me this?"

"That's the point… I'm carrying guilt too. Only I'm the real killer, not you. I made the choice to end a life – paid money for it – but you were doing your job when an accident happened."

They both stared at the view again.

The doctor sighed.

"Putting it like that… perhaps it's you should top himself."

"Oh, there's much worse going on in my life, I can tell you…"

"I'll never forget that poor kid's face…"

Mungo gave the guy's knee a comforting pat.

"Look chum… This country needs doctors – go get your job back… you're very special. One of a kind. Believe me…"

"You really mean that?"

"Course I bloody do. I'm the killer; you're the life saver…"

The stranger looked silently at the stunning London skyline, at the kids playing ball, listened to the blue tits singing from a nearby beech, then stood and held out his hand to Mungo.

"Thanks," he said with a smile. "You've made me think twice. Guess there's always someone worse off… carrying a bigger burden… it's you who needs a strong drink, fella… Go well."

"Not wanting that cash?"

The guy smiled, shook his head, and walked away across the heath, a spring in his step.

Mungo stared after him, wondering if he should confess to the murder, when his phone rang. It was Monica, telling him they were having his favourite venison sausage stew that night and she was serving at six so don't be late.

That call snapped him out of the self pity and reminded him that already that day he'd saved a stranger's life.

He sat for another hour soaking in the panoramic view, then made sure he returned to Harrow-on-the-Hill just before six as instructed. He loved those very English, very patriotic, street names… Nelson Road, Trafalgar Terrace. Expect they'd be changed soon.

As he opened the front door, he could hear laughter from the dining room.

He entered, saw Monica, the kids, and his world suddenly came crashing down around him.

For there, sitting at the head of the table, holding hands with daughter Donna, was someone he never wanted to see again… his young Kiwi step-son Noah, whose million dollar inheritance he'd stolen for himself.

CHAPTER SEVENTEEN

"Mungo darling – meet Donna's new friend - all the way from New Zealand – Noah!"

The chubby charmer froze like that rabbit in the headlights, or was it a snake?

Noah stood politely with a big grin and held out his hand.

"I've heard so much about you… sir."

Mungo cleared his throat, and shook the lad's hand.

"Noah. What a lovely surprise."

"Thought it time you two met Dad – I just know you're going to get on!" laughed Donna.

Mungo sat carefully beside Monica, not taking his eyes off his step-son. He wondered if Noah had told them anything. About his deceased wife in Auckland, about him nicking that million dollars. The next few minutes would tell. And could wreck his whole family life in the U.K.

"I hear you travel a lot Mungo… you been to New Zealand?" asked Noah innocently.

So. You're playing games, for the moment, thought Mungo.

"I have. On my travels. Auckland mostly. Had a dip at Mission Bay."

"Wow. Just round the corner from where we live?"

"We?" asked Mungo.

"My Mum and I. But, she just died, so on my own now."

"I'm sorry," muttered Mungo through gritted teeth.

"Donna tells me you do undercover stuff… 'hush hush'… that mean you're with the CIA or MI6… or driving a nuclear sub… or what?"

"Ah. As my Monica knows, I can't say too much."

"He's certainly away a lot," added his wife. "Sometimes I think I'm a widow without him."

"And you Noah, what are you doing over here… apart from seeing Donna?" asked Mungo. Two could play games.

"A lot of Kiwis love to track down their rellies back here – they still call the U.K. 'home'… so that's what I'm doing… tracking down a wicked step-father who ran off with the family jewels."

"And… you found him?" asked Mungo carefully.

"You know Mungo…" Noah paused a moment. "I think I have."

"So? What next. How do you get these 'family jewels' back from him?"

"Depends really," answered Noah.

"On what?"

"On how he behaves."

"Meaning?" asked Mungo warily.

"Meaning he can simply hand over the jewels… and that's the end of it."

"Or?" asked Mungo.

"Or, I'll make sure his whole life comes crashing down around him like a pack of cards."

"Mmm…" Mungo was enjoying the venison stew. "Let's hope the rascal sees sense and hands you back the money."

"Who said anything about money – you said 'family jewels' didn't you Noah?" said Monica.

"Same thing really."

"And when will this happen Noah – sounds like two cowboys shooting it out in the Wild West somewhere," laughed Donna.

"Well, I reckon he's got the message babe. He's got 24 hours to transfer the cash he stole from me, or his world is shattered!"

"Sounds like you mean what you say Noah... wouldn't like to be that step-dad of yours right now."

"No. Talk about a rock and a hard place."

"So. Once you done that, you staying in town or going home?" asked Mungo.

"I hope he's staying in town," said Donna." We only just met – don't want to lose him yet!"

"Not made my mind up yet."

Mungo felt something throbbing in his left pocket. Must have been a text from California or Cannes or Amsterdam.

He excused himself and went upstairs to the bog.

It was a message from Janie in L.A. She was getting very confusing calls from Dakota about her movie script. When the fuck are you coming home honey, she asked.

Mungo promised to be back in 48 hours... little bit of investment stuff going down in London. Plus... wait for it... for a bit of fun he asked if she could book a skydiving course for them both... something he'd be longing to do for years.

Next he contacted his bank. And transferred that million dollars he'd taken from Noah over to his step-son's Kiwi account. It hurt, but not so much as the boy revealing he'd been married to his Mum in Auckland for several years.

When Mungo entered the dining room everyone was laughing.

"What have I missed?" he asked.

"Noah just got a message..." smiled Donna.

"There is a Santa after all," smiled the Kiwi.

"Eh?" asked Mungo.

"My wicked stepdad just transferred back the family

jewels!"

Mungo sat and smiled.

"I'm pleased for you Noah... expect now you've got what you came for, you'll be heading back home Down Under?"

"You know what Mungo. I'm beginning to like it here... with you away so often doing your 'hush hush' stuff, perhaps I should step in and keep an eye on these guys?"

The chubby charmer and his stepson stared at each other with fixed grins.

"When you going away again Dad?" asked young Sam.

"And for how long?" added son Riley.

"Yes Mungo – what next?" asked Monica.

"I feel I'm being attacked here gang," said Mungo.

"So?" said Donna.

"Tomorrow night. Quick trip to L.A. Help out on a mission, then back soon after."

"Well, when's the cat's away," smiled Noah. "I'm quite happy to stay here a few days... already sitting at the head of the table with my feet under it. Sweet as..."

Mungo could see what the Kiwi shit was doing. Taking over his role as head of the family. Sleeping with his daughter. Flirting with his wife. Being a hero to the kids.

"Perhaps I'll cancel this trip... they can do without me?" he said faintly.

"No you will not dearest. You're one of the good guys out there defending the Western world – a boy's gotta do what a boy's gotta do – isn't that what they say in America?" answered Monica.

Mungo nodded wearily.

He didn't like the way this had turned out in the last hour.

The bloody stepson making him pay back his inheritance. Then realizing how controlling that money made the boy feel. He wasn't shooting home to Auckland as Mungo had hoped. Instead he was getting great satisfaction, and revenge, by suggesting he moved into the Harrow-on-the-Hill home while Mungo was away.

Which meant much of the time… He also worried that Noah might find out about Janie or Margot or Putri, if he hadn't already.

No, Mungo didn't like the way this had turned out in the last hour, one little bit.

"Can I help myself to more of your delish deer stew Monica," said Noah, reaching over and giving himself a generous portion. "And a wee bit more of your lovely wine." As he filled his glass to the brim and ignored his stepdad.

*

"I just called to say I love you
And I mean it from the bottom of my heart…"

Duffy ended Stevie Wonder's greatest, slid off the stage, and joined the Kate and Izzy at the corner table.

It was a girlie night out with about ten hen parties all crushed into the Battersea basement. It gave a whole new meaning to 'shrieking'.

"Lucky you didn't bring baby Byron along… he'd have been up there bawling with the rest of them," he laughed.

"He's being looked after by a friend," said Izzy. "My night off."

Duffy topped up the fizz in their glasses. He felt tonight of all nights he wanted the tongues to loosen so they could talk about stuff they couldn't do while sober.

"Just for once Duffy, reckon you could give up the day job

and do the singing," said Kate.

"Keep drinking babe… keep drinking."

"No, I mean it," she insisted. "Make more money than being a bloody private dick."

"What happened the other night?" asked Izzy suddenly.

"At your place?" said Duffy.

Izzy nodded.

"Had a great nosh with your Mum and Dad. A cigar with Patrick. Then Blanche put me in a guest room."

"And you were gone by dawn."

"Up with the birds, me."

"They were both very quiet over breakfast, fidgety I'd say. Knowing you'd up and gone. Had something happened?" asked Izzy.

Duffy and Kate shared glances.

"Are you ready for this?" asked Kate.

"What?" said Izzy.

"We… thought your Dad might have been involved in the baby scam."

"What!?" cried Izzy. "No bloody way!"

"OK OK," soothed Duffy.

Then explained exactly what had happened.

How they'd seen Patrick exit from Rachel Storm's home, though they didn't realise it was him at the time. They'd followed the mystery lover home… to the family estate. Duffy had then confronted him with this info as Kate was preparing a midnight police raid but Patrick insisted he'd simply been doing a cash deal with Storm to buy the baby and ensure Izzy could keep Byron as he had made her so happy. Duffy said he'd sort of accepted this story and aborted the raid. Then he'd spotted mother Blanche having a bonfire around midnight, burning a load of files… It didn't look good so they were both wondering if the original thinking was true. That Patrick was in fact Storm's lover and the mastermind behind the baby scam.

"You are joking... my Dad?" seethed Izzy again.

"We went into your garden during that night... searched the bonfire," said Kate.

"What? And found?"

"We found part of a hire document for a boat in Greece... receipts for mooring at the Lymington yacht haven... and a very old property invoice relating to purchase of the hospice building," answered Kate. "All a bit charred, but recognisable and could be used as evidence."

"Shit shit shit..." sighed Izzy.

"We needed to run this past you before... before..." stumbled Duffy.

"Before you arrest my bloody parents!" mumbled Izzy.

"Was Patrick your Dad, seeing Rachel Storm romantically?" asked Kate.

Izzy went quiet, very quiet. Stared at her feet, at the ceiling, then Kate.

"I always thought there was someone. He's such a charmer, such a flirt.

There had to be someone tucked away out of sight. Though Mum probably knew about it and simply ignored it. That way they'd stay together... But Rachel Storm... certainly his type."

"But he seems an upstanding guy... that military background... said he was doing charity work," said Duffy.

"He might simply have been bored... away from the action... stop him going mad," added Kate.

"Ah... his Army days... he might have known the SAS nutter, Psycho, from fighting abroad... he'd be a great asset if he was on your side," mused Duffy.

"Dad certainly was sent to all the main theatres in the Middle East... he worked with all sorts... the good and the bad."

"As you do," said Duffy.

"And... I have to admit, when we were kids they took us sailing around the Greek islands... Ios, Santorini, Lesbos... can't remember a summer when we weren't drinking ouzo and eating hummus."

"And so the jigsaw comes together," said Kate softly.

"So. What's next – you really arresting my bloody parents?"

Kate looked at her watch.

"Three hours ago we caught Rachel Storm boarding the Poole ferry to Sàint Malo. She's already saying that she and Patrick have been an item for years and that he was behind the baby business... She seems to worship your Dad."

"Jeez," sighed Izzy.

"And in the last half hour we've taken your parents into custody for questioning."

Kate leant across and squeezed Izzy's arm. "Sorry Izzy..."

The tall blonde choked a moment. "Fuck fuck fuck."

Duffy topped up her glass.

"I think we three should slope off for a quiet curry. What you say?"

"I'm not keeping Byron," muttered Izzy.

"What?"

"After all this, how could I keep that poor little thing."

"Let's decide that later babe," urged Duffy. "This is a shit moment."

Suddenly Dexys Midnight Runners interrupted :

"Come on, Eileen

Come on, Eileen…"

It was Duffy's new ringtone. He answered pronto.

Abigail.

"I've been chasing you for weeks Mister Duffy – been to that ruddy Fortnum bar but you're never there - it's time we met," she chided.

The singing detective looked at the face on his phone. Pensioner. Posh.

Bright. Interesting…

"Sorry love – trifle busy," he replied.

"Do you like gardening?" asked Abi.

"Not much," answered Duffy. "Why?"

"Tomorrow morn at nine. The Palace Gardener in Fulham. They do a first class sourdough toastie in the café. See you there."

And hung up.

Duffy looked across at Kate. No Izzy.

"Where's she gone?"

"Poor girl rushed off. Not every day your Mum and Dad get arrested for selling babies."

"Shit. Fancy that curry?"

Kate silently nodded and followed Duffy to the door.

*

As Duffy parked his Harley at the Fulham garden centre the next morning, he remembered he must chase Kate to get that bloody watch back from Rachel Storm otherwise Zandra his ex-wife would probably have him for theft. Well, not really, but he always tried to keep in her good books in case he needed her again in the future.

And there they were.

Two old biddies waving at him from beside the farm shop, hidden partly by the giant palm trees and the stacks of manure.

They nodded as he approached.

"Don't get up, please," cried Duffy, as he shook their hands with them both.

"Mister Duffy... Abigail – I spoke on the phone."

"And I'm Hanny," said the other.

Duffy couldn't quite work out their relationship. Were they workmates, sisters, or even lovers? The answer soon came.

"It's a long story so we'll make it brief as possible. But first, order your breakfast... the chicken toastie is sublime," suggested Abi.

Duffy did what he was told and sat back to hear the old girl's tale.

"So? How can I help you – burglary... budgie gone missing?"

"Slightly more serious than that Mr Duffy, slightly more serious."

"I'm all ears ladies."

" Well... Normally we wouldn't reveal this ... official secrets and all that... but, as a fellow professional and someone we'd like to work with..."

"Go on," urged Duffy.

"We've known each other for yonks... both started together at GCHQ... then progressed into working for the Government."

"At home and abroad," added Hanny. "MI5 and MI6."

"I'm impressed ladies, most sincerely," said Duffy. And he was. Not often you met two mature female spies, least those who'd admit to it.

"What this is all about, is getting you involved in our latest mission," continued Abi.

"Ah?"

Abi sipped her flat white and crunched into her toastie.

"As we all know, one of the main threats to our security right now is Iran.

They're constantly making mischief in the Middle East, with Israel, the Red Sea, you name it. If there are assassinations or bombings in that arena, then Tehran's fingerprints are all over it.."

"And now the problem has come nearer to home," said Hanny.

A waitress served Duffy his chicken delight which he immediately bit into with gusto.

"Iran is tracking down its enemies on our home soil by using useful idiots, proxies, to do their hunting for them, then, once found, they themselves close in for the kill."

"Clever," said Duffy.

"And the two main groups they're using..." said Hanny. "Wait for it..."

"Are criminal gangs... and... private detectives," smiled Abi.

"For real?" asked Duffy.

Hanny nodded. "For certain. Which is why..."

Abi added. "We came to you."

"So. Already two of their top agents – we'll call them Soraya and Darius – have entered the U.K."

"Shit."

"They've contacted a gang working out of an East End pub, paying them to track down a distant relative, as a 'surprise'... though the target is in fact an anti-Iran activist they want to terminate," said Abi.

"We're in touch with the gang who are going to alert us

259

the moment they find this chappie - they think we're writers – and we hope to get to him before the Iran agents."

"Jeez," breathed Duffy. "So where do I come in?"

"We want to try hook them in through you too... as a private detective... hoping they'll get in touch, asking you to find another of their targets like they've done with the gang..." said Abi. "Get you to give them the victim's address, then soon after, an 'accident' will happen."

"Bloody hell," breathed Duffy.

"Don't worry, we'll be right there at your side... waiting to pounce."

"You'll be the bait that draws them in," smiled Hanny.

"So we suggest we feature you in the press... place some publicity blurb about you in the dailies, that should get them running to use you."

"Like bees to honey my dear," added Hanny.

"We want to catch them in the act."

"Or just catch them."

"And how dangerous are they, your Soraya and Darius?" asked Duffy.

"Oh, lethal, dear Duffy," smiled Abi. "Our two bad actors are the best of the best... the finest Iran has in the field... a trail of bodies from Washington to Rome.

But never been caught."

"Have you ever killed?" asked Hanny sweetly.

Duffy stopped munching his toastie.

"Caught a mouse this morning... but not really. Only in self defence. When it was him or me, know what I mean."

"My last time was on a window sill in Belgrade – he was garrotting me and about to push me off when I took a nail file and rammed it where the sun don't shine. Did the trick," shrugged Abi.

"I was dozing in the bath when he came through the window with a monkey wrench – took one look at my face covered in blue cream – and fell backwards down his ladder, poor boy," said Hanny.

"Suppose if you're in a corner... you do what you have to."

"So. Mr Duffy, are you happy to be involved with us in our little game of cat and mouse?"

"Try stop me ladies... definitely up for it," said the singing detective.

"Splendid," replied Abi. "We'll get you featured in a few newspapers and hopefully you'll get a call from our Iranian friends."

She handed Duffy her contact card.

"Let me know when you hear anything."

Abi's phone rang.

She listened a moment.

"Perfect Derek. Come straight in. Usual table. We've a friend with us, but that's not a problem." Then hung up and turned to her sidekick. "It's Derek, Hanny, with the shoe boxes as promised."

"Shall I go?" asked Duffy.

"No no, please stay dear boy. You might find this interesting."

Within seconds a smart young man in a pinstripe suit joined them at the table, carrying two cardboard shoe boxes.

"Duffy – meet Derek..."

Both men nodded politely to each other.

Derek passed a box to Abi and Hanny.

"I think this is what you ordered ladies."

Abi smiled and gently took the lid off her box.

Inside lay a shiny gleaming new pistol.

"Sig Sauer P365..." said Derek with pride.

"Wow," sighed Duffy.

Abi caressed the gun affectionately like an old love.

"Ah… my little darling… Striker-fired subcompact semi-automatic, with

Tritium XRAY3 Day/Night Sights and two 10-round magazines. Lovely."

"You sound like a sales rep dear," whispered Hanny.

"I googled it… But then, always been my favourite friend in need."

"My turn," said Hanny, as she edged open her lid as if there was a live hamster inside. Then let out a loud sigh. "It's my birthday and I'll cry if I want to."

There in her shoe box lay another bright new pistol.

"A Glock 42 .380 automatic…" said Derek, again with pride.

"Good old Glock," said Duffy.

"Six rounds… that'll do just fine," said Hanny, giving her weapon an affectionate pat.

Derek leapt to attention.

"Job done ladies. Hope you both satisfied."

Abi and Hanny nodded as one.

"I'll tell Sir Geoffrey…" Bowed to the trio and vanished as quickly as he had appeared.

"Well Duffy… Methinks, we're ready for action."

Abi's phone rang again.

She answered and listened. A very long moment. Then killed the call.

"Think these little beauties arrived just in time," she said. "The guns."

"Yes?" asked Hanny.

"That was Eddie, from The Blind Beggar. They've got an address for this

Hassan Bijan… the reporter the Iranians are desperate to find."

"And?" said Hanny.

"Council estate in Ealing. Eddie's given us a heads-up then is calling his smoothie contact in an hour… better get moving so we get there before them."

"Want me along? asked Duffy.

"Why not?" replied Abi. "But stay out of sight. Don't want the assassins spotting you."

The two pensioners, trudged from the garden centre, each with a shoe box under their arms, as if they were off to play a game of bridge at a care home.

Duffy wondered what on earth he'd let himself in for, as he trailed along behind.

CHAPTER EIGHTEEN

When Mungo landed at LAX for once his mood was far from ecstatic. Usually the sight of the Hollywood sign across in the Santa Monica hills would send his heart thumping, knowing that he had arrived, that he was once more in this magical kingdom where the sun shone bright, the tall palms swayed, where anything could and would happen.

But not today.

As he'd driven from his home of many years at Harrow-on-the-Hill, he'd left that little Kiwi turd standing in his front door, waving goodbye with a nauseous grin all over his dial. That little shit had weaponised his family against him. The young lad he'd stolen the million from, had blackmailed him into returning it, in front of his family without them knowing what was going on. From now on, the stepson held the upper hand because he alone in the house knew Mungo was a bigamist who'd secretly married his Mum in Auckland, despite the family in the U.K. And now, with this knowledge, he could do anything he liked in his stepdad's home. Anything.

This was why Mungo was inwardly furious.

Sooner or later he'd have to find a way to tame this kid.

But that would have to wait.

Right now, Janie was waiting at the Arrivals barrier with open arms to greet him.

"Have I missed you honey!" she cried, hugging him so hard he nearly passed out.

Mungo stared at her. She'd had another face lift. He

could see the strings from her ears down under her chin. And botoxed her eyes to Mars. Not a wrinkle on that loving shiny bright smooth face. Like she was dipped in candle wax, Mungo quietly thought. Almost a death mask. With a permanent smile.

"And you look just a-maz-ing, my little beauty," he chirruped.

She led him by the hand to their waiting gold limo.

"This is new," said Mungo, thinking what ghastly bad taste this was.

"I got Hank to drive us," as she nodded to the clean-cut young chauffeur. "It just purrs along... you'll love it babe."

Once in the back, Janie firmly pulled the curtains between them and the driver and ripped off her new husband's trousers.

Before he could say "easy tiger", it was all over.

He was puffing away as he did up his zipper and she was smiling as she checked out her lipstick in the mirror.

"There now, welcome home my love... that didn't hurt did it now?"

"Janie... what can I say... you are one helluva... whore!"

"Love it when you talk dirty... Want another go?"

"No no... save it for later babe."

Janie sat up straight beside Mungo and got down to business, now that the dirty stuff was out of the way.

"Your writer girl..." she said.

"Dakota?"

Janie nodded.

"There may be a problem... with her. She keeps phoning about when are you back home, wants to discuss script changes."

"No worries - I'll see her tomorrow."

"I think she might be drinking… she repeats herself a lot… slurs, know what I mean babe."

"I'll nail it domani, promise. This girl has huge talent – we don't want to lose her, or the project."

"Talking of which, did you get more investment from your Dutch buddy… Wim, was it?"

"Ah. We were about to sign, when he had a terrible accident – hit and run… Dead, Janie, dead. Poor bastard."

"Oh my God… sweet Jesus… that is so terrible Mungo, and you just met the poor guy… Was he married?"

"Sure. Cute girl from Bali. She's devastated."

"You should keep in touch… she might want to invest."

"Good thought. I'll do just that… keep in touch."

"Now. Good news… You wanted to try some skydiving… We're booked on a course tomorrow morning… eight a.m."

"Shit! That is fantastic – something I've always wanted to try before I drop."

"Oh, by the way… we're heading for dinner at Geoffrey's in Malibu… that place always brings back good memories… our wedding party."

Mungo loved the place too. The perfect setting to help forget Noah and his shenanigans back home.

Two hours later, the sun was setting over the Pacific Ocean as they sat at their special balcony table salivating over their filet mignon when he saw her. Sitting in a far corner with a very balding old guy. Willow. She with the balletic legs who he'd entertained weeks earlier at the Chateau Marmont. Her dinner date looked like he was choking on a bone… bent over like he was dying… The girl had got up and was banging him on his back. Waiters huddled around looking important. Somebody yelled into a phone. Too late. Willow's partner must have had a heart attack. Minutes later an ambulance arrived and carried the old geezer away. Mungo hoped for Willow's sake that he'd paid the bill... to eat there was far from cheap. But, looking at the age difference, he must have been rich. Very.

"That is just terrible... the poor man died," whispered Janie.

Mungo nodded, and, ever the hero, walked briskly over to Willow. Spoke briefly then returned to his wife.

"What you doing?" she asked.

"I paid for the meal. Somebody had to. With him gone, she probably couldn't afford it."

What Mungo didn't say was that he also promised to call her the next day to arrange another love session on Sunset.

"My darling boy, you never cease to amaze me..." Janie leant across and kissed him on the lips. "You are a very special person."

Mungo raised his glass and emptied his chardonnay. He'd drink to that.

And twelve hours later that same chubby charmer was... in heaven.

Well...

So it seemed.

In fact Mungo was two miles high above the Pacific Ocean and freefalling at at 120 mph.

Everything around him was dazzlingly bright blue, the sky and the sea.

And cool, he could feel his finger tips tingling and freezing.

Not to mention his thumping heart.

They said the adrenaline would kick in once he jumped out of the plane and fell into nowhere. They were bloody right.

He could taste his honey and oatmeal breakfast at the

back of his mouth.

Attached to Mungo, just feet away, was Marty, his hunky unshaven skydive instructor, as both soared in tandem for what seemed minutes before turning inland, opening the chute, and gliding in to land gracefully at a local football field.

It had been one long day. Up at dawn then across to the skydive club for three hours of intensive training before getting into the plane.

He and Janie had started with the ground school and first jump course where they identified the parachute gear, how it worked, learnt the freefall body positions, all about flying the canopy, learning the turns, backflips, and different exits.

They were both mentally and physically exhausted by the time they boarded the Cessna 182 and soared high, almost vertical, towards the midday sun.

Then first Janie, attached to her tandem coach, Zara, made the leap into the blue, followed by Mungo and Marty.

Their hearts were in their mouths as they fell... and fell... and fell... about to die in seconds... waving goodbye to each other... terrified to look way down at the ground below them where cars were smaller than ticks... and the air rushed past them at over 100 mph... it just couldn't end well... as the ground got ever closer.

But it did.

Three minutes later they were standing in that football field holding glasses of champagne and thanking their tandem partners for the best experience of their lives.

Well, it was the least they could say.

It was certainly unique.

Mungo and Janie hugged each other hard.

"Was that what you wanted babe?" she asked.

"Certainly was..." smiled Mungo, putting on his hero's

face. "But next time

I want to fly solo."

"Count me out… c'mon, let's go get a martini," and dragged her weary husband off to the waiting gold limo.

It took at least an hour in that cocktail lounge for them both to unwind, for the breathing to calm, and the nerves to settle.

"Damn, just remembered…" said Mungo. "Said I'd meet Dakota at two to catch up on the script stuff."

"Can always cancel?" said Janie. "We could have a sleepy afternoon?"

Mungo stood, slapped his cheeks to wake him up, and persevered.

"Nope. You got me worried about her… want to see what's going down."

And he was off.

To The Ivy in West Hollywood, where he and Dakota had fallen across Brad Pitt all those weeks earlier. A lifetime ago. So much had happened.

Mungo was sat at a table near a couple of starlets he recognised from that Netflix horror series where neighbours ate each other, dogs and all. It was gross.

Though the actors were tasty.

He looked at his watch. He was twenty minutes late and wondered if his screenwriter had been and gone before him. He swore quietly into his scotch.

Then he saw her.

Crossing the street outside the restaurant.

Well, not so much crossing as zigzagging through the traffic.

Taking her life in her hands with a painted smile on her lips.

As she neared, she spotted Mungo sitting at his table, waved, and nearly got rammed by a bus.

"Sorry I'm late, partner," she slurred. Then slumped opposite Mungo.

He looked at her carefully. Was this drink or drugs?

"You OK?"

"Sure, why not? What about you – the man with a wife in London and a wife in L.A?"

"That's our little secret honey."

She nodded slowly.

"Course it is, I promise," she giggled.

"I'm only here a few days – want to drop by, see Brett in the office… but thought we should talk about our script first."

"It's all good Mungo… I'm doing a new rewrite… giving it more pizzazz… putting in new characters."

"Does it need new characters – thought you had it just right Dakota."

"Chang thought it needed more action… perhaps a Chinese girl?"

"Chang?" asked Mungo, puzzled a moment.

"Chang Yi… see the ring… see the ring!"

Dakota waved her left hand slowly to and fro in the air. A large diamond ring was on her finger.

"The wind turbine Chang Yi who you dated?"

Dakota burst into a radiant smile.

"My one and only," she giggled.

"But Daks… you hardly know the guy… he just took you out eating."

"And dancing… and bedding… and everything."

Mungo reached for her hand.

"Baby, baby, you know I care for you… we are good buddies… believe me, but… are you back on the booze?"

"I am clean Mungo, promise. No drink."

"What about drugs – you're taking something?" asked Mungo quietly.

She shrugged. "Sometimes… sometimes Chang gives me a little pill to make us both happy… and… it works… You should try."

"No no, please don't… you been there before… it won't end well babe."

"And. I think I am leaving work."

"What?"

"Chang says now I'm a screenwriter that's what I should do… not sit behind a desk working for Brett."

"Fuck Chang – it's me who's giving you the break Daks… don't you dare leave Brett… not yet anyways… Let's both do the movie and see how it works out… Please… give it time."

"Gotta go to the john…" said Dakota and left to go to the bog.

Mungo didn't like what he was hearing or seeing. Daks was on something and it was changing her behaviour. Something this bloody Chang was providing.

His worries were confirmed when she came back to the table.

Like she was up there in the clouds doing her own skydive without a chute.

All over the place.

Freefall.

"He's got so much money Mungo… he's got so much money Mungo."

"Yeah yeah…" he soothed.

"Said he might become a movie producer himself."

"Chang?"

"I said if you can do it, if funny old Mungo can do it with

271

his two wives… so can he." And she laughed hysterically.

"Thanks a bunch."

"Anyway, got to go… I'm late for Chang."

She stood unsteadily.

"But we haven't eaten. Or talked more about your script?"

"That can wait sweetie pie. Chang comes first."

And walked out of the restaurant.

Mungo watched her stumble off and hoped the world was not closing in on his little friend. This girl had a massive talent but deep down was a sensitive flower who could easily take the wrong turning and, like Icarus, burn by flying too close to the unforgiving Californian sun.

*

While Noah was pedalling like crazy on the gym bike, his mind was buzzing. In his personal war with Mungo Swift he knew that he had won. He'd come all the way over from New Zealand to London, discovered he was happily married to a second wife with a family and a sweet daughter, and forced him to repay his million dollar inheritance.

As Mungo had departed on his next mystery overseas trip, Noah knew he had him in the palm of his hand. Knowing now what he did, he could destroy this reptile and get his total revenge, or be generous, and let it go. Let Monica and family pass their days without finding this rat had been married to his own Mum at the same time.

The problem was Donna. He didn't want to hurt her.

Which was why she was pedalling away on the stationary exercise bike next to Noah in that same gym.

He'd figured they should quietly go out for a posh lunch in Mayfair, shoot the breeze, and see what they both felt about life in general, starting with their parents.

After the bikes the two played with weights, did some rowing, then spruced up and headed for the high life.

Once seated at The Wolseley they ordered two flat iron steaks and a bottle of Prosecco, then looked around to spot the stars… over there was Emily Blunt… in the corner was Andrew Scott… and two tables away was the ever effervescent Biggins.

"So," sighed Noah, "here we are."

"Yup," smiled Donna. "Enjoying the good life now you got that money back… Question is, what next… you go back home or stay here for a bit?"

"Tough one. If my Mum was still alive I'd probably go back tomorrow… we'll see."

"Funny thing, families…" said Donna.

"Yeah. They all bring their own problems, one way or another."

"What was yours?"

"My stepdad – bit of a dick… we never got on… thought I could trust him, but I was wrong."

"Where's he now?"

Noah shrugged. "Fuck knows. Travelling somewhere."

"That's the other thing, family secrets."

"We all have them."

"But some secrets," said Donna. "They lie under the surface… never spoken about, but you know they're there all the time."

"Like crocodiles waiting to bite you…"

"Too true. My family secret is that…" She hesitated.

"Go on," said Noah.

"… when I was sixteen, Mum took me walking up on the hill and told me, Dad wasn't my father."

"What?" said Noah. "She had a lover?"

"No silly – I was adopted. But Dad apparently was all funny about it… they'd tried to have babies but it didn't work. So decided to adopt. Think Dad saw it as his fault, so it's never discussed… then few years later, the dam bursts and Mum has the two boys – problem solved. Whatever it was."

"Wow. That's some secret Donna… Ever wonder who your real parents were?"

"I think it was a girl in Leeds… had to give me up… or something… anyway, I'd rather stick with my Monica and Mungo… bless them both."

Inwardly Noah felt relief at this news. Dating his stepdad's daughter always had a queasy ring to it. Too close for comfort. But now she was not related so he could put that to bed.

"And another secret," teased Donna.

"Surprise me."

"Mum and I know what Dad really does."

"What?"

"All this 'so very hush hush' stuff… the games he plays with us… we know the truth."

"You do?" Suddenly Noah wondered where this was going… Did Monica and Donna know about his Mum's marriage to Mungo back home?

"A few months ago I followed Dad."

"Followed him?"

"On my scooter."

"And?"

"He went to this industrial estate in Pinner. That's a real crap area not far from us… and walked into Solar Global."

"Solar Global?"

"Dad doesn't work for the CIA or MI6… He's a bloody salesman… selling solar panels around the world… a travelling salesman!"

Noah's mouth dropped open as he slumped back in his chair.

"Bloody hell!"

"Thought you'd find that funny... So I go home and tell Mum who thinks it's hilarious... All these years he's been conning the family about his missions overseas... going undercover... when he's simply out there selling sun panels!"

"And he doesn't know you two know?" asked Noah.

"Mum and I thought we'd keep it a secret. Otherwise he'd really lose face... don't know how he'd take it... This way we're all happy."

"And he still lives in his fantasy world."

"Off today to Europe. Then the States," added Donna.

"Seems to have a gifted life."

"But. He does have a gun."

"Eh?"

"Pistol. Found it last week. But I haven't told Mum that one."

"Shit. All I can say Donna... those are some crazy family secrets!"

Noah emptied his Prosecco glass and thought.

What else was there to discover about his stepdad? All that commanding a nuclear sub for six months under the oceans was for the birds.

What other innocents was he bullshitting? Like his Mum, did he have another woman somewhere else believing she was the only one? Apart from Monica.

And what's a travelling salesman doing with a gun?

He decided to chase up that private detective, Duffy, and see what he could uncover, though was still reluctant to upset the lovely Donna.

Which was another dilemma he'd have to solve in the not-too-distant future.

*

The sun was slowly slipping behind the grey tenement blocks by the time Abigail and Hanny arrived in their Uber at the dingy council estate in Ealing where the Iranian activist Hassan Bijan was hiding.

Duffy had followed at a discreet distance on his Harley, determined to stay out of sight, in case the bad actors approached him at a later date. But not too far away, just in case.

The two old girls knew that Hassan lived in Apartment 44, on the second floor. From the small grubby piece of lawn below they could see his front door, painted red. By now Abi was sitting, a rug covering her knees, in a collapsible wheelchair, pushed by Hanny. They appeared to be feeding the birds. Except there weren't any.

They heard a van approaching.

It parked near them and a young man in overalls got out, carrying a tool box, and climbed the stairs to the third floor where he disappeared from sight.

"He could be a proxy killer," whispered Hanny "On hire to them?"

Abi shook her head. "Too real."

They both kept feeding the invisible birds.

Duffy kept shivering twenty yards away in the corner of the car park.

Another vehicle drove up and stopped. A small rusting Skoda.

A young Mum with two howling kids. Looked like North

African. She clipped the boys around their ears and both went quiet. She hauled them off to a door on the ground floor.

It must have been fifteen minutes before more movement.

Two black teenagers, a boy and girl, walking slowly and kissing. Walking slowly and kissing. Up the stairs, midst roaring laughter.

Next an old grey-haired gran pushing a large pram. Shopping bags piled on top, baby crying inside. She nodded to Abi and Hanny, shook the pram, but the baby kept crying. Dropped a bag of tomatoes onto the ground. Stooped awkwardly and picked them up. Then dropped an apple.

"Should I help her?" whispered Hanny.

"No, keep your eyes peeled for the others," replied Abi.

The old gran retrieved the fallen fruit, muttered 'hello' to the ladies, and limped with the pram to the lift.

Then reappeared on the second floor.

Walked past Hassan's door, out of sight.

The baby stopped crying.

Abi and Hanny and Duffy all stood in the gloaming, all shivering, for another half hour. Nothing.

Then Abi spotted Hassan's red front door had blown open.

"C'mon!" She leapt from the wheelchair, followed closely by Hanny, and raced as fast as her creaking limbs could carry her, to the second floor.

Just past Hassan's door was that large pram.

Just inside his doorway lay his body.

A single shot through his forehead.

"Shit! Shit! Shit!" spat Abi.

He was stone dead.

They walked to the pram.

It had a deeper inside than most.

The shopping bags had been thrown onto the ground. Fruit everywhere.

And there by the pillow was a tiny tape recorder.

Abi turned it on.

A baby crying.

Duffy joined them carrying something in his hands.

"Found this…"

The gran's long grey wig.

"Soraya and Darius!" cried Hanny.

"He was coiled up in that ruddy pram… under the shopping."

"She even spoke to us!"

Abi looked at Hassan's dead body, and back at the pram.

"So Mister Duffy… Now you know what we're dealing with."

CHAPTER NINETEEN

Mungo squeezed Putri's hand as they sat drinking Heineken at an outside table of The Black Cat coffee shop beside the Keizersgracht canal in Amsterdam.

"I was sitting at this very table when you called to tell me about Wim," said the chubby charmer. "I still can't believe what happened."

Putri shook her head in silence.

"Did they ever catch the hit and run driver?"

"They never will, not now. Something like that happens every week and no-one gets caught."

"I am so sorry..."

Putri smiled at Mungo. "Did you kill him?" she asked sweetly.

"What!?"

"I wouldn't be surprised. Nobody liked him. He had many enemies."

"How are you coping my dear?" asked Mungo softly.

"The first week, terrible. But now... I can smile again."

And she did.

"You see Mungo, my Wim was an absolute shit... When we met I found him a bit crazy, a bit of fun... but, once we got married, he became a bully. My life with him was hell... and now, I am free... I feel happy again... I feel happy especially with you at my side."

"You are very beautiful Putri... you deserve a happy life."

The Balinese girl's eyes softened.

"You could give me that Mungo... you and I could be

good couple?"

"You think so?"

"Deep down, I know so."

And leant across to kiss him on the cheek.

"But first I need get divorced..." she said. Then added "You are not married are you my darling?"

"Do I look married Putri?" replied a wide-eyed Mungo.

"Then let me see my lawyer, and we can talk about sharing our lives?"

"That would be delicious."

"I know you working in Hollywood as a big producer... but you could live here with me?"

"Why not baby – you have a beautiful home... and I could still do business trips to L.A. and London, now and then."

"Perhaps I come too?" suggested Putri with a wide smile.

"And why not, my darling, why not..." replied Mungo, crossing his fingers under the table. "Let's get another drink then plan our lives together... This is beginning to look rather exciting."

By the time the Dutch sun had set over that canal, the two were onto their tenth pint and their world was taking on a very happy glow, enhanced by the strong whiff of hemp floating from the tables behind.

"So where would we honeymoon?" asked Putri, beginning to slur her words.

"Perhaps the Maldives or Aruba or Bali?"

"One step at a time my dear... Remember you are a grieving widow, then you must get a divorce."

Putri grabbed his arm.

"Not grieving Mungo. I want you. Want you now!"

The chubby charmer felt his head throbbing. It was either the Heineken, or the fact that events were threatening to engulf his highly regulated and very disciplined lifestyle. In a few hours he was flying off to Cannes to get married to Margot, and here he was, halfway to the altar with another young love he barely knew. It was everything he wanted, but he had to keep the lid on, otherwise this little sizzling pot would boil over and he would get very very burnt.

He snapped out of his dreams and wondered where he was.

Putri was almost violently pulling him from his café chair. "Now Mungo!"

He gave in and was led by the hand to a cab where he fell in and out, was pulled into Putri's apartment, up her stairs, felt his clothes being torn from his torso, and thrown onto that Super King Size water bed.

His last thought was he was going to miss his flight to France.

And her saying teasingly as she ripped off her red satin bra... "And did you kill my husband darling?"

Then everything went pleasantly blank.

*

Duffy sat with Izzy chomping burgers at McDonald's on Waterloo Station. Beside them in his carrycot was young baby Byron.

"So you been playing Action Man?"

"Good to be out in the field again... even with a couple of old biddies."

"They sound rather switched on to me," said Izzy.

"Oldest spooks I've ever met."

The baby suddenly started screeching... sending the other customers scurrying.

"You sure about this?" asked the singing detective.

Izzy glanced at Byron. "Absolutely certain."

At that moment, Rocco Mars, whose baby had died of TB, walked in with a woman. She had a sad look about her, a short dark fringe, and bags under her brown eyes. She looked at the crying baby… and her face lit up.

"Duffy… this is my wife Jade," said Rocco.

Duffy stood and shook her hand. "Heard all about you… the TB… back to normal now I hope?"

Jade nodded. "It was touch and go, thanks."

"And this is my friend Izzy, who's been looking after little Byron there."

"Ah… what a sweet kid…" said Jade. "Can I pick him up?"

"All yours," said Izzy.

Jade held Byron high in the air, whose crying turned to gurgling.

"Think he likes you Jade," said Izzy.

"He is gorgeous," whispered Jade.

"Are you two still wanting kids?" asked Duffy.

Rocco tugged on his droopy moustache and looked at his wife.

"Sadly I think we're past that now Duffy… never get through the system."

"If we could, we would," sighed Jade as she rocked Byron in her arms.

"Well," Izzy looked at Duffy.

"Izzy and I wondered… whether you two might like to take on little Byron here?"

"You what?" gasped Rocco.

"Are you serious?" asked Jade, grasping the babe ever tighter.

"Let me explain," said Duffy. "That whole baby selling

business has been closed down and Barnado's is looking after the kids we found at their property."

"However," added Izzy. "This little chap sort of slipped through the cracks…

I was going to look after him myself, but that's not possible now, so we both wondered?"

Rocco looked at Jade holding Byron.

"There's no catch here?" he asked carefully.

"You've got a home and a garden…"

"A small garden," said Jade.

"Well," said Izzy. "Now you've got a home, a small garden, and little baby Byron to play in it!"

Rocco hugged Izzy and Duffy.

Jade welled up and kissed the babe on its cheeks.

"How can we thank you enough?" asked Jade.

"I can't believe this is happening," added Rocco.

"Oh… and I've spoken to the cops about that twenty grand you paid to Rachel

Storm… you'll be getting it back in a few weeks," said Duffy.

"Speechless mate."

"Give us a call and tell us how the boy's doing," said Duffy.

"Better than that Duffy – you are now his godfather!"

"Good luck Byron… for the rest of your life," grinned the detective.

"Thank you thank you thank you," breathed Jade as she headed for the exit.

"We'll stay in touch Duffy, promise!" cried Rocco.

And they were gone, taking young Byron with them.

"Have we just made a terrible mistake?" asked Duffy.

Izzy shook her head.

"Woman's intuition… that wee boy's just found a loving

home."

"We should celebrate!"

"And I've got some news," said Izzy.

"Slay me."

"Next week I'm starting a new life."

"Oh dear?" said Duffy.

"You could be part of it…"

"Tell me."

"I'm moving to L.A."

"La-La Land..? Bloody hell… Why?"

"Couple of mates out there… said come and join them. And I thought I'd start all over again… with Mum and Dad probably going to jail here, it's going to get shitty … so going to reinvent myself… new name, new everything..! "

"I'm sorry about that Izzy… your parents."

"They were bloody stupid… I'll stay in touch… but least it gives me a reason to move on."

"I'll miss you babe."

"You could come with me… you got nothing here… become a singing star in Tinseltown."

"Tempting… but I like what I have here, or don't have… London's got this tacky seediness you won't find in L.A."

"Oh I think I will sunshine."

Izzy pulled Duffy to his feet and held him tight.

She literally looked down at him.

"I really will miss you Duff."

She kissed him long on his lips.

Stared deep into his eyes.

Turned on her heels, and was gone.

Duffy got his breath back and watched this glam tall blonde stunner glide from his life.

She really did look like that Hannah something on the telly.

And he really would miss her too.

L.A.? Who knows..?

*

Abigail and Hanny, wearing their most fashionable suits, exited their Uber, walked into the large soulless grey building beside the Thames, showed their security passes at reception, and carried on up the back stairs to Sir Geoffrey's office.

"We could have taken the bloody lift!" puffed Hanny

"I will not give in to old age my dear… got to keep fighting."

"That's a 'no' to botox then?"

"What?"

They halted outside the large polished door.

"Do you think he's giving us the chop?" whispered Hanny.

Abi shook her head.

"After all these years, wouldn't dare… We know too much!"

And tapped on the door.

A distant "come" came from inside.

They entered and there he was, standing smiling behind his vast desk.

Elegant, refined, grey balding hair, a neat clipped white moustache, red waistcoat, his old Sherborne school tie, and still that twinkle in his eye. The good one.

His left had been damaged in Oman many years earlier when he was still a young undercover agent in a dishdasha and sandals. Bloody champagne cork, he claimed.

The room was like a university library. Books lined every bit of space, except for the large oil painting of The Battle of Trafalgar and The Roaring Lion, a dramatic 1941 black and white photographic portrait of Winston Churchill.

"Ladies! How absolutely delightful to see you both fit and healthy."

He shook their hands.

"Sir Geoffrey…" replied Abi and Hanny in unison, almost bobbing.

"Please sit… The tea's just made, so hope?"

They nodded as he poured from the pot into three cups, and sat again behind his desk.

"Well… here we are," he said with theatrical charm.

"Here we are indeed," added Abi with equal theatricality.

"You're still in your delightful pad beside the river Abi?"

"Not in a care home yet Sir Geoffrey."

"Oh, by the way… I sent in a tiger team to test your security a few weeks ago… the cellotape, the hair on the door, all the old tricks..?" he smiled. "Well done."

"You sent in a tiger team!? I thought that was the Iranians."

"Sadly just us playing games."

Abi looked slightly irritated at being targeted by her own.

"And Hanny… you were with your mother?"

"Yes. She's gone, but still living and loving Battersea."

Sir Geoffrey took a long sip of tea and put on a more serious face.

"What truly dreadful times we live in… the Cold War was bad enough, but this… this is getting to boiling point."

"Dangerous times," agreed Hanny.

"Right now, apart from everyone saying we're lurching into World War Three, the enemy has already arrived on our doorstep… acts of transnational repression, they call it, trying to stifle debate or criticism of their countries… where these bad actors use local proxies to do their dirty work for them, then move in themselves and kill their targets on our soil. But,

286

you two know all about that."

"We do Sir Geoffrey… Now you've re-opened Shadow and brought us out of the cold, we're closing in on the Iranians, Soraya and Darius, as instructed."

"Sadly Abigail, not fast enough. Otherwise our activist chappie, Hassan Bijan, would still be alive today."

Abi nodded. "Affirmative. A sad loss. They fooled us. It won't happen again, I can guarantee."

"Second that sir," added Hanny crisply.

"Well…" said Sir Geoffrey, rather sadly. "Three things ladies."

The two retired spooks held their breath.

"First, my sources tell me that Darius was spotted entering Belgium this morning… so he's already moved on, and probably arranged to meet Soraya somewhere else in Europe."

"Good God…" muttered Abi. "Flown the nest already."

"So I think we can assume their mission here is over, at least for the time being."

"Ah," breathed Hanny with relief.

"Second, because of that, I'm letting you two go once more… free to do your painting, pilates, poetry, whatever."

"Poetry?" muttered Abi. "You think we're too old for this sir?"

"No Abi, I'm closing down this mission as it appears our Iranian targets have moved on… and, to be frank, you messed up on that Hassan job."

"Hang on, what if you're wrong. What if the girl is still here? What if Darius is off doing another job in Berlin or Paris, while she targets someone else in the U.K.?" asked Abi.

"They usually work as a pair, so unlikely."

"And three, sir?" sighed Hanny.

Sir Geoffrey pushed a button on his desk and in came

Derek, the pin-striped young man who'd given the girls their weapons in the garden centre. He was carrying two shoe boxes as before. This time they were empty.

"Derek?" queried Abi.

"Thirdly, your guns. I need them back please."

Abi and Hanny looked at each other.

They really had been closed down this time.

"Sig Sauer and the Glock 42 please ladies," said Derek politely.

The two retired spooks dug into their handbags and handed over their pistols, which Derek replaced in the boxes, then exited without another word.

"This really is goodbye then sir?" sighed Abi.

Sir Geoffrey shrugged. "I thought we'd give it another go, but now I think time's up…" He stood and held out his hand. His right eye twinkled faintly.

"Thanks for that one last fling Sir Geoffrey… it was fun, almost…" smiled Abi through gritted teeth.

"I envy you your lovely office," added Hanny.

"Enjoy the rest of your lives ladies…"

They all shook hands and the two old spooks walked away from their years in the service. Like saying goodbye to a very old friend.

"What was that about his ruddy office?" snapped Abi to Hanny in the lift.

"It's not my fault he dumped us," whispered Hanny.

"Should have taken the stairs!" snapped Abi as she trounced out of the building into the cold damp London afternoon. Then turned to Hanny with a resigned sad smile. "Drink, my dear?"

*

"How much!?" gasped Mungo as he strolled along the Croissette in Cannes with Margot on his arm, avoiding the chic ladies with poodles and their poodle doo-doo.

They had just passed the elegant Majestic hotel on their right, had the shimmering

Mediterranean sea on their left, and were heading for the harbour which would be jam-packed with the most expensive yachts and motorboats on the Cote d'Azur.

"Ten thousand…" said his fiancée lightly.

"Dollars?" he asked hopefully.

"Euros sweetie, Euros."

"I'm not made of money cheri!"

"Of course you are… you travel the globe… you are dirty rich bebi… I know it…" giggled Margot, spinning Mungo around and kissing him on his nose.

They walked beside the Palais des Festivals where the chubby charmer had attended the MIPCOM TV market, and there it was around the corner, the Vieux Port… And all those very classy yachts gently bobbing in the very expensive marina.

"Which one have you hired?" mumbled Mungo.

"'L'Escargot Rapide'…" chirped Margot, leaving Mungo to skip ahead in her barefeet along the cobbled sidewalk beside the moored boats.

"The Fast Snail?"

Margot had stopped beside a shining gangplank with white scrubbed ropes that led onto a massive yacht with stained teak decking. Mungo could see why it was so expensive. Everything looked impeccable. Untouched by human hand.

"You like?" cried Margot as she climbed aboard.

"Do I have a choice?" sighed the chubby charmer.

Mungo deep down was in a foul mood. His drinking

and nocturnal activities with Putri meant he had, as feared, missed his flight to Nice. As a stickler for personal details and planning, this stuck in his craw. His peculiar lifestyle and routine meant that he lived from day to day with military precision. If he got his timing wrong his stack of cards could well come tumbling down. And right now he had the tallest card pyramid he'd ever erected. There'd be a whole bunch of casualties. But he was determined not to let that happen.

"You like?" repeated Margot, snuggling into Mungo's neck.

"What do we get for that money?"

"We have this beautiful boat for the wedding ceremony and the party…

24 hours."

"Let's go have lunch," sighed Mungo, knowing he'd lost this battle.

They trudged back to the Rue D'Antibes, found their usual cafe, and ordered the seafood pizza. Sami, Margot's waiter friend and Mungo's best man at the wedding, brought them a bottle of house red.

"Just a few more days of freedom Mister Mungo, then you are a married man," he grinned.

"Looking forward to it," said Mungo. "And you'll be there at my side."

"Certainement. I will make sure everything goes to plan," as he winked to Margot.

"Don't forget the honeymoon cheri… I have booked the Parachute Club this weekend for the skydive," she smiled.

Mungo shrugged nonchalantly, he hoped. "Great stuff."

"But, before that we should do all our paperwork."

"You mean I write a will leaving you the apartment in case I have a heart attack up in the air," said Mungo glibly.

Margot shrugged in a very Gallic way.

"But you're right babe… I should do just that, it's only fair… At my age, anything can happen."

His fiancée beamed and winked at Sami, still standing there.

"Listen, I need some air… back in five…" And he walked out into the back street, carrying his usual briefcase.

Two minutes away he turned into a cobbled alley, and leant against a bolted fire door. Here, least he had some privacy.

Opened his case and took out burner No.1.

Called Monica in London.

She was busy cleaning the carpet. Something she always did when he was away travelling. And that night Noah was taking the family out for a curry. The little creep.

Took out burner No.3.

Called Janie in L.A.

Woke her up. Still in bed but loved hearing from him. Wanted him back home pronto. He said he was getting sales interest across Europe in the Pig movie.

When she suggested they do phone sex. He said he was in a restaurant and didn't seem appropriate.

Took out burner No.4.

And nearly called Margot.

Took out burner No.5.

Called Putri in Amsterdam.

In the shower and still aching from their night on the water bed. She'd already booked to see her lawyer about the divorce. Couldn't wait to see him again.

Duty done he returned to the pizza joint.

Sami the waiter was sat in his seat, talking animatedly to Margot. Like old loves.

That one glimpse proved to Mungo these youngsters were in cahoots, and the rich old git, himself, was undoubtedly their target.

Sami leapt to his feet when he saw Mungo and returned to the kitchen.

Margot fluttered her lashes and asked what he'd been doing.

He told her the stress of the upcoming wedding had made him feel faint.

"I never asked you my darling," said Margot in a whisper.

"What?"

"Have you ever skydived before?"

"Never. That's why I'm looking forward to it," lied Mungo cheesily.

*

Duffy had almost sunk a whole bottle of French white burgundy with Noah in The Fortnum's wine bar.

"You drinking and driving mate?" chirped Toto the barman.

"Nope, I'm probably sofa surfing at yours again Toto."

"Welcome…"

"So?" said Noah. "My wicked stepdad, Mungo Swift. I come all the way from Godzone to your frigid little country. Find the prick not only married my Mum but had a family and kids here for bloody years!"

"And you're dating his daughter, sunshine!"

"Donna's adopted!"

"So she says."

"I threaten to reveal all to Donna's Mum – which I'd never do – and he gives me back the million he stole from me."

"Job done then. And you go back home to the sun."

"Na. I think there's more to find out… Which is where you come in."

"Go on."

"He lives in a fantasy world, pretends he's a spy… when in fact he's away selling solar panels."

"That is so funny," said Duffy.

"And I think he's hiding a whole load more secrets."

"Is this Donna important to you?"

"Very."

"Then be careful what you wish for mate… don't want to hurt the family."

Noah emptied his glass.

"Agree. Here's where he works. I want you to sniff around and find out what other secrets he has in his cupboard… then we'll decide what to do."

Noah handed Duffy a card with Solar Global's address then left the bar.

"Looks like you're on a roll old son," said Toto, clearing away Noah's glass.

"Eh?" said Duffy.

No sooner had the Kiwi walked out, than someone else had entered, heading for the singing detective lounging at the bar.

"Mister Duffy?" she asked in a very feline foreign accent.

Everything about her was dark. Her long black fur coat, her long thigh high boots, her long black silk gloves, her chiffon scarf, her jet black hair tied back in a silk chignon, the outlandish lashes, but mostly those deep dark smouldering eyes.

Duffy recognised her immediately.

Abigail had shown him photos of the Iranian assassins.

And standing there so close he could smell her Dior perfume wafting around him, was the very seductive, very dangerous killer from Tehran.

Soraya.

CHAPTER TWENTY

Duffy froze a moment, assessing the situation. He'd been warned by Abi and Hanny that the Iranians might approach him to track down one of their targets, to do their leg work for them, then, once found, they'd go in for the killer punch. They'd already done the same with an East End gang. They'd been paid to find the guy, Hassan Bijan, leaving the assassins to visit his address and finish him off. Which they did. So now it was his turn. To be approached.

He could feel his heart thumping.

As Soraya's dark eyes burned through him he realized that in seconds he could grab this murderer, have her on the ground, call the cops, and Abigail.

He also realized that she looked fit, physically fit that is, and must have been trained in unarmed combat back in Tehran. If he jumped her there and then it was him who'd probably come off with the broken arm or neck. So, softly softly, for the moment.

"Yeah, I'm Duffy – how can I help you?"

She sat on the stool next to him at the bar.

"Can I get you a drink?" she said softly.

"Another white wine, thanks," said Duffy. "You having one?"

She shook an elegant neck.

"Too early in the day. Just a fizzy water with a slice of lemon," she said to Toto.

"Very sensible," said the detective.

"I like sensible, but... I also like crazy..." She looked deep into Duffy's eyes.

This bitch is flirting with me, he thought.

He smiled back, hoping he wasn't twitching.

"So?"

"I see on your advert, you do singing."

"Oh yeah... clubs, pubs, weddings... you want to book me?" he joked faintly, never forgetting who this person was, and how he should deal with her.

"I would like to see you perform Mister Duffy, certainly... but I'm here for other business."

Toto handed both their drinks.

"OK?"

"You are a private investigator."

"Sure."

"You find missing people?"

"People, dogs, cats, even a parrot once."

"Perfect. I have an aunt who has disappeared. She is very old... about 80.

She lives somewhere in London. One year ago she moved address, from Notting Hill.

But never told us where she went. My husband and I are really worried. At that age she might have dementia, might be in a care home, and forget who she is. Forget to contact us, forget who we are... I want to find her Mister Duffy. Urgently."

"Shit, I'm so sorry... Mrs?"

"Ah. I am Lucie. Lucie Clayton."

Fuck, thought Duffy. She's gone and nicked that name off Google. Lucie Clayton was the name of a charm school started years ago – Joanna Lumley went there - and now was history. Perhaps she thinks I'd never heard of it.

"Nice to meet you Lucie. Tell me a bit about yourself... I

always like to get to know my clients."

"Me? Oh, not very interesting. I live in Sussex, Brighton, with my husband, who's a knee surgeon. Atticus. And I'm from Turkey. Istanbul. Did a bit of modeling here when I was younger, but now I collect antiques... We're lucky to live in an old rectory, so we have plenty of room... and breed alpacas."

"Alpacas... They are just so beautiful."

"We sell the wool... so much warmer than sheep's wool... But I digress."

You certainly do, thought Duffy. But what an impeccable legend you and your Iranian masters have concocted... The detail of Soraya's dossier was made to impress, and it certainly did.

"One of my more interesting clients I must admit," said the singing detective.

"Thank you. You're very kind."

Her gloved hand squeezed his. Again that long glowing dark stare. She's definitely hitting on me, mused Duffy. If only... if only... but no.

"Sorry, back to business," he said reluctantly. "You sure I can't persuade you to have a real drink?"

She shook that head again.

"My aunt."

"Of course... When I find her... what do I do? Get her to call you?"

"No no Mister Duffy. I want it to be discreet. Don't approach her. We simply want her new address. Not to alert her, so Atticus and I can surprise her... in a nice way. We love her dearly and are genuinely concerned about her welfare."

Those dark eyes were almost looking tearful, noted the detective. This girl was a class act.

"I understand," said Duffy. "So once I find where she's living now, I give you a call?"

Again she shook that head, this time more firmly.

"No no. I prefer to call you… in one week."

So that's it, thought Duffy. You can't be tracked. And you will contact me.

"I have one week?"

"If that is not enough, we give you another week?"

"Suits me." And it did. This way he could charge her on a weekly rate.

Bigtime.

For a brief moment Duffy was curious just who this old aunt really was.

So important that the Iranian spies wanted to find where she lived. And deal with her.

Then came the answer.

"I'd better show you who you're looking for."

Soraya took out her phone and showed him a photo of a woman around eighty years old.

"And here she is… My dear old aunt. Her name is Abigail Clements-Brown."

*

At least the Mediterranean sun was shining down on Mungo as he stood on that polished teak foredeck of the "L'Escargot Rapide" in Cannes' Vieux Port beside his barefooted fiancée. As promised, he wore top hat and tails, while his young gamine bride was draped in a light silk white dress, transparent in all the right places. Beside them stood Sami the waiter, acting as best man, dressed in a lavender velvet tuxedo, looking more like a pimp than the groom.

A young black priest, Ntoki, originally from the Congo, conducted the wedding ceremony, with much sentimentality and passion and chanting. Margot had found him a year earlier, selling folding umbrellas on the Carlton Hotel beach, but he had seen the light and changed his life for ever.

Beyond them a small choir made up of hippy artists from a commune in the hills near their apartment, and a trio of moustached pizza waiters with violins, provided a frenzied backing for this rather bizarre occasion.

In the sky above, a small plane towed a fluttering banner saying "Je t'aime Margot"... speedboats roared up to take a peek... and all along the marina sidewalk tourists gaped and shoved, taking photos of this very exotic French happening.

"And I name you man and wife!" bellowed an exhausted Ntoki, flinging a bible high in the air over his shoulder and into the sea.

The boat cheered as one, its siren whooped for joy, while Mungo held the new Mrs Swift in his arms and gave her their first married kiss.

He looked into her mischievous eyes.

"I think I really love you Margot," he whispered sincerely. Despite all he knew about her, she excited him more than any of his other ladies. It was her streetwise energy, her inexhaustible lust for life, her intense flirtation with those hovering on the fringe of the city's bohemian underbelly. She was the supreme risk taker. In fact, Mungo realized looking at her swiveling on the dance floor, she was the risk.

"And I love you bebi," she replied wide-eyed.

He knew this was a wild little minx, but least now she was his little minx.

Margot stood back, whipped off her dress, and, standing in a tight red bikini, shouted : "It's party time!"

And so it was.

For the next eight hours the newlyweds and their fifty or so eccentric guests rocked and rolled on that massive yacht like there was no tomorrow.

There was the tattooed belly dancer contorting on the snooker table, the naked acrobat swinging from the chandeliers, the magnificent bearded baritone down from Paris who did armpit farts and sang songs from the shows, plus the Bee Gees tribute band who had everyone singing falsetto.

It all ended when Ntoki the priest leapt from the bow into the dark waters and was never seen again, but they all hoped it was part of the act.

By four in the morn, Mungo and Margot sat looking at the empty bottles.

"Some party," laughed the chubby charmer.

Margot kissed him on the cheek.

"Merci… that was merveilleux… and now… now we are Mr and Mrs… I think I like it."

Mungo kissed her back.

"Should get to bed before the sun comes up."

"And our honeymoon surprise," she smiled.

"You really want to do this skydive thing?"

She nodded.

"A perfect end."

"That's what worries me."

"What?"

"No matter…"

They suddenly heard someone shouting from the sidewalk.

Mungo went to the stern doorway.

It was Sami, dragging a body to the boat.

"It's Ntoki. I saw him floating in the water… I think he's dead."

"Bring him aboard quick!" snapped Mungo.

They dragged the soaking priest onto the deck.

"This is terrible…" shouted Margot. "He must not die!"

Mungo calmly felt the pulse in his neck.

"He's still alive. Get back…"

He pinched Ntoki's nose and his mouth dropped open. Then put his own lips firmly around the priest's and started blowing into his mouth until his chest started rising and falling.

Within seconds Ntoki convulsed and spewed up half the Med over Mungo.

It was several minutes before he could talk.

"Mungo Mungo… you are a saint… merci merci!"

And struggled to his feet.

"What happened mate?"

"My first time ever."

"Sex?" asked Margot.

"Whisky. I never drink before. I had a whole bottle… Remember nothing."

"I'll take you home," said Sami.

"Merci Sami," said Margot. "See you for the skydive."

"He's coming too?" asked Mungo.

"Bien sur… to hold my hand," smiled his new wife.

"You go have a good sleep Ntoki and thanks for what you did," said Mungo.

The fragile priest held Mungo close and whispered, glancing warily at Margot.

"Coming from the Congo I see things… see things, understand? You take good care mister Mungo, you take very good care…"

And disappeared into the sunrise leaning unsteadily on Sami.

"What was that about?" asked Margot.

"I'm not so sure," said Mungo, looking uneasily at his new bride.

*

Abigail sat fidgeting in her penthouse apartment when there was a light tap on her door. She shot up and listened like a hunted meerkat on the savannah.

Another knock on the door, this time louder.

Abi moved to the door like a panther. Well, a rather old one.

And listened.

Then.

"Who's that?"

"Me Abi… It's Hanny."

Abi quickly unlocked the chained door and let her friend inside.

"Were you dozing old friend?" asked Hanny. "And why are all the lights off – you've been sitting in the dark."

"Sit down and I'll pour you a gin."

Hanny did as she was told and was handed a tall glass of gin and tonic and ice and lemon.

"Mmm… that'll put bristles on my bristles." She took a long sip.

"Now dear, what on earth's going on – you look like you've seen a ghost?"

Abi cleared her throat, took a slug of gin and answered.

"I've heard from Duffy."

"Really? If the Iranians have gone then there's nothing there. Don't tell me, he wants us to hear him sing in some seedy little Soho club, what fun!"

Abi paused. "He's just had a meeting with Soraya."

"What!?"

"She came to his Fortnum's bar."

"Then she hasn't left the country."

"On the contrary, still very much in business."

"Oh?"

"She gave him a job. To find someone."

"No… Who?"

"Me."

"Soraya wants the private detective to find you?"

"Totally as we predicted… as a useful idiot proxy to get an address, then pay them off, and go finish the job themselves."

"But this time it's you?"

Abi nodded.

"Thinking about it, it always was. Those other killings were a warm-up.

The real prize for the Iranian spies was an old Brit spy, who caused them a shit load of trouble over the years… getting revenge… making their Tehran masters very happy indeed."

"So you're their prize target… Which is why you're sitting here in the dark, behind a heavily locked door."

Abi nodded sweetly.

"We must tell Sir Geoffrey!"

Abi shook her head.

"No way. Right now we two are 'persona non grata'… put out to grass… given the gold watch and retired off."

"But you're in danger… they're out to kill you Abi!"

"I have a plan."

"I feared you would."

"We're going 'rogue'. Off the radar… we're going to take on these brutes on our own… no help from Sir ruddy Geoffrey… and we're going to win!"

"How might I ask?"

"Wait and see…"

"Hang on. If the Iranian princess met Duffy in his bar, why didn't he grab her there and then? Then we'd just have Darius to contend with?"

"He feared she'd get away and that by agreeing to hunt me down, he'd get closer to her."

"So he has her number – we can track her?"

"No no – she's too shrewd. Each week she will call him, to see if he's found my address. Then he gets paid, they say farewell, and she comes visiting."

"So simple. And Darius? Is he in Belgium or not?"

"If he was, it was a false trail to make Sir Geoffrey relax and stand us down... it worked."

"And now we've handed our guns in... how do we defend ourselves?"

Abi walked across to a bookcase and pulled out a long bundle wrapped in a towel.

"I've got old Charlie..."

"Eh?"

"My lovely Uncle Cuthbert gave me this after World War Two... saw him through the North Africa campaign... Desert Rats and all that."

She pulled an old rifle from the towel.

"This is his companion. Kept him alive. An old Lee Enfield .303."

She kissed its barrel.

"Let's hope it'll keep me alive too."

"It must be eighty years old!" breathed Hanny.

"And what's wrong with that dear?" retorted Abi imperiously, once more channeling her inner Maggie Smith.

"Does it still work?"

"Follow me."

Abi walked to her balcony overlooking the Thames, with Hanny trailing behind, looking puzzled.

"Do you like pigeons?"

"Not really... too many in London."

"See that little blighter, sitting on that beer can on the far bank?"

Hanny peered across the swirling brown river.

"Just. Though my eyes…"

Abi pulled Charlie gently into her shoulder and slowly took aim.

"No, don't kill a bird for me old thing."

Abi held her breath a moment and eased the trigger.

There was a loud crack.

As the beer can flew into the air, and the pigeon quietly flapped away.

"You missed!"

"Aimed at the can, dear."

"Bloody hell girl, damn good shot!"

Abi turned to Hanny.

"Now. Let's have another drink, then work out exactly how to catch these muppets before they catch me!"

*

Duffy sat in reception at Solar Global on the dreary Pinner industrial estate, waiting to meet the boss.

His head was buzzing. Only hours earlier he'd been inches away from one of Iran's top killer agents, and had let her go. He could easily have slammed a bottle across her head in the bar and called in Abi and MI6. Or could he? He'd had this fear that she would have got the better of him. Been fitter and deadlier when it came to combat skills. And he was probably right. He was here to prove it. He'd alerted the old girl Abi, who was now aware she was top of their kill list. Job done, for the moment.

Right now he was doing another job for his young Kiwi

client Noah. Checking out more details on the mysterious Mungo Swift. He already knew he was a bigamist, with a deceased wife in Auckland, Noah's Mum, and a family of three living in Harrow. Adopted daughter of which the Kiwi was dating.

Sheila, the receptionist, woke Duffy from his daydreams.

"Charlie will see you now Mister Duffy."

He followed her through into the big office beyond and met Mungo's boss.

"Hello mate… you had lunch?" asked Charlie, turning off the racing on the telly.

Duffy shook his head with a smile. Liked the way this was going already.

"Let's go down the Shaggy Lettuce… have a few pints."

Ten minutes later they were sat at a table beside a roaring fire sipping lager.

"So how do you know our Mungo?" asked the boss.

"He saved my life," said Duffy.

"No way."

"Let's just say I'd be feeding the fishes if it weren't for him."

"Well, dear old chubby… good man!"

"This is all rather awkward for me," said Duffy diffidently.

"I'm all ears mate. Friend of Mungo's is a friend of mine."

"Can we talk off the record?"

"Course we can."

"I have a young client. He knows Mungo, and wants to find out more about his personal life. Where he goes abroad, who he visits."

"So you're a copper?"

"Detective. But you can refuse to answer. Remember, he's my hero."

"Mungo Swift. What can I say? Top salesman. Travels the world. And has made our company very rich, especially in recent months."

"How so?" asked Duffy.

"He connected with some Chinese in L.A. and we're importing stuff of theirs, making a bloody fortune… but that's… off the record."

"Anything odd about his personal life?"

"Nope. Lovely wife Monica here… and, if he plays away, I don't know nothing about it… don't want to."

"Fine. Sounds like our Mungo's a pretty straight guy then."

"Yep. Well… there is something I spotted recently."

"OK..?" said Duffy.

"He carries his briefcase everywhere… but one day, months ago, he left it in the office. And it fell open."

"Yes?"

"Inside were four burner phones, all numbered. I thought should I ask him about them, then decided no, none of my business."

"Burner phones..? Usually have them if you're doing something dodgy, like smuggling in bog rolls or gerbils."

"Yeah. Guess it was something crazy. Has a great sense of humour, does our Mungo. Sometimes think he lives on another planet!"

"Food for thought as they say," said Duffy. "But I agree with you, probably some game he's playing when he's away."

"Another pint mate?" asked Charlie.

"Thanks but no thanks," said Duffy. "I think I can tell my client that Mungo Swift's a normal boring guy living a normal boring life…"

*

To go skydiving after partying through the night till dawn and suffering a heavy hangover was hardly a no brainer. To go skydiving when you suspected your new young wife was somehow scheming to bump you off while in the air was sheer madness. But Mungo was determined to follow it through nonetheless. Perhaps, just perhaps, he had got Margot all wrong. Perhaps he'd misheard her plotting. Then again she was very insistent that he signed a will leaving her his apartment, should anything terrible happen to him. Time would reveal all. Which was now pressing as they had already been at the Cannes Parachute Club for an hour and were doing warm-up exercises on the floor before strapping on their chutes.

Sami, Margot's waiter friend and possible co-conspirator, had greeted them on arrival. Which almost confirmed Mungo's suspicions. This guy was real flaky and seemed to hold some influence over his new wife.

Then Jacques, the skydive coach, had taken them through the routine. They'd persuaded him to let them fly solo rather than tandem, attached to an instructor. It was against all the rules, health and safety, but, with a little greasing of the palms, he'd agreed. He took them through the movements over and over… how high the plane would climb before each would jump out… fall at over 100 m.p.h., float on air for a minute or so, then release their parachute. It seemed basic enough.

He handed Mungo and Margot safety helmets and their chutes.

They would board the plane in ten minutes. So if they wanted to take a final coffee or use the toilet, now was the time.

Mungo, who insisted on wearing his wedding top hat and

tails, had already worked out what Margot and Sami might do if they were up to no good.

Cut his parachute strap so it wouldn't open.

So. He decided to give them a chance to do anything disruptive and went off to the loo. For five minutes.

Then returned.

He noted his chute had been moved a tad.

Margot then went off to the toilet, leaving Mungo with Sami.

"Shit! I left my bag in the loo," said Mungo.

"No problem – I'm going – I'll get it," replied the waiter.

And left the chubby charmer on his own.

Whereupon he quickly swapped the two chutes.

Just as Margot returned.

"Have you signed that will darling... just in case?" she smiled.

Mungo took some papers from his pocket.

"Nearly forgot."

As Jacques entered and announced it was time to board the plane.

The two pulled on their chutes.

Margot now wearing Mungo's, without her knowing.

Sami wished them both luck.

As they left the shed and walked across the tarmac to the waiting Cessna, Mungo got out his pen to sign the will, when his phone suddenly beeped.

He'd had a text from Janie in L.A.

Urgent.

"Shopping today in Rodeo Drive when saw writer Dakota. She collapsed in front of me. Now in hospital. Urgent you come home soonest."

"Fuck!" Mungo cried.

"What bebi?"

"Sorry. Problem. I have to go to L.A. right now. No skydiving today…"

He flipped his topper onto Margot's head and rushed back to the shed, leaving she and Sami gobsmacked.

He hadn't even got to sign that will.

CHAPTER TWENTY-ONE

Duffy was sitting drinking cold coffee and shivering in the Red Funnel Ferries office in Southampton with a seriously intense Abigail and Hanny.

His left shoulder was still aching from a very uncomfortable night sleeping on his ex-wife Zandra's sofa. Kate had extracted the mega expensive Hermes watch from the baby scam trial, allowing Duffy to return this twenty grand bauble as promised.

Zandra had showed her relief – she was convinced that knowing Duffy she'd never see it again - by taking him to Sheekey's fish restaurant to drown in some very expensive Chablis. Then, knowing he had nowhere to sleep, back to hers, as they say.

Trouble was, our singing detective could never relax in her super luxury apartment.

As a top London barrister she was on a very good whack which meant everything in her home was the best of the best. Once through the door Duffy had to take his shoes off in case he dirtied the carpet, then drink his coffee like a child in case he spilled it, and was told not to rumple the sofa cushions, etc etc. It was like still being bloody married to her, and reminded him why he wasn't.

As a result he'd hardly slept a wink and it was only, having got an urgent call from Abigail, that he could steal an hour's zizz on the train down to Hampshire.

The imperious tone of the retired MI6 agent shattered his daydream... back to business.

"So you're certain Soraya will call you tonight to get my address?" asked Abi.

"That's what she said," sighed Duffy.

"Excellent. So here's the plan..." continued Abi. "Very simply, you're getting the ferry across to the Isle of Wight. About five miles outside Cowes you'll find the farmhouse. Take the case and spread my stuff around inside as if I'm still living there."

"What's inside the case?"

"My life. Everything from dirty knickers to Sherlock Holmes... gin and tonic to a school photo when I was ten... an old bikini to a chicken risotto from Waitrose... dirty toothbrush to my first Glenn Miller record... Fling it around as if I was there hours earlier... They must believe you've tracked me down and this is my home!"

"Then what?"

"When you've scattered that stuff all over... make yourself a coffee as if you're me... make yourself a ham sandwich... then leave it half-eaten and get the hell out of there waiting for Soraya's call," said Abi.

"And don't leave behind anything that's yours," added Hanny.

"So. Our killer lady calls. I give her the farmhouse address. She asks, how did I find you?"

"And you say you went into all my addresses online... found this one, going back to my days at GCHQ... and reckoned I might have retired there," said Abi.

"You recced the place and deduced this was indeed Abi's home... family photos... dirty bath... even the kettle was still warm," added Hanny.

"Hope she believes it," muttered Duffy.

"We think she will Duffy... Here's hoping," said Abi,

drinking from a hip flask.

The singing detective stood and grabbed the large leather suitcase.

"Here's the key to the farmhouse... you've got the map," said Abi.

"And then?"

"Once you've spoken to Soraya, call us immediately."

"It might be better if you stay here in Southampton Duffy," said Hanny.

"Nearer the action."

"Why?"

"Why?" answered Abigail. "Because if she takes the bait... hook, line, and sinker... you're going to join us two for a very old fashioned stakeout!"

*

Mungo had just collected his bags from the carousel at LAX and was heading for Customs, knowing that Janie would be waiting for him outside with the limo. He'd changed out of his wedding tails on the plane and was back in t-shirt and jeans.

He stopped and checked the time.

It was 4pm, so France being nine hours ahead, it would be 1am in Cannes.

He smirked a little to himself.

For he hadn't told Margot that there'd been one wedding present that she didn't know about.

The secret camera he'd installed in the bedroom ceiling light.

Just for fun. Well, not exactly.

It was so clever that he could tap into it via his phone,

from anywhere in the world.

Which is what he did there and then.

And observed two bottoms heaving in his bed.

One was white and silky smooth. And recognized his new wife, Margot.

The other was darker and spotty. And recognized his best man waiter, Sami.

For a moment Mungo was transfixed.

Deep down he knew this was going on, but to have it on your phone?

"Honey!" he heard through the welcoming faces at the Arrivals gate.

Janie was there looking pleased to see him, but serious too.

Mungo switched off the phone and hugged her tight.

"You watching porn babe?" she joked.

"Yeah, French porn," he joked back.

They collapsed into the limo.

"We're heading straight to the hospital," said Janie. "She's in a bad way."

"Dakota. What's wrong with her?"

"They think it's drugs… not sure what… It was terrible Mungo… There I was shopping on Rodeo… about to try on this drop dead sexy cocktail dress – you would just adore it – it just shimmered seduction, passion, sensuality."

"Yeah yeah…" nodded Mungo, wanting to hear more about the girl.

"And there she was outside on the sidewalk, shuffling along like a zombie… I couldn't believe it… I had to leave my dress behind!"

"Like a zombie… that is bad," said Mungo.

"I run out to her. She sees me. Comes closer and falls flat on her face. All bruised. I call 911. Her eyes – this great screenwriter of ours – her eyes are all glazed. Gone. They pull her into the ambulance and take her to Cedars-Sinai.

I follow her there and she had a quiet night."

Mungo leant across and kissed Janie on her cheek.

"A guardian angel. You probably saved her life."

The limo pulled into the hospital on Beverly and the two went inside to visit Dakota.

She was sitting up in bed, weakly smiling, with tubes into her arms.

Bags under her eyes, face bruised from where she fell.

Mungo thought she looked haunted.

But they were not the only guests.

Sat beside her, also smiling, in a spotless white suit and silk kerchief, was the Chinese businessman, Chang Yi. Who'd given Dakota a massive diamond ring.

Shit, thought Mungo. This guy knows me from Solar Global… not as a movie producer. He could blow my whole story.

Chang put out his hand in an oily greeting.

"Mister Mungo. We meet again… Small world."

"Chang Yi. Good to see you… See you're taking care of our Dakota."

"My fiancée… Of course."

"Hi guys," wheezed Dakota faintly. "Thanks for coming."

"Hope you're getting better babe," whispered Mungo to her.

"Out of here, no time," she smiled back.

Janie looked at Chang Yi. "You know my Mungo, but don't think we met?" she said.

"Sorry. I am Chang Yi. Mungo and I do business together."

Mungo interrupted swiftly. "Movie business. Chang might invest in Dakota's script… That right Chang?"

Chang looked long at Mungo then at Janie, and gauged the atmosphere. He also noticed an almost imperceptible wink from Mungo.

"Of course. I love movies. I love Dakota. So why not?"

"That would be fantastic, wouldn't it honey?" said Janie.

"Fantastic it would be," nodded Mungo.

"We hope Dakota will be out by tomorrow – we celebrate Chinese New Year."

"But I thought that was months ago?" said Janie.

Chang Yi shrugged. "Perhaps. But for me, it is every month."

"Anything we can get you Dakota?" asked Mungo.

"Bottle of rye… No. Just kidding… Mungo, you can get me out soon as."

Mungo kissed her on the cheek.

"We'll leave you in peace… come see you again tomorrow… Bye Chang."

And the chubby charmer left with Janie on his arm.

"I'm worried about her… what'll happen to the script if… to the whole project… our contact with Brad Pitt… if?" said Janie.

"Babe, I'm just worried about her. We've got to keep a real close eye… And I do not like that Chinese slimeball… He's controlling her… and I know he gave her pills."

"Trouble is," added Janie. "Whatever he's doing to her… whatever he's giving her… I think she likes it."

*

Duffy had taken Hanny's advice and was holed up in a cheap Southampton hotel near the waterfront. It was the sort of dump where the only person in the bar was a football supporter down from Ipswich for the week, or the guy changing the chocolate bar machine. So he'd kept to his room, watching a tacky game show on the tiny telly in the corner, and eating crisps with a bottle of warm white which was all they could muster downstairs.

Then he thought 'fuck it' and walked into town.

Past the kebab cafés, the spaghetti houses, and the chic French bistro, was The Oily Spoon with a flashing sign outside… 'Talent Night. Win a Grand.'

Duffy froze. Thought it over. Then entered.

It was mayhem. Some half-naked girl with two snakes round her neck was just leaving the tiny stage.

The crowd was loving it.

Duffy looked around in the gloom searching for a guy with mountains of dandruff on his shoulders, who'd be the manager.

And there he was.

Greasy long hair, gold necklace, and a red waistcoat.

"Am I too old for this?" Duffy asked him.

The dandruff looked him over and grinned wide.

"Never too old mate! What you do?"

"Try and sing…" said Duffy.

"Up next?"

Duffy nodded.

"Name?"

"Duffy."

Dandruff leapt on the stage and announced the singing detective.

Duffy took the mike.

"Hi everybody."

The room roared then waited.

Duffy cleared his throat and gently sang Lionel Richie's 'All Night Long"…

"Da Da, ooooh Well, my friends, the time has come

To raise the roof and have some fun..."

Three minutes later the crowd nearly grabbed him and carried him round the pub in their arms... they liked him.

He went to the bar and sat another hour, as other acts came and went.

Then Dandruff took the stage and announced the winner. Duffy.

He diffidently took the brown envelope and exited by a rear fire door, in case they wanted to claim it back.

No sooner had he collapsed on his hotel bed when his phone rang.

Another new ringtone.

"Don't Cry for Me Argentina..." Had to change that one he thought, and answered.

It was the young Kiwi lad, Noah.

Wanting the latest gossip on wicked stepdad Mungo.

"Well," said Duffy, coughing on the stale crisps. "Not much to report. I went to Solar Global as you suggested. Met his partner Charlie. Had a pub lunch.

And concluded he was a normal boring guy, living a normal boring life. Two small things I learnt. He's in business with some Chinese through their L.A. office which is making them a fortune... didn't say what... and... wait for this... in his briefcase he carries, or carried, burner phones, all numbered... God knows why. Usually burner phones you're using to keep something secret, so you can use them then throw them away... so absolutely no idea what to make of that my friend... So. There you go Noah... And remember I'm biased... the bugger saved my live!"

Noah thanked Duffy and transferred a fee to his account.

As they were signing off, the detective reminded him to be careful what he wished for... don't hurt that girl Donna and her family… priorities, priorities.

Then the phone rang again.

"Don't Cry for Me Argentina."

It was Soraya. As promised.

Duffy tried to sound as calm and professional as he could.

He explained that he'd gone deep into Abigail Clements-Brown's background and discovered she owned a farmhouse on the Isle of Wight, not far from Cowes.

Made more enquiries which seemed to back up she was living there now.

Soraya was quietly pleased.

Transferred Duffy's fee.

And hinted that perhaps they might meet again, on a more personal basis.

Duffy bit his tongue, and agreed.

"That would be most interesting."

Then she killed the call.

He immediately dialed Abigail.

"The Eagle had Landed."

"What?" spat Abi.

"Your little Iranian sparrow hawk has taken the bait. She thinks you're in that farmhouse on the Isle of Wight."

"Have you got a gun?" asked Abi.

"Does a bear…"

"We'll be down with you in a hour… Stand by."

*

Mungo awoke that next morning, still anxious about Dakota. He didn't care about the movie, and the script, all that shit… he worried about her. And what Chang Yi was doing to her.

He told Janie he was going for an early workout at the

gym and drove off towards Beverly Hills.

His plan was to pop into the hospital and see if he could learn more about her illness or whatever, then drop into Brett at the office to find out more about the Chinese.

As he drove he realized he had to make a decision about Margot in Cannes.

Whether or not she and Sami had tried to bump him off during the skydive; now he'd never know. What he did have evidence of, was them bonking in his bed while he was away, thanks to his secret camera feed.

So. Should he right now text his estate agent in Cannes and sell that property soon as, or, should he continue as if nothing was going on between Margot and the spotty waiter, and simply keep everyone happy. He could have Margot while in France, and what happened behind his back he didn't see. When actually, with that camera, now he did.

It was one of those moral or immoral dilemmas you had once or twice in life.

Call the estate agent and end the whole fake relationship, or, let it run along a bit longer until he made a firm decision he wouldn't regret later. After all, his gamine waif in her bare feet was much younger than him… and was now his wife.

There was only one red line not to cross.

Do not sign a will leaving the property to Margot, which is exactly what the children wanted!

He agreed with himself there were more pressing issues as he entered the hospital, and would deal with the Cannes threesome at a later date.

He went straight to Dakota's floor and her room.

He'd stopped off to buy flowers and grapes and licorice. He knew she loved those allsorts.

And went in waving his goodies.

But the bed was empty.

No Dakota.

He raced to reception and they said she'd left an hour earlier. Simply got up and walked. Couple of days before she should have. No note, no nothing.

Mungo stood, heart thumping, wondering where she'd gone.

And decided to hike it across to Brett's office at Global Energy in Glendale.

Seemed there was no ending to this Dakota drama, and, if there was, he prayed it was a happy one, and he didn't even believe in God.

Brett was there to welcome him, bright-eyed and bushy-tailed as ever, throwing his basketball into the hoop.

"Welcome home kemosabe!" he boomed through the hug.

"Good to see you fella," retorted Mungo.

"Those Chinese making you rich yet?"

"Seems so, the blades have started coming, and what monsters they are!"

"Time for lunch?"

"Want to chat first… about Dakota."

"Daks? Why – you're not going soft on her?" grinned Brett.

"I think she needs help."

"What?"

Mungo brought his mate up to speed about the drug taking and her ending up in hospital. As ever he was walking a careful tightrope re the truth. Dear Brett knew nothing about wife Janie in Bel Air… nothing about his receptionist writing a movie script for Mungo…nothing about his salesman buddy playing movie producer.

He also revealed that one of the Chinese, Chang Yi, was

dating Dakota and had given her a massive diamond ring.

"He what!?" cried Brett.

"And I think he's giving her pills…" added Mungo. "That's what she said."

"I don't like the sound of this."

"She was in hospital, then she vanished." sighed Mungo.

Brett was gazing out his windows.

"No, no my friend. She's not. She's coming in here right now…"

Both men rushed out of the office, through reception, to meet Dakota in the car park.

She was alone and walking very slowly, like in a daze.

"Hi there," she whispered. "Hi there," she repeated.

Then collapsed on the gravel.

"What is it babe, what is it?" cried Brett.

"Dakota – what's wrong!?" asked Mungo softly, taking her in his arms.

"It's fentanyl… it's fucking fentanyl."

And stopped breathing.

*

Duffy, Abigail, and Hanny were hiding in a dark wooded copse, drinking black coffee and munching chocolate, on the edge of the farmhouse field five miles from Cowes.

It was two in the morning and so far there'd been no suspicious movements around the property, save for a yapping fox and three roe deer snuffling for food. Apart from that, all quiet.

Abi had her cherished Lee Enfield on a duvet beside her, Hanny a small crossbow, and Duffy his pistol.

"Starting to bloody rain…" whispered the singing

detective.

"Always does," sighed Abi. "Just when you don't want it."

"So what's their battle plan?" asked Duffy.

"Well," said Abi. "We're talking two very hardened killers... 'pro's'... First, Soraya could come alone... thinking I'm in there sleeping... Or, if he's back in the country, Darius could back her up."

"They'll both have NV gear – night vision scopes, rifles, goggles... recce the farmhouse and decide where's Abi's sleeping," added Hanny.

"Then ram the door open, stun grenade in, boom...and job done... The target'll be taken away alive or shot on sight."

"Nice one" breathed Duffy, impressed.

"This your first stakeout detective?" asked Hanny.

"Na... last one was watching over these homeless guys under a railway bridge... While they were sleeping these bastards would drive in, throw them in a van and cut them up for body parts."

"How disgusting," whispered Hanny. "Mine was in the desert. Sahara. I was there dressed as a Tuareg, wrapped in robes, watching these North Koreans selling guns to ISIS."

"Shit," breathed Duffy.

"And my last stakeout was dear old Washington. Hiding in plain sight. In a city park, watching an American senator giving secrets to a Russian agent."

"You girls have lived the life," smiled Duffy.

"Something you can never give up," sighed Abi.

A distant noise alerted Hanny.

"I can hear something..." she said.

The trio held their breaths and listened.

There was a mechanical whirring sound, far off.

"Think it's probably a motorbike down the lane," said

Hanny.

The noise was gently getting closer.

"More like a lawnmower," added Abi.

"This time of night?" said Duffy.

Then Abi recognized the engine.

"Get down! Get bloody down now!"

At that very second the farmhouse exploded in a ginormous flash.

Through the blinding scorching light they could see chairs, toilets, a fridge, a table, a tractor wheel, flying through the air and crashing in the trees around them.

The whole sky was lit up for what seemed minutes.

Then the flames dimmed, the smoke settled, and all was deadly quiet.

"Shit!" secthed Abi. "A drone. They sent in a ruddy drone!"

CHAPTER TWENTY-TWO

"I just can't believe she's gone," choked Brett, swallowing another glass of Jack Daniel's, as he slumped on his office sofa.

"Bless her... she was such a talent," added Mungo.

"She was, she was... A great receptionist."

"No, what I never told you matey, she wrote a movie script, for some media friends of mine... it was really good."

"She was a screenwriter too?" slurred Brett.

Mungo nodded.

"Our little Dakota was a genius... a wasted genius."

"Thanks to fentanyl."

"So it's a bad drug... but do you know anything about it?" asked Mungo.

"Oh yeah. I sure do. I have a nephew in San Fran who died from it last year."

"Shit," said Mungo.

"Let me tell you. I looked into it. Two years ago the Taliban banned poppy farming in Afghanistan, which led to a 90% fall in heroin sales."

"Wow... massive. And a good thing."

"Yeah... Trouble is, the Chinese gangs saw a gap in the market and started making their own addictive opioid shit in their labs... fentanyl. They smuggled it across to the Mexican drug cartels who then brought it in as powder or pills, over the border, into the States, and here we are!"

"Jeez!" sighed Mungo.

"I tell you man, it's wrecking society here... kids wandering round the streets like zombies in San Fran, Philly, New York, even here in L.A... It's 50 times stronger than heroin, 100 times stronger than morphine. Last year Mungo, there were over 100,000 deaths from fentanyl overdoses in this country."

"Oh my God... And now Dakota's just another statistic..." sighed Mungo.

"And so bloody young."

"But what can we do about it?"

"I told you – she said Chang Yi was giving her pills... that could have been the start of all this?" said Mungo.

"But you said they were an item – he also gave her a diamond ring."

"If anyone's to blame," said Mungo.

"Sure, but go easy there Mungo. You've a great business deal with these boys – don't go fuck it up... it's making you guys a fortune... and with all this net zero crap in Britain, it's going to grow and grow."

"I know Brett, I know."

"Perhaps this pill thing with Chang Yi started out as recreational drugs – just bit of fun – something with a glass of wine after a meal – we all done it man."

"Where are they now, our Chinese friends?"

"They flew off to the U.K. this morning. Got another big order of blades heading for your wind farms they said. Want to be there to check them out."

Mungo thought a long moment.

"I think I'll head back to London ... maybe have a word with Chang Yi - he doesn't know Dakota's dead."

"Be careful old buddy. These Asians don't like to lose face, know what I mean. Don't rub their noses in it."

Mungo stood and shook hands with Brett.

"I'm used to walking on eggshells matey. Do it every day."

And he exited out into the Californian sunshine, determined to find out what or who killed the lovely young Dakota, well before her time.

*

Duffy handed out coffee in plastic cups to Abi and Hanny and sat beside them as they rocked and rolled their way back to Southampton on the Isle of Wight ferry.

"So. The drone?" asked Duffy.

"Remember when Iran attacked Israel, with over 300 drones and missiles?"

"World War Three, they said…"

"Well, that same drone flattened the farmhouse last night near Cowes."

"What?"

"It's a beauty, built in Tehran. The Shahed 136. Delta wing… explosive warhead in the nose… flies at 180 mph… a range of 1200 miles!"

"Hell. So could easily been launched at night from a field near London and targeted the property without anyone noticing?" whispered Duffy.

"Easily."

"And no-one will ever know who or how they bombed that farmhouse," said Hanny.

"Except us," said Abi.

"Except us", added Hanny.

"Question is, do the Iranian assassins think you're dead Abi?" asked Duffy.

"Well, I'm placing an obit in tomorrow's Times. Give them certainty. Then I hope the wretches will crawl back under their stones in Iran and leave us to live in peace."

"She threatened to meet up again, for personal reasons," said Duffy. "If you get my drift."

"Don't they say when the black widow spider mates, she then kills and eats the male," smiled Abi.

"Mmm," said Duffy. "She was dressed in black."

"And we know she kills," said Hanny.

"If she does call, let me know immediately Duffy," ordered Abi. "Don't want you missing in action."

"So. We'll go our separate ways then... Seems like the fake farmhouse was an explosive success and we'll see no more of these pesky varmints."

"Not so fast pardner," drawled Abi in a cod Yankee accent. "You're coming to my place for tea tomorrow, then I'll transfer your fee, and then, but only then, will we assess if our demon duo have flown off to make trouble elsewhere."

*

Noah felt his personal drama was drawing to a close. He'd got his inheritance back from Mungo and found out the guy was a bigamist with a lovely daughter he had fallen for. Through the singing detective Duffy, he'd also learnt that his wicked stepdad had some numbered burner phones, which was seriously weird, and was making a small fortune through some new deal done with a Chinese company.

But, being a Kiwi, our young Noah was inherently tidy. He didn't like loose ends. So he'd decided that, after dark, he'd take a trip over to the Pinner industrial estate where Mungo worked out of Solar Global and take a peek around.

He'd popped into a hardware store and bought a set of tools... screw driver, hammer, torch, and jemmy. Anything that might be useful on the night.

Hired an Uber to the estate and was now standing outside the Solar Global sign, getting an idea how far the business premises stretched, and where best to get over the wire fence. He waited to see if there was a security patrol with dogs, then decided he was all on his own.

Him and his baseball cap hiding his face because of security cameras, and his burglary bag.

Once over the fence he headed straight for the reception area of Solar Global's offices. Spotted a camera above the door so headed around the back instead.

Then saw the long aircraft-sized hangar, again part of Mungo's company.

And wondered what on earth they could be storing inside.

Again he saw a camera above the main double doors and headed around to the rear.

Through a high window he could see there was a light on inside. Strange. At nearly midnight.

On the ground below the window was a long ladder.

He heaved it against the wall and climbed up to that high window.

And what he saw was curiouser and curiouser.

Indeed he could have been Alice in Wonderland.

For lying the full length of the hangar were dozens of massive fibreglass shiny white blades.

The kind you see attached to those wind farm turbines on land and offshore.

So this was how Mungo was making his new fortune.

Bringing these in from the States for the Chinese, who could see the mountains of cash to be made by erecting these eyesores across this country's natural beauty spots.

And sitting at a table amongst the blades were three burly Asians playing cards.

Why did this place need security around the clock, asked Noah. Not as if some weedy burglar would break in and disappear with one of these blades in his back pocket.

Which is when his phone rang.

He swayed on his ladder and answered as quick as he could, before the guards could hear him.

It was Monica, Donna's Mum.

She was worried as she'd not seen her daughter that night, never come home, and wondered if they were together?

Noah climbed down off the ladder and whispered back.

"Nope. Didn't see her last night. Could she be staying with friends?" he asked.

Monica said she wasn't answering her phone. Not like her. But she'd wait till morning before getting too anxious. And hung up.

Noah was puzzled too.

His Donna was rock solid, both feet on the ground, not someone to get drunk and end up sleeping in the wrong bed or whatever.

A door creaked somewhere in the dark and Noah froze.

Those three guys might have heard him talking.

Torchlight suddenly beamed from round the far corner of the hangar and Noah raced off into the dark.

He heard Asian voices shouting behind him.

Then the dog barking.

He hadn't seen a bloody dog.

Turned and looked back.

All three stooges were sprinting towards him, with a dog on a lead.

Don't let it off, pleaded the Kiwi to himself.

Then they did.

It was a large mastiff, weighing about nine stone.

But it ran like a greyhound.

Ahead of Noah was the Solar Global office.

And a drainpipe coming down off the roof.

The Kiwi leapt at the pipe and pulled himself up as fast as his arms and legs could muster. Been a sea cadet as a kid so knew all about that climbing shit.

The dog just missed his sneakers.

But the three guys were armed and let off a bullet into the moonlit sky.

"Get down!" shouted the largest, his gold teeth glinting.

Noah weighed up the options.

Get down and get eaten by a giant canine.

Or climb onto the roof and get shot in the arse.

"Put that dog on a lead!" he shouted. "And I'll come down."

The guards hesitated then fastened the mastiff back on his leash.

Noah slid to the ground and was pinned to the wall by two of the grunts.

"What you want!?"

"I got lost," said Noah without much credibility. Even he didn't believe it.

"What you want?" they repeated.

Just then a small car crashed through the wire fence and skidded beside them. The passenger door flung open and a voice shouted : "Get in!"

It was Donna.

Noah flung himself past the guards and landed in the car.

"What you doing?"

"Following you!"

"Why?"

"I think I'm pregnant!"

"Shit!"

As one of the Asians crashed a sledgehammer through the car's windscreen.

Right now, Noah and Donna weren't going anywhere fast.

*

Mungo had left L.A. under a cloud. His first domestic with Janie. It had started out all sad and emotional when he told her that Dakota, their screenwriter, had died. But then when he announced he was doing a fleeting trip back to Europe for more 'investment', she blew it. Big time. Almost threw him out of their marital palace on the spot. She hadn't married him to be some kind of fucking Bel Air widow, with him away all the time like a travelling salesman. She wanted him there by her side, day and night. And anyway, she was rich as Croesus, so why the hell did he need any more cash - he had as much as he could wish for, when he'd married her. Or was there some other woman out there that he was seeing, some other bed that he was sharing?

Then Mungo got the alarming text from Monica saying Donna had not come home and was missing. He put the blame fair and square on that little Kiwi turd, Noah. Bet he'd got her drunk and taken her off somewhere. Did kids still drive all the way to Gretna Green to get secretly hitched? Probably not, more likely fly to Vegas and get an Elvis impersonator do the deed.

He'd also heard from Margot in Cannes, who was wondering when to book the next skydive attempt, and missing him like crazy. As if, thought Mungo, remembering what he'd seen on his bedroom camera. He parked that problem for the time being.

331

And from Putri in Amsterdam who sounded like an excited child. She'd done a fast track divorce online, and now was free, suggesting they should make a date for their wedding.

But right now Mungo was trying to stay focussed, paying the London cab driver and heading into his Harrow home. He had to find Donna, and he had to talk to Chang Yi about Dakota.

Monica was holding back the tears as she poured tea and told him about their daughter's disappearance. How she'd called Noah the boyfriend who knew nothing, how she wasn't answering her phone.

Which gave Mungo an idea. He told Monica a couple of years ago he'd put a tracker on Donna's mobile, in case she ever got in trouble while dating. If he activated that, he might find her phone, might find her.

Thirty minutes later the chubby charmer had followed the tracker on Donna's phone to Harrow Breakers, a scrap yard for old cars. He looked around for the guvnor and found a grizzled red-nosed guy in the office, beneath a Pirelli calendar with a bikinied girl bent low, peering under a car bonnet.

"An old Vauxhall?" said Jim. "Yeah, came in this morning son."

"Where'd you find it?" asked Mungo.

"Dumped at that industrial estate out Pinner way. Outside Solar Global it was.

Bloody windscreen been smashed. No good to no-one."

"Where's it now?"

"Right there, me old love. Like I said, no good to no-one."

Mungo peered out the office window at the mountain of rusting wrecks.

And there it was.

His daughter's little Vauxhall was in the car crusher.

Squashed to a metal lump, five feet long and three feet high. The phone was certainly still in there. He just prayed that his darling daughter wasn't.

Mungo's next stop was his London office. Solar Global on the Pinner industrial estate where they'd found Donna's car. But what on earth was she doing there? Had she discovered he didn't work for a 'so very hush hush' organisation?

And who'd smashed up the car and taken her?

He raced through reception and into Charlie's office.

Who was bending over his long desk looking at a business plan with two others in immaculate white suits and silk kerchiefs.

The Chinese, Messrs Sun and Chang Yi.

"Ah! Mungo... just in time," cried Charlie, beaming. "We need your moniker on this here contract old boy... Our friends are doubling their imports from next month... meaning double the dosh for us," he winked at his partner.

"Hello Charlie. Mr Sun. Chang Yi," replied Mungo carefully, not wanting to be railroaded into anything too quickly. He studied the paperwork and turned to the Chinese.

"This is great news gentlemen. But where are all these blades actually going?"

"Up north Mister Mungo," replied Chang Yi. "Great demand in Norfolk, Suffolk, Yorkshire... Everybody wants cheap power and we want to help."

Mungo slumped into a leather chair.

"You going to sign Mungo?" asked Charlie.

"Sure. If everything's above board."

"Everything is legal Mister Mungo, I assure you," smiled Chang Yi.

"Like giving Dakota drugs?" said Mungo.

"What?"

"She told me you gave her drugs."

"Now Mungo, what's all this about?" interrupted Charlie, concerned his partner was going to blow the deal.

Chang Yi hesitated. "OK. One night, one night only, I gave her speed.

Nothing more. We all take speed in L.A... everyone I know," he smirked.

"You know she's dead?" said Mungo softly.

"Dead? No... no... not my little girl," whispered Chang Li.

"As a dodo."

"This cannot be..."

"She died from a drug called fentanyl. You know it Chang Yi?"

"Fentanyl. I read about it... Not good."

"You never gave her some?"

"Course not. Who you think I am. A bad person!?

Chang Yi headed for the door.

"We must leave. You no trust us. Do not sign. We go somewhere else."

"Wait. Chang Yi. I'm sorry. I want to trust you. I want to do this deal," said

Mungo, smiling wide with fake sincerity.

"But?"

"Let's share that trust. I want to see inside the hangar. Where your guards stop us entering... I want to see the new shipment."

"We must leave now Mister Mungo... But. Tomorrow. Tomorrow we show you the hanger. And the blades. Then we sign. High noon. Like the cowboy movies."

"Tomorrow? I can't wait that long."

Chang Yi looked at him a long moment in deadly silence.

Mungo could see he had no choice. "OK. High noon it is," sighed Mungo.

Chang Yi mirrored the chubby charmer's phoney grin, then exited with his silent partner to their helicopter and departed.

"You've just screwed the deal Mungo!" seethed Charlie.

"It's got personal here Charlie. A lot going down… In fact, why don't we go visit the hangar right now!?"

"They've got armed guards inside. About a dozen. We could get shot."

Mungo weighed this up. It was more time wasted, more hours without Donna, but time he could use to get prepped. And now he could play Gary Cooper in his very own version of High Noon…

*

Duffy had chosen one of his better denim shirts to attend Abigail's tea party in her luxury Thameside penthouse. He'd stopped off at a favourite bakery in Soho and bought her a large chocolate carrot cake, hoping it would appeal to the old girl's taste buds. The more he saw of these two old biddies, the more he liked them. They'd done so much more with their lives than anyone he knew. Out there tracking down the enemy, chasing spies on foreign soil, even terminating suspects when instructed.

These days the youngsters, tomorrow's leaders, struggled to get out of bed in the morning, let alone do a day's work. But Abi and her mate Hanny had nerves of steel, were straight-talking, and took no prisoners. No emotive woke nonsense for them. If so, they'd never have survived.

Just then, as he pulled in to park his Harley outside Abi's flat, his phone rang.

"MacArthur's Park is melting in the dark All the sweet,

335

green icing flowing down…"

A new ringtone. Richard Harris. The old ones were always the best. Like Abi and Hanny.

It was his bigamist life-saver Mungo. Duffy hoped the Kiwi lad had not blurted anything out about the numbered burner phones.

"Duffy. Got a little problem…"

"Mungo. I'm all yours."

"Need some advice."

"Go on."

"Donna, my daughter's gone missing. And might need some help getting her back… Like a posse. Muscle. Know what I mean?"

"I think I do… you need to get together some likely lads to help you out."

"Exactly. Trouble is I'm torn. Between going down the East End route… or the cops."

"Off the record or on the record?" said Duffy.

"Precisely."

"Tough one. We talking weapons here?"

"Definitely."

"When's this happening?"

"Tomorrow. Wait for it… High Noon."

"Love it. Perhaps call in the heavies for starters, then get my mate Kate at the Met for afters?"

"Perfect menu… I'll sort it," laughed Mungo.

And hung up.

Duffy smiled to himself. How was it he was always drawn to the action when the going got rough?

But least, right now, he was heading for a refined cuppa with the charming Abigail.

Clutching the cake in its box, he was about to ring her flat number when someone spoke at his shoulder.

"You seeing Abigail Clements-Brown?"

Duffy turned. The guy was in biker uniform with helmet and goggles and holding an Amazon delivery in a cardboard box.

The singing detective hesitated. Never liked taking stuff for others like this.

But the guy looked like a delivery guy, and it was an Amazon box. If it walks like a duck.

"Or you could get her come down here for it?" the guy added.

"No problem," smiled Duffy, taking the delivery, along with his cake.

"Thanks man," said the biker who then rode off on his bike with a smiley wave.

Once upstairs, Abigail opened her door and gave Duffy a bear hug.

Hanny was sitting in the background, already pouring tea from an expensive looking purple clay pot.

"Got some things for you…" said Duffy.

"Well, what have we here?" purred Abi, looking at the two boxes.

"Got you a little cake in Soho," said Duffy.

"What sort of cake?" cooed Hanny.

"Chocolate carrot cake."

"My favourite," said Abi. "And?"

"An Amazon delivery. Biker asked if I'd bring it up for you."

"Amazon? But I never use Amazon. I never order deliveries… I…"

"Oh…" said Duffy.

Hanny grabbed a box from Duffy, opened the balcony

doors and threw it high over the Thames into the river.

"That was my cake!" shouted Duffy.

Who followed Hanny and threw the Amazon box high out over the water.

Seconds later there was a flashing boom as the balcony glass doors shattered, throwing all three to the floor. Then silence, apart from their ears ringing.

They lay there breathing long, hearts thumping, taking in exactly what had just happened.

Then Abi hauled herself off the carpet, flicked off the broken glass, and said simply: "To be brutally honest Duffy, I never did like carrot cake!"

CHAPTER TWENTY-THREE

"Well," sighed Abigail, "I think we can say without doubt that Soraya and Darius now have my home address."

"Nearly gone up in smoke," added Duffy, sipping a fresh cup of tea.

"Your obit in The Times didn't convince, my dear," said a serene Hanny.

"Ho hum. This is it then. Two ruddy attempts to blow me sky high... I must really irritate them."

"But how did they find you... track you here?" asked Duffy. "Somehow they managed to discover your home very quickly."

"Only one possible reason Duffy, you."

"Me?"

"You're the single link to me and Hanny... Once they'd bombed the farmhouse and found no trace of me, they'd have realised it was all a hoax... realised that you were working with us, the enemy. So, they know where you work from...

They'd have followed you from the Fortnum's bar right here."

"Agree Abi. Standard tradecraft." added Hanny.

"Shit. So I was their useful idiot!" sighed Duffy.

"Don't worry dear, they'd have found us sooner or later."

"So what do we do? They know we're all sat in here drinking tea... waiting for them to burst through the door with Uzi's."

"Simple. You'll be our bait," smiled Abi.

"What?"

"Now that you're part of our clandestine package, they'll be after you too."

"Oh shit."

"I suspect our killers will split up. Probably Darius go after you Duffy, leaving Soraya to deal with us."

"Makes sense," said Hanny.

"So, in a few minutes you'll leave the flat Duffy, get on your bike and ride like hell into the blue."

"Where to?"

"Anywhere. You'll look in your mirror and find Darius tailing you… See if you can lose him… or, turn around and confront him."

"You do have your gun?" asked Hanny.

Duffy nodded.

"But what about you two? I can't leave you."

"We'll find a way dear boy… I have a plan that will confuse our Soraya, and hopefully we'll disappear into the London crowds."

"So you can't stay on here – where will you stay?" asked Duffy.

"Better you don't know. In case you get caught… Now. Be a good boy. Do as I say and go get on that lovely bike of yours."

Duffy stood and bowed awkwardly to the two.

"Good luck ladies," and left the flat.

"I hope he'll be alright," said Hanny.

"He can handle himself."

"Should we call Sir Geoffrey? He'll hear about the bomb."

"That's why I want to leave here soonest."

"How?"

"I've alerted the neighbours…"

"Your neighbours?"

There is a quiet tap on the door.

"Wait," said Abi. She listened carefully.

Five taps on the door.

"As arranged."

She opened the door to two elderly couples, all smiles.

"What fun," said Mrs Hughes. "Never done this before."

"My husband loves dressing up," added Mrs Andrews.

"Through there," said Abi. "You can all use the spare room to change."

On the street below, opposite the flat's entrance, Soraya sat impatiently in a small Fiat with tinted windows.

Duffy the detective had just left the address and rode away on a Harley.

Darius had given him a start, then followed on his bike.

Soraya determined she'd give it ten minutes then enter the building and take the two British agents out. But not for a walk.

Just then two females came out of the entrance, both dressed in black burqas, covering their bodies from head to toe, with only a meshed slit allowing them to see.

"You think you're clever," thought the Iranian killer as she got out of the car, about to follow them.

Then another two ladies in the same Arab dress exited the flats, heading in a different direction.

"Damn!" spat Soraya who was about to make a choice on who to follow.

When a third couple in burqas came out of the building, taking yet another direction.

"Shit shit shit!" seethed the assassin, watching all three pairs mingle and disappear into the thronging crowds of shoppers.

*

341

'I'd better get going love," said Mungo. "Got a meeting at noon."

"How can you go to meetings when our daughter's still missing?"

"That's what it's about – finding our Donna."

"You think she's safe?"

"Hope so, I bloody hope so," muttered Mungo, walking to his car.

"What's that you got?"

Mungo was carrying a long object wrapped in a cloth.

"Not a gun is it?"

"No love, something I ordered online... for the meeting," said Mungo, who got into his car and drove off.

His head was throbbing for two reasons. Both beginning with 'D'.

Finding Donna, and why Dakota died.

He hoped the next hour would bring a swift resolution to both dilemmas.

Back at Solar Global, Charlie was not in a good mood.

To call it foul would be an understatement.

"When the Chinese fly in please don't cock up this new contract Mungo, we could lose millions... I have no idea why you wound up Chang Yi like that – he didn't like it and neither did I! Whatever's going on man, keep your emotions under control... This is a business we're running!"

"I'll do what I have to Charlie. For both our sakes."

Time to bring him up to speed, thought Mungo.

He revealed Donna had gone missing two nights earlier... and that her car had been dumped outside the company offices. No idea what she was doing there.

He also revealed that Brett's receptionist in L.A. had been dating Chang Yi, and just died of a deadly new drug called fentanyl, that was sweeping the States, having been smuggled in through Mexico from China.

"Shit – that's a lot to take in… no wonder you're acting strange Mungo…You don't think… you don't think our Chinese are involved?" asked Charlie.

"No idea mate. Just know this is all starting to stink… and I think the smell is coming from our hangar over there."

"What you carrying in that cloth – not a gun I hope?" asked Charlie nervously.

"Show you later… Listen, if you want to take an early lunch and disappear, I can deal with this on my own?"

"Nope. We'll stand together, whatever it takes. We're partners remember… and this is… High Noon."

"Like in the cowboy movies," nodded the chubby charmer. "Gary Cooper…"

At that moment a helicopter flew low over the building and landed on the lawn behind.

Mungo looked at his watch. Midday. "Bang on time."

Messrs Sun and Yi jumped out and came running towards the office in their white suits and silk kerchiefs.

"Fucking white suits," muttered Mungo, as he walked out to meet their Chinese partners with a rigid smile.

*

Duffy led Darius on a cat and mouse motorbike race across London, eventually heading up to Paddington and the Regent's Canal, alongside the Zoo.

He was hoping that the two old spies had managed to evade the sultry but deadly Soraya who would have been waiting for them outside the flat. They would doubtless be taking her on a crazy chase around the city, or, the Iranian had gone straight to their door with an Uzi and executed them there and then.

A bullet pinged past Duffy's left ear as he parked his bike and started running along the towpath beside the canal.

He reached inside his jacket for his Sig Sauer. Nothing. Must have bloody fallen out on his bike. So, odds were against him. Idiot.

Darius was about a hundred yards behind him and getting closer.

The singing detective leapt onto the deck of a bright red narrow boat moored alongside the bank and hid tucked into the stern door frame.

Darius, also now on foot, raced past him for a further fifty yards on the towpath then slowed, looked back, scanning the canal boats one by one, and started jogging the way he'd just come.

Any second he'd be standing by Duffy's narrow boat, and see him.

He held a pistol with a silencer in his right hand.

At that moment a large long dirty barge carrying coal, was being towed up the river past Duffy's boat.

He looked at Darius getting closer.

He judged the distance between himself and the moving barge, then leapt.

Landed on the side of the barge, feet in the water, and pulled himself sopping up onto the deck.

Another bullet whirred past his head.

Darius gave him a friendly wave from the towpath. Playing games.

The Iranian peered upriver where the barge was heading, spotting a bridge across the canal, and sprinted for it.

Duffy guessed he intended to either jump onto the barge

from the bridge, or simply shoot him from the higher position, while he had no cover.

Without waiting to find out, the singing detective stomped through the cargo of coals on the barge to the other side, leapt into the water, and swam to the far bank.

Darius, still running towards the bridge, had not spotted Duffy's new ruse.

Once on dry land, Duffy ran down the towpath away from the bridge, and spotted an alleyway, leading to a main road.

A double-decker bus was just leaving the stop as he jumped on.

Heading to Waterloo Station.

Out the window he spotted Darius reach the end of the same alley.

Waved at him smiling from the bus.

Game over, or so he hoped. He didn't want to die, not yet, and certainly not like this. As a pawn in some international grudge match. And anyway, getting too old for this lark, thought Duffy. He was seriously puffed, chest wheezing like an asthmatic, thighs aching, and clothes sopping from that filthy canal water. Wonder he was let on the bus.

He was already halfway to Waterloo. There he'd get a cab back to the bike and see if he could spend the night with Toto again. Probably not visit the bar for a while though; these guys knew where to find him.

At the next traffic lights he closed his eyes and was dozing off when there was a tap on the window.

A beaming Darius on his motorbike... giving him a friendly thumbs up... and patting his leather jacket where he kept his gun.

*

Monica never ever drank on her own. Certainly not at lunchtime. But today with Donna still missing and Mungo going off into the blue for some mystery meeting, she was at her wits' end.

She went to the cocktail cabinet and poured herself a limoncello.

It sent her pulses racing at first sip. Just what she needed.

She'd put up with Mungo's fantasy world for years, him pretending to be some sort of James Bond, gallivanting around the world, when she knew only too well he was simply out there selling solar panels, a travelling salesman from Pinner.

But she let him have his dreams, if it made him happy. Like any relationship there was always give and take, though sometimes he was away so often and so long, she wondered if she was giving too much.

But together they'd brought up three wonderful kids in a lovely little home.

They had everything, never wanting for money. If she needed a new car or a holiday in the sun, Mungo would happily provide. He'd even offered to pay for a cleaner and a gardener but she'd turned him down. That was her territory. That was what she enjoyed. Not be like some of her nobby friends who spent most of their mornings cleaning up before the cleaner arrived. Once you go down that path you'll end up with a cook and a chauffeur thrown in. Then what was the point of getting out of bed in the morning.

She pottered down the corridor to the loo, again thinking of Donna. Praying that the worst had not happened. Not sure how she'd cope if it had. The strange thing was that Noah's phone was now going to voicemail. They'd spoken perfectly normally the night she vanished and now he wasn't answering. Could they both have fallen foul of someone, both been kidnapped. Though there'd been no blackmail calls asking for money, not yet anyhow. She just hoped they were alive and breathing somewhere.

On her way back from the loo, she noticed the coat cupboard door was ajar.

Went to close it and spotted Mungo's business case sitting there.

Never went anywhere without that. Like it was attached to his body.

She wondered whether to call him and say she'd found it but decided it could wait.

She stood staring at that case.

Wondered what little secret titbits he carried around with him.

Photos of the family?

A closeup of her?

The limoncello had her pulse racing.

Making her do things she wouldn't normally dare.

As she gently unzipped the case and looked inside.

It was almost empty.

Various pieces of signed paper that looked like business contracts.

The odd menu from restaurants abroad.

Old air tickets and customs forms.

Then she spotted them.

Strapped to the inside of the lid were four burner phones.

Numbers 1 to 5.

Monica was instantly curious.

But there was no No.2.

And why did her darling husband possess burner phones in the first place?

Surely these were used by criminals who didn't want calls traced back to them... or cheating spouses not wanting to be caught out.

Monica was sorely tempted to pick up each one and dial.

To enter Mungo's world of mystery.

But then she had a terrible thought.

Perhaps. Perhaps her darling husband really was working for the security services around the globe; perhaps the travelling salesman job was his cover, his legend, as they say on the telly; perhaps this was all a double double bluff. He knew that she knew he was selling solar panels when in fact he truly was a James Bond saving lives in hostile territories.

Hence the burner phones. To contact his undercover assets. To trap foreign spies. To help save lives. Perhaps, perhaps Monica was married to a hero, but she could never shout it from the rooftops, could never reveal she knew.

She went and poured herself a second limoncello and planned her next move.

*

"You ready to sign the new contract Mister Mungo?" asked Chang Yi. "This will guarantee three more years us bringing in our blades here, for the wind farms...

plenty good profit for you and Mister Charlie."

"Very ready Chang Yi... But, like we said, first we'd like to see inside the hangar... your new shipment... as promised."

Chang Yi shrugged. "Nothing to see. Just many big blades."

"And your security guards," added Mungo.

"To keep our product safe. We do not like snoopers."

"You had any snoopers recently?"

"No no, never."

"We really would like to look at the hangar," said Charlie.

"OK OK," sighed the Asian. "Follow me."

And Chang Yi with Mr Sun strutted across the neat lawn to the doors of the giant hangar.

Mungo noted that a ladder was standing beneath one of the high windows.

Normally that was dumped on the ground.

Chang Yi took out his phone and shouted something in Mandarin.

The massive double doors slowly opened.

So big in there it could have housed two Boeings.

But what they saw nearly bowled Mungo over.

These new blades were gigantic, compared to the few he'd seen earlier.

About eighty yards long and a yard wide at the connection end.

Shiny white fibreglass beauties, lying gleaming in neat rows of ten.

At a glance Mungo counted about sixty of them.

"You are looking at the latest shipment Mister Mungo. Came in just last week," said Chang Yi proudly.

"Very impressive," said Mungo.

He moved forward to stroke one of them, still carrying that long object wrapped in a cloth.

As if from nowhere, two Chinese security guards leapt forward and held his arms.

Mungo looked at Chang Yi.

The Asian again shouted something in Mandarin.

The guards stood back, looked surly.

Mungo saw they carried guns, but ignored them.

"And when do you move these blades out Chang Yi?"

"Tomorrow morning. Then new shipment arrive next day."

"So it's already running like clockwork?"

"We proud that very efficient," said a smiling Mr Sun for the first time.

Mungo looked at all the blades thoughtfully then turned back to Chang Yi.

"These blades are hollow Chang Yi?"

"Of course. Make the wind turbine turn faster, make more energy for the British people."

Quick as a flash Mungo moved to the nearest blade, dropped the cloth from what he was carrying, revealing a yard-long very sharp fireman's pick axe.

And smashed it hard on the outside rim of the blade.

The fibreglass cracked but did not split open.

The two guards were at his side in a flash, wrestling with Mungo.

Four other Chinese guards appeared from nowhere, all armed, rushing towards the chubby charmer who had put his two fingers to his mouth and whistled, loud.

At that second, through the main doors of the hangar, in charged half a dozen bruisers carrying baseball bats, led by Eddie, the friendly gangster from The Blind Beggar pub.

The High Noon posse.

Mungo was thrown to the ground as the Chinese guards squared up to the East End mobsters.

The Asians took out their pistols but had no time to fire as three of the Londoners had tiny crossbows with lethal silent darts.

Immediately two of the guards fell, as the burly thugs attacked the others with bats and knuckle-dusters.

Mungo, in the heat of the battle, grabbed his axe and

again smashed the nearest blade.

At first it wouldn't break, then slowly started to split and crack open, and finally, a large plastic chunk fell to the ground.

Leaving a hole about two feet wide halfway down the blade.

And there was something inside.

Mungo shoved his hand in and pulled out a bag of white powder.

And another.

And another.

He ripped one open and threw it over Chang Yi, turning him into a petrified snowman.

"No!" he shouted through the white dust. "This kill me!"

Mungo grabbed the Asian's arm.

"What is it – tell me Chang Yi!?"

"Is…" he choked.

"Tell me!"

"No!"

"Say it!"

"Is… is… fentanyl," he whispered.

"Fentanyl! You got Dakota's blood on your hands - you bastard!"

Charlie's face fell. "Drugs! Fuck me!"

Chang Yi broke loose from Mungo and raced out of the hangar followed by his partner Sun towards their helicopter.

Mungo nodded to Eddie, who was triumphantly standing over the Asian guards.

"Get them!"

Eddie's crossbow boys chased after Messrs Sun and Yi and brought them down.

Bolts in each bum which turned their pristine white suits

impeccably red.

They were dragged back inside, tied, and dumped in a corner like yesterday's trash.

Mungo and the posse had won his showdown at High Noon.

"Wait!" cried Eddie from the far end of the hangar. "Shush – I hear something!"

"Shtum!" cried Mungo.

And there it was. A tiny noise from one of the blades, like a woodpecker on a tree. Tap tap tap. Hardly audible, but insistent.

Mungo ran to the blade.

It was at the wide end, where it connected to the turbine.

There was a large plastic cap screwed across the opening.

He tried to open it. No go.

Then used the fireman's pick axe.

Seconds later he'd prised the cap open and there, lying inside the tube, was someone, bound and gagged.

Noah.

Dragged him out quickly and ripped off the mouth tape.

"Where's Donna?" cried Mungo.

"Dunno... they did me first..." panted the Kiwi. "But I was running out of air... so quick... if she's..."

Mungo shouted loud. "Shuddup everybody – listen... let me know if you hear anything!"

The whole hangar went quiet and listened.

Peered around the sixty blades.

Ears strained for minutes.

Eddie looked at Mungo and shook his head.

Mungo slowly turned pale.

Then one of the mobsters shouted from the far end of the hangar.

352

"I hear tapping…"

They all ran to him and the nearest blade.

Mungo smashed the plastic casing with his axe and there she was.

Daughter Donna, bound and gagged like Noah.

Mungo heaved her out and pulled off the tape.

Then hugged her tight for a very long time.

At first she was motionless, then she slowly stirred.

And in the end it was a good day… for Donna, for Dakota, and for Mungo.

*

When the bus reached Waterloo Station everyone got off. Except Duffy. He'd crouched down out of sight on the backseat, waiting for the driver to get out. He knew that standing out there somewhere with his gun was Darius, waiting to shoot him dead. The P.I. who'd been working hand in glove with M16. He just hoped he'd get a good obit if the worst happened. That they used one of his younger pix.

At long last the driver exited and Duffy raced down to his seat, jumping out of his door, on the opposite side from where Darius was standing.

And ran like hell.

Past the taxi queue outside the main entrance to the station.

Knocking over a beautifully groomed woman with an ebony cane, and kicking her pink poodle in the butt.

Across the main road, dodging the buses and bikers.

Down that narrow lane with the buskers and beggars.

Slug And Lettuce pub to his left. Could murder a pint, he thought.

Don't say 'murder' he told himself.

His clothes squishing as he ran, still sopping from the canal water.

Still stinking like a dead fish on sale from last week's market.

Looked about quickly and dodged into an alley to his right.

Held his breath.

Nothing.

Commuters breezing past, loving couples, rowdy tourists.

But no Darius.

"Hello Duffy..." said a foreign accent behind him.

The singing detective turned.

He was ten feet away pointing his pistol in his direction.

"As they say, you can run but you can't hide..."

Duffy threw a bag of empty beer cans at Darius's head and hared off down the lane towards the Thames.

Looking back quickly he spotted Darius down on one knee, taking aim.

The bullet grazed his right shoulder, but it bloody hurt.

Still running, there it was, in front of him.

The London Eye.

That weird monstrosity that looked like a huge spoked bicycle wheel, over 400 feet high, and carrying 32 capsules for passengers to view London. It moved so slowly that a snail could move faster.

Trouble was, Duffy didn't have time to go sightseeing, nor anywhere else to turn.

Behind him was the Iranian assassin with his shooter.

In front of him this ludicrous tourist attraction.

If he jumped into one of the passenger pods, Darius would stroll in, do the job, then stroll out before anyone noticed.

Duffy was out of choices.

He hated heights.

So our singing detective started climbing.

Up the outside of the wheel on its steel gantry.

Right now he wished he'd picked up a few tricks from Spiderman.

Looking down he saw Darius was still following him with that same bloody smile.

Probably more lethal than the gun.

Already Duffy was feeling queasy from the height.

He steeled himself and simply looked upwards, not down.

Already halfway up the outside of the wheel.

Tourists were taking photos of him from their capsules. Laughing and waving. With each flash Duffy thought he'd fall.

Another twenty feet higher.

And the dizziness kicked in.

His knuckles were whiter than white.

Stomach starting to heave.

But no more bullets. Just a really painful shoulder where he could feel and smell the blood soaking his shirt. He'd never get that out, not even with bleach.

Why no Darius?

Had he… had he fallen?

"Say your prayers Duffy…"

The singing detective looked up.

Somehow the Iranian had got ahead of him on the gantry and was just a few feet away, pointing the pistol and its silencer at his face.

"What?" mumbled Duffy.

"End of the road old buddy," smirked Darius. "Next time choose the right team."

He took a long breath, shrugged as if to say, sorry but this is my job, and went to pull the trigger.

A distant crack from the ground below.

A trickle of blood from between Darius's eyes.

A final smile at Duffy, then he fell in slow motion to the ground.

The singing detective peered below, trying not to retch.

And saw a small creature holding an old Lee Enfield rifle.

Abigail Clements-Brown had just saved his life.

CHAPTER TWENTY-FOUR

Mungo at last felt his world was coming together. Mostly in a good way. He'd brought the family out for an Indian in Notting Hill to celebrate being alive. And then some.

He was mighty relieved to have survived the High Noon showdown with the Chinese business partners... He'd paid off Eddie and his boys for winning the gun fight, then called Duffy's mate Kate at the Met to take away Messrs Sun and Yi. He regretted losing those outrageous profits from importing the blades, but was quietly satisfied Chang Yi was caught smuggling the deadly drug fentanyl into the U.K. which would put him away for years, and was a day of reckoning for dear young Dakota.

So there he was, passing round the poppadums to his sons, Sam and Riley, with daughter Donna back home from her kidnapping ordeal, and, beside him, his long suffering wife Monica.

Plus of course, Noah.

Donna had insisted he come along too, as she had something to announce.

Deep down Mungo was feeling more relaxed about the Kiwi boy. He obviously knew Mungo had been a bigamist, but, in return for getting his inheritance back, was staying schtum. And, to be fair, the chubby charmer had to admit he was a pleasant young lad, and that it was he himself who'd been in the wrong.

Donna tapped a knife on her wine glass.

"Shush everyone..."

The table quietened.

"Dad… what can I say… but, thank you. Thank you for saving my life yesterday – I had no idea what those crazies would have done to us… and for saving Noah too."

Noah nodded, smiling at Mungo.

"You here at this table, are the most important people in my life… But, sometime soon, there might be one more."

"Oh no, don't tell me dear," said Monica.

"You up the spout Sis?" chirped Sam.

"You're hearing it first… Yup, I'm having a baby!" smiled Donna.

The family cheered.

"That is wonderful darling!" cried Monica.

Mungo sat a little dazed, realising Noah was about to stay part of his life.

Then. "Beautiful news love, just beautiful," he sighed, almost welling up.

"And…" interrupted Noah. "I've got some news."

"You having a baby too mate?" hissed Riley.

"I'm taking Donna for a trip Down Under… show her how the other half lives."

"To Auckland?" asked Mungo nervously. Suddenly alert to the fact that his daughter didn't know about his marriage to Noah's late Mum. If she met the old gang like Sal and Rosso in the Chim Chim Thai Kitchen, it would all come out and his house of cards come tumbling down.

"No Mungo. To the Bay of Islands… going to the paradise up north. I'll give Auckland a miss."

Mungo caught Noah's eye. They both understood the deal. The boy didn't want to hurt Donna, or the family, so he'd play it safe in Godzone. No worries there.

"And I've decided something too Mungo," said Monica.

"You're leaving me?" joked the chubby charmer.

"Next Saturday I'm taking you out for a very special wedding anniversary dinner… at The Savoy!"

"The Savoy? Is it our anniversary?"

"Nope. But I want to celebrate all those years we've been married."

"You sure love – that'll cost," said Mungo.

"Very sure Mungo. It's all organised."

Mungo was quietly bemused. This was a first for Monica. She'd never organised a night out on the town before. Or, was she up to something?

*

It was early afternoon in the Okavango Delta as the Botswana sun burned down on this breathtaking natural wilderness. A fish eagle soared high seeking out its next dish, a lion roared his masculinity somewhere deep in the bush, while in the river grunting hippos played hide and seek around the wooden mokoro, steered effortlessly through the gently rocking waters by the local guide Patience, carrying its precious cargo of three eccentric Brits from across the seas.

Duffy, his arm in a sling from the Darius bullet, wiped his sweating brow, took a swig from the Kingfisher beer bottle, and turned to his hostess.

"What did I do to deserve this?" he asked.

"You were part of the team Duffy… our team… to rid us of those ghastly Iranians," replied Abigail, looking quite regal in a khaki safari jacket.

"Our way of saying thank you," added Hanny, from under a pith helmet with a leopard skin band.

"First time on safari… loving it, ladies," beamed Duffy.

"And Abi, if I may be so bold… You and your Enfield saved my day… again, huge thanks."

Abigail nodded quietly.

"I come here to re-energise," she said. "Recharge the batteries… Works every time."

"So what next. When you get home. Another mission?" asked Duffy.

Abi shook her head and looked at Hanny with a long smile.

"A new life."

"What?"

"I'm selling my London flat and moving to Umbria."

"Italy?" said Duffy.

"Little place in the middle of nowhere."

"Next to a ruddy vineyard," grinned Hanny.

"No telly, no radio, no newspapers. Just my oil paints, my old records, a few good thrillers, and a little Italian wine."

"Little?" laughed Hanny.

"Sounds perfect."

"I'll send a postcard to my old boss Sir Geoffrey and say ciao."

"You really are starting over," said Duffy.

"Hanny's coming along as cook and gardener."

"And you can come and stay whenever you like Duffy…"

The singing detective emptied his bottle of beer.

"Food for thought ladies."

As a giant bull elephant thundered through the reeds towards their dugout canoe, skidded to a halt on the edge of the water, where it thrust back its huge flapping ears, raised its trunk high in the air, and trumpeted loud, silencing all around for several ear splitting moments.

Abi gazed at the testosterone monster towering over her, sighed deeply, and drily observed: "You're all mouth and trousers dear…"

Just two hundred yards away, dressed head to toe in jungle camo, a big game hunter lay flat on a wildlife viewing platform, carefully adjusting their rifle's scope.

They'd patiently been waiting an hour for their prey to move into their line of fire.

It had taken meticulous planning but they knew they had only one shot.

A five second window.

Their target would move slowly left to right and then be gone.

The hunter gripped the rifle tight and breathed slow.

Waiting.

Watching.

Any moment now.

Then, on cue, through the savannah scrubland and palm trees, the target drifted into shot.

On the water.

Abigail Clements-Brown.

Laughing in a canoe.

Soraya concentrated and went to squeeze the trigger of her sniper rifle.

When suddenly a massive bull elephant blocked her view.

Allowing the canoe to glide happily away into the far wetlands.

The Iranian assassin swore.

She'd wanted it to look like a hunting accident.

A stray shot.

Now her one chance was lost.

She bit her lip and drew blood.

"Another time, another place," she seethed, and slunk back into the bush.

*

"What do you think babe?" asked Noah, back home in t-shirt, shorts and bare feet.

He and Donna had flown into New Zealand three days earlier and were standing in the dazzling bright sunshine on the neat cut lawn of a new property for sale near Kerikeri in the Bay of Islands, at the top of the North Island, looking out over the flat calm Pacific Ocean.

It had five bedrooms, a vast kitchen, open log fire, swimming pool, and, of course, a barbecue. Plus a couple of fields for ponies, deer, or alpacas.

"After Harrow, Noah, takes my breath away," replied Donna. "Where's the pollution? Where's the rain? This is heaven on earth."

"Sweet as... Bought it this morning love."

"You what?"

"While you were in the shower. Saw it online. Looked beaut. Did the deed."

"It's ours?"

"All ours Donna. If... if you don't like it we can look at other places, but I just thought..."

"But. What about your family business, in Auckland?"

Noah shrugged with a smile.

"All gone. Sold up. You and I are going to start up together here. With the baby. If you want to?"

"You know what I'd love right now?" asked Donna.

"Fly back to London?"

"A beer. I could kill a beer."

"Shit babe – you're turning into a Kiwi sheila already!"

For the first time in years Noah felt happy. He knew he'd made the right choice. They'd stay in this new home and raise a family together.

He took a couple of bottles out to Donna on the wooden

deck overlooking the sea.

They each took a swig then silently hugged each other.

No need to say a word.

*

Monica had insisted that she go ahead for the special wedding anniversary dinner at the Savoy Grill, and meet him there.

Mungo arrived a few minutes after eight, dressed in a smart pinstriped suit and crimson silk tie. Even had a haircut and shower. Not often he went to a posh London eaterie with his first wife, so had made an effort. As obviously she had too. What was strange was Monica arranging this dinner, almost out of character. She hated snooty places, preferring to have cod and chips down the pub, but obviously with Donna and Noah an item, daughter pregnant, and now away Down Under, these two oldies had to make a special effort to renew their marriage vows.

Mungo was told that the Swift table was at a private booth over on the right.

He peered into the restaurant then froze.

Monica was sat at the head of the table.

With three surprise guests.

On her left was Mungo's Californian wife, Janie, looking like a Hollywood movie star, who'd overdone the botox.

On her right was Mungo's new young wife from Cannes, Margot, looking like a bohemian street urchin dressed for Vogue.

And opposite her was Mungo's future wife, Putri from Amsterdam, the china doll from Bali, looking very fragile, if not bewildered.

A waiter was pouring champagne for each of them.

Mungo, momentarily, felt a stroke coming on. His heart pumped faster and began to hurt. But it passed. He held his breath as he watched the drama unfold in the far corner booth.

Janie was shouting at Monica.

Margot was quietly drinking the fizz then shouting at Monica.

Poor Putri looked petrified.

And Monica was yelling at them all.

Each of the four women kept glancing in Mungo's direction, expecting him to join them at the table.

But he was carefully standing in the gloom outside in the corridor, not wishing to be seen by any of them.

Not wishing to join them and be the sacrificial lamb.

He could see them ripping out his heart.

Slicing off his balls.

Then chopping off his head.

Janie suddenly stood, threw her champagne at Monica, and made for the exit.

Margot picked up the fizz bottle, poured it over Monica's head, then left.

Putri burst into tears and followed the others.

The minute he'd seen them leaving the table and heading his way, Mungo had leapt into the loo and counted to ten.

Minutes.

Then peered in again.

Monica sat quietly sobbing alone at the table, still drenched in champagne.

Two waiters stood over her trying to dry her with towels.

Mungo thought quickly. Or tried to.

This is it.

End of.

She knows everything.

But. He had to face it. She'd been the first... So many years ago. They had kids.

He walked across and sat beside her without saying a word.

She looked at him, wiped her eyes, and looked away again.

Mungo waited an eternity, then whispered: "I am so sorry."

Monica looked at him and started laughing.

"You disgust me."

"It was a terrible thing to do..."

"You had two other wives, possibly three, and leading a young girl on to be the next... What sort of an animal are you Mungo?"

"It just... happened..." mumbled her husband.

"I found your burner phones. Numbered 1 to 5. Who was No. 2. She didn't answer?"

"She died."

"One down then."

Mungo just sat shaking his head in shame. He had nowhere to go.

"So I phoned them all. The other three. Told them I was setting up a surprise dinner for you... just you and each one alone... and they came running."

"Ah..."

"Then we met for the very first time... and we all waited for you to join us, but I expect you were outside hiding."

"Yes."

"I simply cannot understand why you did it... all those lies... bluff and double bluff... all those silly stories about working as a spy when all along I knew you were a bloody travelling salesman!"

"You knew?"

"Of course I knew Mungo… I just didn't know about the other wives, did

I?"

"We'll get a divorce…"

Monica nodded slowly, then looked him in the eye.

"Is that what you want? A divorce?"

"What?"

"You'll never see those other three tramps again in your life. That's all over.

Which just leaves me."

"What are you saying?" asked Mungo, somewhat baffled.

"I've had a few days to live this down. I understood immediately I called the other Mrs Swifts, what was going on… But now. Now it's sunk in. I either live my life alone with the boys… Or, we try to make it work, just married to little old me… and no-one else this time?"

"You mean that? You'd forgive me?"

Monica took the four numbered burner phones out of her phone and placed them in front of Mungo.

"Your move."

Mungo looked at the phones then called a waiter over.

"Could you destroy these please."

"Certainly sir," replied the waiter, scooping up the burners.

"And we'll have another bottle of your best champagne please."

"Am I mad?" asked Monica.

"We can make this work love… and I am so sorry."

"So you keep saying."

Suddenly everything felt very flat for Mungo. His fantasy world had been burst. Bang went being a movie producer in L.A. and living in luxury in Bel Air.

Bang went walking the Croisette in Cannes with the gamine and mischievous Margot.

Bang went marrying the delicate beauty from Bali… From now on he'd have to survive in the real world. With Monica and no-one else. And right now she was behaving like a saint.

"You drive a hard bargain love… but it'll work," he promised.

"It'll have to," said Monica as she leant across to peck him on the cheek.

Then froze. "Be a good boy. Or you walk…"

*

"I would say such wonderful things to you
There would be such wonderful things to do
If you were the only girl in the world
And I were the only boy…"

The whole room had joined in on the chorus, abandoning their salmon fish cakes and bandol blanc, as Duffy, midst deafening applause, joined Kate at her table near the bar.

It was Sunday night in Mayfair's super chic restaurant, Arlington, newly opened on the site of Princess Diana's favourite watering hole, Le Caprice, that had closed down during the Covid years.

"Think they like you Duffy," smiled Kate. "You're a star."

She was wearing an off-the-shoulder black party dress, anything to get out of that sodding uniform.

Duffy nodded to the nearby diners and sipped his chardonnay. He loved this place, its people, a glitzy home from home after dark.

"I got a letter from Izzy today from L.A." He threw an air

ticket on the table.

"What's this?" she asked.

"One way ticket to California… if I want a bed for the night, she said."

"Mmm… are you tempted?"

"Depends on you…"

Duffy then threw a postcard onto the table.

"What's this?"

Kate picked it up.

"From Tehran?"

"Soraya. My Persian assassin. The one that got away. Threatening to call me when she's next in town."

"Shit… Wants to sleep with the enemy… Sounds dangerous."

"Very. I think I'll be indisposed…"

"So. Where next young man?"

Duffy stroked her hand.

"You like Italy? I've some dear old friends who've invited me to stay."

"I love Italy… But…" She paused long.

"Where are you sleeping tonight?"

"I thought you'd never ask."

"I'm asking…"

They gently kissed.

The restaurant went silent…

Then cheered as one.

*

Mungo had told Monica he was popping round the corner to buy a bottle of red, then hailed a cab for Heathrow Airport.

He had tried, tried so hard, to knuckle down and live a

quiet normal life with his first wife. But without those trips away, without the risks and the danger and never knowing what would happen around the next corner, he was going quietly bonkers.

He knew it would hurt her if he disappeared; but he also knew she would understand.

She'd given him a chance to make good his bad behaviour, but he simply couldn't help himself. It was in his DNA, his nature. The chubby charmer.

He'd gone straight to the International Terminal and looked at the destinations.

Made a decision.

Somewhere he'd never been before.

Bought himself a paperback thriller and a new burner phone.

And right now was sitting in Seat 1a in First Class, Virgin Atlantic, en route to Shanghai.

He'd pinged Charlie, saying he was off to find new markets in the Far East, sipped his chilled glass of Moet, then turned to the lady sitting next to him.

She was about thirty, Asian, dressed in a very stylish black and white satin cheongsam dress, with diamond earrings the size of chandeliers. She had a neat black fringe, ruby lips, sparkling brown eyes, and was sipping a campari on ice.

"My first trip to China..." said Mungo with a friendly grin.

"Ah... my home. You will love it." The smile was blindingly white.

"I remember reading, a few years ago, that Shanghai was full of young ladies, worth millions, looking for husbands... Is this still true?" he asked with a twinkle.

"Sadly no," she replied. "They are now worth billions...

Like me."

"Ah…" replied Mungo, beaming like he'd just won the lottery.

"And what do you do?" she asked.

"The arms trade. I run a very big weapons firm."

"Oh that is so fascinating… You must tell me more," she said.

As Mungo ordered more champagne and campari, then snuggled back to enjoy the rest of the flight with his new best friend.

Printed in Great Britain
by Amazon

42680769R00212